D0108376

Praise for
JOSIE BROWN

SECRET LIVES OF HUSBANDS AND WIVES

"If you like *Desperate Housewives,* then you'll fly through this gossipy novel. . . . Brown entertains up to the satisfying ending . . ."

—Examiner.com

"An enjoyable take on suburban California life, complete with mommy cliques, rebel teenagers, and of course lots of adultery. . . ."

—*Booklist*

"This character-driven (sometimes steamy) book can best be described as the offspring of an affair between *Desperate Housewives* and a Jennifer Weiner novel."

—GoodHousekeeping.com

"A probing, entertaining fishbowl of married life in a well-heeled, wayward neighborhood. Loved it!"

—Stephanie Bond, author of *Body Movers*

"Poignant and funny. . . . A great read!"

—Wendy Wax, author of *Magnolia Wednesdays*

*Unfortunately, the U.S. congressman's wife
is only dimples and smiles when cameras are present.*

"Nothing goes in the baby's room that wasn't made in America," she declares crisply. "Not a onesie, not a rocker, not even the baby monitor."

"Okay," I answer. "But I'll still provide comparisons, so that you can make an informed choice."

She smirks. "Honey, let me tell you something: *all* my choices are voter-friendly. It's why my baby will wear Oshkosh."

"I don't know about that. Sure, Oshkosh is an American company—but the clothes are actually made in Mexico."

This stops her cold. She turns to her aide. "Edie! Go ask Larry in Polling about perceptions of the district voters toward Mexican-manufactured goods, and whether it will hurt Mike's union support. Hell, I can't keep the kid in a diaper for the first year of his life—"

"Speaking of diapers," I add, "you'll also want to consider how your environmentally conscience voters feel about cloth diapers versus disposables."

She closes her eyes with a deep sigh, but signs my contract without giving it a second glance. I guess she figures if there is anything there she won't like, she'll get her husband to pass some law to make it null and void.

It's one of the perks of power.

The Baby Planner is also available as an eBook

"A heartfelt novel about love, marriage, friendship—and sharp, manicured claws. Could not put it down."
—Melissa Senate, author of *The Love Goddess' Cooking School*

"Fans of *Desperate Housewives* will love this story. . . . The quick pace and snappy dialogue make this a fun read."
—*Romantic Times*

IMPOSSIBLY TONGUE-TIED

"Brad, Angelina, Britney, and Kevin may want to check out Josie Brown's new novel for its ripped-from-the-headlines plot."
—*New York Post,* Page Six

TRUE HOLLYWOOD LIES

"Brown captures the humor of working for a megalomaniac. . . . A well-paced, entertaining story."
—*Publishers Weekly*

"The tone is confessional, the writing laced with venomous humor."
—*The Wall Street Journal*

"A fine piece of literary work."
—*New York Post,* Page Six

ALSO BY JOSIE BROWN

Secret Lives of Husbands and Wives

THE
BABY PLANNER

josie brown

GALLERY BOOKS
New York London Toronto Sydney

G

Gallery Books
A Division of Simon & Schuster, Inc.
1230 Avenue of the Americas
New York, NY 10020

First Gallery Books trade paperback edition April 2011

GALLERY BOOKS and colophon are trademarks of Simon & Schuster, Inc.

For information about special discounts for bulk purchases,
please contact Simon & Schuster Special Sales at 1-866-506-1949
or business@simonandschuster.com

The Simon & Schuster Speakers Bureau can bring authors to your live event.
For more information or to book an event contact the Simon & Schuster
Speakers Bureau at 1-866-248-3049 or visit our website at www.simonspeakers.com.

Designed by Davina Mock-Maniscalco

Manufactured in the United States of America

10 9 8 7 6 5 4 3

Library of Congress Cataloging-in-Publication Data is available.

ISBN 978-1-4391-9712-7
ISBN 978-1-4391-9713-4 (ebook)

In memory of my mother, Maria;
and my mother-in-law, Ruth

FIRST
TRIMESTER

1

·······

7:13 p.m., Saturday, 18 February

I SEE HAPPY BABIES.

They are all around me here in this restaurant, seducing me with sleepy winks and dimpled Mona Lisa smiles. Their gleeful squeals are the siren's call that makes my heart go achy-breaky, like a seventh-grader who has been honored with a casual nod from the cutest boy in class.

Today is my thirty-seventh birthday. Forget the metronome metaphor. My biological clock drones louder than Big Ben on New Year's Eve.

My husband, Alex, can't hear it. Even if he could, I know he'd pretend otherwise, let alone acknowledge it. Despite my very broad hints that I badly want a child, Alex has nimbly side-stepped these emotional landmines—for the time being, anyway. Up until now, I've cut him some slack because I know that there is only one child in particular who interests him: Peter, his ten-year-old son. But they can't be together because Peter lives in Holland with Alex's first wife, Willemina, who ignores any and all requests from Alex to visit the boy.

So, while I fantasize about the child we might conceive and love together, my husband mourns a boy he may never see again.

Happy birthday to me.

I remind myself to look on the bright side. Last year on my birthday we both agreed that the topic was still open to discussion; that we'd take stock of how life has treated us and move forward from there. Well, life has been great. We're both healthy, the economy is behaving itself, and Alex is up for a partnership at his venture capital firm, Steadman & Martinez.

It's time to talk again.

Tomorrow, for sure. Right now I'm channeling my maternal urges into close encounters of a toddler kind: a cherub-cheeked boy with ringlet curls, not yet two years old, has locked eyes with me in the mirror behind Alex's head. What has caught the little guy's attention isn't the longing he sees there, but the diamond earrings dangling from my ears.

They are my birthday gift from Alex. He saw me admire them once, when we walked by a window at Tiffany.

Yes, it's going to be a great year, in more ways than one.

As I play with my earring to keep my fickle admirer's attention, I pretend to listen intently to my husband as he grouses about the fact that we are the first members of our party to arrive at the restaurant. "I feel a draft. Why did the hostess give us the one booth under an air-conditioning vent?" Alex asks as he shivers. "Katie, who are you smiling at?" He flips around to see what he's missing. "Are they here?"

"No! . . . No one." Immediately I shift my gaze back to him and in one long swallow empty the last of my glass of wine. It's a cabernet that is so good it should be sipped, not gulped, particularly on an empty stomach. But it's too late for that now.

If Alex has his way, it may soon be too late for a lot of things.

He presumes the adoration he sees in my eyes gives him a green light to keep griping. "Jeez, it sounds like we're sitting in an echo chamber. I can hear every brat in this joint! So much for happy hour. Who chose this place, anyway?"

Brat?

That remark is all the warning I need to stay away from the topic of children—tonight, at least.

It's almost as if my young flirtatious friend also heard Alex over the murmur of diners and wants to prove him right, because suddenly his little face crumples into a sorrowful pout and he lets loose a gut-wrenching wail.

To shush him up quickly, his mother lifts him out of his high chair and hugs him to her generous breasts as she waltzes with him in front of their booth. The dark circles under her eyes attest to late-night vigils with her son. But that doesn't give her immunity from Alex's death-ray stare: the same one he uses on any start-up moguls he's caught puffing up their company's income statements.

Miffed by Alex's sneer, my little boyfriend's mom practically runs away from us, shaking her head all the way out the door.

Her husband shrugs, but his proud-daddy smile doesn't leave his lips. Apparently he is used to the frowns of childless adults, because he winks at us as he raises his hand. I wince, expecting a middle-finger salute. I guess I should be relieved to see that all he's doing is pointing his index finger at us, as if to say *You're next* before scooping up their baby bag and following his wife.

God I hope he's right.

I watch as the departing dad wades through a throng of hungry patrons walking in our direction, including the rest of our party: my twin sisters Lana and Grace, and their husbands, Thor and Auggie. Although they're only thirty-two years old, my sisters are the real estate tag team to be reckoned in the tony little Silicon Valley town of Los Gatos, where humble starter homes go for a million dollars or more. By taking turns showing and selling hot properties, they make a great income and still have time to enjoy the things that matter most: their children, their husbands, and the picture-perfect homes they keep.

Their shouts of "Happy Birthday" are heartfelt. Our husbands exchange backslaps, while we ladies lean in for air kisses.

"Sorry we're late," says Grace. "Our sitter bailed on us. Lana's was sweet enough to watch Jezebel along with the boys."

Between them, Grace and Lana have three children. All of them are blond, like their mothers, albeit different shades: Mario, the oldest at six, is a curly towhead, whereas Max, four, has straight golden tendrils, and three-year-old Jezebel's head is covered in strawberry blond coils.

These communal date nights used to be a weekly event. When Mario was an infant, it was no big deal to bring him along. As he got a little older, though, he'd pull the same sort of early-toddler antics as my little admirer.

It was just as disconcerting to Alex then as it is now.

Over the years my sisters and their husbands picked up on this. Instead of enduring Alex's winces at their little ones' restaurant etiquette, now we'll eat out together only when they can get a sitter—which, in a community teeming with small children, is as elusive as the Holy Grail.

I hug Grace to let her know that, as far as I'm concerned, her tardiness is okay. Both her and Lana's shoulders relax. Their next moves are just as unconscious and uncoordinated: in unison they push aside their bangs. They are identical down to the tiny moles below their ears, although Grace's is on the left, and Lana's is on the right.

The men they married, however, are as different as can be. The gregarious Thor is consistently the best car salesman at the BMW dealership in Silicon Valley's Auto Mall. Eight years ago Lana went there looking for a preowned Z4 and walked out with a marriage proposal. For both she and Thor, it was love at first sight. Grace met the soft-spoken Auggie—a professor in

Stanford's philosophy department—at the base of *The Gates of Hell* in the university's Rodin Sculpture Garden. She already owned a wisteria-draped cottage. Indulging in his love of flowers, Auggie has created their very own Garden of Eden in the tiny backyard.

The cottage sits right off the Los Gatos town square: close enough for Jezebel to pedal her tricycle to the park and play with Lana and Thor's two boys.

Whenever I can, I join them. I can't help myself. Kids are my crack.

"Should we order a few appetizers and a couple of pitchers? Has anyone here tried that beer they call Nutty Brewnette?" Alex yanks a shank of my long, dark curls before scooting me closer for a cuddle.

He leaves his arm around my waist. He is tall enough that when, unconsciously, he tilts his head over mine, somehow the curves of our heads fit perfectly, like two pieces of a jigsaw puzzle.

After six years of marriage, I'd like to think that our desires were just as complementary, but I know better.

When, finally, he holds our child in his arms, he'll realize I was right to insist on having a baby.

That's why I have to change his mind, soon; very soon.

Lana, Auggie, and Thor nod enthusiastically at his suggestion for a beer, but Grace's perfect Cupid-bow lips break out into a sly grin. "Nothing for me. I'm not drinking these days."

At first the significance of her words don't penetrate my wine buzz, but then it hits me hard, in the gut:

One of my sisters is pregnant. Again.

Apparently her remark was lost on Alex, too, because he's more concerned with waving down our waitress than deducing the nuance of Grace's words, or noting her prenatal glow.

I can tell by the looks on their faces that my sisters and their husbands seem much more concerned with *my* response. I have too much pride to confirm what they rightly suspect:

Yes, I'm jealous.

But no, I won't show it. So instead I turn to hug Grace tightly as I give her cheek a quick peck. "Oh my God, you're pregnant? What great news! I'm so happy for you!"

That is not a lie. Granted, I'd have been happier if this announcement had come from me, and everyone there at the table suspects that.

Everyone including Alex. *Especially* Alex.

"Way to go, Auggie! Another little one on the way. Wow. That's . . . awesome," Alex says with a smile. But the frost emanating from where he sits has nothing to do with the restaurant's air-conditioning.

The blush that spreads on Auggie's ruddy cheeks is mostly hidden in his wiry auburn beard, but he can't help but puff up a bit with fatherly pride. "We've always wanted to give Jezzy a little brother or sister. It just happened a little quicker than we anticipated." Lovingly he strokes Grace's arm. She responds with a heartfelt kiss.

I hope that my smile is wide enough that they'll take my glassy-eyed gaze for happiness. For that matter, I'd prefer that they think I'm tipsy rather than guess the truth.

I'll have my wish soon enough. When the waitress asks me if I want another glass of wine, I give her a firm thumbs-up.

Already I can tell that it's going to be a long night. If I'm going to keep this smile on my face, I'll need liquid reinforcement.

When the situation calls for it, there is an advantage to being a happy drunk.

"SO WHAT'S your guess, is it a boy or a girl?" Thor's question, broached after appetizers of fried calamari, avocado eggrolls, and ahi poki, is aimed more at Auggie than at Grace. That's because we all know her well enough to predict her answer: *Either, as long as it's happy and healthy . . .*

On the other hand, Auggie is sure to have a definite opinion, as he does on most things.

Before answering, he pauses to give Grace an apologetic smile. "I guess Jezzy has spoiled me into believing all little girls are angels. But I'd be lying if I didn't admit that I'd like a little boy at some point."

Grace's surprised laughter brings out the giggles in me, too. Or maybe it's that third glass of cabernet, downed with too many fried calamari ringlets.

I dunno. Whatever. I just hope I don't throw up on Alex.

Or maybe I should.

Upon hearing Auggie's honest admission, Alex nods in agreement. "Yeah, boys are a lot of fun." The beer has loosened his tongue. What rolls off of it is honest regret. Distance is yet another way in which to lose a child. The grieving process is just as heartbreaking, and is the reason why Alex is adamant that we stay childless.

He doesn't want Peter to think he's abandoned him.

"I know, because that's exactly what I thought, after my parents split up and my dad remarried," Alex had said, explaining his feelings to me one night, when we had first started dating. It was dark in our bed, but I could feel the damp grief on his face.

I presumed he was thinking of Peter.

He took my empathetic hug as my tacit approval of his decision to stay childless. Did he then presume that the kiss we shared immortalized my agreement to do the same?

Okay, yeah, I'll admit it: I married Alex anyway, secretly hoping that Willemina would relent, or that time would heal the gaping hole left by Peter's departure.

Or that Alex would seek to fill the void with a child that was ours together.

The only real change has been that my desire to have that child has grown stronger.

But I can't let on now. So instead I give Grace a wink and a smile. "I'm guessing you're carrying twins. It's a Harlow family tradition that has never skipped a generation, so tag, you're it."

Grace pats her belly as she considers that. "Ha! We'll see about that. In any case, I've warned the doctor that I want to keep the baby's gender a surprise. It's more fun that way."

As tiny as she is, no one would even guess she was pregnant. Unlike me (when I was in college and my five-foot-seven frame was packing the freshman fifteen, I was called "well uphol-stered" by a boyfriend; we broke up soon after that—all right, I admit it: *because* of that), the twins are small-boned and slim, like our mother.

Thor must be thinking the same, because he gives her a sideways glance, then asks, "How far along are you, anyway?"

"As of today, six weeks and counting." She turns to me. "Katie, I'll need all the help I can get with the nursery and some baby gear. Are you up for that?"

"Sure, you name it." This is my consolation prize. She knows I live to help her and Lana, especially when it comes to doing something for their children.

Before either of them makes a major purchase, it's not un-usual for Grace or Lana to ask my opinion. Not only did I earn my bachelor's degree in interior design from San Diego State, I also am the assistant testing director at SafeCalifornia, the state commission that advocates for stricter safety regula-tions on consumer products sold in California. I'm always the

first person to hear about some toxic toy, mass food poison-
ings, or a beauty product with side effects that make the term
an oxymoron.

"If you're looking for a color that works with either a boy or
a girl, you may want to consider a shade in the melon family," I
say, reaching for yet another calamari ring. "It's the new pink.
Besides, it goes well with most yellows and greens. And if Auggie gets his wish and it's a boy, it'll look great with slate-blue ac-
cents, too." Then I lean in close, as if divulging a hot stock pick.
"But no matter what color you choose, use a paint with zero
VOCs: volatile organic compounds. Consider a milk paint. It's
best for the baby. If we weren't eating, I'd tell you what we do to
rate the safety of paint. It would curl your hair."

Both Lana and Grace nod as they rummage for pens in
their purses to take notes. But Grace is frowning. "Thanks for
that. Gosh, I've been out of infant mode for three years now. I
don't know if our infant car seat is up to today's standards anymore . . ."

I shrug. "It can't be. New legislation was enacted earlier this
year. Car seat safety standards keep changing for the better."

Auggie laughs. "What, now we have to buy another one?
Then I guess we'll need one for Jezzy, too. Damn, what a waste
of money! Hers is as good as new."

"Doesn't matter," I counter. "Don't make me bring the crash
dummy to dinner next time to make my point."

Lana's mouth drops open. "Get out of here! SafeCalifornia
actually uses baby crash dummies in its tests? That's—so
morbid!"

"Hell no, it's cool." Thor takes a swig of beer. "You guys also
test cars, am I right?"

Hearing this, Auggie swivels his head my way, too. Alex,
who has heard it all before, keeps his eyes peeled on the War-
riors basketball game.

I nod. "Yep. That's Helen Crowley's department. She's our executive director."

"Wait, we can talk cars later!" Grace is frantic. "Let's get back to stuff that the baby will need. Have you tested any products besides car seats?"

I nod. "Toys, clothing, strollers, high chairs, you name it. Sadly, a lot of these problems surface only after the products have been on the market already. We then validate the complaints with our own testing. If we find the complaints to be valid, we pass them forward to the Consumer Product Safety Commission and lobby our state's legislators for a recall. Lately our child product testing division has found some real doozies. In fact, Tuesday I'm testifying about a portable playpen that has caused a few deaths. When the parents of victims take the stand—well, it can break your heart."

One father in particular, his eyes glazed over with remorse, comes to mind. He spoke at a recent hearing involving bite-size toy sponges shaped like different fruit, one of which was swallowed by his toddler son. I down my fourth wine in the hope of obliterating the memory of his description of his son's suffocation.

My sole consolation is knowing all our hard work—research and testing, calling for hearings, lobbying for new laws on the book—sometimes pays off, and that we've saved lives.

Grace looks pale. Time to get her mind on something more pleasant. "Listen, you two: if you've got time—say, next Saturday—we'll walk the aisles of Babies'R'Us and I'll give you a few recommendations. It's sad how many toddlers stand up in high chairs when no one is looking, and then fall out because the chairs aren't very stable—"

Oh no, I've said too much again, because suddenly Grace blanches and slaps her hand to her mouth.

Seeing this, Lana pats her hand. "Sis, are you okay?"

"I think I'm going to throw up. You know, my morning sickness"—Grace closes her eyes for a moment—"between that and some of these horror stories, I'm getting queasy. Katie, I don't know how you stand it. Every time one of those poor dummies gets crushed, I'd be in tears."

"Yeah, but you've had a kid, so it's real to you." Alex said that so matter-of-factly. "Katie hasn't. That gives her a built-in immunity." He nudges me for validation. "Am I right?"

I can feel the corners of my smile droop into a grimace. I want to scream at the top of my lungs—above the scrape of forks on plates, and the chatter of diners enjoying their meals, and the ESPN commentators debating the night's top-ten sports plays on the five big TV screens over the restaurant's ornate bar. *Don't you get it, Alex? You may not want me to have maternal feelings, but I do. And you can't stop them by wishing them away . . .*

Instead, I think I'll throw up.

I murmur some lame excuse in order to escape to the ladies' room. Alex slides out of the booth first—and then has the nerve to pat my bum when I slip past him, if only to prove to my sisters that I was okay with his off-the-cuff remark.

And with his decision that we not have children.

If we'd been alone, I would have slapped him.

As I run to the loo, I hear Lana's voice rise above the diners' chatter: "Alex Johnson, truly, I don't know what my sister sees in you. God, at the very least I hope your cock is a lot bigger than your brain."

I CAN'T remember the last time I found myself facedown over a toilet bowl.

I take that as a good thing.

Sadly, this time I'm heaving so hard that one of my new diamond earrings plops down into the flotsam and jetsam that was my birthday meal.

Aw, hell! I must have loosened the post when I was teasing the baby in the booth across from us. "No, no, no," I moan as it sinks to the bottom of the bowl. Frantically I look around the stall for something that might help me pluck it out. Toilet paper won't do any good, and the paper seats they provide would be just as useless. Maybe I can stick my hand in the small coated bag that lines the used tampon dispenser, and fish it out—

Ooh, yuck, no! There's a couple of tampons in there.

I search my purse for a pen or pencil or anything long enough to nudge it out of the bowl—

Nothing.

I can't bring myself to dive in bare-handed. Even if the cost of the diamonds aren't worth my dignity, surely the earrings are priceless if only for the sentimental value, because they're from Alex . . .

I'm sobbing so hard that at first I don't notice Grace's sensible ballet flats peeking out from under the stall door. When I hiccup to a stop, she must realize I know she's there, because she whispers, "Katie, I'm so sorry! Please . . . don't hate me!"

"Why? Because you're pregnant again?" I hope I come off as surprised, but my words, bouncing off the stall's metal walls, sound sad even to me. "Grace, it isn't *your* fault! It's . . . it's . . ."

If I blame Alex, it will only get her started again on why he and I should have continued with our couples counseling. She doesn't understand how difficult he finds it to talk about Peter.

Alex can't handle the pain.

So now, to cover for his grief—which my family can't understand, and I can't help him move beyond—I'd rather take the rap by telling her that, between our work schedules, we had to cancel too many appointments with the counselor, that the timing isn't right for us, anyway, and that hey, if it happens, it happens. And if it doesn't, *it's no big deal . . .*

But yes, it is a very big deal: to me.

Instead, I say, "It's all Auggie's fault."

That makes her gasp. But after too much silence, her giggles come out in spasms. "Yeah, you're right! Let's blame it on him. I told the son of a bitch to quit buying those cheap condoms."

Now I'm laughing, too.

And sobbing. I want her life.

But I want it with Alex.

And I want Alex to want it, too.

The sudden realization that I am thirty-seven and may never have a child has me crouching back over the toilet. I can't stop myself from retching out my future, along with the last of the wine and what's left of any heavily breaded salt-and-pepper calamari.

Hearing me go at it again, Grace loses it, too. The door to the next stall slams shut with a bang. The next thing I know, we're barfing in stereo.

Grace flushes her toilet. A moment later I hear water running in one of the sinks. By the time I stagger out, she is dabbing her mouth with a paper towel. Her eyes glisten even as she tries to smile.

This is quite a moment we've shared. If I weren't still crying, I'd laugh.

As I rinse out my mouth under a spigot, I hear her say, "Katie, you forgot to flush!"

The next thing I know, she's doing it for me.

Damn! Damn! *My earring!* Quickly I turn to say something—

But what? It's too late to retrieve it now, anyway.

Slowly, I remove the remaining earring. Tomorrow I'll track

down a replacement. Tonight, though, should Alex notice I'm not wearing them and ask me why not, my answer will be half right: one of the posts came loose.

That's what I get for flirting with a cute babe.

I hate lying to Alex, but I don't want him to be upset with me, or for that matter annoyed with Grace. But by the sad look on his face during the appetizer portion of our meal, I'd say it's too late for that, too.

2

·······

Children make you want to start life over.
—Muhammad Ali

ALEX RISES WITH the sun.

That goes for all of him.

This means that I do, too.

We are usually spooning. I am on the inside. His arms are wrapped around me, his hands cupped in mine, which, by habit, I hold to my breasts. It seems as if his fingers and his cock twitch in unison as the first rays of sunlight break through the opening between our bedroom curtains.

As the beams grow stronger, my nipples harden at his touch, and Alex grows bolder. I hear him rip open the wrapper holding a condom. Then, a moment later, I feel him, long and hard, sliding into me from behind, and my hazy dream—created from half-forgotten memories and wishful thinking, and the result of drinking coffee before bedtime—rolls into the ultimate fantasy: in it, Alex is blessed with some sort of SuperSperm that can flow effortlessly through the tight weave of any condom, and can counteract the hormonal havoc wreaked on me by my daily dose of the pill that leaves me temporarily infertile.

As the bed rocks to the beat of our sideways tango, the sheets and blankets are kicked into a tangled nest around our ankles. In time, we segue into sexual push-ups. He hovers over me, his thrusts accompanied by a collection of low grunts and growls meted out in metronomic precision.

My soft moans are joyous. I can envision SuperSperm streaming its way through me to the secret lair of my uterus, where a solitary SuperEgg is vibrating to the tune of "Someday My Prince Will Cum . . ."

"Yes . . . yes!" Sharing an ecstatic groan, Alex and I climax together. We lie there, in each other's arms, briefly cherishing the moment.

Then, as if he's read my mind, he asks, "Hon, you're still taking your pill . . . right?"

"Of course I am. Why do you always ask that?" I pull away from him to turn on my side.

Can he hear the quiver in my voice? Let's hope he thinks it's from anger.

Apparently I've fooled him about my own feelings on the issue, because his sigh is heavy with guilt. "I know, I know. I'm just—oh, I don't know! Better safe than sorry, I guess."

But I wouldn't be sorry. And he knows that.

"Get real, Alex. I'm on the pill—*and* you wear a rubber! Damn it, why are you so paranoid?" I sit up. "Seriously, would it be so bad if I got pregnant? You said we'd discuss it again this month. So . . . how about right now?"

He doesn't speak. He doesn't have to. The wariness in his eyes says it all. "If you want my honest opinion, I think we should wait—"

"If you want *my* 'honest' opinion, the waiting game has gone on long enough. You said we should wait to see if Willemina relents and gives you visitation rights. Well, she hasn't. Then you said we should wait until the economy is better. Well, now it's on the upswing, and you'll have your partnership any day now—"

"You know my business. The partnership only happens if my portfolio pays off big. And right now, no one knows how well this new account, SkorTek, will perform."

I shake my head angrily. "*You* know. You're their golden boy, remember?"

"Okay! Okay, if it does . . . we'll . . . talk."

"By 'talk,' do you mean 'Yes, let's do this'?"

"By that I mean, yes, it is an action item on the agenda; that we'll consider the cost of restructuring our lives. When we come up with an endgame that works for both of us, we'll move forward from there."

Action item. Restructuring. Endgame. Whenever Alex talks corporate-speak, I know I'm winning the negotiation.

"Let me suggest the endgame. How about when SkorTek's first-tier financing is finalized?"

He shrugs yes. "We may have to do some drilling down on the ETA, but that's certainly within the silo . . ."

Drill, baby, drill! That's all I need to hear to know that I'm practically home free . . .

"I've got to go, or I'll be late for the hearing," I say gruffly, but I lean down and kiss his forehead to let him know I accept this compromise.

For now.

He doesn't look up at me. I know why.

He hates giving concessions.

At least he knows the sex was good, if that's any consolation.

1:46 p.m.

I'M DIGGING my nail into my fist so that I don't blubber like a baby.

In my job, it's best to leave the crying to the bereaved: those who have lost a loved one to the faulty product that should never have made it onto the market in the first place.

In today's hearing, that product is a portable playpen, built by PlayDay Industries. The victim, a toddler named Ariel Patterson, was strangled in its fishnet mesh as the whole damn thing collapsed around her.

Her mother, Rosalyn, speaking in a voice trembling from heartache and choked with sobs, is nevertheless steeled with a resolve that is unique to grieving parents.

She is flanked on one side by me, and on the other by Helen Crowley, my boss and SafeCalifornia's executive director. Helen gave the opening remarks, which included a rundown of the number of these playpens still on the market (in the tens of thousands); how much they sell for, and consequently the amount of money they have made for PlayDay; the corroborating results for our own tests; the legal shenanigans we became involved in when the company thumbed its nose at our requests for a voluntary recall; and last but not least, the written depositions of two other mothers who reported similar mishaps.

Fortunately for them, their children are still alive. Even one casualty of this war—in this case, Ariel—was too high a price to pay for a measly point or two increase in PlayDay's stockholder dividends.

As Rosalyn speaks, every now and then she glances over at us, as if seeking reassurance that her words are in fact penetrating the placid stares of the legislators in front of her.

I doubt my gentle nods do anything to reassure her of this, but their vote will.

Her words come out slowly, deliberately, softly, as if rushing will trip her up and ruin everything. In truth, anything but a total product recall would crush her.

No one knows how fragile she really is right now, except me.

I talked her into testifying by convincing her that, yes, she could stand up and speak of her grief. I even convinced her to take the two-hour drive with me, from her apartment in Oakland to the state capitol in Sacramento, where our elected officials could hear her sad tale; that the memory of Ariel deserved nothing less.

And I was there at her side, every day for the past two weeks, holding her hand as I coached her on her speech, urging her to raise her voice above a whisper.

Prior to Ariel's death, she was inordinately shy.

Since then, she's been practically comatose.

Whenever I came, I brought sandwiches and coffee. A few times I'd brought a sack of groceries so that she'd have milk and bread in the house.

With Ariel gone, she'd quit going to the store.

I know why. Because there is no one to buy groceries for, to care for.

A mother who has lost her child loses herself, too.

This morning, after I banged frantically on her front door for ten minutes, she finally let me in. She was still in her bathrobe and shaking so hard that her teeth were chattering.

"You aren't dressed yet?"

I couldn't keep the panic out of my voice and it scared her. She backed away as she shook her head adamantly. "W-w-why bother?" she stammered. "It won't bring Ariel b-b-back."

I took her hand firmly in mine, but I didn't speak until she finally forced herself to look me in the eye. "Rosalyn, I know you're scared. *But you have to do this.* If you don't, you'll always regret it. You'll hate yourself."

"I hate myself anyway. I have no life. Ariel was my life."

"Then do this for her."

She sighed and buried her head in her hands for what seemed like an eternity. Finally she rose and headed off into her bedroom. When she came out, she was dressed, her hair brushed neatly, makeup applied.

She was ready to avenge her daughter's death in a new Charter Club ensemble.

The last time Rosalyn stood up and spoke to people was for a book report she gave in high school on *Of Mice and Men*. Crowds scare her. This time around, she is scaring *them*.

The gallery holds just the few reporters we were able to cajole into covering this hearing. Most of the audience is made up of this single mother's friends and family. I can tell that she wasn't expecting such a large cheering squad.

Her shyness has blinded her to the many people who love her and feel her pain. And yet, they are there for her in this dire hour of need.

Their faces are stoic despite their tears. Their muffled sobs are the white noise beneath Rosalyn's testimony. To show their support, they are wearing white T-shirts stiffened with a larger-than-life photo of Ariel. On the heaving chests of those who had loved her, Ariel's dimpled smile once again comes to life.

I try to keep my eyes on Rosalyn, but every now and then I glance at the commission members. The legislators are equally divided along party lines. As she speaks, their faces soften. More than a few are glassy-eyed.

The commission's chairperson is a female state senator from a district in the state's Southland populated mainly by well-heeled retirees who have turned a desert into an emerald sea of golf courses.

It is also home to PlayDay.

The company's CEO has held a sympathetic expression throughout the hearing. He's practicing for the civil suit, which is scheduled for two months from now, since Rosalyn had refused to settle out of court.

She wants her day in court. This is just the warm-up.

His sympathy may or may not be feigned, but his pain is all too real. He winces as Rosalyn relives that day, minute by minute, building to her decision to leave her child alone in the bedroom while she ran to answer the phone.

But certainly her child was safe. After all, she was in her playpen.

When she describes how she found her child—cold and lifeless—she repeats the vow she made to God: should he grant her prayer and bring her baby back to life, she'd make sure that no other parent would have to experience her grief.

God didn't grant her wish, but Rosalyn is here anyway, to keep that vow. It is her selfless gift to other parents.

Madam Senator's face actually goes pale under her heavy pancake makeup when she realizes the legislators on either side of her are wiping tears from their faces.

When she finally finishes, Rosalyn's head sinks slowly to her chest as her eyes close. No matter the results now, her action here has lifted her out of the abyss of guilt that has been her emotional hell since that morning she stepped away from her daughter.

Despite PlayDay's generous donation to Madam Chairperson, the vote to recall the playpen is unanimous. The only person more shaken than Rosalyn is the company's CEO.

In no time at all Rosalyn is surrounded by her supporters. Their hugs and kisses should convince her to feel buoyant and victorious and vindicated—

But no. "For my baby," she shouts through her tears as she hugs my neck.

Finally, Rosalyn has found her voice. I've no doubt it will never leave her.

I relinquish her to her cheering squad, who eagerly volunteer to drive her back to Oakland.

In my ten years as a consumer advocate, I've learned to liken myself to a bandage: yes, victims need me to protect and defend during these hearings; but once they are done, for both our sakes it's best to tear myself away quickly, so that the emotional healing can begin.

WE ARE the champions.

Each victory whets our appetites for the next battle.

But will we live to fight another day? Helen, who had taken the train up to Sacramento yesterday in order to lobby the governor for a reduction in the inevitable budget cutback earmarked for SafeCalifornia, joins me on the two-hour drive back to San Francisco. Thus far she's sidestepped my hints to divulge how the conversation went.

I'll take that as proof that the answer is: not well.

We use the car trip to discuss other egregious products that have gotten too many complaints. A child's bed that collapses on one side is on our hit list, as is a window model that drops shut too quickly and too painfully, and an all-terrain vehicle that flips over too easily.

"The testing for the window is closest to completion, and we've got a large number of consumers ready to testify against the manufacturer," I say. "One got a concussion. The other lost the tip of a finger."

"Ouch!" Helen shudders, then sighs. "So many problems, so little time." She nudges her sunglasses higher on the bridge of her nose. "Oh my God, it's so nice to be in a car that doesn't smell like a dog! This weekend I took Marlowe for a walk in the rain, and boy, did he stink after *that*."

While it's satisfying to play David to corporate Goliaths, our work takes its toll in emotional exhaustion. Our staff has the highest attrition rate of all the state's agencies, with the exception of prison personnel.

Helen's rejuvenation comes from the long hikes she and her significant other, David, take with their Labrador, and tending their patch in a communal vegetable garden. Although she is my age, she's been with the state since she graduated from college.

In light of the budget cuts, which seem more drastic each year, I don't think SafeCalifornia would survive without Helen's determined leadership. I can't imagine the department without her.

But she is not just my boss. She is my friend, too.

4:38 p.m.

WE REACH the city just ahead of rush hour. We'd phoned ahead with our good news. Usually that earns us a standing ovation from the rest of the staff—our testers, Karin, Allison, Marcus, and Lucas; and my associate advocates, Jade and Rory—and a drink at our favorite neighborhood sushi bar, Blowfish.

But not today. When we get there, the place is as solemn as a funeral parlor. Desks are being emptied, personal items boxed.

Without saying a word, Allison hands Helen a printout of an e-mail that came in just twenty minutes before we arrived. It is the governor's final budget for the fiscal year issued by the state's Department of Finance. She has flipped open to the section entitled "Summary of Significant Changes by Major Program Area." Helen and I scan it together, but Helen is the first to find what we both suspect, but pray we won't see:

SafeCalifornia has been eliminated.

Helen goes to her office and shuts the door.

"Should we follow?" asks Karin.

I shake my head. I know Helen won't want anyone to see her cry.

Everyone continues their packing.

When I reach my office, I open my computer to the

archives of our test results—consumer goods, food products, and yes, even children's items—and download them into a memory drive. This is an act of comfort, an emotional security blanket. All of these findings have already been disseminated to the media, so that it can warn the public, in the same way in which we defend and protect.

Who will do that now?

I'm almost done sorting through my files when Helen comes out of her office. Her eyes are red and puffy, but there is a smile on her face. "Who's up for a sake at Blowfish?"

Everyone stares at her as if she's crazy.

"Throw me a bone, people! Heck, it's my early retirement party. Don't worry, drinks are on me."

This elicits some sad chuckles, a smattering of applause, a group hug, and a shout from Marcus that the last one to leave should turn out the lights.

That would be me. Quickly I strip my cubicle's wall of ten years of photos, which include Alex and me honeymooning in Maui, clowning around in Halloween costumes, dressed to kill at the San Francisco Symphony's opening-night gala, and tail-gating at a 49ers-Raiders preseason game . . .

Always, it's just the two of us.

Maybe this layoff was meant to happen. Maybe the timing is right at last to get started on a family. But how do I convince Alex of this, too?

Yeah, like this will work: "Hi, honey! First the bad news: I lost my job."

Of course, he'll answer, "Ah hell . . . Okay, so what's the good news?"

"It's time for us to have a baby."

As I flick off the lights at SafeCalifornia, I'm still figuring out how I'll revive him after he faints.

3
....

7:48 a.m., Wednesday, 22 February

F RANKLY, BABE, I like you in hausfrau mode," says Alex through a mouthful of Amaretto-flavored waffles. "We never ate like this when you were chasing down corporate evildoers." He makes a big show of patting his belly, as if his waistline is about to burst the zipper on his Brioni suit.

As if. His regular evening jogs, five nights a week, keep him perpetually lean.

His eyes have not moved from the waffle iron since I poured in the batter for his second serving. Some day he'll learn that a watched waffle iron never beeps.

I show my empathy by walking over to him and kissing him on the forehead. "Maybe you're right," I answer nonchalantly. "But you know me better than that. I'm not the type to sit home and polish my nails. I'll need something to keep me busy."

This is as broad of a hint as I dare give.

He gets it. I know, because his cheeks turn red as his gaze shifts back to me. "I'm sure I'd be bored, too, after a while," he says warily. "But it's not as if we need more money or anything, right? What I mean to say is that I make enough so that you don't have to rush back into some slave-wage gig." He shrugs.

"Katie, you had one of the toughest jobs I know. If I'd had to comfort all those sad, angry people, I'd . . . I'd—well, I don't know what I'd have done. Baby, you're a saint, not a pragmatic, coldhearted bastard, like me. It's a hell of a lot easier giving out money to cocky techno-nerds and riding them hard so that they quadruple your investment in them."

I touch his cheek with the back of my hand. He shaves close, and it's smooth, like raw silk. "You may be pragmatic, but the last thing you are is a coldhearted bastard."

He hides his embarrassment behind his coffee mug. He knows I'm not trying to flatter him. For the past seven years he has been my rock. If it weren't for him—telling me that I'm beautiful and sweet and funny and the woman of his dreams, propping me up every time I came home in tears after listening to a victim whose story broke my heart, or because of a hearing that didn't go our way—

My job would have left me an emotional wreck.

It's not easy trying to save even one small corner of the world.

"Hey, Katie, I've got an idea: why not go back into interior design? You love it. It's your release."

He throws his arms open wide to make his point. Our town house is always a work in progress. I paint and repaint rooms, and haunt flea markets for great finds. For me, an engrossing read is an auction house catalog. "Just think: no more watching the clock or building up vacation time. You can work for yourself and make some nice dough. We'll use it to run off to a deserted island every now and then, on our own schedule, not because the state allows you two measly weeks off every year. It will allow us to be . . . *freer.*"

Something we'd never be if I were to have a baby.

He doesn't have to say it, but that's what he means.

He may be right. Perhaps if I did something fun and creative, I'd be happier, more satisfied with the reality of my life.

Our life together.

Just the two of us.

"Okay, sure. I'll play with that idea. In fact, Grace said she needed help with her nursery, so I'll make it my very first project."

Relieved that I don't have the nerve to say what I truly want, he smiles and pulls me down into his lap for a real kiss.

And he doesn't let me go, even when the waffle iron whistles.

Friday, 24 February

IT'S ALMOST midnight, and I'm exhausted.

And exhilarated.

I can't wait to see my sisters tomorrow.

It's taken me three full days, but I've done it: pulled together the ideal nursery for Grace.

The first thing I did after Alex left for work on Wednesday was purchase an upgrade to my old AutoCAD software from college, so that I could create a prototype of the room that Grace has in mind for the nursery. I then drafted a room to the right proportions: ten by twelve feet, with a tiny closet centered on the wall opposite a large, deep window that faces west.

Next I went through my notes on baby furnishings that are well constructed, have tested low in toxicity, and are proportioned to fit in her nursery without crowding it. My recommendations include a crib that easily and safely converts into a daybed, a dresser that doubles as a changing table, a rocker for Grace, a play chest with a built-in bookcase, and finally, a portable playpen, which she can take from room to room.

It is *not* one made by PlayDay.

The room will need new carpeting. I'm recommending a

manufacturer that I know to be environmentally green, as is the brand of milk paint I'm suggesting for the walls. For a gender-neutral theme, I chose the ocean, which allowed me to use a soft peach shade as the room's primary color. It was the perfect hue for a sun setting into a gray-blue ocean, the mural on one of the walls. The room's accessories and accent pieces—lamps, pictures, the mobile over the bed—will play off a nautical motif.

Later that afternoon I went out and got fabric samples, carpet swatches, and paint chips, so that Grace could choose the textures and patterns she liked best, and so that we could test different shades of paint against the nursery walls.

Yesterday I researched baby products. Okay, maybe I went a little crazy. Will it freak her out to see a 180-item checklist?

As for product recommendations, I've spent all day today putting together an in-depth analysis of car seats, strollers, high chairs, infant swings, camcorders, learning toys, safety gates, smoke detectors, drawer locks, bedding, baby food, formula, diapers, and monitors. Each category is saved on its own Excel spreadsheet, so that it can be updated electronically, as needed. In some categories, the safety stats were almost identical. Because I want Grace to have a choice, I've rated a minimum of six items in each category.

I've even included some cute baby shower ideas. Oh yeah, and there's also an overview of sitting services, mommy playgroups, Lamaze classes, local doulas, and baby nurses—

And I've put it all in a three-inch-wide three-ring binder.

No wonder mothers are always exhausted.

I found a binder the color of a ripe peach. Under its clear acetate cover I've placed a picture of a cute baby in a tiny sailboat, on which I've written *Grace's Baby To-do List*.

I look forward to the day I'll be updating the binder for Alex and me.

4

·······

I think, at a child's birth,
if a mother could ask a fairy godmother to endow it
with the most useful gift, that gift would be curiosity.
—*Eleanor Roosevelt*

11:05 a.m., Saturday, 25 February

I CAN'T BELIEVE IT!" laments Lana. "The state eliminated SafeCalifornia? Why would it do that? . . . Max! *Maxie!*
Honey, stop hitting your brother! Play nice, or I'll give him
permission to hit you back, and you won't like that, because
he's a lot bigger than you . . . That's my good boy . . . I mean,
there's got to be some kind of consumer backlash for this—
Max! *Maximiliano!* I'm warning you . . ."

I've joined Grace and Lana and their broods on a shopping
safari to snag the best car seats for the boys and Jezebel, and to
scout out the best infant seat for the baby Grace is carrying. She
is adamant that she'll not wait until the last minute to prep for
her new bundle of joy. Frankly, I think she's under the assump-
tion that once everything is in its place, the baby will come all
the sooner.

Wishful thinking on her part.

Lana has a mother's version of ADD: try as she might to
carry on an adult conversation, she can't help but interrupt herself in order to reprimand the younger and more rambunctious
of her two sons. The way in which she stops midtopic and then
changes the tone of her voice as she directs it to a different audience is an ongoing source of fascination for me. It's as if she's

got a built-in radar that locks and loads on any misbehaving child in her gene pool, then torpedoes him with the right verbal command.

Hearing her, Max freezes in place with one leg akimbo, weighing his desire to cause mischief against the hysteria in his mother's tone, along with his threshold for time-outs. The carrot that had been dangled in front of both boys' noses prior to Lana letting them out of the car was her promise to buy them the latest superhero action figure. (Who's hot this year? Batman? Superman? Spider-Man? Iron Man? They cycle back around so often it's hard to remember.)

Max is no dummy. He knows to obey now, then wait it out. A truce between the boys will hold until that superhero is in his hot little hands.

Lana of course knows this. Still, she savors the few moments of peace it buys her while we maneuver through Babies"R"Us. The store is strategically laid out so that we'll stumble upon a variety of products before we get to what we came to find. The section we are in now is filled with boxes of disposable diapers for every gender, size, and shape of baby. As Jezebel skips down the aisle after her cousins, she taps each box of diapers and counts out loud to herself.

Grace may not be showing yet, but hormone surges leave her exhausted. She has dark circles under her eyes. She sighs heavily as she picks up her pace to keep up with Jezebel. "What was Alex's reaction when he heard your news?"

"He's being supportive. In fact, he wants me to take a little time off. Or go back to my roots: you know, interior design. In any case, he wants me to, and I quote, 'do what makes you happy.'"

"Wow, that's sweet of him." Grace points at the big sign that heralds Car Seat Land, but we have to wade through countless strollers for sale before we get to our destination. I can tell that she is taken aback by the battalion of perambulators that greet us, because it stops her cold. "Oh my God! It's like a car mall, only it's filled with strollers!"

She's right. We are standing in front of a rainbow of colors, in all shapes and sizes: umbrella strollers, jogging strollers, urban terrain and travel system strollers. There are doubles, triples, and quads. There is a whole row of Bugaboo Bees, and another of the Britax Chaperone in bovine-themed Cowmooflage.

She closes her eyes and shakes her head in frustration. "I think I'm going to faint. Too many choices, so little time. And this is just the beginning! How stupid of me to give away all of Jezzy's baby stuff. Her crib, her little clothes . . . I guess I thought that when we decided it was time to get pregnant again, it would be fun to start fresh. But now that the time has come, I'm panicking. I can't even think of all that has to be done before I deliver. Oh my God, let's just get the car seats and get out of here!"

All three kids have already run ahead, with Lana in hot pursuit. I put my hands on Grace's shoulders. "You know, this pregnancy was meant to happen. You are supposed to have this child now. If you allow it, this is going to be one of the greatest times of your life. Grace, you're not in this alone. Look."

I pull Grace's three-ring binder from my satchel and hand it to her. "It's all here: some suggestions on high chairs, car seats, strollers, diapers, you name it . . . Don't worry, I've put in catalog tags, so that you can find whatever you need." Quickly I open to the printout of the AutoCAD 3-D room layout. "And I put together a diagram of the baby's room, with the furniture brands I'd recommend. Most of these items come in different styles, so you can choose whichever you like. Oh yeah, there's a checklist of items you may think you'll need, and a listing of local mommy playgroups and Lamaze classes, some referrals for baby nurses . . ."

As I fumble with the notebook, Grace just stands there, awestruck.

If she passes out, I'll have to catch her. Just in case, I put the binder under one arm.

Oh no, there are tears in her eyes. Is this a good sign, or a bad one?

I can't tell, so I start chattering like a magpie. "Look, Grace, please forgive me if I've jumped the gun. It's just that—well, I know how busy you've been, what with all the house closings you've got. And also, seeing your taste as it pertains to Jezebel, I pretty much think I've got it down pat. At least I hope so—"

Transfixed, Grace grabs the binder out of my hand and flips through it. "No, no! . . . Wow, this is so—*thorough*! You've thought of everything! 'Delivery, Nursery, Feeding, Travel Gear, Toys, Hospital, Registries, Friends and Family, Shower Items' . . ." I see her shoulders fall as her smile returns. "Katie, this is *incredible*!"

"Excuse me, I don't mean to interrupt, but would you mind if I take a peek at that, too?"

The woman who has sidled up beside us is in her late thirties and bulky with baby. The dark circles under her eyes are proof of what Grace already seems to know: it's a myth that a second go-round of motherhood is easier than the first.

Then again, her first kid may be the reason she looks so tired. The girl lurking nearby is about thirteen. Make that thirteen going on twenty-one: her long, skinny legs are encased in supertight, low-cut jeans, she's wearing a top that rises up her midriff, and she has on more makeup than a supermodel strutting up a runway. Her thumbs are a blur as they speed-type on her cell phone's QWERTY keyboard. Humans may share the trait of opposable thumbs with the lemur and a few other primates, but we stand alone when it comes to the silliest uses for them.

Grace hesitates only a second before handing over the binder. "No, by all means. But I'll wrestle you to the ground if you try to walk away with it!"

The woman laughs wryly. Her eyes open large as she flips through page after page of my handiwork. "I am so jealous. As you can see, it's been a few years since I've had a newborn." She glances at her daughter, who is still furiously texting away.

The girl gives her mother a pitying glare, but the mother ignores it. "I'm a partner in a law firm. Between my caseload and the fact that my husband is out of town a lot, I've had very little time to think about the baby. One of my associates warned me I'd need a baby planner. I should have taken that as a broad hint." Reluctantly she hands the book back to Grace, then turns to me. "Then again, it's not too late. I still have a few months to go, if you can believe that by looking at this bowling ball I'm carrying under this tent. What do you charge for an initial consultation?"

"What do I . . . *what?*" I hate to sound so stupid, but I have no idea what she's talking about.

A *baby planner* . . . does she mean . . . *me?*

Yeah, okay, I've been planning for a baby the past five years of my life, but still . . .

"Katie's terms are really quite reasonable," Grace declares nonchalantly. Obviously the real estate hustler in her is a lot quicker on the uptake than I am. "I mean, look at this Product Analysis section! And this nursery design . . ." She opens to a layout of her nursery.

"Awww, so adorable," coos the woman. Her eyes light up when she sees the crib I've recommended for Grace: it is hand-painted white, with an inset of sapphire-and-peach gingham.

"Katie charges only six hundred and fifty dollars for the initial consultation. That gives you an analysis plan; then one hundred fifty as an hourly rate after that, for implementation of any portion of it. But I chose the annual retainer because it's a steal: five hundred dollars for six hours a month, for her to research playgroups, child-care options, vacation ideas, preschool applications—"

"Oh my God, that's great! You're worth it for the peace of mind alone. Please, do you have a card?"

The woman clutches my arm as if she won't be letting go anytime soon. Or at least, not until I hand her something with my name and telephone number on it.

"I didn't bring any with me because I didn't know I'd need any—"

"Katie is a stickler about our one-on-one time." Grace winks broadly at me, then hands the woman one of her Realtor cards. "This is Katie Johnson. I'm Grace Welch. Feel free to e-mail me here, and I'll e-mail back with Katie's contact info."

Nodding good-bye, the woman finally gives in to her daughter's whines to move toward the more teencentric parts of the mall.

Yep, the lady needs me bad.

And boy, do I need her, too.

I wait until they are safely out of earshot before murmuring, "Want to tell me what just happened here?"

Grace laughs. "Sure! As of this moment you are a professional baby planner. Ha! Just think, Katie: all these years you've been studying these products and didn't know there were other uses for all that knowledge! Now, thanks to my quick thinking, you'll soon have a second client—me being the first, of course."

"I don't know, Grace. I mean, it's not like I have any real-life experience. Granted, I know consumer product testing, and demographic research, and a lot about what's available in today's market . . . but shouldn't being a mom be a prerequisite?"

Grace doubles over with laughter. "Why is that? Honey, most women are clueless about motherhood before, during, *and* after having a child! Every day brings a new turn in the learning curve: not to mention, with every additional child the marketplace and care options change. No two pregnancies are alike. Our very own nephews are proof of that."

She points over toward Mario and Max. The boys think nothing of ramming the strollers together, like bumper cars, on their way to retrieve us. "Katie, you have the skills to provide new moms with some important information: things we may not have known to ask. So why not make money on your know-how?"

She waves the boys over, then says the one thing she knows will close the sale: "Besides, if Alex sees how much fun you're having, it may change his mind about the whole having-a-baby thing."

As if.

I don't think she's right, but it may just be profitable proving her wrong.

5

·······

7:35p.m., Saturday, 25 February

WAIT, TELL ME again what it's called? A baby *planner*?
Just what the hell is that?"

Alex stares at me as if I've grown horns or something.

We're in the middle of our favorite pizza joint: Little Star,
on Valencia. The place is small and the tables are close. Does
Alex really think I want others hearing him give me the third
degree?

To prove that no exorcism is needed, I've been smiling
politely. The goal now is to keep the tone of my voice as
soothing as possible. No waver, no fear. I *will not* let him intimidate me.

"It's a consultant to expectant mothers on the kinds of
things they should consider purchasing for their newborns.
Frankly I think it's a perfect job for me, since I'm trained to assess consumer products and services. As for the money, I'm
charging six-fifty for the initial consultation, and an hourly rate
of one-fifty after that. I will also take clients on retainer, starting
at five hundred dollars a month."

So there.

I take another humongous piece of the deep-dish pizza
we've ordered. I may not be pregnant, but if he's going to scold
me anyway, I may as well eat as if I am.

"Wow! And all you have to do is recommend a diaper company, and the right formula? That's not too shabby." Alex picks up a piece, too. All of a sudden he's found his appetite again.

Not me. I toss my slice back down onto my plate. How dare he denigrate the amount of work that goes into making a new mom feel at ease! "You've got it all wrong. It's going to be a lot of ongoing research. And I'm sure there will be some product testing involved—which is great, since it's information I want to have at my fingertips . . . for personal reasons, anyway."

Alex stops midbite. Warily he looks at me out of the corner of his eye. "Oh yeah? Why do you say that?"

"For Grace," I answer innocently. "Everything I find out is something I can pass along to her, too."

Or keep for myself.

He shrugs his assent and signals the waiter for another beer. The line for tables snakes out the door, and the noise level is making it difficult for us to hear each other.

That's okay. I have no more to say on the subject, and neither does he.

What more can he ask for? That I somehow restrain myself from falling in love with the tots whose moms I'm helping?

The least he can do is ignore it as I live vicariously through them.

9:10 a.m., Sunday, 26 February

THE WOMAN we met at Babies"R"Us wasted no time getting back in touch with Grace, who must have passed along my e-mail address, because a missive is waiting for me, requesting that we meet sometime on Monday:

From: Joanna Wallensky [JWallenskyEsq@ . . .]: Does
6pm work for you? After work I have to pick up my
daughter from school, but perhaps you can meet me
at our house. We live in West Portal . . .

I write back yes, that will work for me, too. In early evening
traffic, my commute will take an hour or more, round-trip,
from where we live in the Marina. A schlep, for sure, but
still . . . *Yippee! My very first client! Yippee!*

1:30 p.m., Monday, 27 February

I'VE SPENT all day Sunday and this morning preparing for
the meeting with Joanna. I've devised a client questionnaire
and product checklist for every conceivable baby need, a cost
sheet for possible services rendered, and of course a vendor
contract. I also took time to look over the spreadsheets I'd created for Grace. Some of the product recommendations would
be applicable to any new client. However, other categories—
registry items, personal shopping, nursery design, a baby-
proofing assessment of her house—will require input before I
customize a plan.

Good. We have enough to keep us busy for the first session.

Grace and Lana, who I've met for lunch, seem even more
excited than I am over the thought of me working for myself.
"There are always a lot of ups and downs, but being your own
boss rocks," says Lana. "You'll see. It has so many rewards,
too—"

"Just think, now you'll be able to set your own hours,"
Grace chimes in, "and every job is different and challenging."

"Yes, I'm psyched about that. I love the fact that I'll be
working with people who are always happy. I mean, you're

never happier than when you're pregnant, right?" I wait for an enthusiastic *Hell yeah* . . .

But no. Just laughter.

Finally Lana gasps out, "Well, at least you'll appreciate the payday."

That's her polite way of ignoring what I already know: not every client will be sane.

That's okay. With knowledge comes power. Sure, my clients are bound to be a little anxious, what with all those hormones surging. But eventually they will learn to love me and to trust me.

After all, I'm the Answer Gal, Ms. Know-It-All.

And they need me more than I need them.

At least, that's what I tell myself.

5:52 p.m.

JOANNA'S HOUSE is a two-story pink stucco cottage, circa 1930s. The yard is an oasis of velvety fescue wedged between two spokes along West Portal's Taraval Street traffic island: Dewey Boulevard and Montalvo Avenue. A garland of crimson bougainvillea has crept up over the front stoop and entwined itself on the porticos of the front door alcove.

I've knocked several times, but no answer.

Some twenty minutes later, Joanna's Mercedes roars into the driveway and lurches to a halt. She hurls herself out of the car: not an easy thing to do, considering that she's five months' pregnant. Her daughter is close behind and pouting. She ignores me as she overtakes her mother and storms into the house, slamming the door behind her.

Joanna sighs and rolls her eyes. "So sorry I'm late! Emma was in detention—*again*. Ah, the joys of parenting." She runs her fingers through her short, auburn hair. It seems that everything about Joanna is staccato, even down to the way her curls rise straight up from the root, only to bob and weave, like a crackling fire.

I can't help it: I want her to relax, to breathe . . .

To protect her baby.

When the twins and I were growing up, we had a shih tzu named Frankie. He knew he was smaller than every other dog on the block, so whenever he found himself near some snarling alpha-mutt, he'd pull a Gandhi: instead of growling or attacking first, he'd go Zen, letting his shoulders drop limply. This had a calming effect on any number of four-legged bullies.

I try it now, to see if it calms her down.

But she is not a dog of war. She is the mom of a teen.

There is no peace in sight.

This becomes blatantly evident as Joanna bangs hard on the front door, to no avail. Through the big bay window we can see that the earbuds of Emma's iPod are firmly in place.

Exasperated, Joanna slams her hand one last time before resting her forehead against the slab of thick prehung mahogany that stands between her and her firstborn. She doesn't look at me when she whispers "It wasn't always this way."

"Of course not. I'm sure it's just a phase. She'll grow out of it."

Do I sound as ignorant as I truly feel?

I guess not, because Joanna nods hopefully. "We can set up at the table on the back terrace. It's the best place to be on a mild evening, anyway."

As I follow her to the garden gate, I'm glad she has her back to me because that way she can't see the doubt in my face. I may know what products children need, but I'm clueless as to how they feel.

I hold my satchel tightly at my side. Without it, I suspect, I'm a complete and utter fraud.

IT TAKES us half an hour to go through the paperwork I've brought with me, including my description of specific services and my contract, on which Joanna can check off those services she wants me to perform.

She places X's in all the little boxes and signs it in a flurry.

Then we go through the assessment questionnaire. Since she is already in her second trimester, some of my questions—particularly about her current medical care—are answered with a swift "Done it" or "Not to worry, I've got it covered." And this time, unlike for Emma's birth, which was vaginal, she has opted for a C-section; and she won't be nursing at all.

Noting my raised brow, she sighs and leans in. "Look, let's cut to the chase: I really didn't want to get pregnant again, but I did it to save my marriage."

That stops me cold. "Oh . . . 'kay," I stammer. "Hmmm . . . I guess I don't get it."

"It's simple. My husband, Paul, wants to be a father."

"Oh! But . . . isn't he Emma's father?"

"Hell no! *That* son of a bitch walked out on us when she was three." Joanna's laugh is devoid of any mirth whatsoever. "Paul and I have only been married for two years. He feels that—Wait! Oh heck, let's drop it for now! He just came home."

Despite the tall box hedge that hovers over the yard, the street traffic cannot be fully muzzled. We've gotten used to the sound of cars halting at stop signs, then gunning their engines as they maneuver around Taraval's circular concrete island. But Joanna's ears are better trained than mine. She must have recognized the crunch of tire to concrete as her husband's car pulled into the driveway.

In a few minutes' time her hunch is proven correct when a tall, good-looking man opens the back door and steps out with Emma. The girl's scowl is still in place and only deepens as her stepfather nudges her along toward our table.

"Glad to see you two gals out here enjoying the fresh air!" Paul's false cheeriness fools no one, but we both nod and chuckle benignly, as if he's caught us playing hooky. Before I have a chance to rise up, his hand grabs mine in a firm shake. "So, you must be the baby planner. Hell, that's a new one to me! But if Joanna says she needs one, whatever, right? . . . Wow, I'm, like, over the moon about this kid. Never been a dad—oh, except to this little lady here."

He puts his arm around Emma for a quick squeeze. Her response—to wrinkle her nose as if he's the nerdiest boy in class—is not lost on him. He shrugs, but it's obvious he's hurt when he mutters, "Hey, do you know any voodoo that will make it a boy? You know, like an ancient Chinese remedy, or some new technology?" Letting loose with a weak chuckle, he nods toward his stepdaughter. "You know what they say: too much of a good thing . . ."

He is the only one laughing at his own joke.

Joanna and I are more concerned with Emma. The tears roll off the high planes of her cheeks and plop onto my baby product checklist.

Nowhere on it is there any delineation between girls and boys. It's going to stay that way, too.

When he still doesn't get it, Joanna murmurs some excuse to me and drags him back into the house with her, slamming the door behind them. The phrases "insensitive ass" and "just kidding" and "Bullshit! You've said that, like, five times now" can be heard above the ebb and flow of the traffic.

"Maybe he'll take the baby with him when he finally leaves us," Emma says, but she doesn't look over at me.

"Emma, honey, you don't really mean that." I lay my hand on her arm, but she shrugs it off.

I gulp down the hurt I feel for her, and it's choking me up. "They're just working things through. Adults do that when they love each other. You'll see—"

Finally she turns toward me, but from the look on her face I'm guessing it's to see if I believe my own bullshit. "No, I *won't*—because I'm never getting married, or having kids. What's the use? Nobody really wants their kids anyway!"

Before I have a chance to tell her how wrong she is—that parents do want children, badly, if only to ensure that there will always be someone there to love them, too, unconditionally— she is out the gate and running down the street toward the shops on West Portal.

I'll be interviewing doulas, baby nurses, and au pair services for my clients. I wonder if I should check out some family counselors, too.

6

2:38 p.m., Saturday, 10 March

LANA AND GRACE have thrown a launch party for my new business, which, after long consideration, I've entitled Making Mommies Smile. They are holding it at one of their sale listings: a tony estate in Saratoga in which every room has been staged to perfection, including the expansive nursery and the toddler's bedroom.

The invitation list included every pregnant woman they know: their clients, as well as those belonging to other Realtors in their firm, and mommies in their children's schools and play-groups.

In between the ongoing scavenger hunt that takes guests through every room in search of product freebies, waiters proffer trays of organically grown tidbits: samples of the kinds of finger foods that are healthy, delicious, kid-friendly, and quick and easy to make.

The guests' swag bags are filled with some really nice items: bottles of an organic baby lotion, and a baby shampoo; a rattle; a safety ID kit; a tote bag; a CD with lullabies sung by celebrity moms; a tooth chart from a local dentist; a height chart from a local pediatrician; a recipe box filled with tasty and healthy recipes for toddlers; and my very own "Katie's Mommy Must-Do Action Plan."

There are coupons from companies with products listed on my "Katie's Approved Merchandise List," and a gift card that gives 25 percent off an initial consultation with me.

Pink and blue balloons tied with long streamers in the opposing color float along the living room's double atrium ceiling. There is wine for those who aren't pregnant, and flutes of Biota Water (beloved by the eco-aware) and Martinelli's Sparkling Cider for those who are. It all has the same effect: the women seem giddy and relaxed.

As I move through a demonstration on car seat safety, they lean in to catch every word I say. Their heads nod instinctively and in unison, like daisies bending in a gentle breeze.

When I conclude my discourse on the importance of purchasing an infant car seat with a five-point safety harness, questions are tossed out fervently, like bouquets for an actress during her standing ovation. Most of them I could have answered in my sleep: Yes, you should look for a detachable cover because, inevitably, your little one will spill something on it. Yes, the LATCH system compliance is mandatory for both cars and car seats, and has been since 2003. And by the way, it stands for Lower Anchors and Tethers for Children, because that is what is needed to keep them safe. And no, it's not wise to put your new infant in the same car seat you used for your three-year-old.

After the very last question, the room breaks into frantic applause.

I am their guru.

I am a rock star.

That's when I notice the woman with her arms folded just below her chest. She has dark brown hair trussed up in a high ponytail. Her baby bump protrudes just slightly between her midriff top and her yoga pants. I guess her to be three months' along, maybe four. She isn't frowning, but her forehead is etched in doubt.

As the Mother Teresa of befuddled new moms, I can't let her go without feeling her pain. I look straight at her and beckon her forward. "Excuse me, you look as if you have a question. Maybe I can answer it?"

She first glances from side to side, unsure that I may actually be talking to her. When she realizes I am, her cheeks flare bright red. Her ponytail sways as she shakes her head. I presume her reticence is shyness. I need to assure her that she's among friends—

And that I could be her very best friend.

For the right price, of course.

"Hey, don't be shy," I assure her soothingly. "I don't think I caught your name?"

She hesitates at first. "It's Lacie. Lacie Channing."

"Tell me, Lacie, what's seems to be bothering you?"

Suddenly all conversation ceases. No one wants to miss a word of something that might be a matter of great importance for her own child.

"Well it's . . . it's just that"—she takes a deep breath—"I guess I just find all of this so silly! Like this list you've made for us—" She points to my new 310-item checklist, which includes everything from A (air purifiers) to W (wipes warming trays). "So much conspicuous consumption! Why is that? For centuries babies have done just fine on a tenth of this stuff—and in other parts of the world, most still do. Not to mention the fact that you've created a scenario in which you take away from us all the things we should be enjoying about motherhood: planning how our babies' rooms will look, what they will wear, whom they'll play with—even how they'll come out of our wombs! I find that—oh, I don't know: sterile, I guess."

She searches the faces of the others in the room. "Am I the only one who feels that way?"

At first no one moves.

Then all heads turn toward me.

What I say now—and how I say it—will either make or break my future as a baby planner.

"Hmmm . . . well, yes, Lacie, I certainly see your point. It would seem that I'm doing all the 'fun' stuff." My chuckle is joined by a few others that are just as shaky as mine.

What worries me, though, is the number of frowns now popping up throughout the room.

Don't sound desperate. Talk with authority. You are in control. You need their love . . .

"But I don't see it that way," I say, in a voice that is surprisingly calm. "Oh, certainly I'll be saving you time and money by researching what you'll buy for your baby, and picking it up for you, if that's what you want me to do. But the most important role I'll have in any client's life is saving her *heartache*."

Lacie shakes her head in disbelief. "And how are you going to do that?"

I go over to a woman holding her swag bag and pull out a small pamphlet. "With this. It's my checklist of safety concerns you may encounter in your home, your car, and of course your nursery. You see, Lacie, I haven't done my job if I haven't made sure that the environment into which you'll bring your infant is a safe one. Let me give you an example." I turn to the woman. "Tell me, have you already purchased a crib?"

The woman smiles and shakes her head. "My baby will sleep in the same crib I had as a baby. It's been in our family for five generations."

"What a sweet idea! I love the sentimentality behind it. But"—I pause, then take a deep breath—"if it's that old, I'm guessing your crib doesn't meet the standards set by the American Society for Testing and Materials."

The woman shakes her head, confused. "I . . . wouldn't know, but I suppose not."

"Just think: a crib is one of the few places in which mothers leave their child alone. And yet each year over twelve thousand accidents occur in cribs, and fifty of those babies die." I look around the room. "As beautiful as your antique crib is, it may not be the safest place to put your child. For example, the slats may be too far apart. Or perhaps a modern mattress is too small, and your child can get caught between it and the crib rails."

The woman starts to speak, but then stops herself.

So that she knows I'm not passing judgment on her, I pat her arm and give her an empathetic smile. "May I make a suggestion? Instead of putting your baby in that crib, fill it with stuffed animals and use it as a decorative focal point in the room. That way you honor a treasured family keepsake in what is now the most important room in your home, without compromising your child's safety."

The woman nods her head. Yes, she gets it.

So does every other woman in the room. All are carefully reading my baby-proofing pamphlet. "Even if your crib meets current standards, it's also my job to make sure that it's placed in a safe spot; that it isn't, say, next to the cord for the window blind. You're paying me to think about those things, and to make you aware of them. When it comes to your child, ignorance is not bliss."

Although I address what I'm saying to Lacie, it is every other new mother in the room who is nodding her head in agreement. "But what you'll appreciate most about me can't be found on any checklist: *I'll be your best friend during your pregnancy.* You know, the one person you can go to when your girlfriends are too harried, or your mom is too far away, or your husband just doesn't have a clue. I'll give you the straight scoop, even when others are afraid to hurt your feelings. I'm with you through the tears, the hormones, and the anxiety. Even after you're long tired of being pregnant, I'll be at your side, cheering you on until that sweet little boy or girl is in your arms for the very first time—and beyond."

As I scan their faces, I lock eyes with each of my guests, if only for a moment. "This is truly going to be the most important and most memorable experience of your life! My job is to ensure that all those memories are happy ones."

I am spent. I've spoken my piece.

All eyes now swivel back to Lacie. Her sour expression has softened, but I can tell that the doubt is still there.

Grace is enough of a salesperson to know that closing this crowd means drawing the attention back to me. "Hey, everyone, time for the raffle!" she shouts in a voice loud enough to earn her the job of carnival barker. "One free session with Katie! Talk about the perfect gift for any new mom!"

Like a beautiful magician's assistant, Lana appears at my side with a bowl filled with the guests' names on tiny pieces of folded paper. With all eyes where they should be—back on me—I reach inside the bowl and draw out one of the slips.

With a flourish, I open it:

LACIE.

Great. Just great.

There is nothing I can do but read it aloud. "And the winner is—well, well, it's you, Lacie!"

The clapping is halfhearted. Lacie doesn't squeal, but nods as if she's been given a death sentence. Thank goodness no one notices. They are too busy lining up to meet me, tossing out questions, jockeying for my attention, and filling out the clipboards handed out by Grace and Lana for appointment requests.

It dawns on me that Lacie is one mom in a million. She may not feel scared or uncertain or overwhelmed by her pregnancy, but there are many women out there who do.

And my appeal to Lacie convinced a roomful of them to give me a try.

I wonder if Lacie will ever call me to collect her freebie.

Quite frankly, if she does I'll be disappointed. Despite the fact that a world filled with Lacies would put me out of business, I have complete respect for any woman who isn't afraid to find her own answers in the process of bringing a baby into this world, even if it means making a few mistakes along the way.

We'd learn a lot from each other.

7

· · · · · · ·

By far the most common craving
of pregnant women is not to be pregnant.
—*Phyllis Diller*

Wednesday, 14 March

BECAUSE OF THE party, I now have six new clients, each with a different set of needs. Two of them are going to be an interesting challenge for me, to say the least.

For example, there is Carolyn Langford, an art gallery owner who is having her first child. Thus far, it has not been an easy pregnancy: she is five months along, and confined to bed rest because she has already had two miscarriages. Her ob-gyn has warned her that the child she carries now needs round-the-clock care and consideration. Her husband, Gordon, an investment banker, has warned her that he will tie her to the bed if she doesn't stay in it. Besides having hired a housekeeper to make sure Carolyn has everything she needs, she now has me as well.

Carolyn is appreciative, not just for herself, but for Gordon, too. "He's still grieving hard over our losses," she explains. "Before the miscarriages, I'd never seen him cry. My heart would break to see him go through that again."

I nod sympathetically. I'm working from the chaise longue in her bedroom so that she can follow her doctor's orders and stay in bed.

"I'll need you to do a lot of running around for me, in order to get things ready before the big day," she says to me in a forlorn little voice. "I'm sorry about that. I was so looking forward to doing all this myself. Of course I'll pay you extra for your additional time."

"I don't mind. We'll take it one task at a time. Before you know it, everything will be in its place in plenty of time for the big day. Would you mind if I take a look at the nursery?"

Dread fogs her eyes. "Please, feel free to go in there now, if you want. It's down the hall and on the right. Just . . . just be sure to shut the door behind you."

The nursery door is closed. It creaks when I open it. The room is painted a stark white, and it doesn't look like anyone has been in it for some time.

I can't blame Carolyn for avoiding it. The emotions held within its walls must be painful for her.

I do a quick reconnaissance on the baby clothes and gear she's already acquired: crib, dresser, and changing table combo; nightstand and rocker; and a toy chest with a few infant toys. In the drawers are some very cute onesies, and hanging in the closet are a few expensive toddler ensembles. The colors are blue and pink, with nothing in between. None have been worn, and many of the items still have their tags.

There are still plenty of necessary items to consider. In fact, some would make wonderful shower gifts. But considering her miscarriage history, I won't broach the topic of registries or a baby shower until it gets closer to her delivery date.

There is nothing more heartbreaking than returning the gifts for a baby who didn't make it into the arms outstretched to meet it.

When I get back to Carolyn's bedroom, I lead her onto the topic of the nursery's colors. Just the thought makes her tear up. "My first miscarriage was a boy. I'd already painted the room blue. The second was a girl. I had repainted it pink by then. After that miscarriage . . . well, white is safe, isn't it? This time we're expecting another boy, but now I don't know what to do! I guess I don't want to jinx it."

This hour with her is more like therapy than a planning session. She is still grieving her losses. Gordon won't discuss it, and her friends can't relate, since they've never experienced a miscarriage.

I know one thing for sure: she won't stop worrying until this baby is placed safely at her side.

I make a note to get her color swatches in pale yellows and greens. I hope it's a start to giving her a new perspective: anything that allows her to focus on the future.

5:44 p.m., Friday, 16 March

ANOTHER NEW client is Merrie Lovejoy. Unfortunately, this congressman's wife is all dimples and smiles only when television cameras are present.

Maybe her off-camera curtness has to do with the fact that she will have delivered her fourth child by her fortieth birthday: just in time to hit the campaign trail again with her husband, Mike, as he makes his bid for a seventh term in Congress.

She is twelve weeks along, and her baby will be delivered by caesarean, she informs me firmly, in order to take away any birthdate guesswork. Photos of the Lovejoys' other children fill the étagère beside her. They have two girls, ages fourteen and four, and a ten-year-old boy. All look like happy, healthy miniatures of either Merrie or Mike, who are the Barbie and Ken of California's Central Valley political power couples.

Edie, one of her aides, attended my launch party and came back raving about me. Now I have to live up to Merrie's expectations, which include (a) being at her beck and call, no matter what coast she calls from; (b) getting information back to her quickly, even if she or her aides are too busy to return phone calls; and (c) trying to decide if her snap decisions are really what she wants or (more than likely) what she feels will play well in the press.

"Now, some ground rules," she declares crisply. "Nothing goes in the baby's room that wasn't made in America. Got that? Not a onesie, not a rocker, not even the baby monitor."

"Sure, okay," I answer. "But I'll still provide comparisons, so that you can make an informed choice."

She smirks. "Honey, let me tell you something: *all* my choices are voter-friendly. It's why I drive a Ford and not a Mercedes. And why my baby will wear OshKosh."

"I don't know about that. Sure, OshKosh is an American company—but the clothes are actually made in Mexico."

"Oh, crap!" This stops her cold. She turns to her aide. "Edie! Go ask Larry in Polling about perceptions of the district voters toward Mexican-manufactured goods, and whether it will hurt Mike's union support. Hell, I can't keep the kid in a diaper for the first year of his life—"

"Speaking of diapers," I add, "you'll also want to consider how your environmentally conscious voters feel about cloth diapers versus disposables."

"Damn it! What am I supposed to do, lug a diaper pail with me on the campaign?" She closes her eyes with a deep sigh. "Okay, all right! Let's come up with an American-made solution that makes everyone happy."

"Gotcha. How about biodisposables? They are eco-friendly, and there are a few companies here in the States that make them—"

"Yeah, yeah, sure, that sounds good." Merrie shrugs. "Maybe having another kid before the campaign wasn't such a great idea. How the hell did I let Mike talk me into this?"

She signs my contract with a sigh and without giving it a second glance.

I guess she figures if there is anything in there that she won't like, she'll get her husband to pass some law to make it null and void.

It's one of the perks of power.

6:24 p.m.

BY THE time I get home from the consultation with Merrie, I'm exhausted.

Well, too bad. According to a text message from Alex that must've come in on my cell phone during my meeting, I've forgotten one very important appointment:

Where R U? S&M partay in full swing. Need U to spread the LUV—

No, Alex isn't sexting about bondage. It's his not-so-gentle reminder that I've got to get myself over to his venture capital firm, Steadman & Martinez, in order to hobnob with him and his current and potential clients at their monthly cocktail party.

Usually I look forward to it. It's Alex at his best: upbeat, congenial, and ever attentive, both to me and to whichever techies he's wooing at the time.

A lot of those guys don't know how to talk to a woman. That's where I come in. With all the facts and figures that stay in my brain, I can talk to anyone—and usually do, incessantly at these parties, since it keeps things flowing.

It takes me just a second to throw on something that resembles a cocktail frock and head out the door.

The party is in full swing when I get there. I weave through the crowd, looking for Alex, and see him standing with two guys who reek of geek. They are wearing the techie dress uniform du jour: jeans and black T-shirts. It's a sharp contrast to Alex, who is wearing Brioni casual: a beige cashmere jacket over gray wool slacks, with a dark silk shirt. One of the guys is balding, bearded, and homely. The other is too tall, too thin, and too shaggy, but in a cute sort of way. Oddly enough, Shaggy keeps looking at his watch, as if he's got somewhere else to be but is too polite to say so. Thank goodness Alex doesn't notice. When he holds court, others are usually at attention.

He has paid handsomely for that privilege.

I slip my arm around Alex. He smiles and kisses me on the forehead. "Ah, here she is now! Katie, meet Henry Laird"—he nods toward Bearded Guy—"and Seth Harris. S&M will soon be adding SkorTek, their company, to its portfolio. Am I right, guys?"

Hearing this, Henry smiles up at Alex. In the Monopoly game of start-up capital, he's just landed on Park Place.

On the other hand, Seth frowns.

What is wrong with this dude?

I reach out to shake their hands. Henry's handshake is vigorous, whereas Seth's is firm, but at least I don't feel as if my arm will fall out of its socket.

"Hey, Katie, guess what? Seth here is a new daddy! Isn't that cool?"

Sadly, his exuberance is just an act. I've never heard Alex call fatherhood "cool."

Still, I know enough to keep up appearances. I nod enthusiastically. "Congratulations. A boy or a girl?"

Seth doesn't crack a smile. "Girl."

Oh . . . *kay.* "How sweet," I add. "A newborn?"

"No. Five months old." Nothing. Not an anecdote, or even an offer to show me a digital photo on his iPhone.

What kind of father is this guy?

"Hey, maybe what Katie does will be something that will interest your wife," says Alex, without missing a beat. "She's a baby planner. You know, a consultant who helps you get everything you need for your little bundle of joy. Right, honey? I'm sure you can explain it better than I ever could."

From the look on Seth's face, you'd think that Alex had just asked him to turn his firstborn over to the devil.

Before I can even open my mouth, Seth Harris shuts me down with a frown that says he can't believe I'd dare speak to him about this. "Doesn't sound like anything we'll need. Now, if you'll excuse me . . ."

He doesn't even look at me. At least he shakes Alex's hand.

As his new client rushes toward the door, Alex shrugs and murmurs in my ear, "Jesus, if this is any indication of how people react to what you do, I guess you should go back and beg the state for another job."

As if.

Damn it, I need a drink.

"Excuse me," I say sweetly to my unsupportive husband and his new client, as I head back toward the reception area, where the bar is hopping.

As I take my first sip, I happen to glance over at the elevator bank, where I notice Seth is waiting. The excellent cabernet in my hand gives me the liquid courage I need to put that jerk in his place. "Excuse me, Mr. Harris!" I'm not exactly shouting, but I know he hears me, because he turns around and stares at me. But just then the elevator chimes and the doors open. He steps onto it, waving his dismissal of me.

To hell with that.

I practically run to the elevator, reaching it just as the doors slide to a close.

He glares down at me. Now that I'm here, I don't know what to say, except: "I don't get it. Does what I do for a living offend you?"

"No! Seriously, lady, I could care less." He runs his hand through his mop flop and pushes the Down button again and again. Too bad. He's stuck with me, at least for the next sixty-three floors. Realizing this, he releases a deep sigh. "Okay, listen—Katie, right? I—we—"

He stops because his voice has choked up. He turns, but it's too late: the tears move from the corner of his eye and down through his five o'clock shadow until they circle under his chin.

In the mirrored panel of the elevator door, his deep brown eyes seek out mine. I don't know what he sees there, but I know what I feel: shock, concern, pity . . .

Although I don't know why.

It's all he needs to answer what I don't have the nerve to ask: "My wife died a day after the birth of our daughter. An infection. I'm raising our daughter on my own. Alex doesn't know this, and frankly I don't want him to . . . No, what I mean to say is that *Henry* doesn't want him to know about it. He thinks Alex may feel I'm too distracted to run the company and pull our funding."

He closes his eyes for what seems like the longest time, but really it's just long enough to drop another few floors. "There, I've said it. Now, if you want to tell your husband, go ahead. Even if it means S&M drops us, at least I won't be lying."

The elevator pings again when we reach the lobby floor.

"Don't worry, I won't say a word." I open my purse and hand him one of my new business cards. "Here, just in case. But really, don't feel obligated. I simply want to help if I can."

He stares down at the card. For some odd reason, it makes him laugh. When he does, a few more tears fall.

"Obligated? Yeah, don't worry about that. What I'm feeling now is just a lot of anger. Life is so unfair. My wife, Nicole, wanted a baby so badly. I . . . I just went along for the ride." He shrugs. "But now that Sadie is here and Nicole isn't, that kid is the only thing that really matters to me, not even SkorTek—except for the fact that SkorTek has to succeed, for Sadie's sake, so that she'll never have to worry about anything." He turns to me. "So yeah, I'll call you. I guess I need you after all."

For both our sakes, I wish it were under better circumstances.

8

·······

Men are what their mothers made them.

—*Ralph Waldo Emerson*

9:06 a.m., Friday, 23 March

THOR HAS A referral for a web designer for Making Mommies Smile: a guy by the name of Jason Welles.

"The stuff he does is . . . well, it's mind-blowing," says Thor. His voice trails off, as if the thought of Jason's magic leaves him mesmerized. Apparently he does well enough at making pretty websites to buy a new Maserati every year from my brother-in-law. Go figure.

I'll just take his word for it. I don't get the web at all: HTML, PHP, SEO, ALEXA rankings, social marketing, blah-blah-blah, whatever. It all goes in one ear and floats out the other just as quickly.

When it comes to techie stuff, my motto is "Don't ask, just pray."

"He's expecting to hear from you," Thor adds. "I told him your new service is really hot, so he should give you all the bells and whistles. He'll make something that will get you noticed, I guarantee that."

"Great! I'll call him right now."

"Oh and hey, before you hang up, Lana wants to know: are you bringing one of your chocolate walnut pies for dinner on Saturday?"

"What? Why? I didn't know we were getting together!"

"Hell yeah. I left a message yesterday, with Alex."

"He never mentioned it. What's the occasion?"

"Mom and Dad are driving up from Santa Barbara." Thor means my parents. Even their affectionate sons-in-law call them that.

Naturally, the moment they heard about Grace's pregnancy, they'd want to come up and celebrate with the rest of us. Like morning glories, they blossom while basking in the sunny presence of their grandchildren, and the glow of whichever daughter is pregnant at that time. It is their payoff for time spent in those few dark corners one inevitably hits on the parenting journey.

I may have been the perfect angel, but the twins were a handful. I have the last remaining pictures of the two of them in Mohawks and spike collars to prove it. And yes, I look forward to sharing these with all current and future nieces and nephews, someday when they're old enough to appreciate the teenagers that their mothers once were.

Although I'm always happy to see my parents, I'm annoyed at Alex. What, he couldn't have warned me? I'm sure it slipped his mind, because of all that's happening at his job. But still! Now I've got to prepare for Dad's inevitable chiding about when Alex and I will be starting our own "little family."

On second thought, I'll let Alex field those questions. That will teach him to pass along messages, even ones we both dread.

9:32 a.m.

MY CALL to Jason the web designer is going great guns. He seems just as excited to talk to me as I am to him. "Hey, any friend of Thor's is a friend of mine."

"Well, really, I'm his sister-in-law."

"You don't say?" His disaffected mumble disappears. "So, you're his wife's twin? I saw a picture of her on Thor's desk. Twins . . . that's always been my fantasy."

"Really? Because they run in our family. Never skips a generation." I guess I should ask if he's a father, too. But then I realize I never answered his question. "But I'm not Lana's twin sister. I'm her older sister."

"Oh? You don't say." I can hear the disappointment in his voice.

"Only by a few years." I don't need some kid making me feel old. I can do that all by myself.

But not today. Today, I'm feeling great, and Jason is my new best friend.

"Thor really thinks you're going to hit it out of the box with your new business. I want in on your success. How 'bout we work a deal? I'll design your site for free, if you won't mind me placing an ad of my own at the bottom of your home page. You know, to let people know we're affiliated."

"For real?" *Wow! Free website design, for a small ad?* "I'll need you to reserve my domain name. It's Making Mommies Smile."

"Gotcha," he says, "I'll do it now."

The flurry of clicks I hear on the other end of the phone excites me. I can see the site in my mind's eye even now. "Think women, probably between the ages of twenty-five and forty, who are somewhat affluent, possibly work out of the house, and want nice things for the little guys in their lives."

"Cougars! Awesome! I can totally get into that."

"Huh?" I stare at the phone in my hand. "Well, no, not quite. More like . . . Did you ever watch that show *Sex and the City*? You know, about women who love spending money—"

"Ah, gotcha! Skankalicious babes diggin' fruity martinis."

"No! These women are married for the most part. And not 'babes' . . . *babies*. So you see, these women wouldn't be drinking." I feel tiny beads of sweat popping up on my forehead.

There is silence on the other end of the receiver, except for some tapping on his keyboard. Is he taking notes, or building his ultimate fantasy basketball team? Maybe that last remark has him rethinking me as a client?

Oh my God, I hope not. He's cheap and quick and I need a site up on the web, like *yesterday.*

I talk a little louder, to get his attention. "You get what I'm looking for now, right? Oh yeah, and I'll need some category tabs: Baby's Room, Great Toys, Hot Products . . . maybe even one that says 'Advice for Daddies.'"

"Ha! Great idea! Let the dudes know what they're getting into, the fees for various services, that sort of thing."

"Yeah, exactly!" Even if he doesn't get it perfect the first time, I'll have a starting point. And I feel certain that the changes will be negligible, and take just a few moments to make . . .

"And of course I'll have my own personal blog on what's hot and what's not." I plan on writing daily. That way the website will be more than an online presence. I'll create a following, a fan club . . .

"Got it." He's breathing and tap-tap-tapping. "I'll use a PHP platform so you can uplink text, JPEGs, even video. Speaking of which, you'll want to have a video box for a web-cam, too, am I right?"

"Wow, great idea! I can use it for demo clips."

"Yep, *now* you're thinking! Viewers eat that up. Keeps them coming back for more. And you can give a teaser on your welcome page to sign up for an ongoing subscription to exclusive stuff: stories, videos, lots of goodies. Go ahead and set up a PayPal account, and we'll link to that."

"Jason, you're a genius!" Of course, expectant mommies would pay for the privilege of viewing product demonstrations, quality testing, and lots of other uses. "Now, about the color scheme. I'm thinking something in soft pastels."

"That's exactly what I'd planned. Elegant, as opposed to in your face. Nothing gaudy. Don't worry, I've got that covered."

Relief washes over me. Now there is one less thing on my to-do list. "Oh, Jason! One last thing: how fast can you get a test site up?"

"I'll have something for you by Saturday night, say nine-ish."

"Wow! Thor said you were fast, but I wasn't expecting something that quickly. That's great because my parents will be in town. I can get their opinion on it, too."

He snickers. "Your parents? Interesting. Glad they're so . . . I don't know. Supportive? Most of the ladies I know who go out on their own get heavy push-back from their folks—or their husbands."

"Frankly, my husband is still a bit leery about this, but I'm out to prove him wrong. These days you've got to be creative about how you earn money. That's what entrepreneurship is all about."

He laughs heartily. "You're telling me! Hey, if it weren't for all you creative types, I wouldn't have a job. So go for it, I say."

"Thanks, Jason. Here's to both our successes." I mean it.

Jason e-mails me a test URL, but tells me not to look at the site until after nine tomorrow tonight.

I can't wait.

11:35 a.m.

THE CALL on my cell is Joanna. "It's . . . a girl." She sounds as if she's been given a death sentence. Before I can say a word, she adds, "The nursery: *make it blue.* And Katie, you can't say a word. To Paul, or to anyone."

"I think you're making a mistake, Joanna. Why don't you go ahead and tell him? In the big scheme of things, it won't matter! Trust me on this—"

"You're wrong about that. You don't know him. I do." She pauses so long that at first I think she's hung up. But then, in a voice I can barely hear, she says, "Until he sees her *that very first time.* Because then he will have fallen in love with her."

As opposed to having fallen out of love with Joanna?

I don't dare ask.

1:14 p.m.

I HAVE tons of errands to run for my clients. I'm glad, because that will keep my mind off my parents' visit.

I've been given budgets from Joanna, Carolyn, and Merrie, not only for baby gear and gadgets but also for infant wardrobes. I'll take pictures of the products I think they'll like, then order and deliver them if I get a thumbs-up on any of the items that catch my eye.

Carolyn insists on gender-neutral colors for all items. Despite her husband's insistence that she think positive about this pregnancy, she refuses to tempt fate by falling in love with another child who may not make it.

Merrie's sonogram is still two weeks away, but she insists she's having a boy. "I'm carrying the same way I did with our son, Marty. Great, we'll have a balanced ticket—I mean *family.*"

Spoken like a true politician's wife.

I bite my tongue before suggesting that she have Larry in polling put the preferred gender to the voters first.

And of course, Joanna has set the mandate for blue, blue, and more blue. She's going to lie to Paul about the sex of the baby until the day their daughter is born.

Then she'll pray for the best.

Sprout, a children's boutique on Union Street, gives me a wonderful start on organic items in a rainbow of colors. The number of items I've plucked off its wide, welcoming shelves puts a smile on the shopgirl's face. "I'm glad to see you're finding a lot of things you like—and in triplicate, too!"

"I'm a baby planner," I explain. "These are for my clients. In fact, do you mind if we divide them into three separate bags?"

"No, not at all." She reaches under the counter. She pulls out not only three large shopping bags, but the store's business cards and event schedules as well, which include their baby yoga and infant sing-along classes. "Check out our website. From there you can go online and fill out the baby registry application for your clients. And if you want to hold a client gathering here, we'll reserve our playroom for you. In fact, leave a few business cards with me, too. I'll be glad to put them out for our customers—and our suppliers. They're always willing to provide samples to consultants, for feedback."

"Thanks for that." I hand her all the cards I have on me and take hers as well, which I'll pass on to some of my clients. Tit for tat.

I make a point to come back soon, with printouts of the completed registry applications for Grace and my three clients.

But the one thing they all so desperately need can't be bought anywhere: time.

3:55 p.m.

I'VE JUST finished my last appointment of the day: with a painter who specializes in working with eco-friendly paints. I've just gotten into my car when I hear my cell ring. It's from a number that I don't recognize. That's not unusual these days, so

I hit the hands-free button in order to drive and talk at the same time.

"Is this Katie?" The man's voice sounds vaguely familiar. Then I place it: it's that guy Seth Harris, from Alex's office party. "I didn't think that I'd need to contact you so soon but—well, the truth of the matter is that you're the only one who can help me right now."

"Not a problem." I rummage through my purse for something to write on. All I have are the color cards I've stuffed in there from the painter. I choose one of the rejected shades: lemony snicket. "I'm booked up tomorrow, but how does the day after sound to you?"

"No! I mean . . . Listen, Katie, I need you to get over to my house as soon as possible! My little girl, Sadie—apparently she has a fever. I left her with a babysitter so that I could come into the office. Unfortunately, the kid is too young to drive her to the hospital—"

"Wait—what? You left an infant with some kid?" I look down at my cell phone. I don't believe what I'm hearing. "Seth, what were you thinking?"

"I know, Katie! I'm an idiot, okay? But you see, we're under a really tight launch deadline with S&M, and Henry is freaking out. I just had to come in—"

"Look, just give me your address, and your babysitter's cell phone number. Then call her and tell her I'm leaving now. You may want to call your pediatrician to say that I'm on my way. That way she'll see us the moment we get there."

Already I can hear him breathing easier on the other side of the phone. "It's Dr. Dorothy Byron, on Stanyan, near UCSF. Jesus, if anything happened to Sadie—"

"Seth, don't beat yourself up. Let me relieve your babysitter and see what we're facing."

"Thank you, Katie. I don't know who else I could have

called." The sadness in his voice breaks my heart. What he did was stupid, and I shouldn't be covering for him. But stupid things happen to parents every day, even the experienced ones.

The goal is to make sure you don't pay for these lessons with your child's well-being.

4:15 p.m.

SETH HARRIS lives in the middle flat of a three-story Victorian on the corner of Cherry and Washington streets, very close to Presidio Heights, within walking distance of the famed Presidio Golf Club. A wonderful neighborhood.

I'm guessing you could actually see the course from his bay window, if the curtain covering it weren't drawn so tightly, as if the place was a tomb.

It is also a mess. I guess Seth has been working late, and he hasn't had time for a normal routine since the baby arrived.

And he is still mourning Nicole. Her personal effects are strewn everywhere, as if she might be coming home any moment now.

The girl babysitting Sadie Harris can't be more than fourteen years old. Her expertly made-up eyes and her right–out–of–*Teen Vogue* ensemble makes her look older than she is, but the baby spittle that is spattered across one shoulder of her lace-trimmed camisole ruins the effect, as does the mascara-tinged tear trail on her face. "Take her, please," she pleads, and practically throws Sadie into my arms. "She's been vomiting. And I've changed her diaper, like six times! She has diarrhea and it's really gross."

Sadie is too warm, and she is red as a strawberry. She squalls like a hungry kitten, so loud, in fact, that I can't hear the fear in the voice of the poor girl who's being paid ten bucks an hour to sit with her, although I can see it in her eyes. This job has turned out to be far above her pay scale.

"Did you take the baby's temperature?"

The girl shakes her head. "I tried, but Sadie wouldn't let me hold it under her tongue." She runs to the table, picks up the thermometer, and brings it over.

I shake my head. "This is a rectal thermometer."

"*Ewwww,*" the girl squeals, and shivers.

I don't blame her. In truth, I've never done it either, although I once watched Lana use a rectal thermometer on one of the boys.

But I actually don't need any thermometer to know that Sadie is much too warm and needs to be cooled down immediately. I rush into the kitchen. Dirty plates and glasses are scattered everywhere, and at first I don't see what I'm looking for: a dishcloth.

Finally I find one, stuffed in a drawer. Carefully cradling Sadie in the crux of one arm, I run the rag under cold water, squeeze out the excess moisture, then fold it into a square and tuck it firmly under her arm, where I know it will stay and help cool her down.

This small act has a calming effect on her. Sadie's face relaxes some and briefly she closes her eyes.

The girl watches, wide-eyed but relieved.

"I don't know how long you've been here, so I don't know what to pay you—"

She holds up her hand in protest. "No, please! Just tell Mr. Harris I'm so sorry!"

I think at that moment if I'd reached out my hand to pat her, she would have kissed it.

She tosses a sheet of paper at me and hightails it out of the apartment, as if it's on fire. I don't think she'll want to sit for Sadie again anytime soon. She has just been exposed to a parent's worst nightmare: utter helplessness when your child needs you the most.

I put Sadie in her carrier and head down the stairs, making sure to close the door but leaving it unlocked, so that we can get back in after the doctor's appointment. I don't have a baby seat in my car, so I put Sadie's carrier on the floor of the backseat and pray that I don't get pulled over on the short drive to the doctor's office.

4:38 p.m.

"ARE YOU Seth's neighbor?" Now that the infant Tylenol has kicked in and Sadie's fever has subsided, the pediatrician, Dorothy Byron, has time to be friendly.

At least, I hope that's all she's being. I don't want to get Seth accused of neglect. Or me either for that matter.

"I'm just . . ." What am I to him anyway? It seems stupid to call myself his baby planner, and not just because I haven't officially started in that capacity for him, either.

And we certainly didn't plan on *this*.

In hindsight, I realize Seth doesn't need a baby planner. What he truly needs is a second parent for his child. Since that may not be in the cards for him, he'll have to settle for a qualified au pair, and a housekeeper, if he can afford both.

I'll get started immediately on finding them for him. "I'm just a friend. He asked me to relieve the babysitter until he got home from work." I try to smile, but if she can see the quiver that feels like a 6.3 earthquake at the corner of my mouth, I'm not succeeding very well. "She was in over her head."

The doctor nods sadly. "Incidents like this—when an infant is left with an underage caretaker—should be reported. But I won't be doing that. I'm very aware of Seth's loss."

My relief must be obvious to her because my lip has finally quit quivering.

"For future reference, fevers are more serious in babies under six months old because they haven't yet developed the antigens needed to fight off bacterial infections, which I'm guessing is Sadie's problem today," she says. "More important, however, is the reason as to why the baby has a fever in the first place. So please encourage Seth to bring Sadie back in if her fever returns. In the meantime, I'm going to grab a couple of things for you to take and give to him. Some infant Tylenol, a rectal thermometer—"

"Not to worry. He's got the thermometer."

She smiles. "Well, that's a step in the right direction." She leaves the room and returns shortly with a small care package.

I'm just about to leave with Sadie when Seth comes rushing in. Seeing her sleeping so soundly and peacefully in her carrier stops him cold. Relief softens the worry that lines his face. Suddenly he looks a decade younger.

He takes the carrier from me with one hand and guides me out the door with the other. "I got here as fast as I could. She looks fine, but tell me I'm right—"

"Yes, everything is okay. I just think your babysitter was in over her head. She didn't know what to do with a sick infant running a high fever."

"How sick is Sadie?" His eyes cloud over with concern.

"The fever was caused by some infection. You'll just have to watch her for the next forty-eight hours, to make sure it doesn't come back."

"Of course." Then he frowns. "That means missing work."

"I don't know about that. Let me see if I can round up a pediatric nurse to watch Sadie for you tomorrow."

I feel his relief: not in his nonchalant nod, but in the way he closes his eyes, as if praying his thanks.

"I'll call you first thing in the morning with the information on a nurse who can be here tomorrow, before you leave for work. And Seth, I think we're going to have to have a very serious talk about some basic needs for Sadie, and as soon as possible. Maybe Monday? When you get off work, I'll meet you at your place. I'll have a few forms to go over with you, so that I can start your assessment immediately."

He nods absentmindedly. All the while he's been stroking Sadie's tiny fingers with his thumb. It is big enough to cover her whole hand and then some.

It's hard for me to believe that, someday soon, her fingers will grasp that thumb with no problem, and when they do, she will never want to let go. As the years move ahead, as her fingers grow longer and stronger, they will be entwined with his in that special bond that only parents and their children share.

When he takes my hand to shake it good-bye, any indentation Sadie may have made on his calloused thumb is long gone.

But the impression she has made on my heart will never fade.

9

·······

If your baby is "beautiful and perfect, never cries or fusses,
sleeps on schedule and burps on demand,
an angel all the time," you're the grandma.
—Teresa Bloomingdale

5:20 p.m., Saturday, 24 March

MY MOTHER DOES cartwheels for her grandchildren.

I mean that figuratively as well as literally. Forget Zumba. Ruth Harlow is a marathon runner and a former USC cheerleader, a whirling dervish of physical awe and can-do attitude. If Mario, Max, and Jezebel aren't crawling onto her lap and begging her to break from the staid stance of the typical affluent Santa Barbara matron by making those goofy faces she does only for them, they are cheering her on as she spread-eagles her sixty-six-year-old body to form a human pinwheel, then hurls herself, head over heels, onto Grace's velveteen green lawn.

Her grandchildren follow suit. Like little rubber balls tossed helter-skelter onto the ground, they bounce before tumbling into a giggling heap at her feet.

Grace, Lana, and I can't help but laugh, too. We know that in due time, they'll soon rival her in turning cartwheels.

Her true legacy to us, however, is not dexterity but the fearlessness to strive for what we really want in life. And that is why my inability to convince Alex to have a child with me disappoints her, although she has never said so.

She doesn't have to. Dad does it, loudly, and often enough for both of them.

I was always my father's favorite: his happy little Katie, the eager stand-in for the son he never had. I've got a mean curveball to prove it. Dad, God love him, taught me how to throw it without giving the batter a tell. His signal that the time was right was a double wink, followed by a nod. Seeing it, I'd let it rip, and strike 'em out every time. After the game, we'd both laugh, as if our special plan had once again won the day.

Even now, as he huddles with Alex and the twins' husbands over the Ultra-Premium E-Series Viking grill in Thor's state-of-the-art outdoor kitchen, I'm still catching Dad's signals. In this case they are thinly veiled barbs aimed right between Alex's pale blue eyes. It's not Alex who winces when Dad says things like "Those beautiful sons of yours are your legacy," ostensibly to Thor; and then, to Auggie, "The more, the merrier! You'll see. The fun never stops."

But yes, it has, for Alex, because he is still mourning a son far beyond his reach.

That is why, under the pretense of wrapping up the scorched corn on the cob in its foil nest and setting it on the picnic table alongside the platters already laden with our steak and burgers, I move close enough to my husband to wrap my arms around him, and I look up at him adoringly. "Hey, everyone, guess what? Later tonight we should all be able to log on to my website for a first peek!" I say this with enough enthusiasm to shift the tide of conversation.

Thor perks up. "Oh, great! You connected with Jason?"

"Yes, and he certainly sounds like he knows what he's doing. Thanks for the lead."

"I don't think you'll regret it. His work is highly regarded—at least the stuff I've seen." He smiles broadly. "Seriously, he can set you up that quickly?"

"He claims he can. I gave him the lowdown on my target audience, then suggested a few category tabs and a color scheme. He sounded as if he could run with that in developing the test site. Of course, I'll be in charge of adding the actual content: you know, the recommended products, a list of my services, getting a blog started, that kind of thing. But I'm guessing that the cleanup will take a few days at the most, and then we can launch it to the public within the week. Isn't that exciting?"

The guys all nod approvingly, especially Alex. More important, I can tell he appreciates my little diversion because he tilts my face up toward his and gives me a long but gentle kiss.

Yes, deep down in my heart I know that eventually he'll see things my way:

Because he loves me as much as I love him.

Dad knows this, too. It's why his eyes moisten and his frown softens. He reasons that if Alex makes me happy, he can't be so bad after all.

Or maybe he thinks Alex has won me over to his way of thinking, and I'll give up on the one thing I want most in my life: a child.

To assure Dad that's not the case, I pull Alex deeper into our kiss.

At first his instinct is to resist, but then he gives in.

When I look up, I see Dad smiling at me. I give him a double wink and a nod that tells him, *See how easy that was? All it takes is a little persistence . . .*

I'm still at the top of my game.

7:45 p.m.

"WILL IT be hard for you?" Mom doesn't look up from the pot she's scrubbing. I turn and watch her face in the paned window over Lana's kitchen sink. The wrinkles in her forehead are etched deeply, like the dimples on either side of her mouth—which the twins are also blessed with. Jezebel has them, too.

What I share with her is less physical and more emotional: the need to please those around us.

I pause over the dishwasher, where I've been lining up Lana's plates: a beautiful Villeroy & Boch pattern called Flora. Each one sports a different bold flower: poppy, cornflower, rose, or sunflower. "I guess so. It's the first time I'm not working for a large entity, so certainly it will be different for me. On the other hand, it will be exhilarating to try something different."

She sprays the suds off the pot and shakes it before setting it on the drainer, then turns to face me while she dries her hands on the full-body apron tied around her waist. "I wasn't talking about your new company. I have no doubt you'll be wonderful at that. You know your stuff, Katie, like no one else. And you're such a people pleaser."

I can listen to her tell me a million times how proud she is of me and never grow tired of it.

"What I'm asking is whether you'll find it hard being around so many pregnant women who have what you don't, and yet want so badly." She watches my face carefully for signs that her question may have hurt me.

It has. That's why I opt to tell her what she wants to hear.

Okay, really it's what I want to believe. "Mom, please don't worry about me! So far it's all been fine. I know I'm helping others and myself at the same time." My little laugh almost sounds natural. "I'm living vicariously through my clients, and I'm okay with that."

For now, anyway.

I don't have to say that out loud. She knows it.

She nods and smiles, but her eyes glisten with damp sadness, the way mine feel they will do any moment now.

I turn so that she doesn't know I've seen her tears spill into the dirty dishwater.

IT'S AROUND nine thirty. Mario and Max have been put to bed, and Jezebel has nodded off on the couch. The big-screen television is now hooked up to Thor's Mac so that we can all see my website in eye-popping HDTV color.

Yep, eye-popping is certainly the term for it.

Another word that could easily describe it is *porn.*

The mauve and lavender color scheme does little to soften the fact that big-breasted nude women beckon us to follow them inside the test website, where—at least according to the honey-voiced cougar with the big whip on her hip—"bad boys get what's coming to them from Mommy! *MeOWCH!*"

"What? . . . *Wait!*" I can't believe my eyes. "This can't be right! Even the domain name is wrong! I asked him to reserve MakingMommiesSmile.com, not Making*Mama*Smile.com!"

I don't think my family doubts this.

At least, I hope they don't.

Auggie is no fool. He knows that as soon as Grace's shock wears off and she finds her voice, her first command will be to shut off the set. In the meantime he quickly clicks through the category tabs. As promised, there is one entitled "Babes' Bedrooms." Within it are the individual pleasure—or pain—palaces of women who claim such come-hither names as Mandee, Candee, and Sandee. They strike sophisticated poses despite the fact that their expensive gowns are sheer enough to expose nipples and their nether regions.

"Give me that," Thor mutters as he grabs the keyboard. I'm hoping that he'll log off, but no: he clicks onto "Great Toys," which has such subcategories as "Nipple Rings," "Dildos," "Vibrators," "Lubricants," "Paddles," and "Lingerie."

"Enough already!" Lana snatches the monitor's remote out of his hand. "Katie, how well did you vet this web guy?"

"I thought he'd been vetted for me." I glare at Thor. "Hey, didn't you say he's done some pretty great websites?"

Lana pokes him in the ribs. "I'll just bet you did. Okay, dirty old man, fess up! How many of them are porn?"

Thor looks up at the ceiling before answering. "A lot, from what I could see . . . Hey, but some of it wasn't! He also created the site for our dealership, so I know he does other things, too." He ruins his mea culpa with a smirk. "Look, Katie, maybe I didn't explain your business to him as well as I could have, but frankly, I don't understand it myself. And I thought once the two of you talked—"

"I'm just as culpable, I guess. It's just that I thought I'd made myself pretty clear as to what Making Mommies Smile is supposed to be: a website for pregnant women who want information on products and services for babies, not . . . not *this* stuff!"

At first no one says a word. Then Dad snickers and Alex lets loose with a guffaw.

Soon we're all laughing. In my case, through the tears.

When Alex finally catches his breath, he gasps, "I'm guessing the domain you want is still available. But if I were you, I'd hold on to this one, too. Something tells me you'll get a lot of hits from it."

That has the men rolling on the floor for a whole new reason.

10

....

I remember leaving the hospital—thinking,
"Wait, are they going to let me just walk off with him?
I don't know beans about babies!
I don't have a license to do this." We're just amateurs.
—Anne Tyler

6:13 a.m., Monday, 26 March

I'T'S THE CRACK of dawn, and for some god-awful reason someone is giving us a wake-up call.

Alex is dead to the world. He crawled into bed around three this morning. I presume he was out with clients. I'd shake him anyway and make him answer it, but since it's my cell phone that is buzzing, tag, I'm it.

I croak out something that's a cross between "Hello" and "I hate your guts, whoever you are" only to be greeted with "Good morning, Mrs. Johnson! Stand by for Mrs. Lovejoy, please!"

Merrie?

Oh.

Great. She wants to go over her baby plan *now*? But I'm not even awake . . .

"Katie, hon, quick question: Do I say I'm having sex while I'm preggers? What's the consensus on that?"

"Oh . . . um . . . you mean, some reporter has had the audacity to ask you that?"

"No. What I mean is that I've got to be prepared, in case one of those slimy jerks *does* have the guts to ask." She sighs.

"Mike's policy team here is split on how I should answer it. You're the tiebreaker. Is it a yes or a no?"

Well, this is certainly an eye-opener. Hmmm. Okay, now, how do I answer this?

"Why don't you say something like, 'My doctor assures me that it's safe. My husband's opinion is that I'm as desirable pregnant as I was when I wasn't. My personal opinion is that it's none of your business, so feel free to draw your own conclusion.'"

There is silence on the other end of the line.

I almost fall back asleep before she whispers, "Brilliant! Mike will *love* it! Makes him sound romantic *and* virile."

She's cackling so hard that I'm afraid Alex can hear her through the receiver. I hang up before he wakes up and is raring to go. I just don't have time for sex this morning. I have to meet a new client in an hour, and I've yet to prepare for the meeting. She sounded so together on the phone that I want to be sure that I make a good impression.

7:17 a.m.

I AM holding the head of my newest client, Twila Rappaport, as she upchucks her latte in the restroom of her offices within UniVamp, one of the online fantasy gaming software companies located in San Francisco's SoMa district.

Suddenly I'm glad I skipped breakfast.

I have more empathy for Grace now than ever before.

No one else is in the restroom. Nor has anyone entered it since we've been holed up in here, and it's going on twenty minutes now: proof that gaming is still very much a no-woman's-land.

That's a good thing, since Twila wants to keep her pregnancy a secret from her coworkers. She hasn't told me why, but I'm guessing it has something to do with job security. Despite the way all the joysticks paused while her gamer cohorts admired her as she tottered down the hall on the way here, I've no doubt that every hipster geek at UniVamp covets her job—and the corner office that comes with it.

"First I was told no more margaritas," Twila gasps as she rises from her knees. "Well, I guess coffee is one more thing to add to the list. Shit!"

"Just part of your new life, at least from now until you're through with nursing. It will be hard, I know. But the baby will appreciate it, even if you don't." I hand her back her purse, a Bottega Veneta that sports a two-thousand-dollar price tag.

She heads for the sink to rinse her mouth. When she resurfaces, she scrutinizes her flawless complexion in the mirror. "I'm already getting pimples. Not to mention a muffin top." She pinches imaginary flesh from her still-tiny waist. If she's bulging anywhere, I don't see it. To my eyes, she looks reed-thin all over. Her slim designer jeans, a leopard-print pattern by Dolce&Gabbana that costs over a thousand bucks, fit her like a second skin.

"How pathetic is this? And my tops are already getting tight, too. I guess that's a good thing when you're as flat-chested as I am."

She strikes me as the type whose body will snap back in no time. Both Grace and Lana claim that it took them a full year after having their babies to get back to fighting weight. Then again, neither of them have this woman's wardrobe.

If they did, maybe they would have been motivated to try harder.

Twila was one of the guests at the launch party Grace and Lana threw for me. Apparently she heard about it through a friend of a friend of a friend. Afterward, when she e-mailed me to request an appointment, I remembered her immediately because she was one of the few women present who worked a nine-to-five gig, as opposed to those who didn't work at all. I'm fascinated with what she does for a living: she is a digital animator. To date, her most celebrated project is a virtual universe for wannabe vampires called the Fangdom, which has hit the zeitgeist with over a million hard-core online gamers. Now it—and she, whose elegant mien and porcelain features are the model for its most popular avatar, albeit with the addition of fangs—has legions of fans all over the world clamoring for the latest, greatest version of the game.

Her child will be the luckiest kid on the playground, what with a mother who knows all those keyboard shortcuts gamers covet.

But that day is sometime far off in the future. Today is about her waves of nausea riding on a tsunami of doubt.

"This pregnancy wasn't supposed to happen. Not now, anyway," confides Twila. "Of course I've always wanted to be a mother, but I thought—well, you know, that when it did happen, I'd be ready for it; that everything would be 'perfect' in my life. I guess I was fooling myself. Life is never perfect, is it?" Twila's gloss wand is suspended over her top lip, which, I've just noticed, is trembling. You can also hear the quiver in her voice.

"I've yet to meet a woman who claimed that the timing was perfect." I hope my laugh eases the tension etched on her face. "Seriously, no need to worry. I do hear that once the hormones start surging, you realize that perfection is no longer important; that the only thing that matters is the baby. And you'll instinctively love this time, no matter how sick or misshapen or uncomfortable or ugly or tired you'll feel these next few months."

She smiles back at me, but her eyes still hold out for the catch. "How about you? Did you have a good pregnancy, or a bad one?"

Ah, the moment of truth.

I pause and take a deep breath before answering. "I haven't had a child yet."

"Oh." As I'd anticipated, she is surprised to hear this. "It's just that . . . well, at the party you seemed in your element among all that baby gear and all those mommies with their adorable little toddlers."

I shake my head. I wish desperately for some excuse to change the topic as soon as possible. Have I talked myself out of a client because I haven't been there, done that? Although she gets paid well for it, she hasn't really killed any vampires, so I hope she'll cut me some slack regarding the gaping hole in my life experience.

Her empathetic gaze tells me she already has.

For some reason I feel compelled to come clean. "Don't get me wrong! I still plan on having children . . . someday." My chuckles seem hollow, even to me. "Frankly, it's my husband. He's reluctant for me to get pregnant. I'd love it if he'd change his mind, but for the time being he won't. It's complicated."

She glances up at me curiously. "So, he doesn't want kids?" Her snicker is more an expression of disgust and resignation. "Join the club."

I almost tell her the truth—that he has a child but is reluctant to risk his heart on another—but I don't need to burden her with my issues, let alone Alex's. "You mean, your husband didn't take the news well?"

"I'm not married." With that declaration, her grimace drops into a full-blown frown. "And I haven't had the guts to tell him about this latest development. I'm breaking the news to him to-night. I don't think he'll take it very well. You see, he's married."

"Oh. Wow. I'm . . . sorry." Truly, I don't know what to say. That would explain her reluctance to tell her coworkers about the pregnancy. I wonder which one in the clutter of man-boys who work here might be her baby's daddy? By the look of lust in their eyes, it could have been any one of them we passed on our way to the ladies' room.

"Don't worry, my baby and I will be fine without Mr. Wrong. Ironically, when I found out I was pregnant, all I could think of was how badly I wanted this in my life—with or without him. But he claims that kids won't be part of his life, ever. They don't have kids, so I guess he means what he says." She shrugs. "He's not happy in his marriage, and yet he doesn't even have the excuse of children to stay in it. Just my luck to fall in love with an emotional coward. And since this pregnancy will ensure that he never leaves his wife, I guess his opinion doesn't matter anyway." She pats her abdomen.

Do I see a slight bulge, or am I imagining it? The mind has a way of playing tricks. This is one of the good ones, if you embrace it. I'm happy for her that she does just that, even if her lover doesn't.

Twila flips open my portfolio of services and pretends to be engrossed, but I know she's thinking about what and how she'll tell him when the time comes.

It won't be easy being a single mom. But she wants her baby, so I hope she sticks to her guns, no matter what his opinion ends up being on the matter.

9:12 a.m.

MY NEXT stop is Carolyn, my bedridden client. Her housekeeper—Marta, a stern Jamaican woman with copper-hued skin and a no-nonsense demeanor—warns me, "The missus is moving slow today."

This is her way of warning me to make the visit quick and painless.

My nod convinces her that I understand. The lines around her eyes soften with that assurance, but I can hear the weight of her concern with each lumbering step she takes as she escorts me to Carolyn's bedroom.

Carolyn seems to be sleeping when I enter, but no: her eyes are open, albeit as tiny slits. Still, through them she views a life growing fuller every day, along with her belly.

When she realizes it is me, she wills herself to rise into a sitting position and motions to the plate of cut fruit on the small table beside her bed. None of it has been touched.

I realize she's offering to share it in order to fool Marta into thinking otherwise, but I won't be her coconspirator. Despite a grumbling stomach, I shake my head. "Thanks, but I had a big breakfast this morning."

She smiles wryly. "Ha! So you're onto me."

I nod. "You're eating for two now. Remember?"

She shrugs. "I still don't believe it."

I ignore that. If she fails to carry this child to term, then I fail, too.

To change the topic along with the mood in the room, I pull the paint color cards I've brought her from my satchel. Carolyn's eyes open wide. She takes her time looking each one over before choosing a soft sage green for her nursery. "Can we give it an undertone of blue, so that it looks more like this?" From her nightstand she picks up strands of a thick grass that has been tied into a bundle with thread, and hands it to me. "I've been staring at it for so long outside my window that I sometimes actually think I'm out there, too. I want the baby to feel that way in the nursery; to have nature all around."

"You're right! That's a gorgeous color." I recognize the species, because it grows in my own yard: *Festuca glouca,* or Boulder Blue. "What do you think of either a soft yellow or a bright cranberry as the accent color?"

"*Oooh,* I like the idea of cranberry! Something different." She leans back onto her pillow. Despite her small frame—or maybe because of it—she looks as if she's holding a balloon under her T-shirt. She is breathing heavier, as if it is weighing her down. Of course it is. She is tiny and frail to begin with.

And much too pale.

"I can have the painters in here by the beginning of next week, if you like." I reach out and pat her hand. "I'd also like to go through the baby-proofing checklist with Marta. I'd like to discuss green-proofing with you as well, and go over some organic recipes that are great for prenatal nutrition."

"I'd like that," she says. "But aren't we jumping the gun? With talk about baby-proofing, I mean . . ." Her voice trails off weakly. Is it because she's tired, or because she's afraid of tempting fate yet again?

"No, not at all. Your little one will be out in no time," I say brightly. "Trust me on this."

She smiles her relief. I've given her hope, which certainly is much more valuable than suggestions for nursery colors or children's clothing.

If anything I say or do can help her through this pregnancy, I'll be worth every dollar she spends on me.

Already what I've learned from her is priceless: that the undying urge to be a mother is worth any heartache that comes with it.

I RUN the rest of my client errands until the early evening. It's six o'clock when I get to Seth's apartment. By then he has already relieved the pediatric nurse. When he opens the door, Sadie is sleeping comfortably in the crook of his arm. His wide, warm smile does a lot to lighten the long entry hall, which seems to be in a perpetual state of darkness.

As he holds out his hand to welcome me, he shifts his daughter from his right arm to his left. She stirs a bit: just enough to yawn and gurgle. There is no trace of last week's fever, thank goodness.

He must see the relief on my face, because his chuckle isn't completely guilt-free. "The nurse says that her fever broke sometime before noon last Friday. I've asked her to stay on through the end of this week."

"That's great." I follow him into the living room and strip off my coat. It's not unusual for the ocean fog to creep in this far beyond Presidio Park. I was shivering all day, so I appreciate the fact that Seth has a fire burning. The glow gives the room some much-needed cheer.

"Hey, are you hungry? To put your mind at ease that I'm not a complete and total screwup, I took the liberty of making us a bite to eat. Just a few appetizers, to get us through the next hour." He points to a large platter on the dining table. On it is a spiraling row of finger foods: goat cheese crostini, some mini-turnovers, mushroom caps topped with spinach, and coconut beer-battered shrimp with a dipping sauce.

"Wow, I'm impressed! Did you really make all of this today, and just for me?"

"Hard to believe, isn't it?" Gently he cradles Sadie's head as he lays her down inside her infant rocker. In no time at all she is purring in her sleep. "My mother died of cancer when I was fourteen. Our father wasn't much of a cook and I was the oldest, so I got the job of house chef." He plucks a little of this and that for a plate soon filled with goodies, and hands it to me. "I guess we were lucky. It kept us off a diet of Froot Loops and Swanson's Hungry-Man TV dinners."

"Well, it's obvious that Sadie won't starve to death."

As I dig in, I see his smile flicker into a grimace. "Seriously, did you presume that I'm totally helpless?"

"Of course not. It's just that—well, I can just imagine how hard it is to balance a full-time job with caring for an infant." I swallow quickly. Stuck in my throat isn't goat cheese but embarrassment. "I guess now that S&M is funding SkorTek, they'll be putting heat on you to work less from home, and more in the office."

Seth frowns. "You're telling me. The word has already come down from the top."

Meaning Alex.

"Look, Seth, I hope you don't mind, but I went ahead and called a few of the top-tier nanny services on your behalf. Unfortunately we're behind the eight ball: most people give themselves a few months to interview candidates, in order to line up the one they feel the most comfortable with. Still, I'm guessing we'll find someone who fits your needs: dependable, knowledgeable, and self-reliant. If you want, I'll start interviewing tomorrow."

His smile is jubilant. "Seriously, you wouldn't mind? That would be such a relief."

"No problem. All part of the service." I put my plate down and wipe my hand on a napkin. While everything else on it looks tempting, I know it's time to get down to business. "I've also got some forms we need to go over. It will help me assess all the things you'll need for Sadie in the coming months. For example, I'd like to go over the baby gear you've already acquired, as well as her wardrobe: coats, dresses, play clothes, sleepwear, shoes, that sort of thing. And toiletries. I'm sure you've got most of the bases covered, but there may be some gaps that need to be filled before she quickly grows into a toddler. By the way, what kind of diapers does she use?"

He guffaws as he shakes his head. "Disposables. Are there any other?"

I nod. "Cloth is greener. If you go that route, you may want to look into a diaper service. Or you can go with biodisposables. I've designed a simple necessities list that we can go over first. Then we'll discuss items to put on Sadie's activity planner."

One of Seth's eyebrows goes up in disbelief. "She sleeps all day, except when she wants a bottle! She barely rolls over. What kind of activities are you expecting her to do, skateboarding or bungee jumping?"

I laugh. "I know you find this hard to believe, but before you know it she'll be sitting up and crawling. Even at her age, there are all sorts of mommy-infant playgroups . . . I mean, *parent*-infant groups—"

"I know what you meant to say. You're warning me that I'll be in the minority when I sign up for these things." He shrugs as he runs his hand through his hair. Is there some gray there? I'm sure Sadie's fever scare took its toll on him. And it was just the first of many emergencies he'll have.

"Believe it or not, there are quite a few dad-and-kid groups out there, too. I'll make sure you tap into a couple of them. It's the best way to create a support group for the long-term. By that I mean other parents who can reciprocate with babysitting, or sharing sitters' names, or lending opinions on things like toddler-friendly restaurants, or preschools—"

"Why do I need them when I have you?"

At first I think he's kidding, but no: his eyes are wide with panic.

For the first time I realize my role in his life: *I am his lifeline.*

Without me, he's afraid he'll drown in a sea of personal doubt and parental ignorance.

And then who will take care of baby Sadie?

I have to make him realize that he is not alone, that everything will be okay.

To that end, the first thing I do is smile. And breathe. "Seth, just about everyone you meet is as new to parenting as you are.

They're going to want to network with you, too. You'll see. You'll end up with some wonderful friendships that may last a lifetime."

He nods slowly but I can see he's not totally convinced.

His life is becoming more complicated by the minute.

Sadie is now fussing in her rocker. At first Seth stands there just staring at her. Then, as if in a trance, he moves toward the kitchen.

As he rummages through a cabinet for a container of formula, a sudden urge to pick her up overwhelms me. I can't help but give in to it. She is light as a feather and responds immediately to my touch: first stretching, her little fingers wiggling like ribbons in the wind; then snuggling deep into the crux of my arm. Her mouth stays pursed until her tiny eyes open. When she sees me, a tiny crescent of a smile lights up her lips.

It's a glimmer of light in an otherwise dark situation.

Until this moment I haven't even realized Seth is back beside me. I can feel the heat of my embarrassment even before I have the nerve to glance up at him. "I'm sorry. I had no right to pick up Sadie without your permission—"

I am stopped midapology by the look of tenderness in his eyes. It overwhelms me.

He is looking at Sadie.

No, he is looking at me.

When he grazes my forehead with his lips, I know I need not apologize for falling in love with his daughter.

Embarrassed at his own impulsiveness, Seth takes a step back. "I'm sorry. I know that was inappropriate of me. Look, it's getting late. I guess we should start to work on that first list."

Reluctantly I hand Sadie back to him. She is greedy for the bottle he places on her lips.

I am equally hungry for her.

* * *

IT'S EIGHT o'clock by the time I get home. Apparently Alex hasn't been here that long. I can tell because he's yet to turn on the heat, and he still has his coat on.

I can also tell he's been drinking by the way his forelock drops over one eye. He is too lazy—no, make that too drunk—to brush it away.

And he's crying.

He tries to cover it up by turning slightly away from me. Or maybe that's not what he's hiding after all. He has something in his hand that he's afraid I'll see. What is it?

A picture?

He cradles it in the palm of one hand. The other one grasps a tumbler. I assume it holds Johnnie Walker Blue, his drink of choice.

Now that I've seen this much, he is likely resigned to the fact that I'll expect some sort of explanation. And yet he doesn't say a word. When I see who's in the picture, I know why:

It's his only photo of Peter.

When Willemina left, she took the photo albums with her. He had kept that one in his office. Back then Alex wasn't of the mind-set that his computers, either at home or at work, were for leisure activities such as storing digital images. Even with the convenience of his trusty iPhone, to this day, I'm the designated photographer.

In the snapshot, he is tossing his son, then four, up in the air. Both wear unabashed smiles. Peter's trust in his father's ability to return him safely to earth is so complete that his eyes are closed, as if fatigued with bliss.

Only when Alex finally turns to me can I take full measure of the chasm of his sorrow in the depth of his eyes. "I've forgotten the color of his eyes," he says as he hands me the photo. His sobs weigh him down. It's as though he'll never rise above his regrets.

"They are blue, just like yours," I say as I gently tuck the curly lock of golden hair off his forehead. "At least, I've always imagined that they are."

"If you say so." He takes my face in both hands and looks me in the eyes, as if he's afraid he might forget them, too. "Ah, Katie, I've fucked up so badly! You have every right to hate me. I'm a jerk, a selfish, stupid—"

"Don't, Alex . . . don't beat yourself up. What happened was not your fault. You did everything you could." I stroke his arm gently.

He's about to say something, then stops himself. Did he want to express his regret? I guess I'll never know. Instead, he shakes his head, then takes my hand and kisses its palm. "Aw, baby, you don't know the half of it. Just tell me you forgive me. That you love me, and always will . . ."

Alex's hands fall to my waist and he pulls me closer. His lips find mine, but his kisses are tentative, as if exploring new territory. We both are: I've never met this contrite Alex.

Soon his mouth is relentless, moving from face to neck to breast to groin. His hands, however, aren't so gentle as they shove me down onto the couch and tear at my blouse. One button flicks off, and then another. Instinctively I reach down to the floor for them.

"Where the hell do you think you're going?" He means it as a joke, but actions speak louder than words. He flips me over and pulls up my dress around my waist. My face is flattened up against the seat of the couch: a Roche Bobois with thick, unforgiving cushions. All I can think of is that its white leather will now always be marred with the hue of my foundation and the memory of this sexual encounter.

He breathes heavy in my ear as he enters me. Even drunk, he is rock-hard. The first plunge makes my heart leap into my throat and my groin tightens. Soon, though, the flap of flesh to flesh finds its rhythm. As the tempo slows, he grinds into me.

He needs me so badly.

That's okay because I need him, too, and just like this: raw, and wanting me as if he'd die without me.

I know I'd die without him.

As if sensing this, he murmurs into my ear, "Don't worry, baby, I'll never leave you, no matter what. We just have to ride this out—"

With a groan he signals he is done, but there is no joy in it.

Too bad, because it has meant the world to me.

He wants me to forgive him. He wants me to bear with him while he processes his loss.

Yes, I can do that.

The minute it is over, he is snoring on top of me. Gently I inch out from under him and make my way into the bedroom, where I crawl into bed, naked.

I leave his semen inside of me. That's stupid, I know. I'm on the pill, so it's not like I can get pregnant.

But just in case . . .

7:15 a.m., Tuesday, 27 March

IT'S DAWN. I feel his arms around me, keeping me warm, safe, and comforted.

Suddenly his snoring, which has been rocking the room like waves, has stopped. He tenses up. Fear loosens his scotch-thickened tongue. "Jesus, Katie! Did I forget to wear a rubber last night?"

I turn to look at him. "Damn it, Alex. I'm on the pill! You know that."

"Yeah, okay, I know! I just . . . *want to make sure.*"

I turn my back to him and scoot to the far side of the bed.

He knows better than to reach out for me, or to beg me to forgive him.

What's to forgive, anyway? His guilt?

And if so, over what? Maybe some irrational fear of abandonment?

I would never abandon him, and neither would our child.

If we get the chance to have one.

Right then and there, I make the decision to get off the pill, once and for all.

And now that I realize how much Alex forgets when he drinks, I'm also making sure we have lots of JW Blue in the liquor cabinet.

11

. . . .

Every baby needs a lap.
—Henry Robin

10:30 a.m., Monday, 2 April

S ETH'S DAYS AS a work-at-home dad are numbered.

I know this because Alex is less than subtle about it, even if Seth won't admit it to himself, let alone me.

"For God's sake, we're investing ten mil in that dude's company," grumbled Alex this morning. "He sure as hell better show up every day."

Seth insists he isn't sweating it, but I am. The rest of last week was spent doing my homework—surveying working moms on the local playgrounds, lurking on their online group loops—and it has paid off. The number one recommendation, bar none, is the Bebe Sitter & Au Pair Service.

When I get to Bebe's offices, I can see why. It is housed in a sweet little Noe Valley cottage that is painted pale blue trimmed with mauve fretwork, and surrounded by a white picket fence leaning slightly under a mantle of pale pink rosebuds.

The receptionist, a dowdy Mrs. Doubtfire type lacking only the Scottish brogue, sports a headset that allows her to hand out clipboards holding either employment applications for aspiring au pairs, or needs assessment sheets for anxious parents. She beckons me to make myself at home.

This is easy to do, since the large, high-ceilinged room could pass for the library in a private club. Two large wingback chairs flank a roaring fireplace that is fronted by kid-friendly safety glass. Above the wainscoted walls is a pale yellow wallpaper with a birds-of-paradise pattern. Queen Anne sofas are cornered into conversation pits. Off to one side of the reception area is a glassed-in playroom with enough toys to fill an FAO Schwarz showroom, allowing mommies to watch their precious tykes interact with prospective nannies through a two-way mirror. None of the nannies checking in for their assignments are carrying parrot-handled 'brellies or oversize carpetbags, and yet their calm and determined demeanors would do Mary Poppins proud.

"Mrs. Johnson, dearie, will you follow me back to mam'selle's office now?" Doubtfire's tone is gentle but firm.

Like a child caught staring out the window when she's supposed to be studying multiplication tables, I snap to posthaste, practically leaping out of my seat.

Doubtfire ambles slowly down a wide hallway, and I have to match her pace. This gives me plenty of time to peruse the candid snapshots, framed and under glass, which line the walls. All show well-coiffed, conservatively dressed Bebe sitters cuddling their beaming little charges in their laps. The pictures were probably taken by ecstatic mothers who have realized that returning to their careers was the right move after all, despite the fact that more than half of their after-tax earnings go to covering their nannies' fees.

That's okay. Any fears these mothers may have had that they'd left their children in the hands of Talbot-couture-wearing ax murderers with blue-rinse coifs who would sell their beloved tots' organs for bingo cards have been laid to rest. Proof positive are the glowing letters that accompany these pictures: "Little Eddie just adores his 'Auntie Carol'" and "Amy cries whenever Miss Lorelei goes home on weekends."

I now have no doubt that Sadie's guardian angel has walked down this hall as well.

Finally we reach the door at the end of the hall. Doubtfire knocks gently. We hear a lilting "*Entrez, s'il vous plaît*" and we follow suit.

I am greeted by sweetness and light in the form of Mademoiselle Simone Sartré. She is small, chic, and pseudo-French, down to the miniature poodles tucked under each arm of her little black dress. "Bonjour, Mrs. Johnson! So pleased to have you here! Sit! Sit, please!"

All three of us obey her. As the poodles have leaped out of their mistress's arms and onto the silk-embroidered tuffets in front of the room's fireplace, I take the chair in front of her French Provincial Louis XIV desk.

"So your mission, as you described from our phone conversation this morning, is to secure an au pair for your client." She reaches across to pat my hand. "You've certainly come to the right place! Everyone on Bebe's staff holds state-certified teaching credentials. Many are licensed nurses as well. We've worked with the children of celebrities, royals, and executives whose companies are atop the Fortune 500." Her slight nod leads my gaze to the wall behind her: In one of the photos there is a rock star renowned for the large entourage he travels with, and his even larger family, blended from two previous marriages. Those wives still live with him, too. The older woman in the middle—between the current wife (a former *Playboy* Playmate) and the three kids under the age of ten, with Mohawks and nose rings—must be the nanny. And I easily recognize our mayor. Oh, so his little ones have a Bebe sitter, too!

And isn't that Posh and Beckham with their arms around a polished and petite Bebe au pair? If so, does she get any of Posh's hand-me-downs?

Now I'm stoked. "The child in question is a five-month-old girl of a single parent: a father who works in the high-tech field. He is trying to stabilize his hours so that he's out of the house just hours a day. But because he is one of the founders of a new company, his days may run longer of course, particularly during this start-up phase. He's hoping that the nanny will be flexible, and will also cover one weekend day as well."

"I see." Mademoiselle Sartré wrinkles her brow. "That will mean overtime, of course."

"He understands." I shift uncomfortably in my chair. Despite the cash infusion from S&M, I really don't know how much has been allocated for the founders' salaries. For his own peace of mind, though, Seth insisted that the nanny's fee be on the high side of the going rate, which works out to about twenty-five dollars an hour.

"Can you really swing a thousand dollars a week?" I asked him.

"Best-case scenario is that you'll find someone who just wants thirty hours, so that it's more like seven-fifty. I'd prefer to work out of the house a couple of mornings a week anyway." He sighed. "I guess that means I'll be packing PB and J for my lunch until Sadie is in high school. Then again, with what I'm reading about private school tuition, I guess I'll be down to bread and water by the time she's five."

That remark gives me an even stronger incentive to ensure he gets his money's worth. "The ideal person will also have to do some light housework and laundry. She must have a car, in case of emergencies. And it would be preferable if she spoke a second language, perhaps French, Italian, or Japanese. Have you a few candidates who are available for interviews over the next couple of days?"

"No, I'm sorry, I don't." Her smile is pleasant, but dismissive nonetheless. "I hope you have a pleasant day."

"What . . . no . . . *wait!* What do you mean you have no one? I saw a league of au pairs in the reception area not ten minutes ago—"

"Oh yes! We employ over two hundred of them. They all have wonderful qualities. Unfortunately, not one on our roster fits your specifications. I'm so sorry."

Something must have caught her eye beyond the palladium window, because she turns toward it. Who can blame her? It's a perfect spring day, and the roses on the trellis right outside are the size of grapefruits.

Besides, watching the bees dancing delicately on their petals is certainly preferable to watching me stutter and collapse onto her antique Persian carpet in a convulsive state.

If Seth is to keep S&M happy, I've got to get him a nanny. *Today.*

Even the poodles turn their backs on me. I take that as a good thing, as I'm sure they have the ability to smell fear, and may attack.

"Please, Mademoiselle Sartré, that was merely a wish list! My client certainly has room for flexibility."

"Ah." Once more she graces me with her attentions. "Well, that's different. *Hmmm,* let me think . . . Maybe there is a candidate who fits some of your requirements." She floats down onto the delicate chair behind her desk and flips through a drawer filled with possible candidates. "The language skills may be hard to match, of course—"

"Then don't bother. Not an issue, believe me."

"Housework may also be a bone of contention with some of our staff."

I want to object, but think better of it. "Okay, well, we can work around that."

"She drives, but you'll be providing the car, I presume?"

Ouch! Okay, maybe Thor can scrounge up something on his lot that's cheap and reliable. He owes me big-time, anyway, for his brilliant web designer, Jason. "I think that can be arranged."

"Voilà. Fanny Price it is."

"*Fanny?* Wow. That's a name you don't hear too often."

"Yes, well, she's as unique as her name. An original if there ever was! A diamond in the rough!"

"I get the picture." But really I don't.

I guess I will soon.

"Fanny can start tomorrow. Just sign here." She hands me a contract that already has been made out.

I peruse it quickly and gulp when I see Fanny Price's weekly fee—and the clause that states we have to give her four weeks' notice *and* four weeks' severance should we want to terminate her employment.

All of that, sight unseen.

I've got the pen poised to sign, but that gives me reason to pause. "Let me understand something: she is capable of taking care of a baby, am I right?"

She shrugs. "Madame Johnson, let me assure you, we haven't yet made a bad match."

"You mean you haven't once lost a client?"

Her laughter has the lilt of Christmas sleigh bells. No angels have been granted wings, but another au pair is employed, and another baby will be placed in competent hands. "Ah, you have the wit of the arcane!"

There is a first time for everything.

Still, the odds are a lot better than the roulette wheels in Vegas, and Seth needed someone yesterday, so I sign.

Seeing me do so, one of the dogs gives a low whine.

Now he tells me.

12

....

A child needs a role model, not a supermodel.
—Astrid Alauda

T WILA INSISTED THAT we meet at the crack of dawn in front of the Starbucks closest to her office, so I can't understand why she's kept me waiting for half an hour. Because Uni-Vamp's corporate campus has its own Starbucks, I presume she wants our meeting to be away from prying eyes.

If she doesn't show in the next five minutes, however, I'm going to have to leave if I'm to make the first-day meet-and-greet between Seth and Sadie's new nanny, Fanny Price.

Just as I'm gathering up my things to go, I hear the faint buzz of my iPhone. It shows me that VampGrrrl, aka Twila, is calling. But what I hear barely sounds human: a litany of gut-wrenching sobs, a garbled moan, then silence.

"Twila? Dear, are you there?"

For the longest time there is no sound at all, but the connection is still strong.

By that, I mean my connection to her.

Finally there is a gasp, then: "He . . . hates me. He wants me to abort."

I hold my breath. "Well, what are you going to do?"

"I've already done it."

"Oh." My heart drops into my gut. I'm mad: at her idiot lover, and at her for not being strong enough to choose what she really wants and needs in her life.

Someone who could have loved her and her child.

"Did—did it happen today? Is that where you are now?"

"What? No!" Despite her being confused at my question, a degree of clarity and calmness returns to her voice. "We fought about it a week ago. In fact, it was on the day I first met you. What you said gave me the courage to put my foot down—"

"Wait . . . what? You say you blew him off? I thought you said that—well, that you went through with it."

"I did go through with it. *I dumped him.* Just like you suggested."

The silence we share is permeated with relief—at least, I think it is, until she adds, "I haven't stopped crying since. I haven't even gone to work, I'm so depressed. I just sit in my apartment and . . . *cry.*" With that, she's at it again. Her sobs crescendo into gasps of despair. "Can you come over here?"

"Of course I can." I look down at the time stamp on my iPhone. Even if I left now to go back into the city, I'd be half an hour late for Seth's meet-and-greet.

But there is nothing I can do about it except text Seth to start without me.

That's okay. I'm sure Fanny will have things well in hand, whereas Twila clearly needs me now: not as her baby planner, but as her friend.

7:43 a.m.

IT'S ONLY been a week since I saw her last, and already she looks different to me. Her legs are still stork-thin, but her breasts seem fuller. Then again, maybe it's just the oversize Raiders jersey covering them and her belly, which she wears over a pair of flannel men's boxers.

Her thin, white-blond hair is shoveled up to the top of her

head and held in place by two tortoiseshell chopsticks. Without makeup, her lashes have all but disappeared. Even against the tear-parched circles under her eyes, she looks like a lost little girl.

But she lives like a teenage boy: not at all as I'd expect, in some posh, cloud-grazing penthouse with a view of the bay and possibly a bridge or two, but a studio walk-up in the heart of the Mission District.

"Nice place," I say. But really it isn't. Her bed is an open futon. Against one wall is a patchwork of metal shelves that hold a library of computer games from seemingly every era, going back to Donkey Kong. Dishes litter the sink and counter. From what I can see, her diet isn't necessarily a healthy one because there are too many empty pizza boxes and Chinese food containers in the kitchen trash bin. I can't really walk around because the floor is a sea of junk. Some of what I wade through is clothes, but I also trip over a bike with a flat tire, boxes filled with books and photos, a couple of pieces of luggage.

Does she really have room for a baby in her life?

As if reading my mind, she laughs. "You're being too kind. But I figure I've got nine months to clean up my act . . . okay, make that seven. That's why I've hired you, all right?"

"Yes, of course. By the time your baby comes, we'll be ready." I plop down on the bed beside her. "I guess my biggest question to you is, where will the baby go?"

"I can clear out my closet."

Taking note of my incredulous look, she rolls off the bed and stumbles over to the mirrored wall on the other side of the room.

Turns out it is really two doors, both of which fold in the middle. Behind them is a compartmentalized closet tricked out with all kinds of hooks, bins, rods, shelves, drawers, and cubbies. Crammed throughout is her wardrobe. Designer shoes, lined up straight like soldiers, fill the bottom and most of the glass cubbies. Necklaces, belts, and scarves hang on hooks.

"Oh my God! That's got to be the most beautiful closet I've ever seen! And so—*neat*!"

"I know. Shocking, isn't it?" The thought of it actually puts a smile on her face. "Clothes are my passion. I'll hate to part with any of my couture finds, but I've got a new priority in my life now."

I nod. "Just wondering: have you ever thought of moving to a larger place? Even a one-bedroom would do until the baby is a toddler."

She shakes her head adamantly. "This place will do just fine. Maybe forever. I don't owe a dime on it. Look, my mother raised me in a tiny apartment. If it was good enough for her, it'll be fine for me and my baby."

"But—" I look around. It is such tight quarters that, all of a sudden, it feels like a jail to me.

I wonder if that's the point: maybe Twila is trying to punish herself.

For what? Falling in love with the wrong guy?

"Listen, Twila, you make a good living, so why not bite the bullet and look for a two-bedroom place now, when the market is low and there are some good deals to be had? Parents need their own space, too. And eventually you'll want privacy. I know you've just gone through a breakup, but there will come a day when you'll start dating again—"

"Are you kidding me?" Her mouth tightens into a grimace. "Ha! I doubt that's going to happen! Not with a kid on my hip."

"Twila, lots of single parents date and find relationships that work. Come on, you're young. And just look at you! You're gorgeous. And smart, creative, and successful. I'll bet men come on to you all the time—"

"No, not men. Just *boys*. Peter Pans who never want to grow

up—like my Mr. Wrong. I look great, and I'm a great playmate—both in bed and out." She shakes her head. "But I do
know how to pick 'em. Immature assholes. Well, now I have to
grow up. For both of us."

She grabs one of the boxes on the floor and flips it over,
emptying its contents, a mishmash of electronic games from
UniVamp. Frantically she grabs some sweaters out of one of the
built-in cubbies and tosses it into the box. I watch her until
she's crammed it full with the contents of three drawers.

I can't stand it anymore. I walk over and put my arms
around her to stop her, letting her collapse against me.

Her sobs roll over both of us. We stay that way for what
seems like forever. When, finally, she's done, we are both spent.
I can barely make out her mumble. "Okay, you're right. I'll call
my Realtor today and get the ball rolling. Aw, damn it! Why
can't he be the kind of man I need in my life?"

That's the question I'd want to ask my Mr. Right—my
Alex—if I could.

8:55 a.m.

I AM forty minutes late getting to Seth's place. He must have
heard me clomping up the stairwell because he throws open the
door even before I have time to knock. I hear Sadie gurgling in
the background, and the soft crooning of a lullaby.

I take that as a good sign.

But no. Not if the frown on Seth's face is any indication.

"Well, well, well! Glad to see you could make it!" His tone
isn't exactly sarcastic, but there is certainly an edge to it. "Fanny
is already here. I have to say, Katie, that I was somewhat disappointed to learn that you two hadn't met *in person* prior to your
signing the contract with the agency—"

"Yes, I'm so sorry about that, Seth! But I can explain. You see, Fanny came highly recommended by the owner of the au pair service, Mademoiselle Sartré. She guarantees that Fanny will meet all our expectations—"

A brow raises when he hears that. It lifts his frown into a knowing smirk. "Oh, I'd say Fanny goes above and beyond any expectation I had. I'm wondering if you will think so, too."

He ushers me in.

Fanny's back is to me, but I can see that she's a big, broad-shouldered woman. Her hair is cut in a long bob, right at her neckline. She is wearing a navy dress with a white collar. When she turns around, I see that the collar is long enough to be tied into a bow, making her outfit a cute sailor ensemble, what with its double row of big white buttons and drop waist. I also notice that she's cradling Sadie, who is cooing and listening, fascinated, at Fanny's song.

I am, too, now that I can make out the lyrics.

And the *voice*.

Fanny Price is singing "My Man" as if her heart is breaking. And as she belts out the chorus, there is no mistaking the fact that she is a dead ringer for Barbra Streisand.

Or at least Barbra as Fanny Brice in *Funny Girl*.

Not just the voice and the haircut and the retro twenties garb and all the theatrical gestures (at least, with the arm that isn't holding Sadie), but also the nose.

If this Fanny were to go ahead with a sex change operation, the illusion would be complete.

Okay, and better lighting, too.

That last note is a high one, and held long enough to have impressed even the original.

My jaw must have fallen open because Seth has to nudge me back to life. I turn to find him staring at me. I can read his mind:

Should we applaud?

If we don't, Fanny may hold that pose forever.

Or at least until Sadie poops.

As if reading my mind, Seth claps tentatively, and I join in.

"Thank you, my darlings! Thank you! A girl can always use an extra hand, if you catch my drift." Fanny gives us a broad wink. "Oops! Our wee one feels a bit wet! Time for a diaper change!"

With that, she exits stage right, into the nursery, Sadie still in hand.

I wait until she's gone, then murmur, "So Fanny is—a manny?"

Seth nods slowly. "You get an A plus. Go to the head of the class. And a tranny manny at that."

My face is flaming, I just know it.

Obviously not as much as Seth's au pair.

"Look, Seth, if you want me to figure out some excuse for dismissing Fanny, I'll certainly pay her contracted severance out of my own pocket." I bury my head into my hands. "I guess I rushed things because I knew you were under the gun to find someone quick. In hindsight I should have never agreed to her—I mean *him* . . . no, I guess I mean her—aw, hell, *whatever,* sight unseen—"

"Whoa, whoa, slow down, Katie! If you think I'm put off by Fanny's—by Fanny's, um, unique qualities, I'm not. I've always been of the philosophy that you've got to live and let live." He smiles down at me. "Although I have to say that when I opened the door and saw her standing there . . . By the way, Fanny made it quite clear that she is under no uncertain terms a she, and I'm certainly not going to argue with her because she's twice my size and could easily take me two out of three falls. Anyway, what I'm trying to say is that I don't mind that she's not a woman per se. I'm a guy, so obviously I don't see that as a detriment to raising an infant. Besides, Fanny's got so much female energy that I don't feel Sadie will be missing that in her life. At least, not anytime soon."

"You don't? Well . . . good to hear that." I don't want to tell him this, but that severance would have wiped out my operating capital.

He laughs when he sees my relieved smile. "Just so you know, I've already gone over Sadie's routine with Fanny. Also, I told her that you will be her go-to person if she can't reach me on my cell. By the way, she's more than willing to do laundry and the grocery shopping. When she offered to help me clean up around here, she cinched the deal. In fact, she doesn't mind working late a couple of nights a week, or even staying over when I travel—as long as it isn't on either Mondays or Fridays. Those are the nights she's onstage at Divas. Hey, and guess what? Turns out she speaks French fluently."

"You don't say." My smile may be curdling on my lips, but Seth doesn't seem to notice. He's just relieved to have Sadie in capable, not to mention large, hands. "If Fanny hangs in there, I guess that will be a bonus, won't it?"

"Hell, forget the French. Just think how many show tunes Sadie will know before she starts preschool. Hey, do you think you can research some good dance schools? I'm guessing that Fanny can handle the voice lessons . . ."

13

· · · · · · · · · · · ·

Making a decision to have a child—it's momentous.
It is to decide forever to have your heart
go walking around outside your body.
—*Elizabeth Stone*

8:12 p.m., Tuesday, 3 April

ALEX AND I are eating at home, by candlelight: poached salmon over braised greens; morel mushrooms atop garlic mashed potatoes; and for dessert, a warm walnut cake topped with Andante Minuet. I made all the dishes fresh, just this afternoon.

I'm dressed in a Diane von Furstenberg silk wrap dress. It is Alex's favorite, not just because of the color (an aquamarine and green tiger print: it matches my eyes) but because he can open it easily with a quick twist of the wrist. Underneath, I'm wearing a black metallic lace Victoria's Secret Miraculous Push-up Bra with a matching thong.

Hopefully, not for long.

Unfortunately he's had a hard day. He and his partners have discovered that the founder of one of S&M's start-up investments has been cooking his books to cover up payments for some mail-order bride from Bangkok. In geekcentric industries, this is an occupational hazard.

I nod sympathetically while listening to his indignant rants, knowing that within the hour he will be both sated with all this rich food and sotted with his favorite scotch. Already he is slurring his words. When he stops in the middle of cursing his partners for their negligence to stare longingly into the abyss of the deep V of my décolletage, I realize my little plan is working.

Once again he is falling in love with me, or at least in lust.

I've been holding off on having sex with him all week—since our last encounter, in fact. When it comes to getting pregnant, timing is everything. According to my ovulation chart, today is the fourteenth day of my twenty-eight-day cycle, when conception is most likely.

Yes, I'm being coy right now, but no doubt about it: tonight Alex is going to get lucky.

In fact, he'll think he initiated it. That way he won't get too suspicious about my game plan: what I call Operation Oops.

Granted, I've only been off the pill for eight days, but if all goes according to plan, I'm guessing I'll be breaking the news of our little oops to him within the month.

I know he won't take it well at first. But once the realization that he'll be a father again hits home, I'm sure he'll come to accept the idea, perhaps even embrace this turn of fate.

I'll make sure he understands that this isn't a do-over, that no other child will ever take the place of Peter. If anything, our child—the one we're making together: tonight, tomorrow, whenever—will grow up revering his older half brother.

There will be one more person in this world to love him, without question and wholeheartedly.

I'm somewhat relieved, however, that I don't have to say that to Alex tonight. He'd be too sullen to hear it. Between all the issues at work and his recent melancholy, he welcomes the drink I put in his hand the minute he walks in the door.

And yes, I keep the liquid aphrodisiac flowing through dinner. Like last time, maybe he'll forget that psychological security blanket so near and dear to him: a condom.

When I'm not pretending to hang on his every word of corporate derring-do or grazing against him while serving second helpings, flirtatious remarks roll trippingly off my tongue.

This makes him smirk and volley with bawdy innuendo. His eyes are heavy with lust. By the time the last cake crumb on his plate has vanished, he makes his move. He stands up and yawns, but by the bulge in his pants I know he's not all that tired. I shiver as he draws me up for a caress. Then his hand snakes through the slit in my dress and finds my panties. Slowly, with a hooked index finger, he pulls them halfway down my thighs and waits.

It's my move.

I take his hand and inch it up between my legs. That's all he needs to know that it's okay to probe me, first with only his thumb, but soon it's joined by his index finger. Together, quickly but gently, they move in and out of me until I am damp with longing. As I bend slightly to push my panties down to my ankles and kick them off, his fingers wander across my outer thighs until they are cupping the cheeks of my ass.

The heat from his hands makes my heart race. "So smooth," he murmurs, "like a baby's."

My chuckle is low and soft. "I wish."

Suddenly I feel him tense up.

Was it the word *baby* that did it?

Damn it.

To keep his mind where it belongs—on me—I grind my hips into his cock. It has no remorse and has stiffened in anticipation.

Good.

Slowly I back into him until I feel him, hardened, between my legs. Grabbing the table, I bend forward just a bit so that he more easily hits the sweet spot he seeks. His hands steady themselves on my hips. The head of his member, now thick, seeks the damp darkness that is my very core . . .

But no, he doesn't plunge. Instead, he encircles my waist with his arms. With a sigh, he rests his head on my back.

I know why, of course.

Oh, hell.

"You want a rubber." I say this in a self-defeating whisper, just audible enough for him to hear me.

He doesn't speak, but when he nods, his five o'clock shadow tickles the small of my back.

At first I don't move. After a while, though, I sigh, resigned to his phobia: my pregnancy.

There will be no memory lapse like last time.

"Do you mind?" He points toward the bedroom. "I'm too drunk to get it."

Talk about adding insult to injury.

"Sure, yeah."

I know he's watching me as I walk away.

I don't rush to Alex's nightstand, where he keeps his damn rubbers. Why should I? Whichever condom I choose from Alex's stash—be it Trojan or Durex, ribbed or silky smooth, flavored or lubed—it is the sentry that stands between me and my true desire.

Without looking, I reach into the drawer and pull one out. It is black, studded, and promises to be extrastrong despite being supersheer.

Once it's on Alex, I have a 98.12 percent chance of staying childless.

I will never feel that surge of hormones and love and destiny growing inside me.

I will never hold my own child in my arms.

I will never be a mother.

And I will never forgive Alex for making this decision for me.

The bile rises in my throat.

I am about to walk back into the living room when it hits me:

If I prick it, I still have a chance of getting pregnant.

I'm so scared that I'm heaving as I hurry over to my vanity table with it. Can he hear me? There, in a round glass container, are my safety pins. I pause as it clicks open, hoping he hasn't heard a sound.

If he found out, he'd never trust me again.

Okay okay okay, let me think this through rationally. First of all, we've already agreed on the fact that we're getting pregnant this year. It's just a matter of *when*. So, this really isn't an issue of trust! It's about *timing*—

Tick. Tock. Tick. Tock.

My hands are shaking as I flick one of the pins open. *It's now or never . . .*

The first prick goes through the wrapper, right where I presume the head of the condom has been pressed flat. Unfortunately I stab too fast and too deep, and spear my finger at the same time—

"*Ouch!* Crap—"

"Hey, you okay in there?" Alex sounds impatient.

I want to curse both my pain and my stupidity. Instead, I say in what I hope sounds like a sultry come-on: "Just putting on a little perfume. It makes me shiver."

He grunts back with obvious satisfaction.

More carefully, now, I stick several tiny little holes through the wrapper, but this time I keep my fingers out of the line of fire.

When I'm done, I walk casually out of the bedroom. For his benefit, when I get to the doorway, I pause. With a shrug, I'm out of my dress. It flutters to the floor. By the time I've reached the couch, I've unsnapped my bra and casually let that drop, too, leaving me naked except for my heels.

Seriously, my act is worthy of an Academy Award.

Alex's eyes roam from my pout to my breasts to my groin, but never to my hands. He looks flushed, ashamed, and lustful all at once.

When I reach him, I push him gently onto the couch with one hand, while undoing his belt buckle with the other. He is so relieved I'm not angry at him that he lets me take control.

Perfect.

I straddle him backward. Holding the rubber wrapper so he can see it, I open it and lift it out of the casing, then roll it gently onto him, stroking him all the while. He settles back into the cushions. I can just imagine his giddy grin.

When I mount him, my gyrations take on a determined rhythm. He joins me, and I lift up from him just slightly so that he can see himself thrusting inside of me. This makes him move even faster, and now I'm following his lead. In a few minutes he releases a deep, satisfied moan, and I imagine that the hot, white surge shooting up within me is more than an orgasm.

This will be our "oops."

Or, at least I pray it will be.

And I feel no guilt. Not one little bit.

14

. . . .

People often ask me, "What's the difference between couplehood and babyhood?" In a word? Moisture.
—Paul Reiser

I KNOW WHAT YOU'RE thinking: that I'm quite a piece of work, some underhanded bitch who will do anything to get my way—

Please believe me: I'm not. If what I do seems selfish or callous, take my word for it that I'm doing this for Alex's sake as well as for my own.

Despite our differences about this issue, I love my husband. Truly I do. I mean it when I say I owe him everything.

You see, he saved my life.

I mean that figuratively, if not literally.

So you see, the child we will have together will be payback: a new way to jump-start his life.

Or, if I'm to be honest, to save the life we've built together.

I MET Alex purely by accident, twice.

The first time was on the Friday before Labor Day, eight years ago. He had wandered into SafeCalifornia's offices. "I need help, like, now," he demanded.

It was lunchtime, and I was holding down the fort in an office that was working with a skeleton crew that day. With this being the cusp of a three-day holiday weekend, most of my coworkers had taken a vacation day in order to stretch it into an end-of-summer miniholiday.

Even agitated, Alex was mesmerizing. The way he towered over my cubicle, I guessed him to be at least six-two. His eyes were deep-set and blue. Back then he wore his blond hair cropped short. His suit fit him perfectly, and it was obvious that the material was expensive.

I worked with guys who wore pen protectors in the pockets of the short-sleeve shirts they purchased from Sears. This man had a handkerchief folded squarely in his suit jacket pocket.

Because my mouth was filled with a bite from my shrimp burrito, I don't know if he could make out my words as I mumbled "What can I do for you," but he got the hint that he was welcome to sit down when I motioned to the chair beside my desk.

Unfortunately, it was stacked with a mountain of manila file folders. I scurried to move them and in the process succeeded in shoveling half of them onto the floor, and smearing the other half with salsa. "I'm sorry! Um . . . wait while I . . . So, now, how can I help you?"

He shrugged off the offer and took a step closer.

I didn't mind at all.

"It's my wife," he said, his voice gruff with anger. "I think she boarded a plane this morning for Amsterdam and took my two-year-old son with her. It's her way of getting back at me. I need help getting her detained when the plane lands, or I may never see my son again."

I hope I had the decency not to stare at him with my mouth open. Truth was, I could think of nothing to say. This wasn't the usual kind of complaints we got at SafeCalifornia. Defective products were the norm, and in our office, this kind of agitation was usually caused by an injury to a loved one.

"I'm sorry, Mr. . . ."

"Johnson. My name is Alex Johnson. Her name is Willemina. Her last name is Johnson, too, but she never got her passport changed. It's still in her maiden name, which is Sieffert. S-I-E-F-F-E-R-T. But our son's passport is Johnson as well, because he was born here—"

"Oh! So, what you want to do is to report an international parental child abduction."

"Yes! Haven't you heard anything I've said?"

It was then that I realized that this tall, handsome, highly agitated man had wandered into the wrong department. He thought he'd entered the Bureau of Consular Affairs, a federal agency that shared our floor. Apparently he had taken a wrong turn in the maze of offices between the two very different agencies.

I dropped the remains of my burrito onto its foil wrapper and tossed it into my trash can. "I certainly sympathize with your dilemma. But I won't be able to help. Let me direct you to—"

"Oh, let me guess: you want me to fill out some missing person's report with the cops, then wait for thirty-six hours to see if she shows up." He leaned in angrily. "Don't you get it? By then she'll be well beyond airport security. I'll never find her then—"

"Yes, yes, I hear you! But I'm serious. You're in the wrong department—"

"Aw, hell, you bureaucrats are all alike! Always pointing fingers, and sending us—*the people who pay your salaries, by the way*—on wild-goose chases." He ran his fingers through his thick hair as if he was going to tear it out. "Look, just let me speak to a supervisor!"

No wonder his wife ran away, I thought. He doesn't listen to anyone.

The only thing that stopped me from calling security and

having them explain the situation to him was knowing that under the same circumstances, I'd be panicking, too. I stood up and simply said, "Follow me."

I ran him back through the labyrinthine hallway until we were in the right department. "I think this is what you're looking for," I said, pointing to the sign on the wall that read BUREAU OF CONSULAR AFFAIRS. "I work in SafeCalifornia, the state's consumer affairs advocacy department."

He stared at the sign, then back at me, all the while biting his lip in frustration. "Look, I'm sorry. I didn't mean to be such a jerk."

"Under the circumstances, you're forgiven."

He shrugged. "Well, then, I guess the least I owe you is this much." He took the handkerchief from the front breast pocket of his suit jacket and dabbed it against my chin.

I pulled back, startled.

He held it up for me to see. There was a streak of salsa on it. "I presume you'd have wanted to know."

"Yes, thank you." I'm sure my face was as red as the small bit of chopped tomato he'd just wiped from my chin. I thought I saw the hint of a smile on his lips, but it was there for just a moment. Then the department's receptionist came back from the break room, and Alex had the most valid excuse in the world to forget about me.

But I couldn't forget him so easily.

Later that day I stopped by the receptionist's desk and wheedled out of her the outcome of his meeting with her superiors. What they'd told him must have sent him off on another frustrated tirade. If in fact his wife had gone overseas, the process of recovering his child would be arduous at best: he'd have to fill out a request with the United States embassy in Holland before they could send a staffer to conduct a welfare visit with his soon-to-be ex; then he'd have to sleuth around as to her whereabouts, through credit card, phone, and bank statements, and fill out even more paperwork requesting the return of his son.

And finally, he'd have to pray that she'd adhere to any terms that had been mediated.

In the coming months, at various times, I wondered what if any progress Alex had made. But of course he'd been successful in stopping her, I told myself. He'd been so determined, so desperate.

Although I presumed I'd never see him again, my heart went out to him.

SIX MONTHS later, on the evening of my birthday, I found myself on the Golden Gate Bridge, staring down into the choppy waves below me.

It hadn't been a good week. The guy I was dating at the time had conveniently dumped me just three days before. That week was also my parents' anniversary, and they had booked a cruise to Mexico, so were nowhere around to tell me what a jerk the guy had been. As for the twins, they were still in graduate school halfway across the country and studying for exams.

"What do you mean you won't be in town on my birthday?" I had groused to Mom. "No one loves me."

"You're being silly, Katie love. If we hadn't loved you, why would we have plucked you out of the cabbage patch, instead of some other little girl?"

That had always been my parents' joke with me. By the time the twins came into our lives, I was too old for the stork, let alone another cabbage patch fib. That's okay. When the twins were three, I had them convinced that Mom and Dad had found them in a nearby garbage can.

Now their own experiences with childbirth had them joking with me that Dumpster diving would have been a lot less painful.

Noting my silence, Mom pleaded, "Katie, honey, please don't be mad at us! Besides, we'll be home in ten days. By then the twins will be done with their final exams. Tell you what: we'll fly everyone home that weekend, so that we can celebrate your birthday in style. What do you say to dinner at Bouchon? You love their bourbon and maple-glazed duck—"

I mumbled something to the effect of "Yeah, okay, whatever" and hung up.

And cried myself to sleep.

The morning of my birthday, Helen's gift to me was my first solo presentation at a SafeCalifornia hearing—and I failed miserably. I'd left home without a key piece of evidence: the video testimony from an irrefutable source that a plastic container manufacturer had just released a product with a higher toxicity level than was legal and had tried to cover it up.

The commission chair had his C-SPAN-ready sound bite ready. "Miss Harlow, you've wasted our time and, worse yet, the California taxpayers' dollars."

The voice mail Helen left me only said, "Don't bother coming into the office when you get back into town."

What did that mean? Was I to take the rest of the day off? Or was I fired?

And if so, what did it matter? No one loves me anyway, I thought.

The height of my personal pity party was watching the tears that rolled off my face disappear in the cold mist that roiled between the bridge and the bay below it.

"Hey, you're not going to jump, are you?"

I guess I was leaning so far over the railing that the jogger coming up behind me was worried—enough to slow down and circle back around, positioning himself close enough to grab me if I did something rash.

I sighed loudly, then turned to face him. "If I want to, what is it to you?"

There was something familiar about him, but I couldn't place it at first.

Then it hit me: *This is the guy with the runaway wife.*

At that exact same moment I knew he recognized me, too, because the look on his face went from wariness to surprise, and then softened into concern . . .

Someone does care about me.

"It's you," we both said at the same time.

We stood there for a while, embarrassed at the circumstances in which we were meeting again. I didn't want it to be that way, so I asked, "Did you ever find your wife?"

As if reminding him of the circumstances in which we'd first met would make things any better.

"It's a long story," he said as he took a tissue from his running pants and dabbed my cheeks.

"Seems like you're always having to clean me up," I murmured.

We both laughed.

"You know, the story of what's happened since I last saw you sounds a hell of a lot better over a drink," he said. "Can I buy you one?"

That night, over a bottle of wine, we swapped tales of woe. No, he never saw his son again. And yes, his divorce would be final in a couple of months.

Two months later to the day, we exchanged house keys.

And on the Friday before the next Labor Day, we moved in together, and were married the next day. That long weekend was the start of our commitment to each other.

I've always wondered if, after Alex got to know me better, he thought I'd have really jumped.

If you want to know the truth, I don't know the answer to that myself.

All I know is that now I can't imagine living without him.

He's my rock, the center of my universe.

So yes, I guess I owe him a chance to be a dad all over again.

15
....

Babies don't need fathers, but mothers do.
Someone who is taking care of a baby
needs to be taken care of.
—Amy Heckerling

JOANNA, MY ATTORNEY client, sends me an e-mail, apologizing for having to cancel on me this evening:

> Flying to Chicago. I'm as big as a house, so I hope they show some pity and upgrade me to first class. At this point I give you proxy to get started on the room, however you see fit. All the bells and whistles! Emma should be home studying after 4pm, so feel free to go over any time after that.

I'm glad I can still drop off all the baby gear I've purchased on her behalf. Every time Alex glances into the guest bedroom where it's been stashed, he winces.

Now that I'm off the pill, I need him amorous, not grumpy.

10:31 a.m.

MY PHONE interview with a new web designer, Abby, starts off on the right note: one in which a toddler is crying in the background.

"Yeah, hello—Jeremy! *Jeremy, honey, hush!* Mommy's on the phone . . . No, you *cannot* have the M&M's now! You know the rules! Candy is for dessert! . . . Hi, hello?"

"Um . . . hi. My name is Katie Johnson. I noticed on SocialMoms.com that you're a work-at-home mom who designs websites. I have to say that I'm very impressed with your online portfolio—"

"*Jeremy!* I said *no!*"

The next sound I hear is her receiver clattering to the floor. I whip the phone away from my ear, but even from two feet away I can hear her arguing with a little boy trying to satisfy a fierce sweet tooth. I wait patiently for their negotiations to end. A minute later they do, with a sobbing boy telling his mother that he will hate her forever for being the meanest mommy in the whole world.

"Hi, Katie? You still there?" Her tone is light and breezy, as if she has no doubt that I have nowhere else to go.

She's right. At this very moment, I need her more than even Jeremy does.

"Yes, well, as I was saying, I'm very impressed with your portfolio, and your fee schedule seems quite reasonable. Just to let you know, I've just saved my domain name, and I'd like you to help me build my site. I'm a baby planner, so I'll need something that reflects that."

"Gotcha! Soft, nurturing, friendly, but competent, confident, and professional, right? What categories are you considering?"

"Let's see: 'Service.' Oh yeah, and one for my bio. And 'Resources' and 'Tip of the Day.' Also 'Baby's Room,' 'Hot Products,' 'Great Gear,' 'Safe Toys' . . . and of course I'd like one leading to my blog. I'll send all of this to you in an e-mail, along with the copy that goes under each category."

"Super! I'll start work on it today. What was that domain name again?"

"It's MakingMommiesSmile.com. No hyphens—"

"I'm on it! . . . Oh . . . my . . . *gawd.*"

"What? What is it?" I'm wondering if Jeremy is back in the room, causing more chaos for his mom.

"Nothing . . . well, okay, you might as well be aware of something: there's a site with a very similar name—have you ever heard of MakingMamaSmile.com?—anyhow, I'm on it now, and I have to say that it has got to be the raunchiest one I've ever seen!"

"Yes, I'm quite aware of the site." That's all I'm saying. Why elaborate?

"Too bad. Wow, I can't believe it! Do you know how many category tabs it has that are named the same as the ones you gave me—"

I sigh. Okay, time for the truth. "Look, that was a test site started by my last web designer. He misunderstood a lot of things about what I'm trying to do here, not the least of which was the URL I wanted to reserve. Now that you know, I'll e-mail you the admin password so that you can point it toward the site you're building for me and clean up that mess."

"Great idea," she says, but I can tell she's somewhat distracted. I'm guessing that the pounding I hear in the background has something to do with it.

This is validated when she adds, "I'm on it, but excuse me for rushing off now. *Jeremy! Jeremy!* No, you are *not* supposed to stack the chairs that way! . . . I don't care that you want the candy on the top shelf! Jeremy . . ."

1:20 p.m.

I GET a text from Seth:

Sadie is six months old today. She sleeps through the
night. She doesn't have colic. She's already laughing at my

jokes. I'm guessing she's the most perfect baby in the world.

I text back: I could have told you that! ☺

Seth: It means a lot to me that you appreciate my little gal—AND my cooking. BTW: it's taco night. And I make my own guacamole. Six candles on a Ding-Dong, and the party is complete.

Don't think I'm not tempted. Why is that?

Because Seth enjoys my company. And Sadie makes my heart pound with joy.

But they aren't my family. Alex is. Maybe one day we'll have a little Sadie of our own—

But not if we aren't home together.

Me: Sorry can't. We have a dinner engagement.

Seth: ☹ We'll save you a Ding-Dong for the next time you drop by. Soon, right?

4:30 p.m.

NO MATTER how hard I knock on Joanna's front door or shout "*Hello . . .* " her daughter, Emma, doesn't seem to hear me.

But through the door's oval window, I can see she's in there.

With her shirt unbuttoned to her waist. Some boy is dry-humping her while he's sucking her neck as if he's one of the undead in *True Blood*.

That makes me pound all the harder.

They must hear me now, because they freeze in unison. The next moment they are scrambling up off the floor. Emma yanks her shirt back up and over her breast, while her boyfriend zips up his pants over his all-too-obvious hard-on. His high-pitched yelp tells me that he didn't tuck in all the way and the zipper has nipped skin.

Serves him right.

As he scrambles out the back door, Emma slowly inches toward the front entryway. There is fear in her eyes, but only for a moment, when she realizes I've seen everything. Then her pupils glaze over with sullenness. She unlocks the door and yanks it open, then stands there with her arms folded at her waist. She doesn't bother to lift a finger as I struggle with the boxes and bags that need to go to the nursery.

"Emma, you know I saw you with—with that boy, don't you?"

"Who cares? Mother is out of town. Besides, it's your word against mine."

"Do you really think that your mother wouldn't believe me?"

Aye, there's the rub. Emma's face goes pale before growing mottled by despair. "What are you going to do, call her?"

I pause as I think through how I'm going to answer her. But before I do, I see her eyes shift from me to out the door. What, is the boy back?

No, but Paul is home. Unlike mine, Emma's ears are attuned to the nuances of the traffic flowing outside her door. I only hear the slam of his car door and his cheery whistle as he charges up the steps.

"Well, well, what have we here? The baby planner bearing gifts? Our little guy is going to be one happy camper." He gives his stepdaughter a quick kiss on her forehead.

She flinches, but he pretends not to notice.

"How do you know it's a boy, Paul?" Her question to him sounds innocent enough. Her role in the family is that of the oblivious kid. It's a part she can play in her sleep, and it certainly comes in handy when she wants to dodge an issue.

Like, say, what I just witnessed.

His smile is uncertain. "Your mom had the sonogram. Remember?" He glances over at me for validation.

Emma turns toward me. She wants to see if I'll lie for her mother.

And if so, why shouldn't I cover for her, too?

My knees buckle. Not because of all the packages in my hand. The weight of this family's pain is too much for me to handle.

"Jeez, sorry, Katie. Let me help you with that." Paul grabs a couple of the bags from my hands and starts down the hall to the nursery. Before I follow him down the hall, I hiss to Emma, "I'm not telling your mother, because *you are.*"

The phony smile on her face droops down at the corners as she considers my threat.

"And if you want to tell him your mother is lying, go ahead, because the truth, Emma, is this: your mother loves him. And he loves her. And no matter what sex the baby is, they will both love her, too."

Before she can retort with something silly, I add, "Emma, she will never love either of them any more than she loves you. You already know that. So for both your sakes, *try to be there for her.*"

Her head snaps back as if she's been slapped. Tears rim her eyes but don't yet fall. My words hold them back; even if Emma doesn't believe me now, I know she wants to, ever so badly.

My smile is quivering as I enter the nursery, but Paul doesn't notice. He's too busy setting up the swing that will rock the son he thinks will be joining them soon, very soon.

16

....

Women are aristocrats, and it is always the mother
who makes us feel that we belong to the better sort.
—*John Lancaster Spalding*

IN MY E-MAIL inbox this morning are:

3 queries from potential clients

43 porn site solicitations *(Thanks for nothing, Jason!)*

From Alex: Client dinner. Sorry, will be home after 10ish xx

From Lana: I want to give you a heads-up: Max claims
he "lost" his slug in your purse. You may want to dump
everything out before you stick your hand back in there.
I'm just sayin'. xoxo

And, finally, Seth has sent me a photo of Sadie. She is sitting up, her back straight, her head held high. Her eyes, the
color of sky, are opened wide, as are her arms, which reach out
to me, her tiny fingers beckoning.

The caption underneath it says, "Thanks for keeping my
nutty daddy sane."

I delete the porn, push the client queries into my to-be-read
pile for later, and move Lana's note into a file marked FAMILY.

That's where Sadie's picture goes, too.

I'VE SPENT the afternoon out on an elegant veranda of an estate in Belvedere, sipping organic lemonade sweetened with too much Stevia, while refereeing a battle of wills between two women who for the last three months have shared a fetus but obviously little else.

Elizabeth Auchincloss is one of the Bay Area's better known socialites. She and her husband, Trey, paid Ophelia McConnaughey to be artificially inseminated with Trey's sperm, and to carry the child in her womb to term.

I am being paid by Trey to keep the two of them busy—separately if not together—so that they don't kill each other.

He first called me late last night, asking if we could meet immediately.

"My wife and I have been through hell. Six years ago we found out that Elizabeth couldn't conceive. Since then she's seen an army of fertility specialists. We've tried everything: hormone injections, three different surgeries, alternative medicine . . . even prayer." Over the phone, his voice, husky with pain, had made me wince. "After three years, we finally gave up. But Elizabeth has always felt that a house isn't a home until there are children in it, so we decided to try surrogacy. We thought we had found the perfect person, too. But then—in the middle of the delivery, no less—she changed her mind! We had done everything legally. I would have gladly sued the woman, but Elizabeth didn't feel right threatening to drag her through court. It broke my heart to hear her crying. For a full two weeks she was a wreck. Ms. Johnson—Katie—I can't have her go through that again. To tell you the truth, I can't go through that either. All that yada yada you do: great, whatever. Just keep those two from hating each other, please!"

Now that I'm sitting between them, I don't know if that's possible.

Ophelia and Elizabeth are exact opposites in looks, demeanor, and the manner in which they show their resentment. For example, Ophelia—a twenty-four-year-old with a PhD of questionable worth in Scandinavian languages and literature from Berkeley, and some pretty exorbitant grad-school loans to pay off—wears her surliness on her sleeve, perhaps between the rip in her soiled SAVE THE POLAR BEAR T-shirt and her tattooed forearm.

On the other hand, Elizabeth, an ice blonde whose life is a Ralph Lauren ad, has a thin physique and an even thinner smile.

The one thing they share is a suspicion toward me.

Elizabeth's rejection is polite but firm nonetheless. "Ms. Johnson, I'm sorry we wasted your time. But the truth of the matter is we don't need a referee."

Trey winces—not because his gift is being pooh-poohed so blithely, but because his wife has seen through his strategy of suggesting they retain my services.

From the look on his face, I'm guessing that this is one argument Elizabeth won't win. He can't endure the thought of watching these two women snarl at each other for another six months, so he's sticking to his guns. "Elizabeth, most new moms would jump at the chance to have a baby planner at their beck and call," he says in a voice that might work on a six-year-old child, but not a thirty-nine-year-old woman. "Katie Johnson comes highly recommended. You should think of her as your personal concierge."

In the hope of adding some levity to the situation, I add, "Better yet, I'm your *mom*cierge. I'll be guiding you through all the things you'll need to provide your baby with a safe, nurturing environment, both pre- and postnatal. For example, we'll assess your—"

Ophelia laughs uncontrollably. "You've got to be *kidding* me!"

She is larger with child than she should be at this point in her pregnancy: the result of a diet that consists mainly of (according to Trey) ice cream, fruit pies, garlic mashed potatoes, and Double-Double In-N-Out burgers. Her cocoa-colored hair springs in frizzy coils from a head that seems constantly in motion: if it's not tilted in derision, like now, it's shaking in disgust—more at Elizabeth and Trey than at me. "Jeez, what will you two think of next? I guess Oscar Wilde was right when he said, 'Anyone who lives within their means suffers from a lack of imagination.'"

At her nemesis's cutting remark, Elizabeth's razor-sharp grimace disappears completely. In its coverage of the myriad charity tennis events, the *San Francisco Chronicle*'s society column never fails to mention Elizabeth's pro-worthy backhand. I'd hate to find out the hard way what it feels like, but judging by the way in which she raises her hand, I think Ophelia just might. If she does, the lemonade will go flying, because Ophelia looks like she's got a mean right hook.

It doesn't make me happy that I just so happen to be sitting between them. Today of all days I chose to wear a new dress, and a silk one at that.

Lucky for all of us, Elizabeth's chilly facade drops back into place before I need to duck and cover.

"Listen, Ophelia, no one twisted your arm to be our surrogate. You said you wanted to have the experience of pregnancy without the—how did you put it? Oh yeah: 'the emotional baggage of a long-term commitment to another being.' Well, we're giving you that, not to mention we took you out of that rat-infested hovel you were living in. Now you've got around-the-clock nurses, a great little house with a fabulous view"—a slim, toned arm sweeps out toward the cabana with its to-die-for views of San Francisco Bay—"and fifty thousand dollars for your time and effort. So why don't you just suck it up for the next couple of months? Afterward, you'll never have to see us again."

Ophelia's complexion, already showing the vestiges of hormones gone wild, flames bright red with scorn. "You're just jealous because I've got the one thing you want and couldn't get, no matter how much money you threw at it. You know, if you put a little more meat on your bones, some of those fertility shots might have actually taken—"

"Whoa whoa *whoa*! No need to be cruel, Ophelia!" Trey practically leaps between the two women, as if that will shield his wife's heart from a truth that hurts so much more than the childbirth she will never experience. His eyes go from the solitary tear rolling down the high plane of his wife's cheek to me. I know what he's thinking:

Please, help us, before they destroy the joy we were meant to share during this time.

As he leads Elizabeth away, I place my hand over Ophelia's. "Do you really hate her so much?"

I know the answer to my question. I just want to hear it from her.

She glances away quickly, but the tears fall anyway. "No, of course not. It's just that . . . well, you see for yourself: she's such a selfish little bitch! Just look around at this place! She has—*everything*."

"No, you're wrong. You know better. You just said it yourself. She doesn't have the one thing you have, and can give her: their child."

Ophelia considers this for a while, then shrugs with a smile. "Yeah, that's great. And the minute I give her what she wants, I'll get kicked out of the Magic Kingdom. They don't see me as a person. To them, I'm just a brood mare. You know, I was a size eight. Now look at me! I eat like a horse. I don't know if it's the hormones, or the anxiety—"

"Maybe it's your resentment." I look her in the eye. "Yeah, I get it: Elizabeth is a cold fish, and Trey is pussy-whipped. But

Ophelia, *none of that matters.* What does matter is that they're honoring their commitment to you. They're doing all they can to make you comfortable throughout your pregnancy. They're giving you enough money to pay off your debt. And most important, *you're* giving *them* a wonderful gift. You've got to find some satisfaction in that, am I right?"

She nods grudgingly, but then says, "Yeah. I'm providing them with the ultimate accessory: a kid—who will end up spoiled, just like her."

Ophelia crams her Double-Double into her mouth.

So much for compassion.

It suddenly dawns on me that Ophelia doesn't need my pity. She needs my respect.

And I need hers, too.

That's why I snatch the burger out of her hand and toss it on the lawn.

When she gets up to protest, I push her back down. "After you deliver the baby, you're welcome to as much cholesterol as your body can handle. In the meantime, do the poor kid a favor and lay off the garbage food."

I wipe the mustard off my hand with her napkin. "And by the way, I've already given your nurses a recommended diet plan for you. And the personal trainer starts tomorrow: three times a week. Trey's agreed to pay for her, up until three months after your delivery. You'll be back in a size eight in no time. Maybe even a size six."

I almost make it to the door when I feel the burger smack me on the back, right between my shoulder blades.

I don't turn around. I just keep walking with my head held high.

I'll have to add dry cleaning to the Auchinclosses' bill.

17

. . . .

Women who miscalculate are called mothers.
—Abigail Van Buren

MY CELL PHONE buzzes with a text message.

At this time in the morning, I can only guess from whom: Merrie.

I fumble to click onto it before it wakes Alex. The message reads:

> CongressmansWife@ . . . : What's my stance on surrogates? Don't want to get in trouble with the Right-to-Lifers, so keep it simple.

Hmmm. Interesting question.

> Katie@MakingMommiesSmile: How about saying that every child is a gift from heaven, no matter which stork delivers it?

> CongressmansWife@ . . . : You're wasted out there. Move to DC!

I laugh out loud.

Then I get serious. If she's really intent on having this baby here at home, we need to do some nursery planning:

> Katie@MakingMommiesSmile: When will you be back in the Bay Area? I've already got deliveries coming in for your nursery, fyi.

CongressmansWife@ . . . : Edie is at the Stockton house now. She can let you in. In fact, I'm sending her to that little meet-and-greet you posted. Do you mind if she passes out Michael's campaign literature?

How do I put it to her delicately? Um, no.

Katie@MakingMommiesSmile: Gee, Merrie, I don't know if that's the right forum for political discussion. Besides, without you there to answer any questions they may have—like, say, about that little banking bill scandal, or that out-of-context piece in the LA Times, it may not have the effect you'd like.

CongressmansWife@ . . . : Great point. Damn that man! I wish they'd invent some kind of Kaopectate for diarrhea of the mouth. Oh, and BTW, I'm definitely dropping this kid in our district's local hospital, as opposed to DC. A room filled with local nurses is a great photo op because they've got a strong union . . . Aw, hell, that reminds me: Michael made a campaign promise to the Natural Childbirth Advocacy League that I'd do this thing without drugs this time. I guess I'll have to tape my mouth shut when the nurses are in the room. Don't want to come off like some sort of potty-mouth banshee dragon lady.

That's good to know.

In fact, I think I'll recommend that she hire a nurse to accommodate her 24/7.

Or at least, whenever I'm within hearing range.

1:01 p.m.

My webmistress's son, Jeremy, is taking his after-lunch nap: the perfect time to call her in order to have an uninterrupted conversation about the design of my new website.

Yes, I love it. The flash graphics that welcome viewers show sweet little babies floating through the air. A stork swoops across the screen, bearing a banner:

Making Mommies Smile:
For All Your Baby Planning Needs

Each of the alternating pink and blue tabs is correct. In fact, Abby is so meticulous that she's already laid in the necessary category copy and photos under each one.

"I took the liberty of rating some wonderful products I've used for Jeremy, and I programmed it so that all items can be rated by others, too."

"I'll test it right now . . . Oh my goodness! Abby, thanks for doing this! I can start adding blog posts, right? I really want to get on that."

"Sure, it's all set up for you. In fact, I've tied your blog to a Facebook fan page for Making Mommies Smile. That way you'll build visibility to your site quickly, and you'll be able to post upcoming events, that sort of thing. Oh, and Katie"—she hesitates—"if you'd like, I could monitor it for you. When you're the mommy of a toddler, sometimes it's nice to touch base with real people, even if it's only online."

"That would be a big help. Why don't you take a couple of days and think about what would be a fair price and let me consider what I can do as well. And Abby, I'm also happy to throw in some swag."

"Swag? You mean gifts?"

"Sure. I'll be reviewing products, and since I'm not pregnant and don't have children—at least, not yet—I can't use them. I certainly wouldn't mind sending them to you." I laugh. "I wanted some sort of forum or community in which we can gather opinions from mothers such as yourself, so you're one step ahead of me. I don't have to tell you that moms are a wealth of knowledge. As of this minute, you are a charter VIP Mommy Tester for Making Mommies Smile."

"Freebees? Heck yeah I'm in!"

"Okay, good. Let's make this work." I'm elated. Granted, Grace and Lana can also test-drive some products, but it's still nice to have another pair of hands on deck.

"Your ID is your e-mail, and your password is—*Jeremy!* Honey, what are you doing out of bed so soon? No, you *cannot* watch *SpongeBob SquarePants*. Now get back into bed! Jeremy, I'm warning you! . . . Look, Katie, I've got to run! I'll e-mail everything else you need to know."

She hangs up, but not before I hear Jeremy wail that she is the meanest mommy ever!

Terms of endearment. Truly they are.

I can't wait to have my own little Jeremy.

I wonder if my pregnancy will slow me down. Right now, with all that has to be done for my current clients—Twila, Seth, Ophelia, Joanna, Merrie, and Carolyn—I'm on the run constantly. Will I be able to handle them, as well as take on more?

Whatever happens, things will work themselves out. Too many clients and getting pregnant are both good problems.

When the time comes, I'm hoping that Alex feels the same way.

I see if I can in fact log onto my own website, despite the fact that Abby was interrupted before giving me my password. I go for simple-stupid first and try PASSWORD. Nope, not that. How about ABC123 . . . No, not that, either.

I think back on my conversation with Abby, and her final words before being dragged away by her son's antics. I try JER-EMY, all caps of course.

Bingo. I'm in.

I think I'll leave it JEREMY.

MY FINGERS hover over my laptop's keyboard, poised to tap out the debut manifesto that will make mothers-to-be find me endearing, compelling, and, most important, necessary.

So why don't I type something? *Anything?*

Because I'm afraid I'll say all the wrong things.

I'm afraid that I'll come off as too cold, or as a know-it-all; that I may bore readers to the point that they won't even consider being clients.

That I'll be too flippant, or maybe too smug.

Worst of all, I'll sound like I'm pleading for a chance to work for them.

So instead, the cursor on my laptop screen blinks on and off, like a heartbeat: *my* heartbeat.

And then it hits me: Write it as if you're talking to Grace. And Carolyn. And Joanna, and Twila and Merrie . . .

Tell them everything you wish you could say out loud, but you feel is either too silly or too sentimental to say to anyone's face.

Just speak from your heart.

Okay here goes:

Dear Mother-to-Be,

You are so lucky! From this day forward you'll have the best reason in the world to smile, the best reason in your life to share your love.

I want to be with you, every step of the way.

Here's how I'll do that:

First, every week, I'll write to you, here. Hopefully I'll be able to give you some bit of advice that you find helpful in your amazing journey to delivery. I'll do my best to give you insights on some products and services you'll find useful, and I'll also pass along research that can help you make informed decisions as to the health and well-being of your newborn.

Best yet, I'll share with you my own thoughts about this wonderful journey you've entered—

And hopefully, you'll share that experience with me, too.

I'm here for you.

In fact, if you're in the San Francisco Bay Area, I'd like you to join me next Monday—along with some of my clients, and a few moms I love and respect—for a meet-and-greet, at Sprout boutique. We'll be talking about the joys and fears of motherhood, and testing a new product, too.

Bring your questions. I've got answers for you.

—Katie

If I have to write something, it might as well be what I really want to say.

God, I hope I'm not making an ass of myself!

3:05 p.m.

I HAD asked the painter working for my bedridden client, Carolyn, to call when he finished painting her nursery, so that I may take a peek. He claimed it would take two days, max. Well, it's been more than a week and no call.

When I ring him to ask what's up, he lets loose with a hysterical guffaw. "Your client is driving me crazy! I've painted that damn room three times already! She keeps claiming it's the wrong shade of blue. Or green. Or whatever it is. Frankly, lady, I've given up on guessing the color she wants."

I sigh. "I'll be right over."

I get there in time to see the painter strapping his ladder onto his truck. "Whoa, whoa, not so fast! Where are you going?" I ask him. "I just got here."

"Well, hon, I've been here for a week. I've pushed back two other jobs to accommodate your client. She doesn't know what the hell she wants, so I'm moving on."

"Look, listen—she's just a bit stressed out about her baby. You know, she's been told to take it easy for a reason. Please, cut her some slack."

He shrugs. "Lady, that's what I've been trying to do. It's not like I don't know the territory. My wife was a bitch, too, when she was pregnant."

My wince only makes him smile.

"Okay, tell you what: you talk her into living with the color on the wall. Or call me when she's ready to make up her mind." He hands me an envelope. "My bill for my time up until today. I'll expect the check within thirty days."

As his truck rumbles out of Carolyn's driveway, Marta opens the front door for me. I can tell by the way she shakes her head that she heard every word. "He's right. She's having such a hard time with it."

"I don't understand. I thought getting the room in order—"

"The problem isn't the room. It's *her*." She points toward the hallway. She's anxious to see if I can help her employer see beyond her fear.

Carolyn is standing by the window. In the past couple of weeks, she's grown bulkier in girth, but her arms and legs are still slender, and her face is devoid of color.

Her guilty look tells me that she watched the interplay between the painter and me. "I guess I'm being hardheaded about this."

I shrug. "You have every right to be. You're paying for that privilege. It's okay to be conflicted about this. About anything. Tell you what: why don't we take a look at it, with a clean eye?" I put my arm around her waist and walk her down the hall.

As always, the door to the nursery is closed. Does she think she can lock out her fears? Well, she can't. She needs to confront them directly.

I'm here to help her.

The room faces west. Right now it's painted in exactly the blue-green color we'd originally discussed. The room's large bay window is bathed in sunlight, casting shadows—distortions of the window's many panes—on the carpet and two of the walls.

The crib is covered with plastic and set in the center of the room. Color chips, in subtle gradations—lighter and darker, softer and richer hues of what is now painted on the wall—are lined up on the plastic sheet.

Carolyn frowns. "You see it, right? There's just something not right with it."

"I think I know what it is. Wait here for a second."

I go out the door, back down the hallway, and out through the back door. I find what I'm looking for in her yard: a clump of the fescue that was the original inspiration for the room's color.

I yank off a handful of strands and run back inside.

Carolyn is staring at the chips, comparing them. I place the clippings beside them, and together we sort through them until we find the one that is the closest.

"That's it," I say. "That's the color."

"You're right," she says, but doesn't sound convinced.

Then I take the chip and place it up against the wall.

It's a perfect match.

Tears rise in Carolyn's eyes. "Why did it take me so long to see it, when it's right here in front of me? I guess I just don't want to get it wrong this time!"

"Carolyn, there is no 'wrong.' You're doing everything you can to safely bring this baby into the world." I place the chip back in her hand. "And when all is said and done, your child will have this beautiful room, where it will sleep and grow and play. But there's so much to do between now and then. We can't stop now. You can't keep doubting that you'll one day be a mother."

I turn my head, so that she won't see my tears. "I can't doubt it either, for myself. So you see? We're in this together."

She looks down at the chip, then up at the wall again. The next thing I know she's putting it, and the rest of the paint samples, in the trash can. "I'll call the painter tomorrow and beg him to come back at his earliest convenience, to paint the trim with that beautiful cranberry accent color. Next I guess we need to do a walk-through to assess what I need to do about baby-proofing this big old house. Can you spare some time now?"

"Of course."

This time, it is she who takes my hand in hers. When we walk out of the room, she leaves the door open.

18

....

Women's Liberation is just a lot of foolishness.
It's the men who are discriminated against.
They can't bear children.
And no one's likely to do anything about that.
—*Golda Meir*

9:09 a.m., Friday, 13 April

NO TWO BABIES poop alike.

Texture, smell, weight—even in babies who are the same age, size, and gender—can be as different as . . . well, as black and dark orange, depending on which one ate pureed carrots for lunch.

That is the conclusion I've come to as I test Happy Hemp, a new organic cloth diaper, for durability, absorbency, and that ubiquitous wow factor that ignites the sort of viral word-of-mouth raves the press craves.

I know: it's a load of crap, both literally and figuratively.

Then again, so is everything about this assignment. I should have never taken it on, but by my very nature I'm a pleaser. I live for the pats on the head, the brownie points, the pathetic role of teacher's pet.

Or in this case, my client Merrie's pet. "Mike's got some constituent lobbying him to use an eco-friendly diaper. But I don't know," she groused this morning on one of her crack-of-dawn wake-up calls.

I stifled a yawn, then muttered, "It's a great idea. Go for it. The press will love it."

"Yeah, I get that. Green is good. But before I bite the bullet, I want to make sure that the kid won't be leaking all over me on the campaign trail. Trust me, it can be brutal out there."

"Don't be silly, Merrie. There are a lot of great eco-friendly diapers on the market—"

"It can't just be any diaper. This constituent—EnviroBest—makes Happy Hemp."

"Oh yeah! I've heard of Happy Hemp." Then again, who hasn't? Thanks to an aggressive promotional campaign waged on the mommy poop loop, word is already out that hemp fibers are softer, plusher, more absorbent, and less irritating than even the finest cotton on a baby's sensitive bottom.

No wonder why it's quickly taking market share from better known nappies.

And yet, no one has done any outside research that tests its claims for absorbency.

I guess that my test, for Merrie, will be the first. "Personally, I have no basis to recommend them, if that's what you're asking. But they must have deep pockets, because they spend a lot on ads."

"Their pockets are as deep as they come. EnviroBest is a new subsidiary of AmeriCorp."

"Oh my God! The tobacco company?"

"You got it. They've been diversifying. And hemp is a more versatile plant than tobacco, that's for sure. Falling profits is mother of invention." Merrie sighs. "This kind of research is right up your alley, so run it through its paces. Just the thought of the number of landfills you'll be saving should make your bleeding heart go pitter-patter, not to mention no more garbage islands floating in the Pacific! If the diaper is as great as they claim, sure, I'm all for it—and whatever quid pro quo they want to swing our way. But if it's crap—literally—there's no way I'm going to put my baby in it. How would I be able to hold him?

I'll ruin my new Donna Karan campaign suits." Merrie wears only homegrown couture.

So now I'm shoveling prototypical poop into a Happy Hemp diaper.

It is the way we eat now that throws my latest test into a quandary. For the best results, I must consider a twenty-month-old toddler as a quantitative mean. But besides sucking on bottles, Mommy's keys, and anything it finds on the floor, really, what do these babies put in their mouths? Is it organic veggies and mother's milk, or Froot Loops and Happy Meals, washed down with Kool-Aid?

For the sake of the kids and their teeth, I'd hope the former is the norm, but I know better, so I compromise and test two diapers.

What will pass for a healthy baby's stool is a little less than four mushy ounces of beans, sweet potato, apple sauce, and oatmeal that has been pureed in a Cuisinart.

But for the kid who salivates every time he hears the Pavlovian trigger "Welcome to McDonald's! How can I help you?" I fill a second Happy Hemp with a good half pound of simulated McSludge, made from mud that is solid as pitch.

I then clip these samples over to the clothesline in our backyard, where they will hang under the intense eye of a digital camera with a timer, which will record, down to the millisecond, any leakage or discoloration.

Let the waiting game begin.

11:13 a.m.

I'VE STOPPED in at Bubble, a children's boutique on Fillmore, in order to pick up some items ordered online for Carolyn, when I notice this sweet little romper for an infant girl.

The thought crosses my mind: *That would be so cute on Sadie.*

Yes, I buy it. It'll be my treat to her. I'll make that clear to Seth, since he hasn't asked me to purchase any clothes for her. This is just my way of being . . .

Of being what? It's not as if she's my niece, or that he's my friend.

He's not my friend. He's my client.

Despite the fact that he kissed me.

Seriously, what's a kiss between . . . working associates?

I can hear my old boss and friend Helen's raucous laugh in my head as I imagine her purring, "Trouble!"

1:15 p.m.

NO MATTER what I imagine Helen would think about my relationship with Seth—or, for that matter, my own doubts about what it is—I've decided to drop off my little present for Sadie while he's still at work. I know this because tonight is the monthly S&M cocktail party, which means he's sure to end up there and not here after he leaves his office.

The text he just sent me confirms this:

You'll be at S&M too, right? Hope so. I need an alibi to get home right after the event, or I screw up Fanny's night. She needs to hit the road by eight. Unfortunately, Alex and Henry are leaning on me to go out schmoozing with them. The Samurai is in town, and Alex insists that S&M is just THIS CLOSE to pulling off a distribution deal between him and SkorTek.

It's Friday the 13th. What are the odds it'll jinx the deal?

Ah yes, "the Samurai." That is the nickname S&M has given Yuju Takahashi, the renowned Japanese industrialist whose appetite for sure-bet start-ups is second only to that for the bawdy gentleman's clubs that clutter San Francisco's Broadway.

No wonder Alex asked me to make an appearance—but then to feel free to leave anytime.

He surely leads a hard life.

I don't mind, because the sooner the Samurai signs on, the sooner I get the official thumbs-up from Alex to get pregnant.

I'll act thrilled so that he doesn't suspect it was just a formality, anyway.

I certainly understand Seth's dilemma. It's Friday night, so Fanny will be pulling out as soon as she possibly can, in order to strut her stuff at the Diva Lounge. If I ask Seth to give me a ride home, Fanny should be stuffing herself into her Super Higher Power Spanx around the same time that the Samurai is cramming some poor pole dancer's G-string with Benjamins.

Will do, but you owe me, I text back.

2:06 p.m.

ACCORDING TO the digital clock, both diapers started their disintegrations even before I got home from Bubble. The McSludge diaper has formed a menacing stain, and there is a slow leak of vinegar pee and pureed faux poo dripping onto the grass from the other diaper.

I jot down the time codes displayed on the digital camera recordings, then unclip the messy diapers and toss them into the trash can.

I guess I have to break the news to Merrie that AmeriCorp

(or EnviroBest, or whatever code name Mike Lovejoy's constituent goes by) is off the hook for its quid pro quo.

FOR THE S&M party, I've chosen a new tight white low-cut sundress. It has thin spaghetti straps and is boned, which means I don't have to wear a bra with it. I pair it with a pair of four-inch white Valentino patent leather open-toed heels adorned with a double bow. Here's hoping Alex loves what he sees, because I'm ovulating again. Why the hell is it taking me so long to get pregnant?

I need him home with me tonight, not traipsing around a strip club ogling some bare-breasted Amazons.

Then again, the later he stays out, the hornier he'll be when he gets home.

Either way, it's a win-win for me.

5:46 p.m.

PERFECT TIMING. I pull up to Seth's place just as Fanny is trudging up Washington Street, stroller in hand. She is a vision in Tartan plaid, tam-o-shanter and all.

She waves frantically as she sees me, as if I'm that Number 24 Muni bus that whiplashes past us like it's being driven by the Headless Horseman.

Inside the stroller, Sadie is chattering. When she sees me, her eyes light up, and she claps her hands. Okay, either she's really happy to see me, or she's got gas. I want to think positive here, so I go for the former.

Fanny swaps Sadie for the gift bag in my hand. Opening it, she coos, "Adorable!"

She then gives an approving whistle to my new dress.

Sadie likes it, too, and gurgles delightedly as she reaches for the sash.

"Just took our little princess out for some fresh air," says Fanny. "Our lord and master keeps that place locked up like a tomb." Fanny's Brooklyn accent is as broad as her hand gestures.

I sigh. "Tell me about it. I'd like to say something to Seth about that, but I'm guessing he doesn't really want to hear it. At least, not yet."

"That depends." The thin brow over Fanny's left eye hovers like a bird in flight.

"What do you mean?"

"If you told him anything, he'd listen. You know, he's got a thing for *you,* doll."

"Oh no, you're mistaken." Even with the chill from San Francisco's infamous spring gloom, I can feel the heat on my face. "Seriously, Fanny, I doubt that."

"Goodness, don't tell me you didn't suspect that, even a little!" My blush puts a smile on Fanny's lush lips. Because they are surgically enhanced, the effect is more Jessica Rabbit than Mona Lisa. "It's a riot the way he talks about you, like you hung the moon or something! Certainly he appreciates all you're doing for us. But the way in which he perks up at your cute little e-mails and all—"

"I think you're wrong about that. He's just, you know, *lonely.* In fact, we met through my husband."

"Ha! Well, I guess I read *that* one wrong." As Fanny shakes her head in wonder, her sleek bob swings gently on her neck. She folds her little charge's stroller with one arm and holds Sadie with the other as she lumbers up the steps. "But you're right about one thing, he is one lonely man."

"If it's any help, I've started researching playgroups but many are moms only. Believe it or not, even in this day and age there aren't many that are coed."

"Yeah, I hear you." Fanny's cackle is mirthless. "My last charge was a little girl. Shy as can be. Whenever we went to the park, it was like pulling teeth to get her to play with the other kids. The au pairs were fine about nudging their charges to give her a chance. As far as we're concerned, the more the merrier. But some of the moms can be pretty picky as to whom their kids play with."

The way Fanny says that makes me wonder if she suspects that they were put off by her. Even in San Francisco, you don't see a lot of Barbra Streisand impersonators in the parks.

Well, at least not ones who are au pairs.

She's right. Seth should have more friends. But *girl*friends? "I don't know, Fanny. Nicole passed away only six months ago. He's still in mourning."

"Dearie, when it comes to a man and his, er, needs, six months is a lifetime. Take it from one who knows." She flutters her fake lashes. "Look, no one here is talking about 'til death do them part. He's had his heart broken once. I don't think he could take that again. All Seth does is work, or look after Sadie. No beers with the boys, no nothing. What's wrong with going out on a date every now and then? You know, a few laughs with a friend. Or better, a friend with benefits—"

"Yeah, okay, I get your drift." I don't mean to be so short with her, but I didn't come over for a lecture on something Fanny feels he needs.

Especially if it's something I can't provide him—

Or wait. Maybe I can.

"Can I leave my car there?" I point to where I've parked, in the driveway. "I want to catch the Number 1 California bus for downtown."

Fanny nods, puzzled. "But why not park it downtown? It's after six, so the meters are free, and they won't tow." She looks at her watch. "Egad! I hope Seth makes it back by eight thirty."

"Oh, he will, on both counts. That's a promise."

"I don't get it. What's the second count?"

"He's going on a date, too." With that, I give Sadie a peck on the cheek and start out the door.

I don't know if she's crying because I'm leaving, or because Fanny's off-key rendition of "On a Clear Day" leaves a lot to be desired.

19

......

I cannot think of any need in childhood
as strong as the need for a father's protection.
—Sigmund Freud

6:38 p.m.

Y OUR MUSHROOM CAPS were better," I murmur just loud enough for Seth to hear me.

After roaming through S&M's massive lobby, which is packed solid with Silicon Valley's best and brightest, I've found him, finally, hovering over the S&M party's infamous gourmet food table.

Millicent, Alex's secretary, spends a full week prior to the monthly party, planning the menu and tasting savory tidbits that validate the impression that the company is as rich as the food it serves. The fact that she's now fifteen pounds heavier than when she started working here is proof she's done a great job.

Seth turns around to face me—too suddenly, as it turns out. His mouth is full, as are his hands. In one, he holds a glass of red wine. In the other, he's got a small plate piled high with lots of goodies: fried ravioli, a couple of crab rangoon cups, figs stuffed with blue cheese, and a veggie feta pizzette.

When a crab cup slides off and lands on my shoe, my point is made.

"Oh, um, sorry!" Seth, embarrassed, chokes down his food as he rights the dish just in time to stop a landslide of appetizers from joining that errant crab cup.

I stare down at the pretty little bow of my new shoe. It will never be the same again.

"Hmmm. I better go get that cleaned up." I turn to leave, but he grabs my arm.

"No, wait. Here, hold this." Handing me his glass and his plate, he crouches down and takes my shoe—my whole foot— in his left hand in order to pluck off the pieces of crabmeat with his right hand. As his long, large fingers wrap around my heel in order to steady me, his thumb gently grazes my instep. It sends a shiver up my leg. Involuntarily I lift my foot, and the glass and plate I'm holding tip precariously—

But he holds tight to me, so that I don't fall.

When I look down, I find him staring up at me.

I am mesmerized by the depth of sadness I see in his face. He doesn't have to say anything. His eyes say it all:

I miss this.

Touching. Holding. Protecting.

All of which you take for granted until you can no longer do it anymore.

At least, not with the one you love most; the one who loved you most of all.

I wonder if, right now, Seth is remembering how Nicole felt the last time he held her.

And then I think about Alex, how he must miss the soft plumpness of a little boy's palm.

Of Peter's hand.

If I wanted to ask him, I could, because suddenly he's there, standing behind Seth. His prideful smile shifts into an uncertain grimace.

Oh, damn. I can only imagine how this looks to Alex.

Or Seth's partner, Henry, who is at Alex's side. He turns white, as if he's just seen a ghost. I guess the last thing he wants Seth to do is play footsie with the money guy's wife.

On the other hand, the Samurai, aka Mr. Takahashi, salivates as he gives me the once-over.

This time when I shiver, I set my foot down on Seth's hand. When he jerks it away from my shoe, I lose my balance and the glass and the plate tip over.

A second later my new dress now looks like a Jackson Pollock castoff.

Nope, I don't think our introduction could have gone worse.

My breasts, soaked with a fine oaky pinot noir, are particularly colorful, not to mention you can now see my nipples through the thin silk bodice of my dress.

Oh, lucky me, they are at eye-level with the Samurai.

Alex sputters out my name, but even his booming voice can't shake his guest from his trance. Finally I snap my fingers in the Samurai's face. He raises his eyes just long enough to accept my genteel smile, which I make before taking a modest bow to show respect, just the way Alex had demonstrated to me.

When I look up again, I see that the Samurai is saying something to Alex. I can't understand it because he's speaking in Japanese. Whatever it is doesn't make Alex happy. His double-wide grin, an involuntary reflex that bares his teeth like a shark, is his poker tell.

He still has it on his face when he turns to me. "We're leaving now."

"Okay, sure, no problem. Let me get my coat." I shake my head at Seth, as if to say *Sorry this screws up your excuse to get home, but there's nothing we can do about that now . . .*

"No, not you. I meant that Henry, Seth, and I are going, with Mr. Takahashi." He shrugs helplessly.

I can't believe my ears. "What? . . . Wait! But—but then I don't have a ride! And I can't get on the bus—like this! What did that guy say to you, anyway?"

Alex starts to answer me, then stops. "You really don't want to know," he murmurs in my ear.

It's the Samurai's turn to snap fingers. "I say it getting late! Time to go to the titty bar!"

Alex leans down to give me a kiss, but I back away. Yes, I'm pissed. And no, I won't forgive him for leaving me here like this.

If I ever doubted that S&M comes first in his life, this incident has put that to rest.

"I'll take Katie home," Seth pipes up.

Henry's glare at his partner is also easy to read: *I'm tired of carrying you, asshole.* Angrily he follows the Samurai toward the door.

Alex looks from me to Seth, and back again. He doesn't like what he sees. It's not my anger that has stopped him cold, but the honest concern for me in Seth's eyes.

Before Alex turns to leave, his poker smile is back. "See you real soon, babe," he says to me, as if he doesn't have a care in the world. "In fact, I'll be home early."

7:22 p.m.

SETH PARKED a few blocks away, at the Sutter Stockton Garage. He's silent on the walk there. I can't say I blame him.

In fact, he doesn't say anything during the ride up California Street and through lower Pac Heights. He doesn't even look over at me.

I don't know what to say, either. Because of me, his partner is now pissed at him.

And so is Alex.

That may cost Seth more than he can afford.

I feel the tears pool in my eyes. Slowly they trickle down my cheeks.

I can feel Seth's eyes on me. The next thing I know, he's pulled over to the curb. He pats my hand gently a few times. When he gets no response from that, he lays his hand over mine and just leaves it there until I'm all cried out.

"I'm so sorry. I blew it for you." I try to lift my hand in order to wipe my face from the dampness and guilt, but he won't let go of it. Instead, he puts it on his cheek. It is the heat and stubble and love I feel there that finally draws my eyes to his face.

He's laughing.

That's when it hits me: "*Oh. My. God.* You did it on purpose!"

"Huh? What are you talking about? Are you saying that I made you spill that stuff on yourself?" My accusation wipes the smile off his face, but he can't hide the guilt in his eyes.

"Yes, so that I'd have to leave as soon as possible. And you knew Alex had to go with the Samurai, so he wouldn't be suspicious if you took me home."

I don't care that I look as if I've run into a buffet table. I can hail down a taxi to take me to my car. I fumble with the knob of his car, but it won't open.

"It's on child lock." His voice is gentle, as if he's talking to a six-year-old.

"Well, get it off, damn it!" I slam my fist against the passenger window.

"All right, just calm down." He taps his finger against the steering wheel, as if he's got all the time in the world.

I can take the hint. I put my hands in my lap. And wait. Two can play this game.

Finally he sighs. "Yeah, okay, maybe I nudged you off balance—just a *little*, though. Hell, Katie, I would have never guessed in a million years that you were so clumsy!"

"Screw you! I'd like to see *you* try balancing yourself on a four-inch heel!"

"I'll borrow one from Fanny and give it a try."

"That's not the point, Seth. Honestly, I don't think you did yourself any favor by bowing out tonight. If the spill hadn't happened, I would have been happy to sit with Sadie until you got home. I could have taken your car, and Alex could have dropped you off afterward."

"That's good to know, and I appreciate the fact that you'd have offered to do so. But Katie, the truth of the matter is that *I really didn't want to go with them.*"

"I know. You're one of the most devoted dads I've ever met. But if you get kicked out of the company, how will you support yourself—and Sadie?"

"If that ever happened, I'd figure it out." His mouth hardens into a frown. "I'll be the first to admit that I'm not as driven as I once was. The company just isn't as important to me as it used to be." He shifts his body so that he's facing me. "Just to let you know: I've already told Henry that when the company is finally put into play, I'm not hanging around. I'll take a buyout instead."

"Wow! How did he react to that?"

"He's not too happy about it. He knows that whoever buys us will want us at the helm—*both* of us. He's got tremendous technical know-how, but the truth of the matter is that I'm the real visionary behind SkorTek, and everyone knows it."

By everyone, he means Alex.

"So you see, they have to play by my terms. And that means cutting me some slack when it comes to Sadie. She'll always be my first priority." He rests his head on the back of his seat. He's staring up through the sunroof of the car, but what he sees there is more than the passing fog.

It's every regret he's had since Nicole died.

"Seth, have you thought about when you might start dating

again?" It's not an easy subject, but there is no better time than now to ask.

He doesn't say anything for the longest time. Nor does he take his eyes off whatever point in the sky he's staring at. As the last of the day's summer light washes over him, shadows accentuate the contours between the bridge of his nose and the hollows in his cheeks. His eyes drop even deeper into the dark abyss of his pain. "Why do you ask?" There is a wariness to his voice.

"I think you need—you know . . . *companionship*." Can he see me blushing? Of course not.

He laughs so hard that the guy walking his dog across the street stops to stare at us. Seth stops only to gasp for air. "Jesus, Katie, if that's what I wanted, I'd be at the strip club—with Alex."

The sarcasm with which he says my husband's name makes me angry. "Alex's only there because—"

"Let's be honest, Katie. We both know why Alex is there."

"Whatever you may think, I know he's there only because his client insisted they go—"

"He's there because *he* wants to be there." Thickening clouds of fog have shifted between us and the setting sun and I can barely make out Seth, but even in the dark, I know he's staring right at me. "Otherwise he'd be here, with you."

I open my mouth to say something—but how can I answer that?

I can't. Because he's right.

"I'm sorry, forgive me for interrupting." His tone is cold. "You were just about to tell me how easy it will be to replace Nicole—"

"My God, is that what you think? Look, just . . . Oh, never mind! Can you take me to my car, please? Alex will be home—

soon, just like he promised—and I don't want to give him any more reasons to worry about his investment in you."

Seth nods stiffly and starts up the engine again.

We drive the rest of the way in silence.

I wait until he pulls into his driveway before speaking again. I don't know if he can make out my words because even I can't hear them, they tumble out in a torrent of regret for what might be the end of a very nice friendship. "No one could ever replace Nicole. I know that, Seth. And I would never presume otherwise." I hesitate, only to choose my words carefully. "But there should be room in your heart for others, too. Friends, not lovers. Just friends."

Slowly, Seth nods his head. "So, what you're telling me is that I should try dating?"

"Yes! Just to make friends, nothing more. At least, not until you're ready for—something more."

His laugh is sarcastic. "Men with kids are damaged goods."

"No, you're not. You're mature, and you don't have a lot of time to waste."

He shrugs. "Oh, yeah? And what woman, pray tell, is going to understand that my weekends and nights belong to Sadie, that she'll always come first, because that's just the way it is?"

"Another parent would. Listen, this is totally out of the blue, but I'd like you to consider checking out a few of the local single parent dating groups. In fact"—I take a deep breath—"one that may interest you is meeting tomorrow evening. It comes highly recommended. A single mom named Kara Kischell runs it out of her home. There will be around thirty people, give or take. Everyone brings a dish and a bottle of wine. No kids are there, just adults enjoying each other's company and letting their hair down. The members in this particular group are all within five years of your age on either side, and it's evenly split between men and women. Most of them have kids under the age of five—"

"Jeez, Katie, slow down!" Well, at least he's laughing again. "Okay . . . I'll make a deal with you: I'll check it out—if we go together."

"You want me to tag along? Won't I cramp your style?"

"That's just the point. I *have* no style."

"What am I supposed to be, your wing girl or something?" I shake my head, emphatically. "Kara seems nice, but she'd never let me in, just to observe."

Seth shrugs. "Either we go together, or I don't go at all. You've got a bad track record of taking other people's word as to whether something is right for your clients." His grin is playful. "You know, Fanny could have been a total disaster."

I have to give him that. "All right, I'll call her up and explain that—well, I'll just say that I want to see what it's all about, so that I can recommend it to others. I'll e-mail you the address. It's at the top of Pacific Heights, so it's easier if you pick me up." I tap the window as a reminder for him to release the child lock.

As I get out of his car I see Fanny. She's sitting on the couch beside the window. Just as I put the key in the lock of my car, she turns around, and I give her a thumbs-up.

She gives me a standing ovation.

8:25 p.m.

WHEN I get home, I put on a new negligee: a sheer black lace baby doll with a G-string bottom.

Then I wait.

And wait.

Until I fall asleep.

6:08 a.m., Saturday, 14 April

WHAT WAKES me is Alex's key in the lock, finally. I can't see the clock, but the soft light melting the room's shadows indicates that it must be dawn.

Because I'm mad, I should pretend I'm asleep.

But since I'm ovulating, instead I pretend I'm horny.

I wait until he sits down on the bed to give a wanton moan, then I roll over and rub the small of his back with my hand. "Missed you. So glad you're home, sweetheart."

He nods, but he doesn't say a word. I've conveniently left a packet with a rubber on his bedside table. He picks it up, but just holds on to it, staring at it. "What the—"

I hold my breath. Cold dread rolls over me. My pinpricks are so tiny that there is no way he can tell it's been punctured . . . or is there?

"Hell, what was I thinking, getting you involved with that guy? If I'd known Seth was such a lazy asshole I'd have never hooked you up with him. At least he's paying you well." He shakes his head in disgust. "I'm glad you're not pissed at me for leaving you with him tonight. Jesus, I can't wait until we go public with SkorTek! That will be one less headache . . ."

Then he rips open the packet and rolls on the rubber.

His thrusts are long, hard, and deep. There are no kisses, no foreplay, no naughty words, no terms of endearment.

What did I expect? Of course he's still angry: not at me, at Seth. I'm thankful about that.

If he has to take it out on *me,* then so be it.

It's what I want, too.

Tonight, anyway.

20

. . . .

Parenthood: That state of being better chaperoned
than you were before marriage.
—Marcelene Cox

6:11 p.m., Saturday, 14 April

ALEX IS still out on his jog when Seth arrives for our mission to scope out the single-parent dating group.

Thank goodness, since they don't seem too fond of each other, anyway.

When Seth gets out to open the car door for me, I notice that he's actually wearing a jacket. His curls are still damp from his shower. All good, all good . . . except for the few dots of shaving cream that still cling to his jaw.

Seeing my concern, he pauses before he closes the door. "What, do I have a zit or something?"

I can't help but smile. "No, silly. It's not as if we're going to some high school dance. Here, allow me."

With the back of my palm, I wipe away the foam. Underneath, his face is smooth.

When I look up, I see he's watching me intently. He doesn't turn away when our eyes meet, but I do.

Maybe Fanny is right.

If so, then I'm glad we're doing this tonight. Seth needs more women in his life. Or at least one who can return his feelings.

Any crush he's got on me is over by the time we make it to Kara Kischell's place. In the short time it takes us to climb out of the Marina to the crest of Pacific Heights, we've yet to agree upon (a) the length of our visit (he wants it to be no more than an hour, I insist he's got to hang in there at least until he makes one new friend); (b) topics that should be off-limits (Seth is adamant that he avoid mentioning Nicole's death, whereas my recommendation is that he go with his gut, judge that on a case-by-case basis); and (c) the appropriate signal should one of us—that would be Seth—urgently feel the need to get out of there.

By the time we reach Kara's street, I'm exasperated with him. "At the very least, we should be able to agree on some sort of signal! I can say something innocent, like 'Kara's garden looks great.' What do you say to that?"

"I'll give you ten-to-one odds that her garden looks like crap," he counters stubbornly. "If so, and you say something stupid, she'll know you're bullshitting. Instead, why don't you just rub your arms together, like you're cold? I'm guessing you'll get goose bumps in that getup." He gives my sundress a grudging nod.

He then takes his hands off the steering wheel in order to demonstrate, and gets honked at by the cab beside us when the car drifts too close to the adjacent lane.

Kara Kischell's home, a gently worn three-story Georgian, is where Pacific Avenue crosses Lyon Street, at the peak of Pacific Heights. Her backyard is, quite literally, the Presidio National Park. The grand old house needs a paint job, and a new walkway—

And yes, her yard looks like it hasn't been tended to in months.

"Okay, you win," I hiss at Seth. "We'll go with your goose bumps act. It is *sooo* original." Just in case my sarcasm was not lost on him, I put on my sweater, which I had tossed on his backseat.

I'm determined to stay at the party for as long as it takes Seth to connect with someone.

Kara's front door is open. As we maneuver around bicycles scattered on the walkway, the ebb and flow of giddy laughter greets us. It is the sound of adults on parole from the one worthy life sentence, that of a true crime of passion: parenting.

Because this shindig is a potluck, I made champagne shrimp pasta salad, but I let Seth carry it in, and I take on the lighter load of his bottle of wine. The steps leading to the front door are crooked and broad, the front stoop lined with all sorts of boy toys: plastic bats and balls, a Spider-Man, not to mention a basket filled with muddy Transformers action figures.

Seth steps on a Voyager Alien that has escaped the basket. Thankfully, it doesn't break. Instead, it slips out from under him, shooting off under a porch swing that holds three oversize needlepoint pillows. Each is adorned with a name: one says KARA, another says KYLE, and the third says KEIRAN.

Seth puts down the pasta salad bowl and crouches down to recover it. Before our hostess finds him on his hands and knees, I jerk him up by the collar of his shirt. "No way! *No stalling.* Your job is to have fun, remember?"

"Someone could have killed themselves on that thing," he mutters, but the way in which he avoids my eyes is my gotcha confirmation. He looks as if he could kill *me,* for getting him into this. "Okay, right. Let's get this over with, then. Ladies first."

I hesitate, albeit just for a moment, as I wonder whether he'll follow me in or leave me stranded.

Then I realize why I have no reason to worry:

He can't hide from me, because I know where he lives.

SETH WAS right: what with the fog blowing in through the Golden Gate and over the Presidio, it's colder than a witch's tit.

Kara leaves not only the door open, but all the windows, too. I'm sure she's trying to offset the heat that comes from so many bodies in one confined space. Who knew there were so many toddlers in San Francisco from broken marriages? Well, their parents are all here tonight.

Babysitters all over the city are having a great year.

For the most part these warm bodies are well groomed, casually dressed, smiling congenially and seemingly captivated by the wit and wisdom of their companions du jour. As instructed, Seth is off mingling. This gives me time to roam from room to room and eavesdrop on the latest pickup lines, observe the best flirting techniques, and wince at the awkward silences between these hopeful couples.

I bless the fact that I'm no longer single.

The conversations sound familiar. Will this be yet another winning season for the Giants? What's the best place to watch Opening Day on the Bay? Did you like the latest Grisham novel? How about the newest exhibit at the de Young?

But every now and again a word pops up that seems out of place. Since when did "baby teeth" and "bed-wetting" become hot topics among those who are single and seeking?

Yes, this will be a good experience for Seth.

As I walk through Kara's home, I pause to study one of her many family photos, which are propped on side tables, hung in groupings on her walls, and taped to her fridge. Her boys, about the same ages as Mario and Max, have been blessed with her dark chocolate curls. In her candid snapshots they pose in superhero costumes, hug and wrestle each other, and smother their mother as if they never want to let her go.

She, too, is holding on to them, as if for dear life.

There is no man in any of the pictures, ex or otherwise. And the photos she shares with her sons are cockeyed and taken at arm's length.

She is chronicling her life as it is now, not the one she presumed she'd have when she walked down the aisle.

I can relate to that.

Like her, I'm doing all I can to change that, as soon as possible.

I don't realize that Kara has come up behind me until she straightens the refrigerator magnet holding one of the photos. "He's a cutie pie, your friend Seth," she says. "How long have you known him, anyway?"

Kara is short, stacked, sultry, and all too obvious in a Retro Bettie apron that proclaims YOU'RE ON MY TO-DO LIST. I'd like her better if she'd stop giving me the once-over, despite the fact that I've insisted at least a half dozen times already that Seth is my client—*and nothing more.*

"I've been working with Seth for a couple of months now." I glance around nonchalantly, to see if I can spot him. The place is packed, and the last time I saw him was a little over an hour ago, so I'm guessing he's enjoying himself.

"Is finding a date for your clients a typical service for a baby planner? I mean, it seems to me that you're going above and beyond the call of duty, if you catch my drift."

Okay, now, how do I put this to her? I realize I should honor Seth's request that I not bring up Nicole's death. At the same time, when it comes to relationships—romantic or platonic—honesty is the best policy . . .

"Listen, Kara, I'm going to level with you. Seth lost his wife. In childbirth. I don't know if he's ready to date yet, but I know he needs friends in his life, people who can relate to his loss, or at least give him the opportunity to talk about it. And everyone here has experienced some of the issues that come up for single parents, particularly when their children are preschoolers or younger."

"Oh my God! How—sad! Well, you're right. Everyone in this room has a story, and I've heard them all." She shakes her head in awe. "Believe me, with that icebreaker, he is *so* going to get laid."

"No, you don't get it! It's not some sort of come-on or any-thing. And the last thing Seth wants is anyone's pity. I think that, at this point, all Seth is looking for is . . . is . . ."

Her laugh rolls out of her in explosive snorts. "Chill out, Katie. I was just kidding. That was just my way of saying that we're all in the same boat. We're trying to paddle with one hand because we need the other hand to keep our kids from falling overboard, emotionally. That's why everyone here takes it slow and easy. No one wants to get hurt again. In our lives, relation-ships have a domino effect."

"Good, then you understand. In fact, Seth asked me to not say anything about his loss, so I hope we can keep this be-tween us."

"Mum's the word." Kara shoves another cookie sheet of ap-petizers onto a rack in the topmost double oven and scrutinizes the timer before punching in the setting. I don't know why she feels it's needed, since the platters of food on her massive dining room table have barely been touched. The women here are in date mode. It's hard to flirt with spinach stuck between your teeth.

Out of the corner of my eye I spot Seth. He is surrounded by three women.

Kara follows my glance and nods approvingly. "See? What did I tell you? He's in good company. The tall one, Teri, is a chef. Has a little boy. He just turned two last week. Her ex was a bar-tender. Decided he could make more money in Vegas—and that it would go farther at the craps table without the baggage of her and their kid." She wipes her hands on her apron. "The brunette with the short hair, Bree, is a lawyer. Her little girl was AI—"

"'AI'? You mean artificial insemination?"

"Yep. That's how badly she wanted to move her life beyond the partner track. Well, now she can . . . Oh, and the lady with the ponytail is Vanessa. She's a photographer. The divorce was dirty. So sad. He's got the money to hammer her—which he did, so he got the kid, too, most of the time: a three-year-old girl. It just worked out that way."

"Oh." I watch as Vanessa leans in toward Seth to catch his every word. Whatever he said made her laugh. She touches his arm seductively.

Does he like it?

Suddenly, to my surprise, I realize how much I hope he doesn't.

But of course, I want him to be happy . . .

And like Kara, surrounded by friends. "How long have you been hosting these shindigs, Kara?"

She lets loose with one of her giddy foghorn blasts. "Too long! Well, let's see: Kent walked out on us with my best friend, Jane, when Kieran was only a year old. Then I went into a massive depression in which I lay in bed for a month and cried myself sick. That was a real happy time around here! But after a while I decided that with friends and husbands like that, who needs enemies? Nope, I needed better friends, ones who actually understood what I was going through. So I put it out there: whenever I was on the playground with the boys, or at their preschool—and this is the result: an instant lonely hearts club." She sweeps her hands out toward her living room.

For the first time since I've arrived, I hear the slightly hysterical chuckles and see the involuntary tics—the way one woman pulls on her earlobe every few seconds, how one man lets out a nervous cough after every sentence.

I also notice the longing in their eyes.

And yet, even as Kara's new friends work hard to like and be liked, couples bend away from each other ever so slightly, as if afraid of yet another emotional blow to the heart.

Despite this, the smile on Kara's peach-glossed lips is wide with fierce pride. She has moved beyond her pain.

She has made it her mission to help others do the same.

Her full, sensual lips pucker into a frown. "Aw, heck! Jordan is honing in on Seth."

"Who's Jordan?"

She shudders. "The biggest blowhard in our group. Jordan just hates it when a new guy shows up. He considers himself cock of the walk. But from what I hear, that is a *massive* exaggeration." She holds her thumb and forefinger an inch apart to illustrate her point.

I turn to see who she's describing. Ick, okay, yeah, I remember that guy. Yes, he's good-looking: buff and broad-shouldered, Ken doll clean-cut, an expensive jacket over jeans, and a smirk that's meant to intimidate any other guy in the room.

Does he really feel that women will find that attractive?

I had my initial run-in when I first walked into Kara's living room. It seemed as if every head swiveled toward us at the same time. I kept patting my hair. It's a nervous habit, sure, but it also kept my wedding ring front and center. Only one man—this Jordan dude—didn't let that keep him from sidling up to me and saying, "That dress is very becoming on you. Of course if I were on you, I'd be cumming, too."

I wrapped my arms around myself and ran.

If Seth had seen it, he would have been right in guessing it was the sign to beat a hasty retreat.

"Jordan is a Class A asshole. He kisses and tells," Kara is warning me now, as if I couldn't guess *that*. "Drives the women crazy. The other guys can't stand him, either. Unfortunately, he won't take the hint that he's worn out his welcome. Come on, let's go save Seth from Jordan's buzzkill."

We make it over to them in time to hear Jordan say to Seth, "A tech guy, eh? Let me guess: your wife didn't like your gamer pals, am I right? . . . No? Then what: did she hate the fact that you spent all your time at the office, so she took off with some other guy?"

Seth's sunny openness darkens to annoyance, then to pitch-black anger. I'm not the only one who notices. Kara actually takes a step back. Teri, Bree, and Vanessa exchange glances.

I know what they're thinking: *Is this a side of this guy I won't like?*

No, I want to say to them, *don't judge him by this. If you knew his real story you'd know that he has every right to be angry . . .*

Seth closes his eyes in disgust. He's just about to say something—something I'm sure he'll regret—when Kara blurts out, "Jordan, you idiot! His wife died!"

Suddenly the room is silent. Seth turns to stare at me. The pain etched on his face makes me go white with shame.

He stalks out of the room.

I turn to Kara. She, too, realizes the seriousness of her mistake. She grabs my hand to lead me through the crowd and out the door. "Katie, please tell him I'm sorry! You told me that in confidence, and I should have never—"

I nod and give her a hug, then run out of the house. I know that I'll be asking his forgiveness for me, first and foremost.

SETH HASN'T driven away, thank goodness, although I wouldn't blame him if he had.

He doesn't say a word as I get into the car. Nor does he look at me. He just starts the engine and pulls away from the curb.

I guess I don't know what to say, either. Considering my betrayal, what could I possibly say that would be adequate, that will allow him to trust me again?

He heads down Pacific Avenue, but instead of driving down

Divisadero to return to the Marina, he veers off in the opposite direction and climbs up one more block, to Jackson.

"Get out," he says.

"You want me to walk home—from here?"

He looks over at me. No, he's looking *beyond* me.

When I turn, I realize we're parked right in front of Alta Plaza Park. One block long and two blocks wide, it crowns the tallest hill in Pacific Heights.

He gets out and walks to the door on my side. Before I can protest, he opens it. "We both need a little fresh air."

I nod silently. I'm not wearing the best shoes for a walk up to the top, but I figure I owe Seth this much.

He doesn't stop at any of the broad benches that take in on one side the magnificent view of the city and San Francisco Bay, with views of the Marin Headlands, and on the other side distant views of the city stretching to the hills of South San Francisco.

Finally we reach the massive playground perched on the far side of the park's hilltop. He stops in front of one of the swings and pushes it gently. I don't think he's waiting for me to say anything, but I blurt out something anyway:

"Seth, please, please forgive me."

"I'm not mad at you, Katie." I can't see him in the dark, but I can feel his eyes on me. He speaks in a voice so soft that I can barely hear him.

"Yes, you are, and you have every right to be! I should have let you tell Kara yourself—I mean, if you wanted her to know about Nicole—"

"No, you don't get it. Yeah, okay, what you did was exactly what I asked you *not* to do. It was stupid on your part, and I'm glad I get to say I told you so, because you can be such a prim little know-it-all, but . . . but I know you well enough to know that you did it because you thought it was the right thing to do at the time."

He holds the swing still. His hands are gripped tightly on its metal links, as if holding firm will allow him to find the strength to make his point. "Katie, this is where I was with Nicole when she told me she was pregnant. Right here. She'd packed a picnic and we ate it over there"—he points to a picnic table on the lawn, just outside the playground—"and then I brought her over here to kiss her—and she said it, just like that: 'We're going to have . . . a baby.'"

Seth's voice cracks when he says the word *baby.*

Just then the moon peeks out from under a cloud. He glances up at it, as if he'll find the words he needs to say somewhere in the cosmos.

No, really, it's so that he doesn't have to look at me. "And you know what I said to her? I said, 'We can't. Not now. You have to abort.'" He stares at me. "That look on your face—it's the same one she had. She couldn't believe I'd said that." He drops his head. "She cried for the longest time. Then she called me a son of a bitch, and said that nothing was more important to me than work; that she'd leave me rather than give up this baby. She meant it, too. I know, because Nicole always followed through on whatever she said."

I can barely make out what Seth is saying because he's so choked up. His tears, running down his face, look like shards of glass in the moonlight.

"Katie, that creep at the party was right. I *was* selfish—"

"No, you're wrong! That jerk didn't know what he was saying."

"Please, Katie, hear me out! Even when I told Nicole okay, sure, keep the baby, that was selfish on my part because I wanted her, no matter what the cost. Well, guess what? *She left me anyway.* Having Sadie cost Nicole her life."

He's standing so close to me now, I feel his hot breath on my cheeks.

"I don't blame Sadie. I don't blame the hospital. *I blame myself.* God help me, maybe I could have talked her into changing her mind. If I had, I wouldn't have been there, tonight, making small talk with some really nice women who have what she always wanted and never will. They'll get to watch their children grow up, and she won't. And she wanted that more than anything. She wanted that even more than she wanted me."

As he straightens up, he brushes his tears away. But still he won't look at me. Instead, he walks past me and down the path, toward the car.

As I stumble after him, it strikes me that Seth and Alex have something in common after all.

Or did, once.

21

....

10:22 a.m., Monday, 16 April

CAROLYN, MY BEDRIDDEN client, e-mails me her disappointment that she can't join me and my other clients for Making Mommies Smile's very first meet-up at the Sprout boutique.

Not to worry, I e-mail back, you can watch it live, on webcam!

The video streaming is Abby's idea. She's been Tweeting, Facebooking, and posting mentions on various mommy blogs and web communities. "I'll take it on my iPhone. Piece of cake," she explains brightly.

Joanna, Elizabeth, Ophelia, along with Grace and Lana, will be my live audience, there to comment on the product I'll be showcasing: a great gizmo called the SwingLo Chariot that is supposed to rock your baby to sleep.

Really, it's a fixed-in-place swing that sports a variety of settings, all with two or three speed levels: Sailboat (supposedly puts the motion of the ocean in this wee rocker); Cruise Control (emulates a long car drive); Hand to Mouth (makes the baby feel like its mother is cradling the baby to her breast); Roly Poly (which has a gentle rolling motion); and then there's my favorite setting, called Wheeeeeee! (babies supposedly love it, because it mimics the sensation of Mommy or Daddy tossing them up in the air).

It didn't toss out my little test dummy, so I'm giving it a thumbs-up.

6:16 p.m.

I'VE TOLD everyone to feel free to bring their little ones, since Sprout has a playroom that should keep them busy while the moms and moms-to-be watch the demonstration. That would have worked out great, except for the fact that Joanna was supposed to bring Emma to sit for them.

As usual, Joanna shows up frazzled and apologetic—albeit this time without Emma. "I'm so sorry, Katie! I've been trying her cell, but she's just not picking up. Do you mind me asking how much you offered to pay her?"

I'm sure her daughter's no-show has nothing to do with the money. It is just Emma's way of paying me back for making her fess up to her mom about having her boyfriend over to the house. "Ten bucks a kid, for two hours. She would have racked up, too."

I nod over to the playroom, where Mario, Max, and Jeremy the Terrible are already wrestling on the cushioned floor. Jezebel, always the little lady, looks on disapprovingly. As the boys roll toward her, she scoops up her American Doll just in time and climbs to safety on a rocking chair.

"Ha! That's why she blew you off. That's only half of what Paul shells out for her allowance."

"You're kidding, right? She's just thirteen! What does she do to earn eighty bucks a week?"

"The usual: her grades, straighten up her room, keep away from alcohol, drugs, cigarettes, joints, sex, and any or all activity that will raise my blood pressure while I'm pregnant."

Ophelia shakes her head in wonder. "So, you have to bribe your kid to be good?"

Joanna's eyes narrow angrily. "We don't consider it a bribe. We consider it a reward."

Elizabeth gives Ophelia a dirty look, but the surrogate is used to it and shrugs it off. "You rich folk slay me! The kid is obviously out of control, and your answer to that is to throw money at her? No wonder it doesn't mean anything to her!"

The only thing stopping Joanna from blasting Ophelia is the appearance of Fanny. Today she is dressed as Barbra a la *What's Up, Doc?:* paperboy cap, paisley wrap top, and all. "Where's the party?" she demands, ignoring the stares from my clients and the Sprout salesclerks.

Abby, whose iPhone has caught everything from the WWE antics of the boys to the near catfight between Ophelia and Joanna, now swings it in Fanny's direction.

Always ready for her close-up, Fanny strikes a blue steel pose that could pass for the real Babs in silhouette.

People tuning in now will presume they are watching lost footage from a Fellini movie.

There is only one way to convince them otherwise. In my best television hostess voice, I proclaim, "Grab a seat, everyone! The demonstration is about to begin . . ."

I DO as Abby has instructed me and talk in a clear, slow voice, looking directly at the camera as I put the SwingLo Chariot through its paces. Its passenger is a demo doll that weighs about thirty pounds: the maximum weight recommended by the manufacturer.

For the most part, the boys have been reined in by the adults. The promise of a walk down the block to a cupcake shop has done the trick (yes, Ophelia, bribes do work), so the room is relatively quiet as I point out the SwingLo's best features: its various speeds and motions, its patented Rock-a-Matic suspension, and the numerous colors it comes in.

"The cushion is removable, and therefore washable, too!" I'm putting too much emphasis on that, but I've just noticed that Max is headed my way.

"Can I try it, Aunt Katie?" He's much too fast for me. With one hand, he shoves the demo doll off the swinging seat and hops in its place.

"No! No! *My turn!*" Jeremy, who has been sitting obediently in Elizabeth's lap so that Abby can keep working the camera, has jumped up and is now trying to pull Max out of the seat. The SwingLo's plastic pedestal base can't support both boys, and over it goes, tossing Max on the floor, and Jeremy on top of him.

Abby, too shocked to turn off the camera, keeps it focused on the melee, which now includes a crying Sadie, a screaming Jezebel, and Lana and Grace pulling the boys apart.

Despite the laughter of the other mothers, I'm very serious as I point out, on camera, the most obvious flaw of the SwingLo: "As you can see, when there are other children around, a floor model isn't as stable as it could be. We'll check in with the SwingLo when there's a bolted tabletop version. This is Katie Johnson of Making Mommies Smile, signing off."

I won't know if the camera caught Fanny singing "You're the Top."

Since Abby has never learned how to edit on the damn thing, here's hoping it didn't.

11:06 a.m., Tuesday, 17 April

Seth@SkorTek: You look great on camera.

Katie@MakingMommiesSmile: I've got a great FX team. They edited out the extra 10 lbs the camera supposedly adds to your ass.

Seth@SkorTek: Oh yeah? Too bad they couldn't edit out Fanny's closing number. Sounds to me like it was off-key.

Katie@MakingMommiesSmile: LOL! I don't know how you were able to hear it over the ruckus the boys were making.

Seth@SkorTek: Hey, if I knew how much fun your little meet-ups are, I'd have come myself.

Katie@MakingMommiesSmile: The only prerequisite is that you can restrain a four-year-old boy, should he get out of line.

Seth@SkorTek: Having been one, it'll be a piece of cake. Next time, count me in.

I don't know if he means it, but in a way I hope he does come, even though I know that Henry and Alex might hit the roof.

8:15 p.m.

"HEY, UM, Katie, have you had a chance to review the website's Google Analytics today?" Abby is whispering, I presume because Jeremy is napping.

"Nope. I've been busy writing up a report for my client Twila. Why?"

"It's crazy! I mean that in a good way! We've had over twenty-three thousand hits!"

"You're kidding, right?" I click onto my computer's browser and scroll to the tab that takes me to my website's admin page. "Can you tell where all this traffic is coming from?"

"Hold on a minute . . . Seems that it's from YouTube! *Oh my God!* Our video has already gotten something like fifty-six thousand hits!" Abby is practically squealing. "And listen to some of these comments: 'What an honest review! Will Making

Mommies Smile be doing more?' . . . And 'This looks like so much fun! I wish I'd been there! Will Katie Johnson be doing these demos in other cities?' . . . Katie, there are over seventy comments here!"

"They're on the website, too, in the comment box under my quotes: 'I HEART@MakingMommiesSmile! Her columns make me remember why I had kids in the first place' . . . Wow! And my Twitter account now has over one hundred thousand followers!"

"Yeah, well, that's the power of SocialMoms. This is what one said: 'Katie Johnson, where have you been all my life?' Wow, talk about a hundred and forty characters of lovin'— *Jeremy!* What did I tell you about drinking out of the dog's bowl! *Get out of there now!* Listen, Katie, gotta go! I'll call you later—*Jeremy!* Not the dog's food! *No*—"

I scroll through my e-mails now: there are hundreds of them, mostly mothers-to-be with questions: about products, about their parenting concerns, about their relationships with their husbands.

I guess I should answer all of them—but when?

I click on an e-mail from something called MeLish:

We'd love your viewers to have the opportunity to sample our latest toddler taste sensation, Mini-Meaties! Not only do they come in baby-friendly bite sizes, but they are organically grown and nutritious, too!

And several others from major advertising agencies, requesting media rate cards for running banner ads on my site . . .

And even a few companies—manufacturers of all kinds of baby products—asking if they could sponsor a speaking tour.

I'm still staring at my computer screen when Alex walks in. He nuzzles my neck. I pat him gently but firmly push him away. "Honey, not now, please. I'm looking at how well my site is doing and—well, it's phenomenal. I'm blown away."

He glances up at the screen. Without asking, he nudges my hand away from the mouse. "Wow . . . Gee, Katie. Seriously . . . this could be big!" He turns to face me. "When did this happen?"

"Just today!"

"Well, well, well!" He goes to the window and opens it wide. "Ma, look at me! I married a millionairess!"

"What are you talking about? Do you think this is worth some real money?"

"I'm paid for what I think—and *hell yeah, baby*!" He sweeps me up into his arms and smothers me with his kisses. "Obviously you've struck a chord in the blogosphere. These companies don't just throw money at crappy little web pages."

He scrolls through my site, clicking onto pages. He looks puzzled. "Huh. It's not as if you're doing anything special. You certainly have good SEO. Your social networking is driving it, that's for sure . . . These blog posts: Do you mean all this crap you wrote?"

"Of course!" My stomach does a flip. I never thought Alex would ever read my posts, where I swear allegiance to all mothers-to-be, and talk about my yearnings for a child of my own—

"Huh. Good . . . I guess. Keep it up." He doesn't believe me. No: *he doesn't want to believe that this is me.*

That's okay. He'll believe it when we're pregnant . . .

"I'll draw up the prospectus for some seed money, so that you can staff up. We don't need you losing momentum, right? If you can sustain these numbers for a while—what do you think, a mil? No, let's make it five . . . I'll pull together a heavyweight board, and we can grow it organically, then at the right time, play out an exit strategy—Jesus, who'd have thought it? Katie Johnson is one hot stock!"

I smile wickedly. "Let's celebrate. Let's make love."

It's his turn to smirk. "Yeah, sure, okay! Anything that turns you on."

"Why don't you pour us a couple of glasses of champagne? You know, to celebrate?"

He nods and heads to the kitchen. While he's gone, I head to his condom drawer—

And pull out one that is touted as both "ribbed" and "warming." It's called Rough Rider for a *very* good reason.

And it pricks just as easily as any of the others.

Alex's new winning proposition will soon be a working mom, and he better not have any objections.

SECOND TRIMESTER

22

....

5:54 a.m., Monday, 7 May

I'M DEEP INTO my favorite dream: Alex stands over me as I deliver our baby. He is all smiles as the nurse swaddles our child in a receiving blanket and places our son in the crux of Alex's arm. There are tears of joy in his eyes. When he speaks, what comes out is—

The ring of our phone. But much too loud, much too long . . .

I'm jolted awake when Alex yanks the pillow out from under my head so that he can cover his ears with it.

"Whattaya want?" I rasp out.

"Please hang on for Congressman Mike Lovejoy's wife, Merrie," chirps an all-too-chipper voice of the aide to my most elusive client.

My agreement is a grunt.

Merrie is wide awake and to the point: "On Mother's Day, *W* magazine is profiling me, along with five other young and fruitful congressional wives, for a piece they're doing called 'The Pregnant Power Moms of Capitol Hill.' We're all with child, so I've got no advantage there. Hell, I don't even have the nursery ready for Twelve!"

"What do you mean? What about all that great stuff I've been sending— Wait, um, Merrie: don't tell me you're going to name the baby after a number!"

She laughs. "Don't freak out. We always nickname our kids after the election years in which they're born—until the polls for preferred names come back. We won't have the final count for this little guy until next week, but as of an hour ago, Matthew is leading over Mark. But get a load of this: Matthias is a close third, and the pollsters think that the Fundamentalists are going to rally—"

I squint at the clock. "Merrie, it's not even six here. Is there a point to your call?"

"I need you here with me, as soon as possible! The interview is in three days—on Friday. I can't have the reporter see how unprepared I am for little Twelve. All the other congressional wives have such cute little nurseries already set up. Of course, none of them have a twelve-year-old daughter who sexts her boyfriend topless photos, or an eight-year-old son who sneaks into her closet and tries on her heels." She sighs. "Hell, two of these women have never had kids before. So you see what I'm up against here. Look, I'll make it worth your while. What's your day rate?"

Suddenly I'm wide awake. Since last week, when *Time* magazine touted me as "a cross between Dr. Spock, Mary Poppins, and the *Good Housekeeping* Seal of Approval," Alex has been riding me to triple any figure that comes into my head.

At first I envision one hundred, then two hundred—

"It's a thousand dollars." I hold my breath . . .

"No problem. I'm sure there's some PAC we can squeeze to offset your expense." She muffles the phone receiver, but I can still hear her as she hollers out: "Edie! Go see what kind of contribution the WASPS are making next month! No, not the DAR! I mean Women About Stable Parenting Skills . . . Great, that works." Her voice booms through the receiver. "Katie, check your e-mail for your flight's confirmation number. You'll leave tomorrow. I'll need you for all three days. We've got to brainstorm something that moves me to the front of the pack."

"I'm on it, chief."

When I hang up the phone, Alex gives me a thumbs-up. "Love it when you say 'I'm on it.'"

"No, you love it when I charge a thousand dollars a day."

"That was *per day*? Damn! You're right!" He points down toward his hips. The sheet is now raised seven inches above them.

I'm not ovulating, but that doesn't matter.

8:14 a.m., Tuesday, 8 May

MY FLIGHT to DC is full. I'm sitting between two businessmen who, like me, have been clacking away on their computers for the last two hours, without exchanging a word. I guess we're in for another three and a half hours of peace and quiet—

Or maybe not. The baby in the seat in front of us has started to wail at the top of her lungs.

"Ah, hell," grumbles Window Seat. "I guess the rest of the trip will be like this."

Aisle Seat, who is wearing earbuds, is oblivious to it all—until the baby's brother, a preschooler, reclines his seat all the way back, and Aisle's scotch rocks tipples into his lap. Aisle stands up and jerks the seat of the toddler's mother to get her attention. "Damn it, lady! Can't you keep your kids under control?"

It is an involuntary reaction to look at wrecks, particularly the emotional ones. I crane my neck to see this mother's reaction.

As I suspected, she is close to tears.

The innocent passenger crammed in the window seat beside Mom with squalling baby cringes in embarrassment. Any doubts he may have had that he'd been awarded the seat assignment from hell just went out that window.

He probably wishes he could have gone with it.

I give him a smile. "How would you like to exchange seats?"

The heads on Window and Aisle swivel toward me, as if I'm some kind of otherworldly apparition. I'm sure Aisle is wishing his scotch were holy water.

But to Mom's unlucky seat mate, I am a saint.

The shuffle is quick. The last time I saw someone move that fast was during the Bay to Breakers race.

Today I'm paying it forward.

I motion for Mom to sit next to the window. "Thank you, thank you, thank you," she murmurs, as she settles her son between us. "I thought we'd be late for the flight. We ran out the door and left Tommy's plane toys in his room. He's been so bored! But it's been hard to give both him and the baby the attention they need."

I nod. "I've got an idea." I turn to Tommy. "How would you like to play I Spy with me?" I ask him.

First he looks at his mother, then he nods shyly.

I take the in-flight magazine from the seat pocket and open it to a beautiful picture of a beach. It's an easy half hour of fun and games for him to spot the items I call out. We keep score on a tiny pad that I've pulled from my valise.

Now that there is another woman sharing her row, Tommy's mom feels free to nurse her baby, as opposed to trying to get her to suckle the plastic nipple of the bottle with her mother's expressed milk. Another hour of Tommy's time is occupied with my iPad, which is loaded with games for Jezebel, Mario, and Max.

When the little guy finally falls asleep, I get back to my work: eventually I feel the mother's eyes on me. When I turn toward her, she whispers, "Are you flying for business, or pleasure?"

"Business. I've got a client in DC who needs me right now."

She nods and sighs. "Yeah, I remember those days. I thought I'd never give them up. Even worked part-time after Tommy was born. But I made the decision not to go back to work after Britanny's birth. Frankly I don't miss the grind. Watching them grow up is why you have kids in the first place, isn't it?"

My answer to her is a low chuckle. "I know what you mean. In my case I truly love what I do, so it all works out."

She nods. "That helps, particularly if you have to travel away from your family. I can tell you're a wonderful mom. I'll just bet your kids are missing you right now."

I start to correct her, then think better of it. We are strangers whose paths will only cross once. For a few hours more I can pretend to be someone I desperately want to be, but am not.

5:14 p.m. (EST)

MERRIE AND Mike Lovejoy's home-away-from-home is an ivy-covered historic brick Queen Anne mansion on one of the prim tree-lined lanes wedged between M and Wisconsin streets, in Georgetown. Not only is it large enough to hold their current brood of three—twelve-year-old Mallory, eight-year-old Mike Junior, and four-year-old Michelle—and the au pair, April, who watches over them, it also has room for a fabulous nursery as well.

As I'd suspected, Merrie has done virtually nothing with it. There isn't any furniture at all, and all the cartons of baby gear, toys, and clothing that I've mailed to her over the past three months are stacked against a wall.

Granted, she has valid excuses: she's been crisscrossing the country with the kids while campaigning with Mike in California. While at the same time, she's been checking out new schools for Mallory and Mike Junior in DC.

"If he wants to run again, it better be for the Senate," she huffs and puffs through her baby weight. "That way we'll have five years between campaigns." She looks at the clock. "We still have time to make it over to Pottery Barn Kids, if you want to look at the dressers and cribs," she says.

"Nope, that's no longer on the agenda."

"What do you mean?" Merrie's eyes narrow in concern. "Don't tell me that too many of their pieces are made overseas!"

"You said you wanted an edge over the other congressional moms, right?" I smile. "Well, what do you say we go over to Goodwill instead?"

Merrie is so shocked at my suggestion that she almost misses the chair that's supposed to catch her. "What am I supposed to do there, distribute alms for the poor?"

"No. That's where we're meeting the decorator who is commissioned to help us put together the nursery. She's already selected some really nice items for the room. From there, we'll go over to the Salvation Army—"

"Are you crazy? Katie, look around you!" She throws open her arms. "Does this place look like some sort of halfway house? That side table over there is pre–Revolutionary War. This chair I'm sitting in was once owned by Dolly and James Madison. Why, pray tell, would I want to go slumming?"

"Why? Because that's where Middle America shops when it's out of a job, Merrie. And right now the biggest issue in your husband's congressional district is unemployment. By finding some treasures on the cheap and using them for the most precious person in your life—your new baby—you'll be showing your constituents that this is not a time for conspicuous consumption, and that you empathize with their real-life concerns."

"Katie, that's sheer lunacy . . . and sheer genius."

"Thanks for the compliment—I think. But that's just half the scheme. The items we choose today will be brought into your basement, where a videographer will shoot digital footage of you and the kids sprucing up the pieces, and we'll put it up on YouTube: you know, painting them, glue-gunning some new cloth over an old lampshade, fixing the seat of a wicker rocking chair, tatting up some cute pillows. A fun arts and crafts project for the whole family."

"Perfect! I'll be the Martha Stewart of congressional wives. Talk about great coverage." Merrie jumps out of the chair, energized. "Okay, let's get on over there pronto. Edie! *Edie!* Call our driver. Now, Katie, I presume the decorator will have time to have the pieces fumigated before she brings them into the basement, right? . . . Oh, don't give me that look . . ."

7:33 p.m., Wednesday, 9 May

WHILE THE videographer is putting Merrie and the kids through their paces, I've decided to sort the baby clothes I've sent and that were never opened.

I drag some of the boxes into the nursery's large walk-in closet. Until the freshly painted dresser dries, I can fold some of the onesies and sweaters and put them in the closet's built-in cabinets.

As is the case in many old homes, the closet door is heavy—it's the original, I'm guessing—and it won't stay open, not even when I try propping it up with a box of toys. It's a cool late summer evening and there is a light in the closet, so it's not like I mind—

The giggle and the loud "Shhhhhh!" tips me off that I'm not alone. When I push open the door I see Congressman Michael Lovejoy feeling up the au pair, April, against the nursery wall.

Is this a rape?

Should I scream?

When April unzips the congressman's pants and drops to her knees, I get the answer to the first question.

My shock eliminates the ability to act on the second.

I close my eyes, but I forget to cover my ears, which is why I hear him groan when he comes. Without thinking I open my eyes just as he leans against the wall to catch his breath, then lifts her off the floor in order to smother her in kisses.

They freeze when they hear the sounds of his children running out into the yard. Mike peeks out into the nursery door, then gives April a pat on the butt that has her scurrying down the hall. He zips up his pants and tucks in his shirt before heading off in the opposite direction.

Now it's my turn to groan.

3:22 p.m., Friday, 11 May

MERRIE'S INTERVIEW goes beautifully. The nursery is in perfect order, just in time for the reporter's grand tour. As an added touch, she allows the children to point out their handiwork, which they do with unfeigned pride. While her photographer takes the photos that showcase the nursery's twenty-four-hour transformation by the decorator, her staff, and me, the reporter lets it slip that she wants to lead with Merrie's interview. "Your take on motherhood is so much more compelling than the others," she gushes.

After she has ushered them out the door, Merrie leans against it with a sigh. "Damn, I can't wait for this pregnancy to be over so that I can have a drink again." She looks over at me and smiles. "And no lectures on nursing, okay?"

Yeah, okay. We got bigger issues to discuss . . .

I have four hours before my flight: plenty of time to break the news to Merrie that her husband is having an affair with her au pair.

I start by closing the door to her dainty pink office. "Merrie, the other day when I was getting the nursery closet in order, I had a couple of visitors."

"You mean ghosts? I don't doubt it. Did you know that Aaron Burr lived in this house? The kids claim the place is haunted. Then again, they'd do anything to get us to move home once and for all."

If a scandal breaks, they may get their wish.

"No, it wasn't ghosts . . . Listen, I don't know how to say this, so I'll just come right out with it: I guess Mike thought no one was in the nursery. He and—and April . . . Merrie, I caught them in—in an uncompromising position."

The grin on Merrie's face fades slowly. She opens her mouth, but no words come out.

They aren't needed. The sorrow in her eyes says it all: her husband has betrayed her. She is carrying his child. They are very public figures . . .

There is nothing more for me to say, either. I'm sure there is nothing right now that she wants to hear.

Instead, I walk over to her and put my arm around her shoulder—

But she shoves it off. Her smile is etched in stone. The tears in her eyes make them glitter like sapphires. "You're wrong."

"No, I wish that were the case, but—"

"But what?" Merrie shakes her head in disbelief. "Listen, I really like you a lot. But I'm going to level with you: *whatever you thought you saw just didn't happen.*"

"Oh . . . kay." She wants me to buy into her denial. Sure. Whatever.

"Wait—" She waddles behind the desk and opens the drawer, where she pulls out a checkbook. She writes one check, then another. "Here is your fee for the project this week. And this second check—it's to cover your services for the next three years."

"Three years? I don't understand! Are you having another baby?"

"No, of course not! That asshole is never touching me again. The way I feel now, no other man will, either." She stiffens her back, but she won't look at me. "Consider this a severance check."

She motions my dismissal with a wave of her hand.

Ah, so that's it: shoot the messenger.

I am almost at the door when she adds, "Oh, and Katie, I don't have to remind you that you signed a confidentiality agreement. Should you breach that with any lies or innuendo that besmirches either of us, you'll be sued into the ground. I'll—*we'll* make your life miserable."

I stop and turn around. "Merrie, I'm not a threat to you. I guess in your world it's hard to know who's really on your side."

Before she can wipe them away, her tears drop onto her checkbook. "If a politician's wife knows anything, it's that money can buy you a hell of a lot of friends. Our husbands are proof of that."

23

....

There are three reasons for breast-feeding:
the milk is always at the right temperature;
it comes in attractive containers; and the cat can't get it.
—*Irena Chalmers*

8:14 p.m., Saturday, 19 May

IT IS SUNSET. Dinner at Lana's has ended with scoops of gelato for all. Jezzy, decked out in fairywear—a velour tutu skirted in a puff of tulle dusted with sequins—has nodded off on Auggie's lap. The tender nylon wings of her costume are crushed between her father's chest and her halo of strawberry curls.

Jezzy's cousins are also incognito. Mario is in full Batman regalia, including the stiff-eared headgear, whereas little brother Max is his sidekick, Robin, except for the mask. He won't come out and say it, but I know he finds the eyeholes uncomfortable. Besides, if he wears it, how will anyone know it's him?

He has yet to learn that some of us don't need costumes in order to hide our true selves.

Jezzy may have pooped out, but the boys have one more burst of energy left in them. I could help Grace and Lana clear the table, but I'd much prefer my We Time with my little nephews, leaving the men folk to grouse about the start of another lousy season for the 49ers.

With the bees now off sleeping in their hives, Max, Mario, and I are free to indulge in harvesting sweet drops of honeysuckle without the boys swatting at everything in fear for their lives.

At six, Mario is old enough to grasp the concept. Max, on

the other hand, yanks the blossoms off the vine by the fistful, ripping them in half. He then sucks on them, only to spit them out. As he eyes his brother jealously, his brow dips along with his pouting lips. "Aunt Katie, none of mine have honey drops!" Max proclaims, and holds up the carnage he has created as proof. "Can I have Mario's? Please? *Please?*"

Mario's eyes narrow at his brother's suggestion. He then shifts his gaze to me, seemingly anxious as to whether I'll acquiesce to the bane of his young existence.

I wink at him even as I shake my head at Max. "Maxie, guess what? Yours have the honey drops in them, too! What if I teach you the secret of finding them?"

He nods slowly, as if uncertain that this could ever be possible. I smile and take his small hand in mine. "Snip it gently now," I murmur in his ear while positioning his forefinger and thumb at the bottom of the flower's neck. He nods and obeys, then gasps when he realizes he is actually pulling the long stamen through the funnel of the small flower. But before it is all the way out of the flower—

"Quick, Max, hold it up to your mouth," shouts Mario.

Max raises his hand just in time to catch the solitary drop, and eyes open wide as his tongue extends to greet this new taste sensation. After a gulp, his face lights up. "Yeah, Aunt Katie I did it! 'Nother, please, please!"

I am just about to pinch another blossom loose when I feel Alex's hand stop mine. He lifts it to his lips for a gentle kiss. "What a good aunt you are."

I smile up at him. "Thank you, my sweet. But as in all things, practice makes perfect."

He winces, then says in a voice loud enough for Thor and Auggie to hear, "I'm glad you feel that way, honey, because I've got some great news. Peter is coming into town next weekend. He'll be staying with us."

"What? When—" Yes, I'm shocked by Alex's pronouncement. "How did this come about?"

"Who's Peter?" Max is suddenly suspicious. He barely tolerates sharing me with Mario and Jezebel.

I squeeze him tightly and quickly and he's all smiles again. He needs no more proof that he is a very bright star in my galaxy.

"I heard from my ex, via e-mail." Alex examines the honeysuckle bloom in his hand. "She and her—her *boyfriend* are coming to town, on business. They'll have Peter with them, and she's agreed to his staying with us—if you'll agree to it, too."

"Yes, of course! Alex that's—that's wonderful!" I still can't believe my ears.

Apparently neither can my sisters and their husbands, all of whom look just as dumbfounded as I feel.

"Wow, Alex, that's fabulous," murmurs Grace uncertainly. Then a smile lights up her face, its fullness a reflection of her fifth month of pregnancy. "We can't wait to meet him, too. There's so much fun stuff to show him: the Exploratorium, the California Academy of Sciences—"

"We'll get tickets to Cirque du Soleil," Lana interjects. "And take him on the ferry, maybe to Angel Island for a picnic!"

I know what they are doing: they want Alex to see that Peter fits right in with the rest of us.

With me.

That he has family who will love him unconditionally: sight unseen, no holds barred.

That there is, and will always be, room for Peter here, in our lives.

So that Alex will see that there is room for other children as well.

Alex's eyes glass over. To hide this fact, he reaches for his beer mug and takes a swig.

I put my arms around his waist and give him a squeeze. "When are you picking him up?"

"You mean when are *we* picking him up, don't you? Noon, next Saturday. They're staying on Nob Hill, at the Ritz-Carlton. His mother suggested that we grab a bite together at the hotel before going our separate ways."

He can't even bring himself to say her name.

"That's . . . nice." I try to sound upbeat, but now I'm wondering if I have to pass muster before Willemina turns over her precious cargo to Alex.

"You don't sound too happy. I thought this is what you wanted, for us to spend time with him, together."

"It's exactly what I want. It's just that—" Of course I can't tell him what I think, so instead I say, "If we're getting him midafternoon, that cuts down on all we can do over the weekend. I guess we can squeeze in a lot, even in a day and a half."

He gives me a quizzical look. "What makes you say that? We're to have him for a full week." Noting my gasp, he mutters low, so our nephews can't hear him: "Don't you get it? She's dumping him so that she has time with her boyfriend." His insincere laugh makes me wince. "But who am I to give a shit? Full-court press, baby, full-court press! Let's just make it so that Peter never wants to leave, ever again."

Yes, let's. That way, you'll see what we are missing.

With Peter, we will be complete . . .

10:06 a.m., Saturday, 26 May

THE MAKING Mommies Smile meet-ups are weekly now. They've gotten so big that I've had to cap the guest list at fifty. I've gotten smart and charge five dollars a head for babysitting.

I now hire at least four sitters, what with all the little ones who come with their moms.

No, I don't use Emma. She avoids me like the plague.

This one is being held on a Saturday. I've dubbed this meeting "The Breast Pump Round-up" because we'll be comparing six of the most popular pumps on the market. Our first step is to demonstrate the right way to pump, then to discuss the best time to pump (in the morning) and why.

Twenty of the mothers who are still nursing had volunteered to quality-test all six pumps, and received them as swag a month ago. After the demonstration, there will be a discussion as to which worked best, and why. Then the women will rank the pumps from one (the best) to six (the worst).

I roam through the crowd, saying my hellos. Both Lana and Grace are here, as is Joanna. I'm surprised to see that Elizabeth and Ophelia are here, too. For obvious reasons, Elizabeth won't be breast-feeding, and I know for a fact that their surrogate contract calls for Elizabeth and Ophelia to part ways on the day of the baby's birth.

Still, it's a good sign that they decided to come together. The therapist I recommended to them, who specializes in postpartum depression, must have them working through some of the issues that stand between them.

I also notice Ophelia's plate is filled with many of the healthy snacks that were prepared by our guest nutritionist, as opposed to the cupcakes and cookies also laid out. Although her belly is bigger, the rest of her is toned: her arms and legs are slimmer than when I last saw her. Elizabeth had mentioned that Ophelia actually looks forward to her three-times-a-week sessions with a prenatal personal trainer.

Things must be turning around for her because the smile she gives me is genuine.

This time Carolyn was able to make it, too. Her husband, Gordon, drove her over and walked in with her, but quickly begged off when he saw one of the women whip out her breast in order to accommodate her hungry infant. He's now waiting in the car out front.

I'm also happy to see that Twila is here. She walks over and gives me a big hug. "Hey, guess what, I've already got an offer on my place!"

I laugh. "Oh, I believe it. Anyone who sees that closet would want it."

"Yeah, you're right. That's what did it. That, and the Realtor shoving the rest of my real life into a temporary storage unit, so that it didn't look so cluttered. Heck, it's so pretty now that I wish I could stay there."

She pauses, as if seeking my approval for this seemingly innocent remark.

Well, she's not going to get it. "We're moving forward, not backward, remember?" I hope I sound gentle but firm.

"Yes, yes, you're right, of course. Well, the closing is Monday. Then I'm homeless. Can I couch surf with you?"

That makes me laugh out loud. I can just see the look on Alex's face, should one of my pregnant clients move in with us. It would be priceless.

"You'll find a great place in no time. And when we get done with it, you'll have a fabulous nursery to boot. It's what you deserve, Twila. And so does your baby."

"That's what I keep telling myself." Her tone is light, but I know she means what she says. "In fact, I have my eye on a little place in Noe Valley. Two bedrooms, a bath and a half. Cute and cozy. I put an offer in on it yesterday, so we'll know tomorrow."

"Perfect!" I give her a thumbs-up. "I'm at your disposal to help set it up, and to do a baby-proof walk-through. Just give me the hi sign. Hey, will you need help moving in?"

Of all my clients, she is my favorite, maybe because of what we have in common. Besides, it's not as if she has a lot of friends right now. Her oblivious coworkers may think she is putting on pounds, but no one has dared to consider that she might be pregnant. I'm sure I can coerce Alex to lift a few boxes. And perhaps Lana, Thor, and Auggie, too, if Grace will watch the boys.

"Nope, got that covered. Starving Students will be my brawn. Besides, I have so little that I'm sure it'll fit into the smallest truck they've got." She glows with satisfaction. "It's adorable. And the baby's room faces the backyard. It's as tiny as a postage stamp, but I think I can fit in a swing set. Should they accept my offer, I'll want you to come by and pull together the nursery, as soon as possible."

"I'm there for you. Just give me a call." I watch as Twila's eyes move toward the door—

Ah, I see why. Seth has just walked in. He's got Sadie around his neck. She squeals with laughter when she sees the playroom: something she knows well, from that very first meet-up, which she attended with Fanny.

Seth glances around the room. Unlike Carolyn's husband, Gordon, he doesn't seem at all uncomfortable in a room full of women, most of whom are pregnant. Spotting me, he makes his way over. He gives Twila a polite nod before squeezing my shoulder. "You see? I've made good on my promise."

I laugh. "Yeah, well, you should certainly get a kick out of this meet-up. Our topic is breast-feeding."

Twila and I watch as his face falls. "Oh . . . okay then, maybe I should skip this one." Seth looks down at his chest. "It's not like I've got the right equipment for it—"

Twila sputters out a giggle.

Suddenly I realize that they've never met. "Oh, I'm sorry! I should introduce you two. Twila Rappaport, this is another one of my clients, Seth Harris."

As Seth reaches out to shake her hand, Sadie yanks hard on his hair. I grab her from around his neck and bounce her on my hip. It feels so natural. "Twila works in high tech, too, Seth. Over at UniVamp."

He laughs. "I imagine it's a Wild West show over there. Those guys are always one step ahead. Do you design, or are you an animator?"

She smiles proudly. "I lead the design team."

"Interesting." He raises a brow. "Then you must know Adam Anders. He's in design over there, too, isn't he?"

The way she wrinkles her nose her smile loses its impact. "Unfortunately, yes . . ."

Their talk segues into technical jargon. I smile and feign interest, but if I'm to be honest with myself, I feel left out.

Without thinking, Seth reaches for his daughter. Reluctantly I hand Sadie over. Immediately I miss her soft, warm flesh against mine, and her smell of talcum powder and baby shampoo.

Mostly I'll miss the attention she pays me when she's in my arms, the way she pats my cheeks, to make sure I'm real.

And yes, I miss the attention Seth pays me when I hold her.

Not that he's paying me much attention at the moment. He is caught up in Twila's glow.

Abby nudges me. "Shouldn't we start?"

I shrug in agreement, then put on my game show hostess face. "Places, everyone! And welcome! It's fun to have you here, at this month's Making Mommies Smile meet-up!" I feign my own smile for the camera. "Today we'll be talking about breast pumps! Does yours suck?" (Pause for the inevitable whoops and giggles.) "Ha! Thought so! Yeah, okay, I'm milking this for a few laughs. All kidding aside, some of my wonderful mommy testers will be giving you the scoop on a few that don't. Let's start with Jeanne Huston, who is joining us all the way from Sacramento. Jeanne, which feels the most natural? Let's talk about your favorite of our six test models, and why . . ."

DESPITE THE topic at hand, Seth has been able to hang in here for the whole meet-up. Every now and then I glance over at him—or, I should say, at *them*. He pretends to be interested in the demonstration, but his asides are directed at Twila, who is quick with a smile if she doesn't outright laugh.

At what, Jeanne's pumping technique? Really, she should be paying better attention . . .

Halfway through the demonstration, I notice that Twila has ended up with Sadie on her lap. It throws me for a loop, and I say the wrong thing: *hump* instead of *pump*.

Seth laughs the loudest at my faux pas, and that embarrasses me even more.

When, finally, the demo is over, the women mingle for a few more minutes over the food table before collecting their children and heading for the door.

Twila and Seth stroll out together, deep in conversation.

"They make a cute couple, don't they?" asks Grace as she comes up beside me. "Hey, you should try setting them up."

She's right. It's the perfect answer to my concern for Seth.

And for that matter, my worries about Twila.

So, why does it make me sad?

"—and Mom are coming up tomorrow. Lana heard from them. Seems that his doctors have referred him to a specialist who can run some tests—"

"Wait, stop. What did you say? Something's wrong with Dad?"

Grace shrugs. "His doctors thought he had a detached retina. Turns out it may have been caused by a rare disorder. They suspect he's got something called Von Hippel–Lindau disease.

Sounds very serious: it causes tumors to pop up all over his body. Right now they think there's one behind Dad's left eye. If it's too late to remove the tumor—well, it may leave him blind." Her nervous cough belies her concern. "Lana's been researching it. Are you ready for this? It's genetic. If Dad is an affected carrier, that means one or more of us may be as well." She looks down at her growing belly. "I have to admit, I'm somewhat concerned. I've asked Auggie to talk to some of his physician pals there at Stanford. You know, so that we get the fuller picture and can discuss our options."

I can't imagine my father without his sight. That means he won't be able to watch his grandchildren grow up.

If I'm so blessed to have my own, he may never see my child.

I shake off that thought. I'm going to think positive. "Okay, well, if they're coming up, I guess we'll all have dinner next week. Do you guys want to come over to our place this time?"

Grace laughs hysterically.

"What the hell's so funny?"

"Oh, you know how it is. Alex springs up like a jack-in-the-box anytime one of the kids gets near any of your art pieces."

She's right, and I know it. He once made a flying leap over Mario in order to protect a beloved Sisley from my nephew's peanut-butter-and-jelly-covered fingers.

"I guess you're right. Then your place?"

"Nope. Lana's. I want to hold off having the boys over, considering I've just painted the baby's room. Remember?" She frowns. "Oh, what am I saying? Of course you wouldn't. You've been too busy with your other clients . . . Don't look so hurt! I'm teasing you. Seriously, my only regret is that I didn't work out a referral deal with you when I had the chance. All those women we speak to . . . Ah, well, at least I can always say I knew you when."

24

....

I feel sure that unborn babies pick their parents.
—*Gloria Swanson*

8:13 a.m., Friday, 1 June

ALEX IS ON pins and needles. Tomorrow is the big day.

I tell him to calm down, take a deep breath. "Seriously, what can go wrong? I'm sure he's just as excited to see you as you are to see him."

"Yeah, yeah, I guess you're right. It's why I love you so much. You're always the calm in the center of the storm."

If only that were true. Right now I'm sweating a lot of things. My father's illness. Peter's reaction to me.

And of course I'm wondering why I'm not pregnant yet.

But I have to stay Zen for Alex.

For *us.*

9:40 a.m.

"HELLO, MAY I speak to Katie Johnson?"

"This is she."

"My name is Evan Gold. I work for EnviroBest. I was wondering if you'd be interested in endorsing a product of ours. It's called Happy Hemp."

I freeze. This guy has *got* to be kidding. "What exactly does endorsement entail, Mr. Gold?"

"You know, chatting up the product with your clients and viewers. Mentioning some of its unique features—"

"You mean, like its leakage factor?"

I don't hear anything. Did the line go dead?

"Pardon me? I guess I don't know what you're asking."

"Mr. Gold, I'm trying to ascertain if your diapers leak, and in what capacity."

"Well . . . I wouldn't know about that." There is a suspicious edge to his voice.

As there should be. "If I were to endorse your product—*anyone's* product, really—I would have to test that product first. Are you willing to allow me to do so?"

"I think you've got it wrong. We want to offer you an endorsement fee—"

"No, I think *you've* got it wrong. The reason we have such great traffic to our site, Mr. Gold, is because we don't endorse a product unless it's been tested first, by our mommy panel. Now, if you're willing to provide sample boxes of your diapers to twenty of our moms—"

"Yeah, sure, no problem! And they'll all comment on how great they are?"

Does he hear me snicker?

Do I care? "That depends, Mr. Gold, on how well they stand up to the testing."

"Oh." He sounds disappointed.

Gee, I wonder why.

"Okay, then how about a simple Twitter campaign? You know, where they all just mention the product for a chance to win a—"

I hang up the phone.

Yes, I'll admit that felt good.

Making Mommies Smile is the one consistently honest thing in my life.

12:33 p.m., Saturday, 2 June

PETER IS angry at all of us: Willemina, Alex, and especially me.

He ignores everything his mother tells him, leaving her to mutter what I presume are threats under her breath to him in her native language, Dutch.

He doesn't scare easy. This is proven when he refuses to go up to Alex and give him a hug, despite Willemina cooing in Peter's ear as she nudges him toward his father, and in spite of the broad, welcoming smile that refuses to leave Alex's face.

Me, he won't acknowledge at all.

I'm not surprised. My guess is that it has a lot to do with Willemina's demeanor. Although he bent down toward her, she did not even deem Alex worthy of an air kiss, settling instead on a stiff nod that left him crouched in an awkward position. Yes, she smiled as she stuck out her hand in order to shake mine, but did Peter pick up on how lightly she touched it before pulling away, as if I were infectious? I'm guessing yes. And the way in which she shoves Bastiaan Van Acker, her boyfriend, forward toward us like a human shield is certainly a telltale sign that it's painful for her to be in our presence.

Bastiaan shakes his head in sympathy. With us, oddly enough.

It freaks me out how much he resembles Alex: tall, golden-haired, with those sad blue eyes. I can tell that Alex has picked up on this, too, because he is still sizing him up, as if Bastiaan is his competition.

Competition for what?

"Shall we?" asks Willemina. She points to the entrance of the hotel's restaurant. We nod and follow her lead. In looks, Willemina is the opposite of me: fair to the point of being pale, she is tall and regally aloof. Though she is dressed casually, there is a formality to her ensemble, which includes a fitted couture jacket and slacks, and very expensive shoes.

Aw, hell, why did I choose to wear jeans, just because it was a Saturday and we'll be playing with a ten-year-old boy?

Of course, I never expected to be intimidated like this.

At least Bastiaan doesn't think I have cooties. Graciously, he takes her elbow in one hand and mine in the other, leaving Peter in the care of his father.

But the mere touch of Alex's hand on Peter's head has the boy scurrying out of reach.

I could cry for Alex. He doesn't deserve this.

1:12 p.m.

OUR MEAL here at the Ritz is superb, but I wouldn't know it.

I am too caught up in the family drama being played out before me.

The two leads seem to have gotten different scripts. Alex, for one, is trying hard to fill the role of congenial host. He does this with interesting asides to the adults, and friendly winks to his son. The other, Peter, might as well be in a silent horror film. Either he ignores his father completely, or he shudders when he hears his father say his name. Despite the fact that our opulent banquette is very large, Peter is practically sitting in his mother's lap on the far end of the table. This makes it all the more obvious that he wants to stay as far away from us as possible.

When he speaks, he only addresses his mother, and in Dutch, despite his fluency in English.

Doesn't it bother Willemina that he is stabbing the fine linen tablecloth with his fork?

No. She ignores his behavior completely.

I feel as if I'm in the only bad Bergman film ever made.

The secondary leads in this tragedy are just as lost. Any attempt toward small talk by Alex's ex leaves a lot to be desired. "It is even colder here than I remember," murmurs Willemina. "Just one more thing I've always disliked about San Francisco."

Alex's back stiffens at the oft-heard criticism of his hometown.

Bastiaan's belly laugh does nothing to defuse the tension. "Well, then I guess it is a good thing that we will be spending most of our time here in the wine country, ja?"

On that note, I take a gulp of my wine in a mock toast. "What do you do, Bastiaan?"

"International investments, for Danske Bank Group. My company has some investments in Northern California, so I thought that Willemina and I could combine business with a little pleasure." He takes hold of Willemina's hand and grazes her knuckles with his lips. She colors slightly and her smile is faint, but there is no doubt to anyone at the table that she enjoyed it.

Apparently Peter is dismayed by Bastiaan's small act of intimacy. He turns over his glass and a churning white river of milk flows downstream: over the edge of the table, and onto Alex's lap.

"Aw, damn it," Alex mutters as he scoots back, but it's too late. The front of his khakis are now soaked with what will soon be the souring scent of slow-drying milk.

Peter slumps down in his seat, as if he's been slapped by the reality of his father's anger. Whatever Willemina is growling at him in Dutch has absolutely no effect. He is whimpering like a lost puppy.

Alex stares at his son. There is no anger in his eyes, only despair. I think it has dawned on him that his worst nightmare has come true:

His son no longer feels any connection to him.

Without another word, he heads off in the direction of the lavatory, leaving me to clean up the mess at the table. My large cloth napkin doesn't cover it, nor does his.

Peter watches my hands intently. When he thinks I don't see him, he glances at my face. I catch him looking at me and say, "It's okay. It was an accident. Your father isn't really mad."

Although he is looking straight at me, he addresses his mother, in perfect English: "Mother, the whore talked to me. Should I say something back?"

No one answers him. Even Willemina is too stunned to do so.

Finally she answers her son: "Darling, this one is not the whore. This one is your father's wife. While you are with them, you must treat her with respect."

I may be speechless, but not Bastiaan. He shakes his head at Peter's audacity and Willemina's directness with her son, but there is still a wry smile on his lips. He leans over toward me, as if we're sharing a private joke. "Don't blame the boy. He was too young when Alex left them. Of course all he remembers is his mother's pain."

"What are you talking about? She left Alex, not the other way around."

He blinks his disbelief. At first he opens his mouth to say something, but then chooses to study his dessert menu instead.

Alex comes back just in time. He doesn't argue when Willemina makes some excuse to keep the boy with them on their trip, as opposed to leaving him with us.

He just shrugs. "Sure, whatever."

I can't believe my ears! So, he is giving up his shot to reconnect with Peter, over a glass of spilled milk?

With a glassy smile, he reaches out for the boy's shoulder, but instead takes the boy's limp hand in his and shakes it gently.

Then he walks away.

Relief lightens Willemina's eyes.

Peter just looks away.

I wonder what he's thinking about his father. I already know what he thinks about me.

I STUMBLE after Alex, but he's moving so fast that I don't catch up to him until he's already reached the car. "Alex, wait! What happened to 'full-court press, baby'? You said we'd have a whole week with Peter! The spilled milk was an accident. Please, don't throw away this chance to be with your son. It may be the last one you get for a very long time—"

He answers without turning to me. "It's over. The kid hates me. He thinks I abandoned him, and nothing I can do will ever change that."

"Just tell him the truth! Tell him how frantic you were, that day she stole him from you! Tell him how it broke your heart. Then explain to him how you had to track her down, and how you petitioned to have him returned to you—"

"I can't do that, Katie!"

"Of course you can. He needs to hear all of that and more from you!" I grab his hand and attempt to pull him back with me.

Alex wrenches his arm away from me. Shocked, I turn to face him, but he won't even look at me.

Instead, he looks down at the ground. "Damn it, Katie, I can't! I can't because—*because it would be a lie.*"

"What do you mean? It's not a lie. I was there—"

"No, you weren't, Katie! You . . . weren't." Tears of shame rim his eyes. "Yeah, sure, on that day we met, I was out of my mind because she'd tricked me! But after they explained all the hoops they wanted to put me through—petitioning our consulate over there for joint custody, the waiting games, that it would

end in some bullshit mediation sessions, with no way to enforce
my rights—it's just bureaucratic busywork. Screw that! I
manned up, let it go. Life goes on, right?"

His shoulders square as he lifts his head. No more pretending. The truth has set him free.

My dry whisper comes out as a quiver. "But Alex, he's your
son."

He shrugs. His confession was a catharsis. It has released
him of any obligation for further pretense regarding the issue of
Peter.

I realize this as I hear him say, "Katie, face it: some of us
aren't cut out to be parents."

He may be speaking for himself, but he is certainly not
speaking for *me*.

Deep down in my heart I know he'll change his mind when
it's our child together.

The sooner the better, so I'll no longer feel guilty about
pricking his condoms.

If he truly wants to be honest with me, now is the time.
"You lied to me, Alex. Willemina said you left Peter and her for
another woman, not the other way around."

He doesn't react. He is so much in control of his emotions
that he doesn't even glance over at me.

We drive in silence as we head west along California, dart-
ing around a tourist-packed cable car. When we cross Van Ness,
he finally speaks. It's not an answer, but a dare:

"Who do you believe, Willemina or me?"

Does it matter? No, of course not. Because I love him, even
if I don't believe him.

Besides, once I'm pregnant, there'll be nothing he can do
about it.

25

....

A man loves his sweetheart the most,
his wife the best, but his mother the longest.
—Irish Proverb

6:15 p.m., Friday, 8 June

"TWILA THINKS YOU'RE cute."

There, I've said it.

Seth looks up at me. By the way his eyes have narrowed, I know he's suspicious.

So that I don't blow this, I look back down at the list of dad-and-child meet-up groups I've brought with me, as if it's going to be a hard decision choosing between the one called Badass Dads (extreme posturing), another called Spirited Dads (meditation with your little one), and the one called Make Room for Daddy.

Then again, we're talking about Seth here, so it's a toss-up.

"Really? What did Twila say?"

How should I answer him? I haven't talked to her because I don't want to get her hopes up. After the fiasco at Kara Kischell's single-parent meet-up, my guess is that Seth will say thank you but no thank you.

I notice that Fanny has quit ironing in order to eavesdrop. Unfortunately, she's put the iron facedown on Seth's only dress shirt, which he had planned to wear to the S&M party tomorrow night. Even gawking at her doesn't get her attention at first. The smell of scorched cotton finally catches her attention, and Seth's.

"It will make a great dusting rag," Fanny says apologetically.

He rolls his eyes at me, then winks. "So, what?"

"You mean, you don't care about the shirt?"

"No, I mean, so what should I do regarding Twila? Should I call her or something?"

So he is *interested . . .*

"Sure . . . I mean, if you're interested, too."

He lets that sink in. "I guess I won't know if I don't call," he says, but he's not smiling.

"Then you should call." I mean that.

I think.

2:12 p.m., Saturday, 9 June

IT'S A beautiful day along the Marina. Grace and Lana have brought the kids over to fly kites. Afterward we'll walk over to All Star on Chestnut Street for some hot glazed donuts.

Mario's kite is a dragon. Max's is a dog with floppy ears. Jezebel's is a colorful kitten. The strings are long enough for the kites to catch the wind, but short enough that the children can still maneuver the kites on their own.

That's a good thing, because Lana is distracted with dire thoughts about Dad's tests, which take place late next week.

"If he tests positive for that disease—you know, that Von Hippel–Lindau thing—Mom is going to be very upset. She'll definitely need our help. We've got to prepare for that." Although the kids are a few yards away and much too young to know what we're talking about, Lana is speaking in whispers anyway. "What did Auggie find out about it?"

Grace frowns. "It's not good. Slow degeneration into blindness; kidney issues, too—"

"I think we're jumping the gun here." I'm trying to act calm, but I can feel my heart flip-flopping in my chest. "Shouldn't we wait until the tests come back before getting upset?"

Lana frowns. "I'm already upset over the thought that we could be going blind, and I'd hate to think that we've passed it on to the kids."

Grace looks down at her bulging belly. "I know. I've been thinking about that all week."

Would it stop me from wanting to get pregnant?

I can't think about that now.

There will be plenty of time to worry after Dad's tests.

10:54 p.m., Monday, 11 June

TWILA CALLS. "You'll never guess who called me and asked me out."

"Don't leave me hanging," I answer. "Anyone I know?"

"That hottie from your meet-up. You know, that Seth guy."

"Is he a hottie? I hadn't noticed." *I am such a liar . . .*

She laughs. "Hey, just because you're married doesn't mean you've quit looking. At least, I hope not!"

"So, did you say yes?"

She sighs. "Yeah, what the hell, right? He's cute, and he knows the score." She lowers her voice. "Speaking about who knows what, I broke the news to my boss at work today. It was a riot. He almost fell off his ergonomic ball chair."

I burst out laughing. "Well, that must have been quite a sight."

"It was. He then had the audacity to tell me that he's glad I'm pregnant because he was worried that I was just getting fat. The nerve of that jerk!"

I'll say. She's already five months along and maybe, *just maybe*, she's up to a size four.

"Okay, then, see you Wednesday! . . . Oh, and by then, I'll have had my date with Seth, so I can fill you in on all the deets."

Do I really want the details?

Of course I do.

12:14 p.m., Tuesday, 12 June

I MISS my old SafeCalifornia colleague Helen, so on a whim, I send her an e-mail: Up for Blowfish? One?

Well, of course she is.

When I get there, she has already wrangled a table for two, up against the back wall. She is sitting on the side that faces away from the TV screens with its Japanese anime running in a continuous loop.

After the requisite air kisses, we both settle down in our respective chairs. "So, how have you been? What are you up to these days?" she asks.

"I'm a baby planner."

"A what?"

"I help my pregnant clients get ready for the big day. I make sure their nurseries are in order, and that they have all the right baby gear—"

Helen almost chokes on a sip of sake. "That term always makes me laugh: 'baby gear.' As if it's a camping trip. I guess, metaphorically speaking, it is a grand adventure, isn't it? Congratulations, kiddo! Sounds like the perfect fit."

I smile as my clients come to mind: Merrie, Joanna, Carolyn, Elizabeth and Ophelia, Twila—and, of course, Seth. Yes, perfect is one way to describe it.

And exasperating.

But certainly fulfilling.

My own grand adventure.

At least until the next adventure comes along. And that should be any day now, considering the amount of time Alex and I spend in the sack.

To lose my smile, I pretend to peruse the menu. "I've also got a blog, where I discuss the best products to buy. Every now and then I uplink a video in which I do product demonstrations. In fact, the demos are causing quite a stir. I've been getting a lot of hits—and believe it or not, some requests from companies for product endorsements. But I won't agree to put my reputation on the line until I know the product is worth endorsing—which is quite a catch-22, since I don't have the time or the money to test all these products before I say yes. Although I did test one at a client's behest: a diaper called Happy Hemp."

"How did it go?"

I frown at the memory of the McSludge debacle. "It was a total disaster! To make matters worse, then I get a call from Happy Hemp's marketing director. He wanted to pay me to blog about it."

"Get out of here! What did you say?"

"I explained that before I could endorse any product, I'd have to test it first. He never called me back. I guess their own testing went as poorly as mine."

"Smart girl." She shakes her head in wonder. "I guess that's what marketing has come to these days. Companies provide the bloggers their products for free, and enough of them are so giddy about getting all the free stuff that they keep the blog posts positive. A win-win for everyone—except of course the poor schmuck consumers who buy subpar products."

There is no humor in her laughter, only bitterness. I can't say that I blame her. Like me, she's built her reputation on fact, not hype.

I pick up a piece of a spider roll with my chopsticks. "How about you? Any grand journeys planned?"

She shrugs. "I'm a lady of leisure. I garden and take Marlowe the wonder dog on long hikes. David and I took a trip to Montana last month. Life is but a dream. But . . ."

"Let me guess: you're bored."

She laughs. "You know me too well." The tears gleam in her eyes. She washes them away with a gulp of sake. "David thinks that there's—and I quote—'more in store for us.' That's his euphemism for getting down to the business of having a baby."

"Really? You're going to try to get pregnant?" Suddenly I'm jealous. She has a man who wants her to carry his child.

"Hardly! Oh, granted he'd like me to, but that's not who I am. I enjoy my life just the way it is, thank you very much." She shrugs as she takes a bite of her fatty tuna sashimi.

"But Helen, maybe this is fate trying to tell you something."

"Don't, Katie, please." She looks me in the eye. "Look, just because *you* want to pop out a kid or two doesn't mean we all do. I'll admit it: I for one love having a size two figure, not to mention sleeping in on weekends as opposed to pretending I give a damn whether my six-year-old's soccer team is in the finals. I'm very aware that this makes me seem selfish in a lot of people's eyes. But isn't it just as egotistical for parents to want their kids to win all those tournament trophies? My God, if I want something of mine to get a blue ribbon, I'll enter Marlowe in a dog show."

I nod my head. I know nothing I can say that would change her mind, just as nothing she says to me would ever convince me that I should live my life without a child.

Or that what I'm doing to trick Alex into having a child is wrong.

Almost as if reading my mind, Helen asks, "And how about

you? Are you any closer to that little bundle of joy you've always wanted?"

"I'm trying my damnedest."

"So Alex has finally come around to your way of thinking?"

"Um . . . not quite."

Helen's brow arches delicately. "What exactly does that mean?"

"Just that . . . well, I'm off the pill. But Alex doesn't know it yet."

"Egad. That's certainly ballsy." She signals our usual waitress, Anna, for another minicarafe of sake. "Well, I guess you can always tell him that you beat the odds and are in the one percent who get pregnant despite being on it—but you'll have to be a good little liar to pull that one off. If he used a condom instead, you could always claim it broke. Then again, you'd have to prick it beforehand or something for *that* to happen—"

In order to hide my shame, I feign interest in the sashimi combo that Anna just put in front of us. It sits inside a bamboo basket on a bed of smoking dry ice and is garnished with a forest of twigs.

Oddly enough, it reminds me of the finale of *Wicked*.

I guess presentation is everything.

I'll remember that if and when I have news to break to Alex. That gives me an excuse to go out and buy new lingerie.

26

· · · · · · · · · · · ·

10:20 a.m., Thursday, 14 June

I HEAR YOU'RE COMING up our way! I can't wait." I try to keep the waver out of my voice, but Dad picks up on it, like a human Geiger counter.

"Your mom is concerned. I'm not. So I'm going blind. Big deal." His breathing is labored.

Or maybe he's teared up. If so, I can't let on that I notice. *Keep it light. Be upbeat.* "So, when's the big day?"

"They pushed it back. A couple of weeks from now, I guess. The doc they want me to see—some big muckety-muck—had to give a speech at some convention next week. Hey, if they're not worried about my prognosis, then why should I be?"

My laugh is feeble, my heart heavy. "Give Mom a kiss for me. Tell her I'm here, if either of you need anything. In fact, I can fly down to LAX and take the airporter to the house, if you guys want company on the drive up—"

"Don't be such a nudge! You were always the little mother of the family . . ."

His voice trails off. He thinks that motherhood is a sore subject with me.

It was, once. But no longer.

I'm working on it. And I won't give up.

9:38 p.m.

MY EXCUSE for being over at Seth's on the night of his date with Twila is that I'm helping Fanny baby-proof his apartment. Alex is out, too—a client dinner—so it's not like I have somewhere to be, anyway.

Truth is, there is nowhere I'd rather be.

"Do you think he'll bring her here?" Fanny asks hopefully.

From her getup—*Yentl* lite, which means a vest over a puffy pirate shirt, short wool pants buckled just below the knee, and a cap over a short tousled wig—I'm guessing that's what she's counting on.

"I'm sure he'll do whatever he can to make a good impression."

Thank goodness that remark goes over her head.

While Sadie sleeps, we've gone room by room, taking note of items in Seth's home—toxic cleansers, toys made of questionable materials, upholstered furniture and carpets, soaps, food—that should be replaced with others that are more environmentally friendly. We are in the kitchen when we hear the front door open.

"Hmmm. It's only nine thirty. That's not a good sign," hisses Fanny.

She's right, of course.

The look on Seth's face bears this out. But when he sees me here staring at him, he does a double take. In a flash the anger I see in him shifts to sadness. "Oh—Katie! I wasn't expecting you to be here." He looks from me to Fanny.

She can take the hint and skedaddles. "See you on Monday," she trills as she heads out the door.

"I should be going, too." I move into the living room. I'm putting on my coat when I feel his hand on my arm.

"Katie, wait. I want to thank you for all you've done for

Sadie and me these past few months. Really, I mean that. But . . ." He pauses, as if at a loss for what to say next. "I've come to the conclusion that we shouldn't be working together anymore. It's just—things are getting too complicated."

"What?" I stop midsleeve. "But—but there's still so much to do! Seth, what . . . why—"

"It has nothing to do with your work for me. I mean that. I just feel that . . . I feel that I'm much too close to you. And that means one of us is going to get hurt."

Too close . . .

"I don't know what you mean." I'm lying. Can he hear it in my voice? Maybe Fanny is right about his feelings.

"What I'm trying to say is—is that . . . Katie, listen, you're a very nice person, but I think you need to focus on your own life and not anyone else's: not Twila's, not mine—most certainly not mine."

"Oh. I see. You two had some kind of gabfest about me. What, were you comparing notes or something? Am I not living up to either of your expectations?"

"Trust me, your name never came up! You'd be the last thing I'd want to talk about with—*with her.* Listen, let's just say it was a fiasco, from start to finish."

So that's it. He struck out, and he's blaming me.

"Seth, I'm sorry things didn't work out as you'd hoped. Frankly I think you guys are well matched. Maybe if you call her again, she'll give you a second chance—"

"You've got to be kidding me!" He shakes his head, exasperated. "See, this is exactly what I mean. *You just don't know what you're talking about.*"

He looks at me as if he's seeing me for the very first time.

It hurts me that pity has replaced the sadness in his eyes.

That only makes me angrier. "You're right. If that's how you feel, then it's best that we not work together. Good-bye, Seth."

As I stumble down the steps, he calls after me.

He's still standing in the doorway as I pull away from the curb.

9:19 a.m., Friday, 15 June

VampGrrrl@UniVamp: FYI: Date with Hottie was a bust. A shame. I thought things were going well at first, but then we ran into a friend, and he acted totally weird. Do me a favor: If he asks about me, tell him I've started seeing someone else. LOL, seriously, that may not be too far from the truth. Don't quote me, but Mr. Wrong may be coming to his senses (!!!) He's asked to see me. What do you think, should I say yes?

Ah, just as I suspected, Seth blew it. Well, to hell with him! He doesn't know what he's talking about. My clients love my input.

He just needed someone to blame.

Me.

Katie@MakingMommiesSmile: I say follow your heart—but remember: stick to your guns!

VampGrrrl@UniVamp: Gotcha! I'll play hardball!

27

· · · · · · · · · · · ·

Children are like wet cement.
Whatever falls on them makes an impression.
—Dr. Haim Ginott

1:14 a.m., Thursday, 21 June

ALEX AND I have made love practically every day this week.

I don't know which of us wants it—make that *needs it*—more. I know S&M has put a lot on his plate because he's been working around the clock. But when he finally gets home, I'm the first thing he grabs: not the remote, or a beer from the fridge.

I'm his sustenance.

Me.

Tonight has been a particularly active lovemaking session. Seduction takes place in the kitchen (who knew leftover borscht was an aphrodisiac?), whereas foreplay happens in the living room (I knew that midcentury Eames rocker would come in handy one day), before we end up in the bedroom.

But we don't make love in the bed. We do it in the walk-in closet.

Unfortunately, yes: still with a damn rubber.

Practice makes perfect. To that end I've perfected my condom-sabotaging technique: now I preprick, in bulk. I can do a whole box in under ten minutes, quickly and seamlessly.

I'd like to think that if there were an Olympic competition for it, I'd win the gold.

"Hey, remember, tomorrow's the S&M party. Got anything sexy to wear?" gasps Alex, sweaty and spent, from the floor of the closet. He doesn't know why I'm so randy these days, but he's smart enough to just go with the flow.

He doesn't know how grateful I am for that. The flow, that is.

"I might have had something, half an hour ago. Let me see what I can find that wasn't crushed. What's the occasion, anyway?"

He smiles slyly. "We're about to make it big-time, with SkorTek."

I prop myself up on one elbow. "Wow! That's so exciting!"

"Yep. It'll make our year."

In more ways than one. Finally, we can dump these damn rubbers.

They're all defective, anyway.

"Well, I guess Seth will be happy about this," I murmur, more to myself than to Alex.

"Ha! I doubt that. By the way, you don't have to worry about that guy anymore. We're breaking the news to him tomorrow that he's being let go."

"*What?* But it's his company! How can you do that?"

"Easy. There's a fiduciary responsibility clause in his contract, and he's breached it several times over. He's just not focused on the work. Henry's been carrying him since—well, since his kid was born. What's the little guy's name again?"

"It's not a boy, it's a girl, and her name is Sadie."

"Yeah, okay, whatever. Doesn't matter, now that he's history."

"Oh." This saddens me. "I—I guess he had some premonition that something like that would happen because he told me last week that my services were no longer needed."

"Well, that makes things easier. If he hadn't I would have asked you to drop him anyway."

Ha. Had Alex tried, I would have told him to get lost. What he's doing to Seth is low and underhanded—

But I don't say that to Alex. What's the use?

After tomorrow, Seth will have yet another reason to hate me.

4:12 a.m.

THE CALL comes before daybreak. Alex groans, then shoves me away.

My subconscious tells me that it can't in a million years be for me, because I no longer work for Merrie Lovejoy, therefore it's got to be for him.

He's snoring again, so I reach over to grab it. "Hello?" I hope my tone is warning enough that this better be good.

"Ms. Johnson, it's Emma." I recognize the voice, if not the tone. There is no sneer, just fear.

"Emma? Is everything okay?"

"No," she howls. "A piece of the baby came out of my mom with a lot of water! I called 911, and we're in the ambulance now, but Mom wants you to meet us at the hospital, as soon as possible! Paul's in Sacramento and won't be home until later tonight—"

"Okay, Emma! Don't panic! Ask the med tech which hospital—"

Through the phone I hear him tell Emma California Pacific. I'm glad I do, because she's crying so hard that it's difficult to hear.

"Okay, Emma, tell your mom I'm on my way! In the meantime, call Paul and tell him when he gets back to town to meet us at California Pacific. Emma . . . Emma, are you still there?"

Her "Yes" comes in between a torrent of sobs. Right before I hang up, I hear her whisper "Thank you."

9:44 a.m.

THE BABY was stillborn.

We are in Joanna's room. She is sedated now, which means all we have to do at this very moment is listen to her breathe, and prepare ourselves for the grief that will rise from her as soon as the drug veil is lifted.

I am holding Emma's hand—the one that isn't still grasping her little sister's umbilical cord. She hasn't said a word since we got to the hospital three hours ago. The emergency staff was too busy rushing her mother to NICU to notice and to take the cord from Emma.

In the ambulance on the way to the hospital, Joanna told Emma that there's nothing to worry about; that the doctors would make sure the baby was all right—

A baby that hadn't kicked or moved since yesterday.

Or was it the day before? Joanna had been so busy at work she hadn't noticed the obvious signs of fetal distress.

But for Emma's sake, she babbled on about everything being okay; that although it was a week earlier than expected, maybe today they'd be bringing home the baby.

My guess is that she was trying to convince herself of this too, even as she was losing her baby.

Paul must have broken every law on the books to get back to San Francisco as quickly as he did. He strides up to us anxiously, his eyes scanning our faces for any sign of relief.

When he doesn't see any, the light goes out of his own eyes.

He takes the chair on the other side of Emma. She lets him put his arm around her. They are huddled like that when Joanna's doctor comes out to see us. The words "stillborn" and "high stress" and "I explained to your wife that over thirty-five is a high risk" roll over us, pitching us into a whirlpool of grief and wonder over what might have been.

Only when the doctor expresses his condolence for the loss of Paul's daughter does Paul resurface from his sadness. "My daughter is right here," he says, pointing to Emma.

At her stepfather's public acknowledgment of her role in his life, Emma blushes. With her free hand, she gives his hand a squeeze.

The doctor shakes his head. "I mean your *infant* daughter."

"But . . . I don't understand! I was told it was a boy."

The doctor gives him a strange look. When Emma lets go of his hand, Paul seems to realize that she was in on her mother's lie, too.

He leans back. His eyelids close, heavy with the guilt he feels over his own role in their duplicity.

It's Emma's turn to comfort him. To do this, she lays her head on his shoulder.

Joanna wakes just at that moment. I see her eyes flutter open, and the awe on her face when she sees them there, together like that. A moment later they see her, too. Paul leaps up to give her a kiss, to tell her his fear that he may have lost her—

That he is sorry they've lost their infant daughter.

Hearing that, Joanna's eyes get big. The knowledge that her secret is out releases a torrent of tears and fears and promises. "Paul, I'm so sorry! Please forgive me. If I told you the truth, I knew you'd be disappointed! But please don't worry. We'll try again. I'll take it easy and we'll get our boy—"

Our boy.

Even as Paul shushes Joanna and assures her that there is no need to get pregnant, because their lives are perfect, just the three of them, Emma heads for the door.

I don't know which is worse: saying the wrong thing at the wrong time, or finally saying the right thing when it's too late.

In this case, I'm guessing the former.

I run after Emma, but before I have a chance to call out, I watch as she pauses in front of a hooded trash dispenser. She pushes open the lid and stares down into it for a moment before dropping the umbilical cord into it.

I'm too stunned to say anything. By the time I find my voice she is long gone.

11:14 a.m.

ALTHOUGH IT'S not even noon yet, I figured right: that the carnage has already taken place at S&M.

The open bottle of scotch on Seth's dining table is all the proof I need.

I'm surprised he opened the door to me in the first place. Now that I'm standing there in his hallway, all I can think of saying is: "I'm sorry."

Seth doesn't answer me. Instead, he watches as Sadie crawls over to me, then uses my legs to support her climb into my open arms.

"Katie Johnson, you're like a bad penny. You always show back up." Seth's words come out slow and slurred. "Oh . . . no, wait! I mean a bad five mil. Because that was going to be my cut—*if that dolt, Henry, and that shark you married, hadn't figured out a way to cut me out of my own company.*"

Sadie's playful slaps can't make me wince, but Seth's anger certainly does. "What happened?"

He shakes his head in wonder. "I came in at ten. They'd already done me the favor of cleaning out my desk for me." He points to the large cardboard box on the table, beside the scotch bottle. "Then they informed me that I'd already marginalized my role in the company by my, and I quote, 'malfeasance and negligence during this very critical start-up period.'"

With Sadie's finger pulling at my lips, the words come out jumbled. "What exactly does that mean?"

"It means that S&M can twist the small print in our agreement to prove their point. For example, when I left one of their blue-sky circle-jerk sessions because Sadie was at the doctor's with her emergency fever, I was 'showing no concern for the well-being of the company,' never mind the well-being of my child was at stake."

"They're being ridiculous! I can't imagine that will stand up in a court of law!"

He tosses back the last third of his drink. "That's just the problem. Going to court means paying a lawyer to represent me. When it came to cash, S&M always kept us on a very short leash. Or as Alex always put it, 'The sweetest payoff is on the back end.'"

I feign interest in Sadie's curls. I remember hearing Alex laughing about the number of clients who fall for that line.

"But isn't it true?" I asked Alex once, innocently.

"Yeah, for a few of those guys. But usually by the time we sell it off, only one or two of them is left standing. There's always a way to pit one partner against the other. We just stand back and watch the fur fly. You know, like at a dogfight. Survival of the fittest, baby, right?"

Wrong. Today it's Seth who is home licking his wounds.

It's not a great day for my clients, and I feel their pain.

I'm sobbing now, and try as I might, I can't stop the tears from coming.

Quickly I hand Sadie my keys to divert her attention from my tears, but it's not that easy for me to get Seth to quit staring at me. "Hey, whoa, let's not go overboard here! I'm not going to just lie down and let them run over me—"

He rushes over to me. I feel his hand patting my shoulder. I turn into him, and suddenly we're in a group hug: Seth, Sadie, and me.

I could stay like that forever.

But finally he lets go of us.

He takes a few steps back and squints, but only one eye closes. I know that look. It's the one he gives when he's trying to figure me out. "Really, Katie: why are you here?"

"I was worried about you." I wipe away my tears. "And . . . I've just come from the hospital. One of my clients lost her baby."

"Oh, man. That's . . . so hard." I can tell he wants to comfort me, but he's afraid to get close again.

As close as we were once, a long time ago.

Before Twila.

Before Alex.

This is all Alex's fault.

When I hand Sadie back to him, she gives a small pout that makes me smile. "I'm going to talk to Alex about this. It's not fair, and I don't like it."

Seth laughs uproariously. "Oh yeah, okay, that just made my day. Seriously, Katie, do you really believe he gives a hoot what you care about?"

"Yes, of course! He loves me!" I hate Seth now, even more than I hate Alex for what he's done to him. "Why would you even doubt that?"

"Why? Because—because . . ." He looks away, ashamed. "Look, I appreciate you coming over here to see that everyone is alive and well, despite all the crap with SkorTek. But considering what just went down, I don't feel that we can be friends."

"Is that the real reason?" I touch his arm so that he has to turn toward me. Sadie giggles. She wants in on the game.

Then again, she doesn't know what's at stake: my friendship with her father.

The joy I get in being around both of them.

His deep brown eyes can't lie to me. Yes, there is something else. But no, he won't tell me what it is.

I pick up my purse and walk out the door.

I suppose Fanny was right, but there's nothing I can do about that, because I love Alex.

11:44 p.m.

I *HATE* Alex.

Hate hate hate the bastard.

The announcement about the Samurai's financing traveled fast. It is big news throughout the industry. Tonight at the deal celebration party, both Steadman and Martinez came up to me to tell me that Alex walks on water, that they expect great things from their new partner.

Partner.

That word is an aphrodisiac. Both Alex and I left the party tipsy and horny.

We're home now, where the real party begins.

I undress him quickly now, then push him down on the bed. My own striptease is slow, better to taunt his prick into a hale and hearty erection.

I've just positioned myself over him when he murmurs, "Whoa, whoa, whoa, girl! Aren't we forgetting something?"

"What?" I look around the room. "Mood music? Do you want me to light a candle or something?"

"No . . . you know. A rubber."

My laugh sputters to a halt when I see the serious look on his face. "But . . . but you're a partner now. Tonight's the night, remember? You said so yourself: 'When I make partner is when we'll get pregnant'—"

He sits up so quickly that I almost fall off the bed.

"Look, there was obviously some sort of disconnect that night. You were expressing a frustration, and I was just letting you air it out. You know, so that you'd get it out of your system and move on—"

"What do you mean, 'get it out of my system'? It will always be there, Alex, whether you like it or not—"

"That's just it, Katie. I don't like it. And I never will." He's not smiling. He's not frowning.

He's not backing down.

Not now, not ever.

All these years, he's been lying to me.

"Katie, sweetie, I know you're feeling some anticipointment here—"

"What in the hell are you trying to say, Alex? Please, just— speak English for once!"

"Honey, I'm trying to tell you that I feel your pain. I know you're—that you're disappointed that you misread my signals—"

"You said it point-blank—"

"What I meant to say," he interrupts, "is that our lives are much bigger than the whole kid thing. You've just started a new business, S&M will expect a lot more hours from me . . . It just wouldn't be fair to have a kid with all of this going on."

"I'll give up the company! I really want to have a child! Alex, it's—it's now or never!" I'm blubbering so much that I don't even know if he can make out what I'm saying, but I've got to make him understand.

He places both his hands on my shoulders so that I'll look him in the eye. "Well then, I guess it's never."

Finally, he's said what I needed to hear.

Years ago. So many years ago.

Fuck him.

I pull open his bedside table drawer with such savagery that it falls to the floor and everything falls out.

Including all the rubbers, which I've already pricked.

I grab one off the floor and tear open its wrapper with my mouth. "Here you go. Let's celebrate."

What I don't say, but what we're both thinking, is *if you can still get it up*. With his penis now at half-mast, it's debatable.

But Alex aims to please. Himself. And since I'm still rarin' to go . . .

When we're done, he cuddles me and whispers, "Babe, I'm sorry if we got our wires crossed before. But I'm glad we're in agreeance now . . ."

Oh yeah, we're in agreeance.

I'm getting pregnant whether you like it or not.

28

·············

Life is always a rich and steady time
when you are waiting for something to happen or to hatch.
—*Charlotte's Web*

8:11 a.m., Thursday, 12 July

M<small>Y</small> PERIOD IS late, now, by a week.

I feel fat. Bloated. Crampy.

And we've had unprotected sex, like what, a bazillion times now since I've been off the pill?

I've got to be pregnant. *I must be pregnant . . .*

Before Alex wakes up, I sneak out of bed and make my way over to my underwear drawer. It slides open silently. My hand slips through cotton and silk and nylon, inside three sets of Spanx Super Power Panties, where I hide pregnancy tests. They are stacked six deep.

A man wouldn't be caught dead looking in there.

I slip out one of the square cardboard boxes that holds the answer to my prayers: a home pregnancy test.

My footsteps are silent as I make my way into the bathroom. Did Alex hear the click of the lock? His snores quicken, so maybe . . .

I've got to pee, and fast.

No problem there. I position myself over the toilet and let loose. The tinkle of urine on water makes me hold my breath. I hope. *I pray.*

This is supposed to be instantaneous—

It is.

No smiley face.

"Damn it!" I mutter.

"Hon—hon? Where'd you go?" Alex sounds groggy.

"Coming right out!" I flatten the box and the applicator, and stuff them under the tissues in the bathroom garbage can.

I find him lying on his back, erect. He's already rolling on a rubber, but stops cold. "Oh, *shit!*"

I'm naked, but that's not why I'm shivering. "What? What is it?"

But of course I know what he sees.

He strips off the condom and holds it up to the light to study it, spreading it wide with his fingers. I imagine he sees a shaft of light as wide as the Rainbow Tunnel.

I close my eyes and wait for him to freak out—

But no. He shrugs and tosses it into the trash by the bedside table. "Wow. Close call! Just goes to show that those things aren't infallible . . . Hey, maybe we should double up on them, or something."

I shove him down onto the pillows. "You were just too rough with it. Here, let me put another one on you."

I reach over him and take another out of his bed-stand drawer. I'm slow and steady and make the sort of moves that get him growing larger with each stroke. Soon he forgets his trouble, comes, and gets happy . . .

When he leaves for work, I'll call Dr. Rankin, my gynecologist, to beg for an emergency appointment later today.

The home pregnancy test has got to be wrong.

I'm pregnant. I can feel it.

Seeing her is just a formality . . . isn't it?

DR. RANKIN can squeeze me in at four thirty today. I can't wait!

When I turn on my computer, there are a slew of e-mails waiting for me: yet more requests for product endorsements, questions from potential clients, and even more questions to the "Ask Katie" column on the website.

But there are two that I open first:

VampGrrrl@UniVamp: Hey, so, I think I'm ready to have you come over and see the new place. How about this evening, like, 6ish? 6:30ish?

That's perfect. I can go over there right after my doctor's appointment. *Hmmm.* Am I already glowing? . . . Ack! Too early in the morning to look in the mirror. Besides, it's hard to tell in this light.

If I am, I wonder if Twila will notice. I can hear her now: "Welcome to the club" . . .

Katie@MakingMommiesSmile: Sounds like a plan. Let's make it 6:00, because I'll be coming from another meeting. Can't wait to see your place!

VampGrrrl@UniVamp: Great! I'll text over the address now. Oh btw, parking is a pain! The driveway only fits one car, but the best parking is down the block in the lot at the elementary school. It should be fairly empty by then.

Katie@MakingMommiesSmile: Will do.

I pause before I open the second e-mail, and pray it's something that won't make me cry, please not today:

JWallenskyEsq@. . . : Dear Katie, I want to thank you for your kind note, and for the beautiful flowers, and mostly for coming to my rescue on that awful day. I don't know what we would have done without you.

Pretty much things are back to normal here. No, I take that back. Things are better than normal. Paul is being very sweet to Emma. Frankly, I think she's mad at me now, not at him. But maybe that's a good thing. I deserve it and he doesn't.

I want to let you know that we've made the decision to forgo my getting pregnant again. I will of course honor the rest of my contract with you. If anyone warned me about taking it easy, it was you (and, yes, Paul), but I've always presumed I was some sort of Superwoman. Well, now I don't have to be. That's a relief, too.

Still, I hope we can stay in touch. And I want you to know if you ever need anything from me, please don't hesitate to call me.
—Joanna

I write back to Joanna that her bill to me is already paid in full, and that I would be honored if we could stay friends.

11:55 a.m.

LANA CALLS: "The tests results are ready today. Mom and Dad are already here. Can you come over tonight, to Grace's?"

"Of course. What time?"

"Later. Around eight. We'll be leaving all the kids at my place, with a sitter. We don't want them to see Mom crying."

"How do we know she'll be crying? Maybe it's not as bad as you're both making out—"

"Katie, I called dad's physician, Dr. Hendricks, this morning. The specialist had already called him with the prognosis. He'll be confirming what Dr. Hendricks already suspected." She sighs. "He realizes Mom is in denial. We all need to be on the same page, to help her through it."

I can take a hint. "I have a client meeting at six tonight, but I'll be there as soon as I can." I hang up.

I can do what Lana is doing—fret and research and presume the worst—but I want to think positive thoughts now.

I want my father around for a long, long time, so that he can watch his youngest grandchild grow up.

I hope I have some good news to share with everyone tonight.

2:11 p.m.

I HAVE errands to run on Fillmore Street. On the way over, I pass Alta Plaza Park, where Seth and I went after that disastrous singles meet-up at Kara Kischell's. While I wait at the stop sign at the corner of Steiner and Clay, I see him, across the street, wheeling Sadie's carriage over to the park. Without thinking, I call his name. He glances up, but just then a van honks me to move on, so I hit the gas.

As I roll down the street, I see him staring after my car. He's not smiling, and I guess he wonders why I made the effort to get his attention if I wasn't going to stop in the first place.

What would we have to talk about, anyway? He refuses to tell me about his date with Twila, and although he won't just come out and say it, I'll just bet he thinks he got shoved out of SkorTek because of something I said to Alex.

The thought of this makes me cry so hard that I have to pull off the road.

He was a good friend, and somehow I blew it. Okay, Alex blew it for me.

Jeez, I swear, I'm hormonal.

I just know I'm pregnant.

4:51 p.m.

I'M WATCHING Dr. Rankin's poker face as she studies the ultrasound monitor. She's been moving the wand inside my uterus as if it's a metal detector looking for gold. Then, finally, she glances over at me. "Sorry, Katie. I don't see a fetus."

I sit up so fast that I rip the sanitary paper that covers the patient table. "Maybe we should have another look—"

"Katie, sweetie, your blood test also came back negative. The purpose of this transvaginal ultrasound was to double-check that. How long did you say you've been having regular sex without contraception?"

"Three months."

She puts her hand over mine. "We shouldn't jump to any conclusions, but it may not be such a bad idea to run some tests."

"Are you saying I may be infertile?" That thought stops me cold. I ease back down onto the table.

"I'm just saying that we should find out what's happening, and the sooner the better, if, like you say, you plan on having children."

"But—I'm healthy! I mean, sure, my periods are always on time. Yeah, okay, sometimes I spot between periods, but—"

"That's an indication that we should take a better look." She looks down at my chart with a frown. "You turned thirty-seven in February, right?"

"Yes. But that's still young enough to have kids! I have friends who are older than me, and are pregnant, or just had babies—"

"Yes, of course, under normal circumstances, there should be no problem. But each year after age twenty-seven, a woman's chance to conceive begins to decline." She gives my hand a pat. "Unfortunately, infertility isn't an exact science. There are several causes, and each one has to be ruled out. Perhaps there's an issue with your reproductive organs. Or your body may be producing too much, or too little, of the hormones that help the ovary prep the egg before releasing it. Or your fallopian tubes may be harboring a bacterial infection, or an STD. A common culprit is chlamydia."

I'm overwhelmed by helplessness. "I've got to know, Doctor. Please, isn't there something we can do today, to start the process of elimination?"

She pauses in thought. "There's another type of blood test that I can run, but it's best to do it the third day of your menstrual cycle, so you'll have to come back for that. Or I can give you clomiphene citrate pills. You're to take them only for a few days, toward the beginning of your next menstrual cycle—"

"But I can't wait until then! We're seeing my parents tonight and—"

"Katie, if it turns out that you are in fact infertile, finding out why may take some time." She smiles, but I can hear the concern in her voice. "One thing we could do today is take a few x-rays—a hysterosalpingogram—which will give us a clear view of any blockage in your fallopian tubes."

"Yes, please, let's do it."

"I'll have to inject you with some dye first. Once we take the x-rays, I'll put in a rush order with the lab downstairs, if you care to wait. Now, lie back down, this will only take a second. Relax and you won't feel a thing . . ."

The injection is gentle, but I flinch anyway. From my perch on the table I look out the window, seeking refuge from my anxiety in the world beyond my fate. The fog rolls past in cold blasts. A mother struggles to push a stroller up the street, but the wind isn't helping her progress. When finally she makes it to the top, she stops to wrap her baby's blanket tighter, then rounds the corner.

I still believe that, someday, that will be me.

I've just got to round a very big corner.

5:39 p.m.

THERE IS a blockage in one of my fallopian tubes: something called a "tubal occlusion at the utero-tubal junction."

It is filled with fluid, what they call a hydrosalpin.

Yes, it can be drained. That's the good news.

The bad news is this: if it hadn't gone untreated all these years, I might have had a decent chance at getting pregnant, through in vitro fertilization.

As of now, I have little hope of ever having a child.

I have to quit crying.

But today, right now, I have to pretend that everything is okay.

I have to be happy for my clients, like Twila, whom I'll be seeing any moment now.

I have to focus on my parents, who need me by their side now, more than ever.

And I need Alex there, for me.

Fat chance. Truth is, when I break the news he'll be relieved. And despite knowing my feeling about children, he won't even have the courtesy to feign disappointment.

I wouldn't be surprised if he dances a jig when he hears.

I guess he'll be happy that he never has to wear a rubber again.

Well, I'll be happy that I don't have to go through the hassle of pricking the damn things.

I check my makeup in the rearview mirror. I'll claim that my reddened eyes are due to allergies.

Twila doesn't have x-ray vision, so she won't be able to see my broken heart.

6:32 p.m.

TWILA'S NEW home is a single-story tiny cottage wedged between two Victorian tri-level co-ops. There is no front yard to speak of, just some deep window boxes over concrete slab.

Over the past decade, San Francisco's Noe Valley has become the neighborhood of choice for young parents too hip for Marin and too cash-strapped for the Marina or Pac Heights. For the most part, the streets are flatter and the area is sunnier than other parts of the city: perfect for wheeling carriages over sidewalks lined with trendy little shops.

Twila swings open her door. Ever the fashionista, she has on a long, gauzy top over leggings and boots. Her baby bump is prominent now, but she is still slender.

She has that glow I covet.

"Yay, you're here!" She gives me a hug.

I hold her tight. I know she'd feel my pain because I've felt hers, so many times.

She pushes my hair out of my face. "Is something wrong?"

"No! Yes . . . you see, I . . . I thought I was pregnant. I was wrong."

"Oh." She pauses, then gives me a gentle kiss on my cheek. "Oh my! I'm so sorry! I didn't know you were even trying. I thought you said your husband was dead set against it—"

"He was. But you can't really stop an accident, can you?"

"Nope, not at all. What's the old saying, 'accidents are meant to happen'?" She laughs halfheartedly. I'm sure she's hoping I'll join her. She takes my hand. "Here, let me give you the grand tour."

There's not much to it, but that's okay. In no time at all she and her baby will fill it with the two most important things a home needs: love and laughter.

I take in all the beautiful wood: the floors, the original cornices, the intricate molding. "It's certainly charming."

"As promised, we've got separate rooms." She points to two rooms off the hallway.

The master bedroom is small; the nursery, tiny. Both have high ceilings. In Twila's room, a queen bed will fit, but just barely. At least now she has more room than she ever had in the studio. There is no more clutter. Everything is in its place.

The baby's room is Realtor beige, a color that shows well in staged homes because it's bland enough not to offend anyone.

"We'll need to brighten this up," I murmur. My mind's eye is already envisioning the room filled with all the essentials: a crib that converts to a toddler bed when the time comes. A changing table that becomes a bookcase. A dresser that is tall, as opposed to wide . . .

We will make it beautiful for her baby.

"I was thinking a buttery yellow hue. It's always been my favorite color."

I nod and walk over to the window. It is ten feet high, like the doors, and faces west, letting in a lot of light.

There is a tiny closet in one corner. "Not much room there,"

I say. "That's okay. We'll find some movable storage pieces that will grow with the baby."

Twila sighs. "I don't miss much about the old place, but the only thing I *do* miss is—"

"The closet!" We say it in unison. Then we both laugh.

We're still laughing when the doorbell rings. Twila looks annoyed. Obviously she wasn't expecting anyone else. She sighs as she excuses herself to answer it.

I stay in the hallway, but the place is so small that of course I can see the door from there.

It's Alex. He looks serious, and he's carrying a bouquet of roses.

Ah, so he knows about me.

He cares.

I presume he got off work on time for once, and Dr. Rankin called the house to check up on me, then mentioned my reaction to the awful news that has ruined my life. Maybe he's guessing how upset I am, and wants to drive over with me to Grace's, as opposed to meeting me over there, so that we can hold hands and talk about it.

Yes, we can finally talk it through—

But no, that can't be it, because he's holding out the flowers to Twila. They are yellow roses. She looks pleased and allows him to take her in his arms and give her the kind of passionate kiss that says *I forgive you* and *Yes, I love you, despite all the hurt you caused me . . .*

Oh my God:

Alex is Twila's Mr. Wrong.

I take a step back, and the floor creaks ever so slightly. The sound is enough for Alex to open his eyes. When he spots me, his mouth falls open even wider than it was with Twila's tongue in it.

He looks at me as if I'm a ghost.

I might just be. All my hopes and dreams just died.

Twila looks up at him, then over at me. Her smile only grows wider. "Oh! Alex, this is Katie. She's helping me with—"

Her baby.

Their baby.

I run past her, but I have to shove him out of the way to get through the doorway. At first it seems he doesn't want to move, that he wants to hold me tight, but no, I won't let him. While shaking him off, I wrench the bouquet out of his hands and hit him with it before running down the steps and out into the street. I imagine I look like a madwoman, but I don't care. I can't stand the way he shouts my name, over and over again, as if that's going to make me wake up and all this will fade away—

As if it never happened.

But I have proof that it's happening. I've ripped my hands to shreds on one of his goddamned roses. Angrily I toss his bouquet at him, but that doesn't stop him from following me.

I still have one rose in my hand as I fumble for my car keys. I get in just before he reaches the car. He begs me to open the door so that we can talk.

I unlock it, although I don't know why.

Before I can change my mind, he jumps into the passenger seat. I wonder, do I really want to hear what he has to say?

"You've been having an affair with her?" I scream. "You got her pregnant?"

"I know you hate me. You should. I'm a jerk, an idiot—"

"Alex, you're the father of her child!" It comes out as a gasp. "How long have you been seeing her?"

He doesn't look at me. He can't. I guess he's too ashamed. "About a year. S&M provided UniVamp with its mezzanine financing. Twila was part of UniVamp's presentation team." He frowns. "Of course, we had to keep it a secret. Then about four months ago she broke the news to me that she was pregnant. I asked her to—to abort, but she refused. She said she was having the baby, with or without me. That night, I was so upset that I drank a whole bottle of scotch. In fact, I almost told you about it, when you walked in on me." Alex finally has the courage to look at me. "Katie, I've been so unfair to you! I've fucked around on you, and—and then . . . this."

I wince. "It was the night I found you holding Peter's picture, wasn't it? I presumed you were thinking about how much you missed him."

"I was thinking about how I'd let him down—and how I'd be ruining any chance of a relationship I could have with another child. *My* child." He's heaving so loudly now that I think he'll die, right here and now.

I still love him, or I wouldn't care this much.

"I wanted to have your child, too! Remember? All these years, I would have done anything in the world—" My eyes are fogged by my tears, which never seem to end. "I found out today that I may never have children. That's all I've ever wanted."

His face twists as he contemplates the irony of it all. I've validated his long-held suspicion. "I know. Having a baby meant more to you than I ever did."

Now I can smile. "You're wrong. Yes, I wanted a child. But I wanted it to be your child, too, Alex. What does that matter now? You love Twila, don't you?"

He does nothing for the longest time, then betrays me yet again, with a nod.

I am too numb to scream. Instead, I let him in on the one thing I know will hurt him the most: my betrayal.

"I've been off the pill for a couple of months now. And I've been pricking your rubbers."

Watching him turn pale is some vindication—but then he ruins it by muttering, "Jesus! Well then, thank God you can't get pregnant. I can't imagine being a father to both your kids—"

Before I know it, I slap him, backhanded, with all my strength.

"Damn it, Katie," he yelps as he pulls away from me. I take delight in seeing his cheek turn a bright red. Instinctively he massages his face, but he's got nothing to stanch the blood dripping from his nose and onto the front of his shirt. The tears are streaming down his face now.

Good. Now he's hurt, too.

"Twila wasn't the only one, was she?"

He shrugs. "Yeah, okay. I've messed around before. But none of them meant anything. It goes with the territory."

I remember Seth's accusation, the night Alex went off with the Samurai, the one I've denied for too long.

It's why Alex lost Willemina and Peter.

Now he has lost me, too.

We sit there together, quietly, for a long time.

Finally I say, "Get out."

He sighs, but he has no reason to argue.

He doesn't even have the decency to hide the fact that he's relieved.

"Don't bother to come back to my house," I warn him. "This is your home now. She is your family."

He watches me as I drive over the crest of the hill at the end of Twila's street.

I have to see my own family. I need them badly.

29

....

A Freudian slip is when you say one thing
but mean your mother.
—Author Unknown

7:44 p.m., Thursday, 12 July

D O YOU WANT to tell us what happened?" Grace whispers.

Despite my resolve to focus on Dad and not myself, the twins pick up on my pain the very moment I walk through the door. Then, like fairies summoned to heal a bruised petal, Grace and Lana cuddle me. Their sisterly concern is their magic dust. Under most circumstances it is powerful enough to fight off the demons of doubt, fear, and shame.

But not today.

Today I found out I am never to have a child.

And, as it turns out, I never really had a husband who loved me, either.

Here and now, in my sisters' arms, I'll never feel alone.

"Alex and I split up. Turns out he's been seeing someone else."

As if not believing what they've just heard, they both lean in even closer. "How did you find out?" asks Lana.

"I saw them together. He kissed her, brought her flowers." My laugh borders on hysteria. I guess I'm still in shock over the vision of another woman in Alex's arms. "Turns out she's one of my clients: it's Twila."

"He's seeing a pregnant woman?" Grace says in disbelief.

Then the obvious dawns on her: "Wait . . . *he* got her pregnant?"

I can't look at them, but I nod. "Small world, huh? All the time she's telling me about her asshole married lover who wanted her to abort her baby, and I'm telling her to stick to her guns and have the child—and—and now . . ." I'm choking on my own sobs. "*I can't.*"

"You can't what?" the twins say in unison.

"Before I saw Alex with Twila, I'd just come from my doctor. Apparently there's some blockage in my fallopian tube."

"But that can be fixed with surgery, right?"

"That's the game plan. But the tube is filled with fluid. Depending on how long it's been there, it may ruin my chances of fertilization. And get a load of this: they won't even conduct the surgery if the additional tests show that something else is out of whack down there. They'll be monitoring my urine, measuring my hormones; if the tests indicate that I've got a high hormonal baseline—well, I may not be able to have children after all."

"That may be a blessing in disguise," murmurs Lana.

Flabbergasted, I turn to her. "How can you say such a thing?"

She shrugs. "I'll be honest with you: since I've been reading about Dad's condition, I've been scared out of my wits. It could mean internal hemorrhaging in the eye, or in the brain! And then there's blindness. Not to mention the high risk of kidney cancer—"

"Hush," whispers Grace. "They're pulling into the driveway now."

We set our faces into neutral smiles. While Grace goes to get Auggie and Thor from the media room, Lana walks over to the door. Suddenly she turns back to me. "What do you want to say to them about Alex?"

"Absolutely nothing! Today is not the day to break that news. In fact, let's wait until after they leave to tell the guys."

She nods and opens the door. Her lip trembles when she tries to smile.

As for me, well, I hope I don't burst into tears.

8:23 p.m.

"ALEX IS where again?" This is the third time Dad has asked me that question. I'm guessing the painkiller his doctor prescribed for his ongoing headaches has kicked in. He is calm, but his mind is like Teflon: nothing sticks for long.

And he looks so fragile. For once Mom does, too. He is her life. She is envisioning what may be left of their future together.

"Alex is having dinner with an out-of-town client," I repeat patiently. "Something he couldn't get away from."

Dad harrumphs. Once again Alex is in hot water.

If only he knew how deep . . .

Mom shakes her head. "We were hoping we could tell you all, together, but . . . well, I guess we should just come out and say it: the specialists have confirmed what Dr. Hendricks suspected. Your father has a rare disorder: Von Hippel–Lindau." She chokes up. "The tumor behind Dad's left eye is inoperable. He's—he's losing sight in that eye. There may be other tumors throughout his body. They'll be monitoring for that, and also his kidneys . . ."

She turns her head so that he doesn't see her cry. When she regains her composure, all she can say is, "I'm so sorry."

Grace strokes her arm gently. Thor sits down next to Dad and pats his knee.

Lana murmurs, "I—I guess we should get tested, too. Just in case."

Mom shrugs. Dad musters his energy to wave at me, but his smile is weak. "Don't worry, baby. At least you'll be okay. But the twins—yes, the twins may want to see what's up."

He is oblivious, hallucinating. At least, that's what I presume until Mom says, "Arthur, no! Remember?" She looks from him to me, then down into her lap, ashamed.

"Yes, of course I remember the day we brought her home with us from the adoption agency, like it was yesterday! So tiny. Not even a month old." He sighs. "Well, at least we know she'll never go through this—"

Mom jumps up and stumbles over to him. "Hush! No! She doesn't . . . *Arthur!*"

But I won't let her shut him up. I move in between them. "Mom, what is it? What does Dad mean?"

Mom stands there, just staring at me with eyes that say *I'm so sorry . . .*

"You mean . . . *I'm adopted?*"

This is all a bad dream. I can't believe my ears.

I take hold of my mother's shoulder so that she has to look me in the eye. What I see there is a broken woman, stricken with guilt.

The twins look just as stunned as I feel. Grace turns white and has to sit down. Auggie reaches over to help her, so that she doesn't topple over.

My heart is racing a mile a minute. "Why didn't I know this? Why didn't you tell me?"

"We— It just never seemed like the time was right." I can barely hear my mother through her sobs. "We were going to tell you when you turned four, but then I found out I was pregnant with the twins. It was such a shock because I thought I couldn't conceive! We felt it wouldn't be right to announce the birth of a baby, and then turn around and tell you that you were adopted. You'd been so used to it being just the three of us. You even asked why we felt you needed a little brother or sister." She stops and shakes her head. "So we decided to wait until a better time. But a better time just never came. You were always so shy with the other kids at school, such an insecure teen. But not at home. But you were so wonderful with the twins! You were their big sis, the one they looked up to the most—"

She stops because she realizes she is failing to convince me that what they did was selfish and wrong.

The light goes on in my dad's eyes. I imagine he now realizes what he's done. He looks so sad. Does he pity me?

I pity me.

"Katie, I never wanted you to hear it this way." Mom's lip trembles so hard that her words come out in little gasps. "We would never want to hurt you. If this hadn't happened—"

"I'm glad it happened." I feel my lips curling into a smile.

"You don't mean that." I recognize Lana's tone. It's the one she uses when Max is overstepping some boundary.

Well, I'm not Max.

I'm not even Lana's actual sister.

I'm nobody. The placeholder. The temp.

I was, in Alex's life. Now I know that was my role in my parents' lives, too.

I give Dad a kiss on the forehead. "It's okay. Everything will be okay."

He places his hand on my face and gives me a soft, watery smile.

But we both know the truth: nothing will ever be okay again.

30

· · · · · · · · · · · ·

Children make you want to start life over.
—Muhammad Ali

10:13 p.m., Thursday, 12 July

SETH'S PLACE IS dark, except for the light emanating from his computer screen. From it, I can make out his face, just barely, in the window.

He looks out when he hears my footsteps on the stairs. I don't wave, or even ring the door buzzer.

He can tell by my face why I'm there.

After he opens the door, he just steps back. He doesn't offer me coffee, or tell me to make myself at home on his couch. He knows better. He sees that I am in pain. That makes me a force to be reckoned with warily, like a hungry lion or a wounded grizzly.

We stand there, just looking at each other, until finally, I blurt it out:

"I found out tonight that Twila is Alex's girlfriend. Her baby is *his*."

"Oh . . . shit." Seth is staring at me so intensely that I blush.

"Seth, the truth: when did you figure it out?"

He pauses. I don't know if he's now reconsidering everything about that night, or just trying to decide what to say next.

Here's hoping what he says is the truth. I don't need another liar in my life right now.

He swallows hard. "The night I had that date with Twila, we ran into Alex. We were at Absinthe, grabbing a bite to eat after a movie. He was there with Pat Steadman. I hadn't realized it was one of their watering holes, or believe me, I would have avoided it like the plague."

"Twila knew, though."

He pauses to consider that. "Yeah, now in hindsight, I guess you're right." His laugh has no humor in it. "I guess she wanted him to see us together." He shakes his head in wonder. "Alex waved at us. When we waved back, of course he had to come over and say hello. Otherwise he knew I'd ask him later why he hadn't." He frowns. "She thought he was coming over to say hi to her, not to me. I realized that immediately, because when he held out his hand to her, she went ahead and introduced us. You know, something like, 'Seth, this is an old friend of mine, Alex Johnson. Alex, this is Seth.' All that time, she watched his face, to check his reaction. But you know Alex. He's a pretty smooth guy, he wasn't going to give her what she wanted: a jealous reaction. So—so she leaned in and kissed me."

I could just imagine that. What is it VampGrrrl told me once? Oh yeah: "I'm a great playmate—both in bed and out."

"Go on," I say.

"Alex has this weird-ass smirk—"

"Yeah, it pops up on his puss when he lies."

"Don't I know it! Around me, he was always smiling." Seth shrugs. "Well, after that kiss, he wasn't grinning anymore. But I was. And then I said something stupid. I said, 'Yo, Alex, we still have that investor meeting tomorrow, right?' Ha! You should have seen Twila's face when she realized we knew each other. It didn't hit me then why she laughed so hysterically about it, but I know now."

I can just imagine how it made her day when she realized her date was one of Alex's business associates.

"I guess dating her got me axed from the deal." He shakes his head.

"No, it didn't. Well, let me put it this way: it might have sped the process along, but Alex's game plan all along was to pit you and Henry against each other, then go with the last man standing. It's standard operating procedure at S&M."

Seth looks at me sharply. "You don't say? Well, that's an interesting tidbit."

"Tell me the truth, Seth: Did Twila know Alex and I were married?"

He considers that for a moment, then shakes his head. "Maybe that would have come up if Alex had asked Twila and me how we met, but he didn't."

"No, he wouldn't." It's my turn to smirk. "He's too arrogant for that. Then what happened?"

"After Alex walked away, she seemed so . . . I guess the word is preoccupied. When we got back to her place, she blew me off pretty quickly. On the drive home, I put it together."

"Is that why you told me you didn't want us to work together anymore?"

"Yes." His voice is low, I can barely hear him. "I was shocked to find you here, and I didn't know what to say. What if I'd told you what I suspected, and it turned out I'd been wrong? For all I knew, she was a close family friend, and the three of you hung out together all the time. It would have been a mess either way. That's why I thought it would be best if we cool our friendship for a while." He looks at me intently. "Besides, I didn't want to hurt you."

"Seriously, you didn't want to 'hurt me'? Or did you think that keeping Alex's little secret for him would help your position with your largest investor?"

"You're wrong, Katie. Since when did I give a damn what Alex thought of me?" Seth grimaces. "But I did care about what you'd think. I always have."

I look up at him. "I know you do."

He seems relieved. No, he's elated. I know this because his kiss doesn't hold back. It's warm and deep and raw. It leaves absolutely no doubt that he wants to have me, to love me, to take care of me . . .

But all I can give him right now is the part of me that wants to feel, to hurt, to be roughed up and avenged.

He doesn't know this, though.

All he knows is that my fingers are fumbling at his buttons and unzipping his jeans, my lips are begging him to enter me; that my nipples are taut because they want to feel his mouth around them; and that I'm mounting him and guiding him into me, and tightening around him as he plunges deep—*so deep*—and swells inside of me—

Then shudders with me as our orgasms erupt simultaneously.

No, he doesn't know that it hurts to hear him whisper "I love you."

Because I can't say it back to him.

I don't know if that day will ever come. Can he live with that?

He's lived with so much already, so I guess he'll take what he can get, which at this point in my life are all the shattered pieces of my heart.

When I get up to go, he asks, "Why don't you just stay?" His voice is husky with happiness.

I don't answer. I just wave as I go out the door.

11:54 p.m.

WHEN I get home, I scrounge around for some stationery, but all I can find are some custom note cards with my name and Alex's entwined on the front in a romantic script font.

Not at all appropriate for telling your family that you need some space.

I grab the only other blank paper I can find: some lined paper that I rip from a yellow legal pad lying on the desk in my home office.

The note I address to Dad and Mom is short and bittersweet:

> I know you both love me, and I hope you realize I love you, too. Still, I can't help but feel betrayed.
>
> I wish I could put the news of my adoption in perspective, but right now it's just not possible. That said, I hope you'll respect my request to leave me alone for the time being.
>
> —Katie

As I scrounge around my desk for an envelope, I notice that the cursor on my computer is blinking to tell me I've got a new e-mail:

> VampGrrrl@UniVamp: I didn't know. I'm so sorry. Please forgive me.

I delete it and put a block on her e-mail address.
I will miss her friendship.

THIRD TRIMESTER

31

What price we pay for the glory of motherhood.
—Isadora Duncan

3:13 p.m., Tuesday, 7 August (ST)

Happy Hemp's Corporate offices are in a nondescript building in a far-flung corporate campus, somewhere off one of the traffic veins that pump commerce into Chicago.

Like its multitudes of consumers, it could be located in Anywhere, USA.

I'm sitting at a highly varnished mahogany table in the company's large glass conference room. The table, an egalitarian circle, fits fifteen of us with room to spare.

Above the heads of those considered least important to this meeting (that would *not* be me, as I am the guest of honor) is a backlit screen that frames a PowerPoint presentation, filled with charts, statistics, and stock photos of happy mommies that flicker whenever it is necessary to make a very important point, at least from Happy Hemp's perspective:

That I'd be the perfect spokesperson for the company.

"—and a retainer of five thousand dollars a month." Garth Kinsey, Happy Hemp's vice president of marketing, smiles grandly. "Of course, we will provide as much product as you deem necessary for the reviews . . ."

Joanna Wallensky, my attorney, shakes her head. "I'm sorry, Garth, but I thought we made it clear: the fee would have to be, minimally, seventy-five hundred a month, plus a kicker for page views over fifty thousand a day."

A few of Garth's posse clear their throats uncomfortably.

Not me. I just smile. I enjoy watching him sweat this one out.

In the end, though, he also nods. Game over.

Is he a loser at the art of this deal? Hardly. He's just got deeper pockets than he's letting on.

And since Joanna knows their financials backward and forward, she knows just how far we should counter.

As he scribbles his John Hancock onto our contract, he says the words I've been dreading all day: "Now, here's how I want you to position our diapers . . ."

If he let me go with my gut feeling on the Happy Hemp brand, it would be repackaged as a biodegradable gardening mulch, not a shit sack.

But what do I know? I'm just the talking head.

When I diaper the toddler talent, I hope I can keep clean hands and a straight face.

IT'S NOTHING personal with good ol' Garth.

Truth is, I enjoy watching them all squirm.

This is our fifth corporate dance this month. The other four wined and dined us, too. Then they whined about our take-it-or-leave-it deal. But they, too, signed Joanna's paperwork, and cut the first of twelve monthly checks right then and there, as stipulated in the agreement.

Now their products flash across the computer screens of the two million unique visitors who come one or more times every month to my website in order to watch videos of my daily audience-packed demonstrations, or send me e-mails about their own little bundles of joy, or uplink photos in our online family photo album.

I (actually a member of my growing staff) write back to

them, cooing about their tots, and giving my two cents on the health and well-being of their babies—

And making subtle suggestions about the products I feel they should use.

Yes, I am a sellout.

It's not that I need the money. Or the power. Or the fame or the glory.

What I need is the love.

And these women love me. They really, really love me.

Thank goodness, because not everyone who is left in my life feels the same way.

1:11 p.m., Wednesday, 8 August

"REALLY? *THAT* piece of junk?" My stalwart webmistress Abby's bluntness about my new policy makes me wince. "Oh, I don't know, Katie. I mean, come on! Jeremy broke that stroller in just one day."

"Yeah, well, let's face it, Abby: Jeremy is the Incredible Hulk of toddlers. Now, if the stroller had been made of, I don't know, Kryptonite maybe . . ."

The phone receiver emits a deathly calm of scorn from this very proud mother. "I hope you're not insinuating that he's fat! Why, Katie Johnson, I'll have you know that Jeremy is in the ninety-ninth percentile in both height and weight for his age group. His incredible strength comes from his strict adherence to his toddler gymnastics coach's regimen—"

By now I've laid the phone down on the desk. I know that Abby will ramble on for only a moment or two, because that's how long it will take Jeremy to find a way to distract her.

But no, she grabs my attention again with the word *cruel.* As in: "I don't know what's got into you! For the past month, you've been absolutely cruel. A total B-I-T-C-H!" She lowers her voice. "I have to spell it, because Jeremy is standing right here. Otherwise I'd—"

She's right, of course. But she doesn't know why.

And I can't tell her, either. Otherwise I'll tear up. "Look, Abby, forgive me, please. Of course he's a sweet little guy. I've been supercrabby lately. I guess I'm under a lot of stress. You know I didn't mean it—"

"Oh. Sorry to hear that, Katie. I guess we're all a little under the— *Jeremy!* No you *don't!* Get those scissors away from the dog! *Jere*—"

There's the inevitable click, and then a dial tone.

I don't know which is worse: that she yelled in my ear, or that she's still calling me by my married name.

Too bad Katie Johnson is already a brand (at least, according to the *Wall Street Journal*).

Not that my adopted surname—Harlow—is any better.

If I find my birth parents, will I take one of their names?

I don't want to think that. Right now, the only name that matters to me is Making Mommies Smile, because that's the name I tell everyone to write on their checks.

10:10 p.m., Thursday, 9 August

BE IT personally or professionally, Lana and Grace have always been a tag team, and in their mission to get me to see them since the incident, they've been relentless.

This week alone they've sent four e-mails, six text messages, and three voice mails, one of which has all three kids hollering into the phone, "*We miss you, Aunt Katieeeeeee!*"

It's been a month. Yes, I miss them, too. But it's still too soon for me to face them.

That doesn't stop me from stalking them: periodically I drive over to Los Gatos in the hope of spotting them, either in their yards or in the park.

Actually I did once: all three of them were playing hide-and-seek on Lana's lawn. I was watching them from a distance. But then Mario turned around and recognized my car. Of course he ran in to tell his mother that Aunt Katie had finally come home to them, but by the time Lana got outside I'd already taken off.

I guess that was stupid of me.

I save the kids' voice mails. It's the only thing that makes me smile these days.

2:15 p.m., Monday, 13 August

ALEX'S LAWYER is trying hard not to be a prick. I give him credit for that because it's not easy to negotiate with me these days, especially if you represent Alex.

Bitter is my new black.

"No, Norman, if I've told you once I've told you a hundred times: Alex cannot have any of his clothes."

"Katie, be reasonable—"

"I don't have to be reasonable, Norman. There's not a stick of his clothing here that's older than our marriage. That makes them community property. That means I get half of everything, so I get half of his suits, too. Don't worry, I'll send him half my dresses." Of course I'm thinking of the dresses that I've got bagged for Goodwill.

Norman sighs loudly to express his displeasure at making his money assuaging the scorn of soon-to-be divorcées. "Okay, then at least send over *his* half of the clothes."

"Sure, okay, that's only fair," I answer.

After getting off the phone, I take a pair of scissors to all of

Alex's suits, slicing them right down the middle. He'll get the left pant leg and right suit jacket arm of his charcoal Brioni, the right leg and left arm of the pin-striped Savile Row.

It's the least I can do. All is fair in hate and divorce.

10:25 p.m., Wednesday, 15 August

"I KNOW when you come," Seth murmurs in my ear. "I can hear you. *I can feel you.* So why won't you kiss me?"

"Because that's not what this is about."

We both know what this is. We also know what it isn't.

He wants to be much more, but that's not happening.

Not now. Maybe never.

Sometimes I'll fall asleep over there, but I get up before dawn so that I can leave before he wakes up.

But not before I slip into Sadie's room: to kiss her soft, sweet cheeks as she sleeps, and to watch her eyelids flutter as she sighs inside some happy dream.

Then I whisper "Good-bye" and pray that Seth never comes to his senses and kicks me out of their lives.

Yes, I'll be honest, I would miss him, too.

But I can't tell him that. He'll take hope from it, and the last thing I can offer anyone now is hope.

1:36 p.m., Saturday, 18 August

A MONTH ago Joanna had put me in touch with Charlie Reynolds, a man who runs a professional search group that works with adoptees.

"He's relentless," she declared. "If your biological parents are still alive, he'll find them."

Charlie may be good at what he does, but when we first met he was also quite blunt as to what I could expect. "If you think you'll find someóne who will fulfill some fantasy for you, forget about it. This isn't some teary soap opera. Your biological mother gave you up for a reason, and that reason had to do with something happening in her life at that time. Whatever it was could still be an issue. Or there may be different ones now. Either way, you still may not be part of the life she wants to lead."

"Okay, okay, I get that I may not be welcomed with open arms. But I still have to find her."

His grudging nod was evidence that I'd passed some initial test.

Whether Charlie is all Joanna claims is still debatable. The proof is in the pudding, and up until now it's been a slim gruel at best. To date, all he has dug up on my adoption is the paperwork filed with the county of Los Angeles; proof that it was handled by a private adoption agency also based there; and, unfortunately, that the place is now out of business.

"So, where are all the files now?" I ask him.

His cough, a combination of wheeze and phlegm, takes a full minute. I can hear the puff of his cigarette a moment later. "I've got a lead on some warehouse in North Hollywood." He hacks out a laugh. "Hey, do you look like any movie starlets? A lot of them used to go away to have a love child so that nobody would know they'd gotten knocked up."

I glance in a mirror. In the seventh grade, my classmates used to tell me I looked like Julia Roberts. But by my first year of college, they were calling me Miss Piggy. That year I was a walking talking living breathing eating example of the freshman fifteen.

Now, all I see in the mirror is a sad woman in need of a new haircut and a sabbatical.

Drink, fuck, mourn.

So I lie. "I've been told I look like Demi Moore."

"Nah, she would have been too young . . . Whoa, wait a minute! Before the Bruce Willis years she was involved with Emilio Estevez—"

"It was a joke, Charlie! She wouldn't have even been in puberty then— Oh, never mind! Just call if something surfaces."

I hang up and put my head down on my desk, and try not to cry.

32

*Being a full-time mother is one of the highest salaried jobs
in my field, since the payment is pure love.*
—Mildred B. Vermont

2:13 p.m., Sunday, 19 August

T HE BABY SHOWER I'm supervising for Elizabeth is everything she wants it to be: coed, elegant, and media-worthy.

More so than she knows: Ophelia has run away.

While the guests chatted on the house's expansive veranda, which has eye-popping vistas of San Francisco Bay and the Golden Gate Bridge, I went to retrieve Ophelia from her lair: the cabana by the infinity pool.

Her "cozy casita," as Elizabeth calls it, is larger than it looks: four rooms, including a spacious media room—

But no Ophelia. There is a note, however. All it says is:

We're gone. Sorry, but I need my baby more than you do.—O

I call the cell phone of the RN who has the weekend shift. "Where are you? Is Ophelia there, too?"

"I'm in the kithen. No, I'm by minthelf." She answers with what is obviously a full mouth. She's found the hors d'oeuvres, but she has lost her charge.

"Get up to the cabana!" I hiss. "Ophelia is gone!"

I hear her gasp as she chokes down her food, then clicks off.

It takes her a full two minutes to get to this side of the estate. By then she's huffing and puffing.

Yes, I'm exasperated with her. "Why did you leave her side?"

"She asked me to get her some food. The kid has been on that diet for months, and behaving herself. She and Elizabeth have become so close. I thought a little piece of cake—at her own shower, for God's sake—couldn't hurt!" The nurse looks around the room. It suddenly dawns on her that I'm not kidding.

"Did she say anything? How has she been acting lately?"

"Well, no complaints, at least nothing outright. But I could tell she's been depressed. You know, it's not easy giving up a baby. Most of the surrogates I've worked with don't want to get attached at first, but that's nearly impossible. The baby is growing inside of you. Of course it's a part of you! Every movement, every kick—" She sighs. "She never showed her true feelings to the Auchinclosses. She knew Elizabeth would start with her little anxiety attacks. That was part of the problem. Ophelia was worried that the baby would *become* them. You know, take on all those nervous tics that they both have. 'If I could do it over again, I'd have seen this coming and I would have said no,' is how she put it."

I shake my head. "But she can't do it over! She signed that contract in good faith! This will break Elizabeth's heart!"

"What about Ophelia? She might harm herself. Trust me, I've seen this before. Birth moms can get very depressed as they get closer to their due dates—"

"Well, then we've got to find her, before she does something rash. She couldn't have gotten far! She doesn't have a car."

I am *so* wrong.

She has my car.

We find this out when we corner the manager of the valet service hired for the party.

"She said she lost her ticket, but described the car perfectly," explains the man, exasperated. "Besides, when was the last time a pregnant lady in this town stole a car?"

Today, I guess. That's what happens when one desperately wants to keep her baby.

I turn to the nurse. "Go get Trey! Tell him to meet me down the hill, in front of the yacht club. I'll run down the hill and head her off before she reaches Tiburon Boulevard and drives out of town."

There are many reasons I love Belvedere. Right now it's because there is only one quick way down from the Auchinclosses' estate, which sits on the island's highest point. Whereas all the streets downhill unfurl like a Slinky, there are several outdoor stairways built into the steep hillsides that provide shortcuts to walkers who may want to reach the bottom more quickly than even the narrow roads will allow.

I break a heel as I run down all fifty-six steps of Hawthorne Lane. The next stairway is five houses away, where a small painting denotes the start of the Cedar Lane steps. It is a bit shorter, but not by much: forty-two stone stairs that must have been put in during World War One. I hobble over them, cursing the fact I'm not wearing sneakers.

That walk ends a few houses down from the last set of Cedar Lane steps, which zig and zag between four landings, but drop me right in front of Belvedere's yacht club.

I'm relieved I've beat my car, which is just now barreling down the final stretch of narrow Beach Road. I flag down Ophelia. She is so shocked to see me standing in the middle of the street that she stops short when I hold out my hand. Otherwise I'm sure she would have run me down.

As she pulls over to the side, I jump into the passenger seat. "Ophelia, where the hell do you think you're going?"

"I've changed my mind! I can't let them have my child! I won't let them have her."

"But—but you have a contract with them."

"That doesn't matter. It was signed under duress." She reaches over to restart the car.

I take the key out of the ignition and toss it out the door.

"That's not true, and you know it. There were witnesses to the contract. You went through a series of videotaped screenings. Please, Ophelia! Don't put the Auchinclosses through this again!"

"You can't stop me, so don't even try! I've got to get out of here, now, because—because—"

She is so upset that she is gasping for air. Will she put her baby in distress? I have to calm her down before she does—

I slap her.

She's so shocked that she starts breathing again.

I wait a couple of minutes. Then, in a low voice I ask, "Ophelia, what do you want, really? I can understand how hard it must be to have a baby growing inside of you, and feel it is a part of you. But looking at the long-term picture, that isn't what this is really about, now, is it? And I know it's not about your feelings toward the Auchinclosses either. You and Elizabeth are getting along now. And it can't be the money, because they are taking care of everything for you: your pre- and postnatal care, your school loans, a full year's rent for your apartment, not to mention an extra fifty thousand dollars. They're even covering the taxes on what they're paying you. So, what is it that you want?"

The trail of tears drips onto her distended belly, which will soon be a thing of the past: by week's end, in fact, when she goes in for her already scheduled C-section.

"After I deliver this baby tomorrow, I won't have anyone. And that's all I really wanted! I want . . . *I want to have a family.*"

It's my turn to cry.

She stares at me while I bawl. Soon we are hugging.

When finally the sobs subside, I tell her the truth, even though I know it will be hard for her to hear:

"Look, Ophelia, I don't know why you took this on, or how the Auchinclosses found you, but I do know one thing. It's not just true for you, but for all of us: *any family you have will start with you.* The people you bring into it are there because they want to be; because they love you. They aren't there out of obligation or fear. They aren't there because you pay them to be there, or because they're your own flesh and blood. It's deeper than that."

"But there's no one in my life now but them, and this baby!"

"Then maybe it's time to ask yourself why. What have you been holding back? When are you going to start giving instead? Family has as much to do with what you create as with what's created for you."

She gulps down her objection. Because she knows I'm right. "How do I start?" Her voice is small, forlorn.

"Take the opportunity they're giving you. It's a fresh start. Begin living the life you want. Now you have no excuses. There is nothing—no one—holding you back."

She doesn't say anything, she just stares out at the sailboats bobbing across Raccoon Strait between Belvedere and Angel Island in the center of San Francisco Bay.

The tap on the window brings us both back to the here and now. Trey stares back at us. He bites his lip, but holds his tongue from releasing threats of lawsuits and breaches of fiduciary responsibility.

Because this is the mother of his child.

The other mother, anyway.

Whatever stubbornness his little girl has will come from her. Just like her elegance and good taste will be Elizabeth's contribution.

I hope my gift to Baby Auchincloss will be an ongoing relationship with her birth mother. If I'd had that, I might be more willing to follow the advice I just gave Ophelia.

I motion to Trey to follow us back up the hill.

Sometime after the party, when Elizabeth is basking in the glow of friends, family, and the anticipation of the coming event, I will lobby Trey to alter their contract with Ophelia to openly acknowledge her role in the birth of their daughter, and to allow for select visitation rights.

If not for Ophelia's emotional well-being, then for their child's.

33

....

I'm not interested in being Wonder Woman
in the delivery room. Give me drugs.
—*Madonna*

Monday, 27 August

MY FATHER NOW leaves little messages like this on my voice mail:

"Honey, was thinking about you today. Remember that time you let our dog, Ralphie, out of the yard, and he fell asleep in the neighbor's driveway, and that idiot, Carl Overton, ran over Ralphie's little paw? Poor mutt was in a cast for weeks! You'd put him in your little red wagon with the twins—how old were they then, four? Five? Anyway, you'd haul the three of them down to Santa Barbara Pier. The tourists thought you guys were so cute, they started giving you dollar bills. Even after Ralphie got better, the three of you would slip that cast back on him and con the tourists . . . Baby, I can see it in my mind, as if it were yesterday . . . I better hang up before this damn thing cuts me off. Call your mom. She misses you."

I don't call Mom. Instead I call Dad's doctor, to check on the progression of my father's disease. The doctor doesn't hold back. He tells me that the sight in Dad's left eye is almost gone now. Thank God the other eye only has the usual problems you'd find in a man hitting seventy. So far, though, no tumor there.

"But he is experiencing renal distress," Dr. Hendricks tells me. "We're doing what we can, but . . ."

But.

What he doesn't do is chide me for staying away.

Good, because guilt doesn't work when there's been a betrayal.

None of us can see into the future. Dad's way of compensating for that is to seek solace in the past.

I wish I could do the same.

11:54 a.m., Wednesday, 29 August

SETH IS into relationships, not booty calls. "I feel used," he mutters after a particularly acrobatic love tussle.

"Oh, really? Could have fooled me. Seemed like you loved every minute of it." I look over at the clock. "Make that *every hour*. Damn, where does the time go?" I jump up and scrounge around his floor for my clothes.

I'd stopped by unannounced. Since his dismissal from SkorTek, he's been scrambling for freelance jobs for high-tech companies that need him to write code. But his income has been cut by two-thirds, so he can no longer afford Fanny. On three mornings a week he leaves Sadie at a wonderful nursery co-op that owed me a favor for giving it one of my online Happy Face Medallions: my site's equivalent of the J.D. Power Award for Excellence.

The nursery is fine for Sadie until Seth gets a full-time gig. Then he'll need Fanny again.

But that doesn't look as if it will happen anytime soon. Seth refuses to sign Alex's buyout agreement, and therefore can't collect the token amount that comes with his doing so. In the meantime he's scrounging to find a lawyer who'll go after Henry and S&M on contingency.

Good luck with that.

"No, I mean it, Katie. I want us to go out on real dates." He sits up on the bed. I love the way he looks when he's naked. That's when you can see just how broad his shoulders really are, and you can marvel at that large scar on his abdomen, which he got while skateboarding, but he insists he'll tell Sadie it was the result of fighting off pirates in the South Seas.

Will I still be in their lives to see her reaction when he tells her that whopper?

That depends on how long I hold on to the pain that formed from hearing the truth of my own surreal past.

In the meantime, I know of one way to keep Seth thinking he's one step closer to me, when the truth is that, for now anyway, I need to hold him at bay:

I'll buy him lunch.

I toss his shirt to him. "Okay, want to go on a date? How about a bite to eat, say, Greek? La Méditerranée, over on Fillmore?"

"I'm in," he says, and buttons up quickly.

Men are so easy when food is part of the equation.

1:22 p.m.

I'VE NOTICED that everything I do these days has an ulterior motive.

This lunch is no exception. True, La Méditerranée's falafel sandwiches are to die for. Literally melt in your mouth. The wines are decent, and the waitstaff are comfortable with one another and their customers.

But today, I'm not here for the hummus.

I'm here for Joanna. This is her favored lunch hang.

Seth and I are just finishing up when she comes in, spots me, and approaches to exchange hugs and hellos.

Now, for step two of my plot. "Seth Harris, meet Joanna

Wallensky, one of the best corporate lawyers in the city. A shark you want swimming on your team."

"Nice to meet you." Seth holds out his hand, and they shake.

Joanna smiles. "No, the pleasure's all mine." She gives me an approving wink.

"Have a seat, Joanna. Hey—in fact, maybe you can help Seth, or provide a referral. He's got what I consider a great suit against Steadman & Martinez. After obtaining a board majority, they voted to dismiss Seth from his own company—all because he's a single parent and couldn't get coverage when his child was ill and had to go to the hospital."

Joanna frowns. "Assholes! But I'm guessing that was just one of the excuses they gave before kicking you out. Did you sign the dismissal contract?"

Seth shakes his head. "Hell, no. I'm not that stupid."

"Good. That's a start." She rummages in her purse and pulls out a business card. "Here, call my assistant to set up an appointment. I'll review your file, and if your case has merit, I'll get the ball rolling."

"But—well, I want to make something clear: I'm strapped for cash. If you don't mind taking it on contingency—"

"Let's talk about that when you come and see me." She digs into the baba ghanoush and lentil salad that have been placed in front of her, as if by magic: obviously one of the benefits of being a regular.

As Seth goes out front to sweet-talk the meter maid out of a ticket, I lean over to Joanna and whisper, "You were perfect! You know I'll cover your hourly fee in the meantime. Just send me the bill, but don't tell Seth. If this thing settles, you can apply your third to what's owed on my retainer."

"Then I presume he doesn't know I'm your attorney. Am I right?"

"No, and I don't want him to know it, either. I just want him to be able to move on. He can't until this is over."

Joanna shrugs. "You're one to talk. Thanks to Alex the Douche Bag, you've become one hard cookie. Haven't you even noticed the way Seth looks at you? He adores you."

I sigh. "Yeah, okay, what of it? Right now, I don't need to jump into another relationship. I need time to lick my wounds."

She shakes her head sadly. "Life is too short. He learned that the hard way. He's healing slowly but surely, and I'm glad for him." She nods toward Seth. "And I've no doubt you will, too. But please, Katie, for your own sake, don't take too long."

I know she's right. And yet my heart is still numb.

I give her a hug and hurry up to catch Seth.

3:35 p.m.

WHEN I get home, there is an invitation waiting for me in the mail:

Carolyn and Gordon Langford
announce the blessed arrival of their son, Gordon Lawrence, Jr.
born on August 2nd
5 pounds 1/2 ounce
Please join us in celebrating his journey into this world.

I tear up. Granted, the little guy came early, but Carolyn made it to term, and that's what counts.

She kept her word and had no shower. That's okay. Now we can celebrate in style with the guest of honor there, so all of us can hold him and coo to our heart's content.

I wouldn't miss it for the world. Besides Carolyn and Gordon, I'll be the happiest person there.

It's times like these that I realize I'm doing what I was meant to do.

"SHE NEEDS to see you," begs Edie.

Her plea is as simple as that.

This call has taken me by surprise, for several reasons: first, it is local, as opposed to coming from DC's area code, 202; second, there is no anonymous voice announcing that this call is to connect me with "Congressman Lovejoy's wife, Merrie."

And finally, I never thought I'd hear from Merrie—or, for that matter, any of her entourage—ever again.

So yes, I'm curious. "Why, Edie? What's up?"

For the longest time, Edie doesn't say anything. Then: "Please, just hear her out. We're not too far away: here, in the city. The Marriott."

I sigh. "Give me an hour."

This ought to be good.

EDIE IS ushering the children out of the suite when I get there.

"She's waiting for you," she whispers, just as the elevator doors close and they are propelled down into the real world.

The suite is opulent. Some PAC is going to be the recipient of a hefty hotel bill.

Merrie's feet have swelled. She is ready to pop. This should be a happy time for her, but from the puffiness around her eyes, I know it hasn't been. She turns her head to the wall so that I can't see her cry. It's rare that someone sees Merrie when she's vulnerable.

I'm not enjoying the privilege.

"April is pregnant," she says, finally. "I found out this morning. And get a load of this: she's already three months along—*and* it's a boy."

I sit down beside her. "Oh. Wow. Well, this certainly puts a different slant on things. Does the media know yet?"

"No. Right now she's sequestered in some tricked-out cabin in Big Sur. It's the second home of one of Michael's inner circle, and quite secluded." Merrie struggles to position herself so that she's not so uncomfortable. "She insists on keeping the bastard. Do you see where this is going? *She will always be in our lives.* Eventually she'll get tired of living in the shadows, and she'll want people to know. And there goes everything! All these years I've put into his career—and the hard work! All the kowtowing to this greedy, crazy constituency and that one—"

"Admit it, Merrie. You enjoy politics."

That stops her cold. A shadow of a smile crosses her lips. "I used to. When it was pure. When Michael was willing to say what he really meant, and stuck to his principles. That was when it was worth it."

"So leave him."

She stares at me. "But—but he's my life!"

"No, Merrie, he is *not* your life. And he's certainly not much of a husband. He hasn't been, for quite some time." I lean in. I want her to read my lips: *No new bullshit.* "Your life is your children. Your life is to be lived for the causes you believe in, not the compromises he asks you to make, and that disgust you."

Merrie glances up at me timidly. "Just what are you saying, Katie?"

"I'm saying that, if you want to stay in politics, do it for yourself, not for him. Whether you wanted to admit it to yourself or not, you've always been the captain of the Good Ship Lovejoy. And he's been the albatross taking you off course. If you're going to play the game, then play it to win."

"You're right. Why should I wait for this thing to blow up around me? Why should I let the two of them control my destiny?" She shoves herself up out of the chair and over to the window. It looks out toward the horizon and the panoramic sunset, where a sherbet sun melts into a deep blue sapphire ocean. "All it takes is one well-placed call to the *Washington Post* from an anonymous tipster, and the jig is up. Michael goes down in flames, right before the election."

"I guess that means the competition will be a shoo-in for his seat."

"Yeah, sure, that guy will hold on to the seat for a while—but not for long. Had he been a real threat, we would have released some dirt on him that would have him heading for the border. If I wait to release the story right after he's sworn in, then when he resigns the state will have to hold a special election." Her smile is triumphant. "By then my memoir will be on the bestseller list, and Michael's constituents will remember all the things I stood for."

I wince at that. Hopefully they'll forget all her waffling on every imaginable issue . . .

"Hmmm, I wonder whom I should have Edie call with the tip: Dana Priest? Alex Birnbaum?"

The thought of a new world order has Merrie quite literally peeing her pants.

I stare down at her feet. "Um . . . Merrie, are you okay?"

Merrie gasps. "Oh my goodness! My water just broke!"

I pull out my cell. "I'll have an ambulance here in a second, to take us to California Pacific. What's Michael's telephone number? I'll call him, too—"

"Don't bother. He's in Big Sur with his mistress." She spits out the words. "Besides, it will read better in the press that he was there, as opposed to being at my delivery." She lowers herself back down onto a settee. "Well, it's about damn time."

"Yeah, I know. It must be hard toward the end. You just want the baby out and into your arms—"

"No, I mean it's damn time I got rid of Michael . . . Oh, by the way, my baby is a girl. How fast do you think it will take to paint the nursery pink?"

34

. . . .

A baby is something you carry inside you for nine months,
in your arms for three years,
and in your heart till the day you die.
—Mary Mason

F OUND HER." CHARLIE Reynolds, my birth parent detective, knows that's all he has to say to me.

I stop what I'm doing, which is some blog post blarney about Happy Hemp's environmental benefits. "What? Where . . . *How?*"

"These kinds of cases are always a little luck, and a lot of persistence. Oh yeah, and payoffs. By the way, I'm tacking on an extra thou to your bill, to cover a little bribe I made."

"You had to bribe someone to get ahold of my birth records?"

"Hell no, that was the easy part. The hard part was getting to your mother."

My mother.

"The big day takes place next week. I'll call you when I have more details."

"Wait! When—"

It's too late. He has already hung up.

* * *

11:30 a.m., Saturday, 8 September

"TRICK OR treat," says Seth.

It's not, really. That is still almost two months off.

And besides, it's broad daylight.

He has stopped by my place, out of the blue. He claims he was jogging through Crissy Field, but I don't believe him. Yes, he's in sweats, but he's not damp or breathing hard.

And he's carrying roses.

I wish they weren't yellow. They remind me of the ones Alex brought Twila that awful night.

Before I can move, he pecks me on the cheek and lets himself in.

"I presume you got an invitation to Carolyn Langford's party tonight," he asks.

"Yes, I got an invitation. I didn't realize you even knew Carolyn."

"Hell yeah, I met her at one of your meet-ups. Remember?"

"No, not really." I hadn't realized he'd talked to anyone other than Twila that evening.

I pretend to look for a vase, but I really don't want the flowers. The minute he leaves I'll walk them over to my next-door neighbor. She is a lonely old spinster whom no one ever visits. I know she'll appreciate them.

"Why don't we go together? It starts at eight, so I'll pick you up at, say, seven thirty? That will give us time to find parking."

"Can you get a babysitter?"

"Fanny would be happy to do it. She misses us. She misses you, too."

"The feeling is mutual."

"Glad to hear it." He moves in for a real kiss, but I hold the flowers and the vase between us.

We can't make love here. I still feel Alex in every room.

Especially the bedroom.

I threw out all the rubbers, though. They were defective anyway.

After the divorce is over, I'll put the house on the market.

That means finding a new Realtor, since I no longer speak to the twins.

6:22 p.m.

WHEN WE get there, the party is already in full swing.

I am greeted at the door by Carolyn and little Gordon, or Gordy, as they are already calling him. He squints and yawns and grips his tiny fists tightly. When Carolyn puts him in my arms, she coos softly to him: "Here is your aunt Katie! She was the one who told me you'd never leave me."

My faith worked then, for her, but I've lost it in the meantime.

Turns out the doctor who was Carolyn's infertility specialist is also the one recommended by Dr. Rankin. Someday soon I'll call her.

But first I have to begin believing again.

Carolyn rises on her tiptoes to give Seth a kiss. He strokes the baby gently with his hand. When I offer to let him hold Gordy, he does so with an ease that makes me smile.

Many of the partygoers are people I know: women from my meet-ups; wives who are, or were, clients of mine; and their husbands, who give cloudy nods when we are reintroduced. They can tell their wives are fond of me, but they forget why.

I guess my legacy to the world is helping women feel inspired and happy throughout their pregnancies. Ironically, it's a journey I may never experience myself.

Seth and I have been mingling with our hosts and the other

guests for an hour when I feel someone staring at me. As it turns out, it is four someones:

Lana and Grace are here, with Thor and Auggie.

For a moment I feel as if I'm in a diorama: it seems that we've all quit moving and stopped breathing at the very same moment.

Grace and Lana turn from me to each other. Their emotions are mirrored almost exactly: surprise, anxiety, hope, doubt, then back to hope again.

But what they hope for is not going to happen.

No, I am not going to wave, or say hello, or embrace them.

Instead, I put down my tiny plate of appetizers and head for the door, walking right past them, even brushing up against Grace, who is now so very big with child.

Seth, who sees the shock on my face, says our good-byes for us. As casually as possible, he heads out the door behind me.

When I reach the car, I slam my fist on the roof—not because I'm so desperate to get into it, but because I'm anxious to get out of this emotional abyss I've fallen into.

I hear Seth's footsteps coming up quickly behind me. "What was that all about?" He turns me around so that I have to look at him. "What is happening between you and your sisters?"

"It's none of your business, Seth!"

"Katie, I'm making it my business." Gently but firmly he pushes me down into the passenger seat and closes the door. Then he walks around to the driver's side and gets in. "Please, talk to me."

The tears start, and it doesn't seem as if I'll ever be able to make them stop. I don't know if he can hear my words through my sobs, but it actually feels good to hear it said out loud, as opposed to keeping it locked away in the dark void that's now my heart:

"We're no longer close. We're no longer family. I'm adopted, but no one told me—not until my father came down with a disease that can be passed along from one generation to the next."

"Did your sisters know?"

It's easier for me to shake my head than choke out the word. When, finally, I can speak again, I add, "I know it's not their fault. But between finding out about that, and about Alex, and the fact that I can't have a baby—"

"What? When did you hear that?"

"Damn, Seth, don't you get it? All of this happened on—*that day.*"

He lets that sink in. Suddenly he's angry, too. At me. "No, Katie, I don't get it—*because you won't tell me anything.* In fact, had I not known Alex had gone out with Twila, I don't think you would have mentioned the breakup, either." He slams his hand down on the steering wheel. "All we do is screw."

Finally, something to laugh about. "Gee, I've never heard a guy complain about *that* before."

"Maybe that's because no man has ever truly been in love with you."

He's so serious that it stops me cold.

"Maybe no man cared to hear about your day—or wanted you to share your problems. Well, I do." He picks up my hand and stares down at it. "Katie, when you came over that night and told me what had happened to you and Alex, I knew your heart had been broken. If I'd even known about the other things, how do you think I would have reacted?"

"Just like this. *You would have cared too much.*" I pull my hand out from his. "Seth, don't you get it? Grace and Lana care too much, too. That's why it hurts me to be around them. I don't want to see the pity in their eyes—"

"Seriously, is that what you think, that they pity you?"

"Yes! They have children. I don't. They have loving husbands. I . . . never did. They know their real parents—*and I don't*. Not anymore."

"Are you telling me your parents told you that you were adopted, then abandoned you?"

"No, of course not!" I shake my head in annoyance. "What I'm trying to say is that in thirty-seven years they never took the time to tell me the truth. Why is that? How could they have done that to me?"

He hesitates, as if wondering whether what he has to say will make sense to me. "Because, in the big scheme of things, it doesn't really matter."

"Yes, Seth, it does matter! *Because it matters to me.* Just like whether I got pregnant with Alex's child mattered—"

"Despite the fact it didn't matter to him."

It comes out before I can stop it: "Well, isn't that how your own wife, Nicole, felt?"

His head reels back. It's as if I've hit him in the gut. "Does it still matter to you, Katie?"

"Having a baby matters, yes. And finding my real mother matters, too."

"What about your sisters, your parents? Do they matter?"

I bite my lip. "I know they will again. Someday."

"How about me, Katie? Do I count?"

Yes, he matters. But like me, he is vulnerable.

And so I don't answer him.

I refuse to be the one who hurts him this time around.

He shrugs. "I guess I have my answer."

He starts the car. Neither of us talks on the way home.

Ever the gentleman, he gets out to open my door when we get to my place. "Good-bye, Katie."

Just like that.

I want to stop him, but I can't.

When he drives away, I want to run after him.

But then, what would I do if I caught him? Could I ever love him as much as he loves me?

Right now I don't have the emotional strength to try.

I have to save it up for the meeting I'll soon have with my real mother.

35

· · · · · · · · · · ·

Biology is the least of what makes someone a mother.
—Oprah Winfrey

2:41 p.m., Monday, 10 September

So, YOU'RE MY big sis. Imagine that."

It's almost three o'clock in the afternoon. The man sitting across from me on a cracked leather banquette in the Mel's Drive-In on Sunset Boulevard in Los Angeles happens to be my brother, Rodney Gardner. He is closer in age to the twins than to me, of medium build and height, and well dressed, but he smells of liquor, which has dulled his eyes and, I presume, loosened his inhibitions.

Why else would he be leering at me, as if I were a hooker instead of his long-lost sister?

I smile politely and try to keep the tremble out of my voice. "I know absolutely nothing of the circumstances of my adoption. If your mother—*our* mother—sent you, please tell her I'd like to meet her, if that's her wish, too—"

He laughs heartily at that. "Oh no! Au contraire! Mother doesn't know I'm here. I wouldn't have told her in a million years—at least, not until I had a good look at you myself."

Rodney hasn't taken his eyes off me since I entered the diner. Not that I blame him. I turn my head in order to avoid my own natural inclination to seek out any and all characteristics we may share: the slant of our noses, perhaps, or the color of our eyes, or maybe the shape of our ears.

I wonder what might be the cause of his obvious disdain for me.

"Do I look like her?"

"There's no doubt about it. Trust me, she won't be able to deny it." And with that, a smile appears on his thin lips.

Relief washes over me. "That's good to know. Look, I know this sounds rushed, but it has been my obsession to meet her since I found out about—about my true circumstances. How soon do you think that can be arranged?"

He smiles grandly. "How about tonight? You can join us for dinner, at the house." He hands me a business card. On the back he's already scribbled an address, on Bellagio Road. I recognize that as one of the premier streets of Bel Air, somewhere high in the hills.

"Tonight? That would be great!" I rummage in my purse and pull out a business card. "You can call me on the cell phone number listed here. You can also reach me at the Sunset Tower, where I'm staying while I'm in town."

He nods appraisingly. "You have wonderful taste. That's another family trait." When he stands up, he takes my hand. But he holds it too tight.

It's all I can do to keep myself from pulling away and running out the door.

What stops me is the overwhelming curiosity I have about my birth mother and my real family. "Can you tell me something about her? Do I have any other siblings?"

"You also have a sister, Claudine. She'll be there tonight, too, believe me. As for Mother, she's a beautiful woman—much like yourself. Laughs a lot. Throws herself into charity work. A free-spirited type." He pauses and smiles. "I guess that's where you come into the picture."

"So, I was a mistake." I already knew this. I just had to say it out loud, once; to yank off this little bandage of reality now, quickly, so that it will never hurt again.

"Isn't it obvious?" He laughs uproariously. "No matter. Father claims he's loved her since the moment he met her. In his eyes, she could do no wrong. Mother is an angel. And now we'll be one big happy family."

One big happy family.

I thought I had that, once.

I hope Rodney is right.

6:33 p.m.

THE FACE that opens the front door of the stately Gardner mansion in Bel Air is mine.

I feel as if I'm looking two decades into the future, and it has been good to me: yes, there are more wrinkles, and a few more pounds. My hair is thinner, and possibly grayer, but that's not easy to tell because any probable white strands have been professionally highlighted.

If our faces were exact mirror images, her smile would have gotten only bigger, instead of fading with the shock, as it does now. I recognize the disappointment I see, as I've seen it on my own face, too often recently. Her eyes, light green like mine, darken with sadness.

No, make that suspicion. I know this when she whispers, "Oh, my sweet Lord! Why you, why now?"

I don't understand what's happening here. "Weren't you expecting me?"

I look from her to those standing behind her: Rodney, and a woman who looks to be around the age of the twins. She is taller than I am, and thinner.

If possible, she is angrier, too.

Only Rodney seems happy and at peace.

"Sorry, Mother, I forgot to mention we'd have a guest for

dinner tonight, but I thought you wouldn't mind, considering she's *family*. This is Katie. *Harlow.*"

He waits for the full force of my adopted surname to hit her.

It does: broadside, reeling her away from me, as if I'm her worst nightmare come to life.

It dawns on me now that I am.

"Who is she?" asks my new sister. What was her name again? Oh yes, Claudine. She peers closely at me. "Should we know her?"

"I'll say," answers Rodney. "She's our *sister*. Or I should say, she's Mother's first child." His wink makes me feel dirty.

I realize I've been deceived, but I don't know how, or why.

Hearing her worst suspicions confirmed, my mother nods slowly. With a tentative wave, she motions for me to follow her in.

I can tell she wants to cry, but won't give Rodney the satisfaction of watching her do so.

If she won't, then I won't, either. If that's all we share today, so be it.

7:13 p.m.

THROUGHOUT THE meal, I am cross-examined by Claudine, who is suspicious and surly. "Funny, how you've popped up just now. But I guess it couldn't be better timing. Despite everything, Father will want to know about this."

I am so upset at the turn of events that I can't eat a bite of the gourmet meal cooked by a chef with Cordon Bleu training, and served by a butler in uniform. That's not why I'm here anyway. "I didn't come to make trouble. I wanted to meet my parents." I look at my mother when I say this, but she keeps her mouth shut and avoids my eyes at all costs.

"Our father is not yours," Claudine snarls. "So don't get any big ideas."

"I'm sorry, I have no idea what you're talking about," I answer.

"Oh, no? You mean to tell me you don't know who he is?"

"How could I? And if he's not my father, what difference does it make?"

She opens her mouth to answer, but then swallows her retort with a spoonful of mashed potatoes.

Good. Like I give a hoot. At this point, she can choke on those potatoes, for all I care.

I look over at Rodney. Yes, he's enjoying this little tête-à-tête. He answers the anger in my eyes with a shrug. "Well, it makes a very big difference to Mother. You see, he may not take kindly to the notion of a bastard child, and write Mommy dearest out of the will."

"Finally," murmurs Claudine.

I can't believe my ears. "What is wrong with you people? Don't you care about your own mother?"

My new siblings gawk at me, then burst out laughing.

Finally Claudine collects herself enough to sputter out, "That's rich! In the first place, she's not 'our' mother. Our mother died when we were quite young."

This memory seems to be a killjoy for Rodney. His cough dies down into an uneasy silence.

Apparently that doesn't matter to his sister. She's having too much fun. "Katherine is our father's *second* wife," she adds as she smiles over at my mother. "He makes us call her Mother. I guess it assuages his guilt for marrying her so soon after our *real* mother was buried."

"Oh, now, cut him some slack, Claudine," says Rodney, but his tone warns us that he'll do anything but. "He was a wealthy grieving widower with a couple of kids under the age of ten. Every woman in town wanted him. She just got there first. And to think, she was the nun who taught us in the first grade! Quite a hoot, now, isn't it?"

I look over at Katherine Gardner. Shame hangs heavy on her head. The tears drop off the tip of her nose, into her delicate Limoges soup bowl. When they land in the bouillabaisse, it ripples out, causing the tiny pink roses hand-painted on the bowl's bottom to quiver, as if they were real.

"But now that Father's dying, maybe he'll finally see dear Mama for what she really is," continues Rodney. "I mean, really! What kind of woman abandons a child?"

That woman—the woman who is my mother—looks from them to me. Then, although she is shaking, she stands up and leaves the table.

I don't blame her at all. There is no place for her here, with them.

I turn to Rodney. "Why are you hurting her this way?"

"Oh, don't take it so personally. She's served her function. She's kept him happy as a lark all these years. Too happy, for our taste. The way his will is currently written, she'll end up controlling our trust funds. When he finds out about you, I guess it will make him rethink that. And not a moment too soon."

"Why? What's happening? Where is he now?"

"Down the hall. He's bedridden. Emphysema. Smoking is such a bad habit." He shakes his head. "Well, at least his condition is not genetic."

NO ONE tries to stop me as I rush after my mother, down a long, stately hall. I catch her right outside a set of large mahogany double doors. Even with the hallway's thick carpet, she must have heard my footsteps because she turns around. Her face is now calm, but her eyes are still steely.

"Please, can we talk?" I beg her.

"I don't think there is anything left to say. As cruel as Rodney is, he's also right. I abandoned you. I got pregnant when I was far too young. When I gave you up, I knew I was doing the right thing." She raises her head. "I still feel that what I did was for the best. For both of us. God gave us both a second chance."

No! This is not what I want to hear. I want her to admit that she regretted her decision, that she wished I'd been at her side all these years.

That I'd been her family, not these horrible people.

But that's not going to happen. I see that now. It's all in her eyes, the ones that look just like mine.

For almost three decades, her second chance has taken place here: on a five-acre gated estate high above Los Angeles, with its two wings filled with French antiques and Impressionist paintings, its emerald lawns with views of the distant Pacific.

And now she hopes that her dying husband will still love and forgive her, and protect her from those who will do her harm.

Not the least of those are Rodney and Claudine. And I am the heat-seeking missile they will use to destroy her world.

So much for second chances.

Does God ever grant a third?

Katherine Gardner holds out her hand. We are supposed to shake now, and say good-bye, I imagine forever.

For the longest time, I stare down at her delicate hand. When finally I take it, I try to hold on to the heat that flows between the two of us, because I know it will be the only pleasant memory I'll ever have of her.

10:47 p.m.

THIS TIME of night, the ride from Los Angeles to Santa Barbara takes only ninety minutes.

When I knock on the door, the face that looks back at me belongs to someone who has loved me my entire life. This face has always comforted me when I was forlorn. From its lips come the smiles that make me laugh, and the words that inspire me.

A lifetime of looking into the depth of its eyes has taught me to read them well. It is not a second language, but rather my first.

What I see in them now is forgiveness.

My mother—the woman who raised me—is granting me that, and asking for my forgiveness as well.

She only has to look in my eyes to know she has it.

Our hug is accompanied by silent tears that commingle, and by sobs that have us trembling in unison.

My father can't see me—the house is too dark, and as I'm to find out later that night, his vision is now totally gone in his left eye.

But when you raise a child, even her silence can be heard loud and clear.

Dad only needs to sense me.

Despite the tears flowing down his face, he smiles and says the words I most needed to hear:

"Welcome home, Katie."

36

A mother is a person who,
seeing there are only four pieces of pie for five people,
promptly announces she never did care for pie.
—*Tenneva Jordan*

10:13 a.m., Saturday, 22 September

I'LL BET YOU don't remember me," says the woman with a dark brown ponytail.

My meet-up is jam-packed. Over a hundred women have come up to me to ask a question, or to thank me for a well-received blog post, or to comment on a product they feel is worthy of my praise.

And yet, there is something familiar about this one woman, but I simply can't put my finger on it.

The newborn boy mewing in the Baby Bjorn strapped to her chest is the biggest clue. Like his mother, he is adorned with dark curls . . .

Ah, yes, now I know who she is.

"Yes, of course I remember you! We met at my business launch party," I say. "Good to see you again, Lacie Channing. And congratulations on this little guy. He's so beautiful." I grin. "You see? You didn't need me after all."

She laughs joyously. I'm sure she was thinking exactly that. But to my surprise she says, "Oh, I don't know about that. I'm sure you've got some tips that keep moms inspired, even during round-the-clock feedings."

Her graciousness is appreciated.

"In fact," she continues, "I'm here to collect on my win."

Now it's my turn to laugh. "Sure, any way I can help."

"I'm glad you said that." Her smile fades and her voice reflects a more serious tone. "Is there a chance we can meet sometime later this week?"

I nod, and we exchange business cards. Whatever she wants has got to be important. This is not the kind of woman who needs help in setting up her son's nursery.

This is a woman who is out to change the world.

Okay, I'm up for that.

2:03 p.m., Sunday, 23 September

MY RENDEZVOUS with Lacie takes place at San Francisco's Homeless Mothers Program. The building, on the outskirts of the Mission District, is teeming with women from all walks of life. Many are pregnant. Others have children in tow.

"The goal here is to get—and keep—these women and their families off the streets," explains Lacie. "It doesn't matter what put them there. They're here now because they're determined to change things."

"But some of these women are substance abusers, am I right?" I know that sounds blunt, but I have to ask.

Lacie doesn't flinch. "Yes, some have been. But part of our mission is to help those who are willing to help themselves. It's a vicious circle. Like all children, they've learned from their parents both good habits and bad. But the people you see here"—she points into the classrooms we pass—"are determined to change. We help them put a roof over their heads, meals, and clothing. Do you know how many of our clients have children with birth defects? The number is much higher than that of the general population, partly because many have never had prenatal care. We introduce them to clinics, where they can get the health care they need, for themselves and for their children."

"But that's just a Band-Aid on the problem. Is there any long-term residual from this program?"

Lacie nods her head. "Through our yearlong employment training program, we teach them the skills they need to be productive, and help them find jobs to support their families."

"So how can I help?"

"Katie, you endorse a lot of products. Maybe you can twist a few arms and get some much needed donations for our moms, who can't afford diapers, or formula, or strollers or toys—or even clothing and shoes for their children."

I think of all the free samples delivered daily to Making Mommies Smile. Some get rejected by my mommy testers because they don't have the time or need for them.

Well, now I've found some women who need all the help they can get.

"Of course, I'll be glad to help. In fact, I've got a truckload of stuff that can be picked up whenever you want."

Lacie smiles. "Great. We'll send a truck over to your place tomorrow, then."

Something tells me this is the start of a beautiful friendship.

10:05 a.m., Monday, 24 September

"LONG TIME no hear from," chides Helen.

"Hey, the phone is a two-way instrument," I counter.

"Fair enough," she concedes. "So, how have you been?"

"Busy. Being single is harder than I thought."

She laughs. "Consider the alternative."

"Usually the punch line to that is 'dead.'"

"You're the one who married an asshole. In hindsight, which would have been preferable to you?"

I snort. "You've made your point. Hey, I've got a proposition for you: what do you think of getting the old team back together? I'm changing the direction of Making Mommies Smile. I feel it needs a professional testing division. My followers deserve it."

"Hmmm. Now, there's a thought. But how will your advertising and endorsement accounts feel about it? I would think they'd prefer the sort of cheerleading they've already been getting from all those viewers who are just grateful to get a few freebies."

"Oh, I'll still give out samples. But from now on they'll only come from the accounts that have earned our MMS Happy Badge, and it can't be bought. This way, we'll have a double rating system. You know, professionally tested, and mommies' choice. In fact, I'm raising the bar even higher: advertisers will also have to donate a small percentage of sales and a minimum amount of product to charities that help homeless mothers get on their feet."

"That shouldn't be such a hard sell. It's a tax write-off."

"Not to mention a great public relations move," I add.

"I love this kinder, gentler Katie."

"I'm not a complete softie. Trust me, I'll be working you to the bone. Here's how I see it: you'll review nursery and playroom furnishings, and me-time products; Allison will get food products, and family fun; and Karin will handle gadgets and gear."

"'Me-time'? I love the sound of that." She pauses. "Let me get this straight: you're telling all ad clients 'no badge, no ad'?"

"Exactly."

"Well then, I guess it's good-bye, Happy Hemp."

"That's okay. Happy Hemp was actually a load of crap to begin with."

Helen has always loved a good pun. Even a bad one. When I hang up, she's still laughing.

37

Father asked us what was God's noblest work.
Anna said men, but I said babies.
Men are often bad, but babies never are.
—Louisa May Alcott

10:36 a.m., Monday, 1 October

I RARELY GRAB COFFEE at the Squat & Gobble on Chestnut Street. My hang has always been the Grove, catty-corner across the street. Today, though, the line at the Grove is out the door, and I need my caffeine fix like now, so what the heck, why not give the Squat a try.

They are coming out the door right as I'm entering: Alex and Twila.

It's been almost three months since that hellish day. His hair is a bit longer, and he seems bulkier than I remember. Twila, though, has lost any baby fat she may have ended up with, and is as stylish as ever, in tight jeans that would fit a teen girl, and sky-high heels.

And here I am, in yoga pants that haven't seen the inside of a yoga studio since—

Aw hell, who cares?

He holds the door open for her while she struggles with a state-of-the-art stroller, so he sees me first. First he turns white, then red, then white again.

If he has a heart attack and dies, does his insurance policy still list me as the beneficiary?

Blood money is bad karma. Of course I'd donate it all to charity . . .

He gives a stoic nod and a wave. I take a secret delight in his look of total discomfort. On the other hand, Twila searches my face, presumably for signs of pain.

Neither, though, is stupid enough to stoop to pity.

"Katie," declares Alex, as if that's some form of hello.

All I can do is nod.

But as I do-si-do past the stroller, I can't help but look inside.

As I suspected, their baby is beautiful.

"You can hold her, if you want," says Twila.

I look up. Her eyes beg me to do it, as if, by my holding her child, she'll finally be granted the redemption she so desperately seeks.

I shake my head and give the only excuse I can think of: "Oh no, I have a cold."

She must know I'm lying. But at least I wasn't blunt about why I'm passing: for me, holding a baby is an honor.

More so because I'll never hold one of my own.

But holding her and Alex's would be no privilege at all, only something I'd regret.

Suddenly it dawns on me that it's ten thirty on a weekday. "Alex, why aren't you at the office?"

He blushes. "I . . . I decided to take a sabbatical. It was Twila's idea."

Well, at least this time he's trying to bond with his child. That's certainly a step in the right direction.

Still, I can't help but smirk.

This seems to annoy Alex. "What are you laughing at?"

"I'm just thinking about all the little ironies of life. Stop me if I'm wrong, but aren't you trying to shove Seth Harris out of his own company with the excuse that he took too much time off for his infant? My God, he's a single dad whose wife died in childbirth—"

"Wait . . . what?" Alex stares at me, as if snapping out of a daze.

"You heard me. 'Survival of the fittest,' remember? What was he supposed to do, let his daughter die of neglect when she had a fever?"

Twila looks from me to him. "Alex, what the hell is she talking about?"

I take pleasure in filling her in. "Seth had to leave one of their bullshit 'strategy sessions' in order to meet me at the hospital. His five-month-old daughter had a dangerously high fever. Alex is using that as grounds to take his company away from him—"

She turns to Alex and glares at him. "Boy, that is low."

Alex grabs my arm. "What do you mean his wife died in childbirth? I didn't know she was dead!"

"That's thanks to Henry. He thought if you knew about it before they signed with you, it would have scared you off and made the deal a nonstarter."

"It's practically a nonstarter anyway," mutters Alex.

"Oh yeah? Why is that?"

He shrugs. "Seth's a smart guy. He's got himself some wily attorney. She's going to drag this thing out for quite some time. The longer that happens, the longer it takes for us to recoup our investment. Not to mention, of the two of them, it turns out that Seth was the brains of the operation."

"Too bad you had to find that out the hard way."

"Katie, seriously, had I known about Seth's loss, I would not have made his absences part of the dismissal."

I pat his shoulder. "Oh, I know that, Alex. I also know you would have come up with some other excuse—especially after seeing him with Twila."

Both of them turn beet red.

At this point, it doesn't matter how great the chicken-apple sausages tasted with their omelets. I've left them with a bitter taste in their mouths.

Now that it's almost eleven, the line at the Grove has disappeared.

Screw the coffee. I'm ready for happy hour.

38
·············

The heart of a mother is a deep abyss at the bottom
of which you will always find forgiveness.
—Honoré de Balzac

9:03 a.m., Wednesday, 3 October

THE LAWYER EXPLAINS that he's calling from some law firm I've never heard of. It's got six names, all of them WASP, and it's located down in Los Angeles.

"The reading of the will takes place tomorrow, two o'clock, our offices," says the man, who also happens to be the third name on the marquee. "Will you be able to attend?"

I feel the bile rising in my stomach. "I'm sorry, I don't know what you're talking about. Can you tell me who . . . who died?"

"Rodney Gardner senior."

"Well, what does that have to do with me?"

He pauses before answering. "You were his eldest daughter."

I promise him I'll be there.

2:08 p.m., Thursday, 4 October

NEITHER VILE Rodney junior nor odious Claudine deem me worthy to look at, let alone acknowledge.

Frankly, that's a relief. Why pretend there is any love lost between us?

Katherine looks even older than at our first encounter. I have no doubt that her love for the elder Mr. Gardner was genuine.

Too bad his other children weren't willing to accept that.

I tune out during most of the legalese. It's nice, though, to discover that my biological father was generous toward many charities, but it makes it even more bittersweet to me that I did not get to know him before he died.

When junior and sis's names are read, the amount of their trust funds would have the average guy on the street quitting his day job and checking real estate prices for small South Pacific islands. Not these two. They gnash their teeth and harrumph loudly.

Something tells me that it will do no good. From the looks of this law firm's plush formal offices high over Wilshire Boulevard, I'm guessing that Gardner senior's will is as tight as a condom.

Okay, probably tighter.

"—and to Katie Harlow, my long-lost daughter, whose existence was not made known to me until it was too late for me to demonstrate the affection she deserves, I hope this trust, with an allowable withdrawal percentage of five percent or five hundred thousand dollars per annum, whichever is greater, will provide some comfort for her."

The reasoning part of my mind switches off for a moment. *What? Five percent, or half a million dollars?*

My heart skips a beat. As astounded as I am, though, the thought still occurs to me that I would trade all of that to have known my biological father.

Yes, I have a part of his estate, and his blood surging in my veins, his genetic pool. But do I have his sense of humor? How about his laugh?

Katherine would know this.

Afterward, I invite her to coffee. It pleases me greatly that she accepts.

3:13 p.m.

"I HAVE to apologize for how I treated you the first time we met." Katherine's eyes moisten at the thought. "What with my husband—your father's—illness, Rodney junior's deception brought out the worst in me."

"Thanks for that," I answer.

My attempt at graciousness is to forgo telling her how crushed I was by her rejection.

For the next hour, I satisfy her curiosity: about my adoptive parents, the siblings I grew up with, my childhood, my company, and even my broken marriage to Alex.

She keeps silent throughout. Melancholy leavens her smile. I presume that like me, she regrets losing out on all the time that we could have spent together.

But as she said before, she wanted a second chance for both of us.

Seems we're getting a third chance as well.

"Your turn," I declare, as I signal our waiter for refills.

She tries to sigh away her tears, but can't. "He was my first and only love," she explains. "We met in high school. He went to a private prep. I was at a Catholic school. Our basketball teams played opposite each other one night. But once we laid eyes on each other we were inseparable."

They were also naive, especially when it came to contraception. "My parents were livid. They sent me away to a home for unwed mothers. It was Catholic, of course. I was ashamed, and felt abandoned. In truth, I'd never told Rod about . . . about you."

Whereas her parents were unforgiving, the nuns were kind. Giving me up was a sacrifice that encouraged her to look deep inside herself. Taking her vows seemed like the next natural step.

"I was happy in my faith. I taught at the same elementary school I'd attended as a child."

She knew who little Rodney was, that very first moment he entered her first-grade class. "Besides sharing Rod's name, he was a miniature of his father," she says sadly. She tried hard not to show him any favors, but how could she not?

"And of course, I thought about you. How different things would have been if I'd kept you, if you could have met your brother, played with him."

Her relationship with the first Mrs. Gardner was cordial. Rodney senior, a hardworking captain of industry, never came to parent-teacher conferences. For this she was glad. "It would have been too hard on me."

By the time little Claudine entered her class, the fact that the first Mrs. Gardner's cancer was inoperable was already a foregone conclusion.

That's when Rod took over the duties of meeting with his children's teachers.

"Our reunion was sad. He was in mourning. Our friendship was his solace. I was his *friend*." She emphasizes this last word in order to make that clear to me. "As we became comfortable with each other again, he asked the question that always comes up: why did I become a nun?"

Knowing that the true reason would have devastated them both, she lied.

She didn't tell him about me.

She was too ashamed. I would always be her cross to bear.

Had he known, would he have cared? Would he have tried to find me?

I have my answer in his very generous gift to me.

"From what you told me, Katie, you strike me as very self-sufficient. I presume you'll put your inheritance to good use."

I nod, thinking about all that I can do with the money. Dad

will see the best doctors. I will set aside trusts in the names of my niece and nephews.

That's when I tell her about my new grand scheme: creating a Making Mommies Smile Foundation. It will give grants to organizations like the Homeless Mothers Program.

She leans over and gives me a kiss. "If you want, I'd be honored to sit on your board."

"Thank you, Katherine," I answer. "The women I have in mind for it are an inspiring group, one in particular. I can't wait for you to meet my mother, Ruth."

39

....

A baby is God's opinion that the world should go on.
—Carl Sandburg

1:10 p.m., Saturday, 13 October

I S IT SOUP yet?" That is my way of asking Grace if she feels as if today will be the day we welcome the newest member of our family into this brave new world.

She sighs. "Nah. *Nada.* The doc says everything is as it should be: the baby has dropped and is in position. So I guess it's only a matter of time."

No one knows that better than me.

All is revealed in the fullness of time.

"Are Mom and Dad there?"

"No, they're over at Lana's. Dad is letting Mario read to him." She sounds a bit melancholy. I know what she's thinking. A month ago Dad would have been reading to his oldest grandson instead of the other way around.

As I toss another log in my fireplace, I remind her, "I'm here if you need me. Have Lana or Auggie text my cell if I don't pick up my phone."

"Just don't hold your breath." She laughs. "I said that to Jezebel, and she now does it just to spite me."

"It's good practice for her, before she starts swim class."

"That's easy for you to say! You're not the one who has to catch her when she passes out!"

We've just hung up when I hear the door buzzer. I'm guessing it's UPS because I get deliveries every day, thanks to all the advertisers who are willing to have their products tested and touted on my site.

But no, it's not Mr. UPS.

It's Mr. Seth Harris.

This time, however, he doesn't have flowers.

Not that I blame him. I don't deserve them.

"May I come in?" Seth's question is simple, but his tone is formal.

I nod and open the door wide.

Although I walk into the living room, he stops in the foyer. "I just wanted to tell you that S&M settled the dismissal suit."

"Oh . . . wow! That's great . . . isn't it?"

My question puts a faint smile on his lips. "Yeah, in fact it is, because they agreed to all our terms, which included Henry's dismissal and my reinstatement. Oh, and I get Henry's equity as well."

"And what does Henry get?"

"He doesn't get sued for, quote, 'withholding vital information about the well-being of the company prior to S&M's equity buy-in.'"

"What exactly does that mean?"

"It means Alex found out about Nicole."

I can't hide my smile.

"Ah," he says, "I thought so."

"Are you upset with me?"

"Upset over that? How could I be? It encouraged him to settle. Of course it was a gamble. Who knew Alex had a conscience?" It's his turn to grin. "Then again, Nicole's death would have come out in the countersuit that Joanna was going to file next week. Frankly, I'm happier it came from you."

"Why do you say that?"

"Had it not been settled favorably, just think of all the money you'd have lost."

"You mean, Joanna told you about that?" I turn away, embarrassed. "She promised she wouldn't tell you!"

"Yeah, well, all bets went out the door when she realized the potential for SkorTek. She felt this case was a slam-dunk, and she'd rather have a small equity share than the billable hours—"

"So, now Joanna has a piece of your company? Ha! . . . Hey, is it something I should get in on, too?"

His smile fades. "I've always wanted to be in partnership with you. You know that."

I'm at his side in a flash.

He takes me and holds me tight, then gives me the sort of kiss that has me wanting to take him, right here, right now.

"At least let me get inside the doorway," he mumbles as my hands yank his belt from his pants.

He slaps them away. Yep, he's in complete control. This means choosing the place (the carpet in front of the fireplace) and the position (we start with him on top, but I know we won't finish that way).

His hands explore every bend, every curve, every nook and cranny of my body, as if I'm a highly valued work of art. The touch of his fingertips on my breasts sends shivers that make me quiver, and my nipples become taut with anticipation. When his fingers probe deep inside me, I gasp. I know my dampness excites him because I see him grow large—

Before entering me.

I don't know who needs this worse: he or I.

If it's Seth, then I suppose he's being a gentleman, because he takes his time, increasing his tempo slowly, waiting for my gasps to guide his strokes so that my orgasm can be timed with his . . .

When, finally, he explodes inside of me, I collapse with him onto the floor. His eyes are open and the love I see within them has me blushing and sobbing and babbling about my own foolishness; about what life could and should be about; that love and family isn't blood or law, but trust and action.

He hushes me with his lips and holds me in his arms as we fall asleep in front of a fire that is on its last embers.

Like love, energy doesn't die; it just takes different forms.

6:30 p.m.

SETH AND I are sound asleep when I realize my cell phone is buzzing. It's dark outside, but the digital clock on the phone shows that it's only six thirty, so it can't be Merrie . . .

Oh my God, that means—

I flip open my phone. The message reads:

It's soup!

I poke Seth. He bolts awake. "What the hell?"

"I need a lift to the hospital, like now! . . . Hey, on the way there, let's pick up Sadie from Fanny. I've got someone I want her to meet."

7:54 p.m.

GRACE WAS right to forgo the knowledge of the sex of her child.

For one thing, it gave us all something to bet on.

Jezebel was the only one allowed with Auggie in the birthing room. Like a miniature doctor in tiny pink scrubs, she marches out to make the grand pronouncement: "It's a girl, thank goodness!"

There is shouting from those with winning bets, and grudging nods from the rest.

We all gather around the nursery window as the nurse holds up the newest member of our family.

Sadie takes her favorite perch: Seth's shoulders.

Mom holds Dad's hands and murmurs in his ear what she can see but he cannot. He smiles anyway. This new baby's birth is one more milestone he's been blessed to share with his family.

Lana leans back onto Thor. "Honey, what do you think? Should we go one more round?"

Thor slaps his hand to his forehead. "What, are you crazy?" He jabs a thumb in the direction of Mario and Max, who are shoving each other as they jockey for what they believe is the primo spot in front of the window. They are just tall enough to see through it.

Jezebel throws up her hands to me so that I can carry her over. "I bet you can't guess her name," she teases me.

I go for the obvious. "Ruth, like Grandma?"

She shakes her head adamantly, then cups my ear and whispers, "*Katie.*"

So that she doesn't see my tears, I hold her close and give her a big kiss.

You don't need a baby of your own to make a family. You just need love.

ACKNOWLEDGMENTS

··

IT TAKES A village to raise a child—and to create a book. My own support group is populated with a metropolis of friends and family. Special thanks go to Angela and Tom Johnson; Jean and Berney Neufeld; Wanda and Jim Collins; Karin and Gary Tabke; Tawny Weber; Poppy Reiffin; Stephanie Bond; Kate Perry; Holly Cless; Wendy Tokunaga; Helen Drake; Robbie Wright; Allison O'Connor; Allyson Rusu; Sharon Conn; Emily Kischell; Patricia Steadman and Mario Martinez; Darien and Don Coleman; Andree Belle; Rita Abrams; Bob Freedman; Linda May and Andy Brown; Vera and Ron Gott; Kelly and Doug Gott; Wendy and De Brown; Norma and Michael Martinez; Carmen Martinez; Jacklyn and Sean Brown; Heather and Seth Brown; Elizabeth Jones; Sheryl and Rich Levy; and Bonnie and John Gray.

A special thanks to my dear friend, Lissa Rankin, MD, for sharing her professional experience with stillborn births, and for departing some pertinent insights on infertility.

I have a marvelous professional team: My literary agent, Holly Root, is the brains of the operation, and to whom I owe my focus. My editor at Simon & Schuster/Gallery, Megan McKeever, is its soul. Her insights to my plot and prose are always spot-on; Kristin Dwyer, my publicist at Simon & Schuster, has been my biggest cheerleader. I am hers as well. If any of my heroines are ready for their close-ups, it is thanks to the hard work of Jon Cassir of CAA.

I will always revere my publisher, Louise Burke, for her

wisdom, and her enthusiasm for her authors' labors of love. My deep and sincere appreciation to Jennifer Bergstrom, Gallery's editor in chief, for her unwavering support. It is always an honor to have Gallery Books' hardworking sales force by my side.

Finally, I want to thank my children, Austin and Anna, for their endless abundance of love and friendship, and for all they've taught me about the real-life demands of parenting; and my husband, Martin, for being the hero of my own story.

AFTERWORD

································

MY RESEARCH LED me to some wonderful resources, which I'd like to share:

Regarding Von Hippel–Lindau

Von Hippel–Lindau is a very real disease, caused by an inherited mutation. It affects around thirty-two thousand people born in the United States each year. Symptoms of this disease include hemangioblastomas in the eyes and brain, and it can result in kidney cancer, pancreatic cysts, and pancreatic neuroendocrine tumors. For more information, go to www.ninds.nih.gov/.

Regarding International Parental Child Abduction

The U.S. State Department offers assistance in cases of international parental child abductions through its Office of Children's Issues. For more information, check out travel.state.gov/abduction/abduction_580.html.

Regarding Homeless Prenatal Programs

For whatever reason, some pregnant women have no jobs, no homes, and no prenatal care. One organization that works to help find all three for new and soon-to-be mothers who are willing to help themselves is San Francisco's Homeless Prenatal

Program, which welcomes volunteers and donations. Visit www
.homelessprenatal.org.

Regarding Product Safety

Although most states have consumer affairs departments, in an
ideal world, SafeCalifornia, the fictional state commission that
employed Katie and specifically focused on consumer product
safety, would indeed exist, and it would be working hand in
hand with the following wonderful organizations. I hope you
will lend them your support:

The U.S. Public Interest Research Group (www.pirg.org)

A federation of nonprofit, nonpartisan advocacy organizations
that exist in every U.S. state and Canadian province; their mission
is to uncover consumer products that are a threat to public health
and safety, then lobby state legislatures for their removal and recall.

KidsInDanger.org

Another nonprofit organization that makes parents aware of
product recalls involving child safety.

The U.S. Product Safety Commission (www.cpsc.gov)

The federal agency that creates product safety standards and recalls products that don't meet those standards.

Regarding Baby Planners

Baby planner is not a fictional profession. Such services actually
exist; they are time savers as well as provide the emotional sup-

port system many new mothers need. To find a baby planner, check out babyplannerinstitute.com, the website of the International Academy of Baby Planner Professionals/Baby Planner Institute. There you'll find a member directory, as well as a listing of events where you'll meet a host of experts and specialists to help you plan a safe and happy journey into parenthood. They also provide online classes, certification, and business organization information, if you're thinking about becoming a professional baby planner. SeedPlantGrow.com also offers classes and provides organizational assistance.

THE BABY PLANNER

josie brown

INTRODUCTION

Acting as a consultant for new moms on the latest baby gadgets, the best play groups, and the most socially desirable mommy-meet-ups, professional baby planner, Katie Johnson, is finding it difficult to ignore the ticking of her own biological clock. However, the success of her marriage to husband Alex means squelching her own maternal urges and living vicariously through her sister's and her clients' pregnancies, until, as Alex puts it, "the timing is right."

When she finally realizes that Alex will never budge from his stance to remain childless, Katie takes fate into her own hands and plots an "accidental" pregnancy. But things don't turn out exactly as she'd hoped, and Katie is taught an important life lesson: how we nurture is the true nature of love.

TOPICS AND QUESTIONS FOR DISCUSSION

1. The author uses quotations to introduce each chapter of *The Baby Planner*. Which quote, if any, resonated with you? Discuss how these quotations reflect the events or emotional undertones of the chapters? How did they contribute to the movement of the narrative?

2. Readers learn how badly Katie wants to become a mother. How does this shape her character and her interactions throughout the story? Do you think Katie's longing to be a mother holds her back from living life to the fullest? Give examples from the book to illustrate your opinion.

3. In the opening scenes of *The Baby Planner,* the author illustrates how having children forces changes that parents might not expect. Discuss how children complicate, influence, and disrupt the relationships in this book. Consider romantic relationships as well as relationships with other children, friends, family members, and even business partners.

4. How might Katie's life turned out differently if she had never lost her job?

5. Katie married Alex knowing he was resistant to wanting more children, but she hoped he might change his mind. Have you ever wrongly assumed someone would change their mind?

6. On the other hand, by the time we meet Katie and Alex, he clearly knows she wants a child, his child, more than anything. Yet he continues to withhold that opportunity from her. In fact he even leads her to believe he might change his

mind. Why do you think he acts this way? Compare and contrast Alex's behavior to Katie's.

7. Does this discovery validate Katie's covert actions to get pregnant? Does it influence your ability to sympathize with Katie?

8. One character, Lacie Channing, points out that Katie's baby planning service encourages "conspicuous consumption," and makes the early months of motherhood less enjoyable and more "sterile." Do you agree with her? Why or why not? Discuss the pros and cons of industries like baby planning, which capitalize on consumer mindsets and stressful, life-changing events (think wedding planning, event planning, and even personal shopping services).

9. Katie displays her social conscience as she regularly recommends green products to her clients. Do Katie's recommendations make you reconsider the types of products you buy and use? Why or why not? If you're a parent, did having children influence the choices you make about the kinds of products and food you bring into your home?

10. Katie's mother worries about her new career as a baby planner. How does Katie deal with the conflicting emotions she feels? Discuss the ways in which Katie's exposure to moms-to-be influences the decisions she makes in her own life.

11. On page 112, Katie makes the decision to stop taking "the Pill" and starts "Operation Oops." While Katie had hoped to help Alex overcome his previous parenting mistakes, her decision is ultimately a deceptive one. How did Katie's choice to "accidentally" get pregnant change or reinforce your ability to sympathize her character? With Alex's character?

12. Throughout *The Baby Planner,* the author depicts mother-hood from a variety of perspectives. Compare and contrast the mothers in this story. Are their desires and expectations similar, or do they view motherhood differently? Which characteristics of the mothers do you feel are most desirable? Which mother did you relate to most, and why?

13. Discuss the various insecurities that Katie's clients feel. How do these insecurities influence their actions? What are the consequences, both positive and negative, of the choices the mothers in *The Baby Planner* make?

14. Seth's single parenting has the added dimension of his griev-ing his wife's death after childbirth, and his initial reticence for becoming a parent in the first place. Discuss how his re-lationship with his baby daughter may have been different, had his wife had lived.

15. Katie eventually discovers that she was adopted. How does this discovery change how she views motherhood? Identify and discuss the lessons she learns through the experience of seeking out her biological mother and, eventually, coming to terms with her own adoption.

ENHANCE YOUR BOOK CLUB

1. The theme of motherhood is the obvious core of this book. Consider the mothers you know and discuss how becoming a mother has changed their lives.

2. Explore the field of baby planning by visiting *http://baby-plannerinstitute.com.* Go to the "Members" section and

visit some baby planner websites. Write down your observations and feelings about the industry, its benefits (or detriments), and how baby planners market themselves. Compare what you find to how Josie Brown illustrated the profession in her novel. Discuss your findings with your book club. Have you, or would you, ever considered employing a baby planner?

3. On the whole, Americans purchase and bring into our homes a large number of consumer products each year. While Safe-California, the consumer product safety commission that Katie worked for, is fictional, there are several ways you can learn more about the products you bring into your home. Take some time to visit the U.S. Consumer Product Safety Commission's website *(http://www.cpsc.gov)* to check out current recalls, read the "On Safety" blog, or watch some of the videos and webcasts. Share some of what you find with your book club and then make a commitment as a group to be more conscious of product safety before you buy.

4. To learn more about Josie Brown, visit her website at *www .josiebrown.com.* You can also read her blog and interviews to gain more insight into her writing process and influences. Discuss with your book club how much (or how little) Josie's personality and background seems to have found its way into *The Baby Planner.*

F Brown Josie
Brown, Josie.
The baby planner /
22960000369347   OAFI